D0269257

HEIRS OF THE BODY

HEIRS
OF THE BODY

A Daisy Dalrymple Mystery

CAROLA DUNN

Constable & Robinson Ltd
55–56 Russell Square
London WC1B 4HP
www.constablerobinson.com

First published in the US by Minotaur Books,
an imprint of St Martin's Press, New York, 2013

First published in the UK by C&R Crime,
an imprint of Constable & Robinson, 2013

Copyright © Carola Dunn 2013

The right of Carola Dunn to be identified as the
author of this work has been asserted by her in accordance
with the Copyright, Designs & Patents Act 1988

This is a work of fiction. Names, characters, places and incidents are either
the product of the author's imagination or are used fictitiously, and any
resemblance to actual persons, living or dead, or to actual events or
locales is entirely coincidental

All rights reserved. This book is sold subject to the condition
that it shall not, by way of trade or otherwise, be lent, re-sold,
hired out or otherwise circulated in any form of binding or cover
other than that in which it is published and without a similar condition
including this condition being imposed on the subsequent purchaser.

A copy of the British Library Cataloguing in Publication
Data is available from the British Library

ISBN 978-1-47211-083-1 (hardback)
ISBN 978-1-78033-142-3 (ebook)

Printed and bound by
CPI Group (UK) Ltd, Croydon, CR0 4YY

1 3 5 7 9 10 8 6 4 2

To all the readers who have kept Daisy alive
through so many adventures

LANCASHIRE COUNTY LIBRARY	
3011812793094 3	
Askews & Holts	06-Dec-2013
AF CRM	£14.99
SPA	

ACKNOWLEDGMENTS

My thanks to Kerry-Ann Morris of Jamaican Echoes; Nancy Mayer, my consultant on matters of inheritance; Pat Jones of the Railway & Canal Historical Society; Doug Lyle M.D. and Larry Karp M.D. for matters medical; RAC librarian Trevor Dunmore; Malcolm of the Telephone Museum; Dominique Bremond for checking my French; Mary Jarrett for her kind hospitality; and last but not least, my ever-faithful companion in my research jaunts, Carole Rainbird.

HEIRS OF THE BODY

ONE

"*Darling, what* on earth are 'heirs of the body'?" Daisy enquired, frowning at the wad of blue Basildon Bond writing paper in her hand. She had been busy all day and was only now, after dinner, opening the afternoon post.

"Postmortem effluvia?"

"H-e-i-r."

"Coroners?" Without looking up from the *Evening Standard*, Alec reached for his whisky, an indulgence usually reserved for celebrating the end of a big investigation. "Undertakers? Worms?"

"Ugh, Daddy, that's disgusting!" Belinda's Easter holidays had started just a couple of days earlier, and her father was apt to forget to mind his tongue in her presence.

"What, worms? Just think, if they didn't do their work we'd be up to our necks in bodies."

"Alec, really! In any case, 'heirs' is the important word here. Cousin Edgar's coming up to his fiftieth birthday and apparently it dawned on him a few months ago that he hasn't the faintest idea who is heir to the title and Fairacres."

"Your letter's from Lord Dalrymple?"

"No, Cousin Geraldine. She's frightfully scathing about 'heirs of the body,' but I can't make out why."

"It'd be because she and Lord Dalrymple have no children. It's just a legal term for legitimate offspring, and their legitimate offspring, ad infinitum."

Daisy cast an anxious glance at her stepdaughter.

"It's all right, Mummy," Bel said indulgently. "I know what legitimate means, and illegitimate. It's whether the mother and father are married or not."

How did children find out such things? Daisy wondered. She was sure she hadn't been aware at the age of thirteen that procreation without matrimony was even possible. Times had changed between 1911 and 1927!

"I read it in a book." Bel answered her unvoiced question. "And looked it up in the dictionary."

"Well, darling, I'm glad you're using your dictionary. But I was rather hoping you didn't know what it means."

"Oh, Mummy, how positively Victorian!"

Since Daisy frequently decried the persistent influence of Victorian attitudes in older generations, she was left speechless.

Alec had set aside his paper to fill his pipe. Now, between the vigorous puffs required to get it burning, he said, "I'm not really up in all that stuff, but the 'body' bit must mean that step- or adopted children don't count. And the original entail, or patent, or will, or whatever must have specified heirs *male* of the body. Otherwise, your brother having died, love, I think your sister's eldest son would have inherited the estate and title from your father. Or perhaps Violet first, and then Derek. But don't quote me on that."

"Derek?" said Bel. "Oh, wouldn't it be fun if he was Lord Dalrymple!"

"A new law was passed just last year, though, and I'm not sure what effect it has in a situation like this."

"Tommy Pearson must know."

"He's your cousin's solicitor?"

"Yes. Cousin Edgar always felt Father's lawyer—the old family firm since forever—condescended to him because he'd been a school-

2

master, not brought up to his new station in life. He was very impressed with Tommy's part in that kidnapping business. . . . You didn't hear that, Bel."

"I think I'd better go and read in bed," said Belinda with dignity, "if you're going to keep talking about things I'm not supposed to hear."

"Heavens yes, it's after ten. Past your bedtime."

Belinda kissed each of them goodnight, then said, "Mummy, may I go and see the twins? Just a peek?"

"Of course, darling. You don't need to ask. Quiet as a mouse, though."

"I know. I just like to ask in case Nurse Gilpin catches me. She can't fuss if you've said yes, can she?"

Alec grinned. "I wouldn't count on it. Every victory over Mrs. Gilpin is temporary."

"I don't care much if she does fuss. They're my brother and sister, after all. Daddy, is Oliver your 'heir male of the body'?"

"He would be if I had a title, pet, but you can't inherit a job with the Metropolitan Police. As it is, you're all my heirs."

Daisy was not prepared to go into the business of a father's part in the bodily side of parenthood. "Run along and tackle Nurse, now, darling," she said firmly.

Looking determined, Belinda left the room.

Daisy sighed. Sometimes life seemed to be a perpetual battle with Oliver and Miranda's nanny, whose Victorian attitude dictated that parents had no business in the nursery.

She returned to consideration of Lady Dalrymple's news. However unrewarding, it was bound to be infinitely preferable to the letter that had lurked beneath it in the pile, from Daisy's mother, the dowager viscountess.

"I'm surprised Pearson didn't find out who the present heir is when he took over." Alec poked disgustedly at the bowl of his pipe with a used matchstick, then reached for the matchbox and started the flare-puff routine again.

"It may not have crossed his mind. Cousin Edgar probably has a perfectly sound will leaving everything to his wife, and Tommy doesn't go in for aristocratic clients. In fact, I think he does his best to avoid them, because of Madge being Lady Margaret. She told me he's too independent to want to take advantage of her family connections."

"I expect all he really wants is to avoid the complications of entailed estates."

"I wouldn't blame him," said Daisy, trying to make out what Cousin Geraldine was going on about. Her writing was the kind that looks very neat but is difficult to decipher. "Oh, she's complaining about the Dalrymples not being prolific in the production of sons. What cheek, when she hasn't produced a single heir of the body herself, male or female. Besides, it worked to her advantage. If I'd had lots of brothers, she wouldn't be a viscountess."

"What exactly is Edgar's relationship to you?"

"I've never worked it out." Daisy had next to no interest in the ramifications of aristocratic family trees, unlike her friend Lucy. Possibly as a result, Lucy had married the younger son of a marquis and was now Lady Gerald Bincombe, whereas Daisy had married a Scotland Yard detective. "Some sort of second cousin, I think. Or third. Once removed, I'm pretty sure of that. Geraldine says they're having to go back to my great-great-grandfather's descendents now. That would be my great-grandfather's brothers, I suppose."

"Great Scott! They must have been born about—let's see—1800, or so." Smoke spiralled up and Alec sat back contentedly.

"The second brother was Edgar's grandfather. Apparently the third never married. The fourth and youngest got a governess into trouble and was shipped off to the West Indies—at least, that's the family legend."

"Not one either your father or your mother would pass on to you."

"How right you are. Gervaise told me." And Gervaise had gone off to war when she was sixteen, so perhaps she had known about unmarried mothers when she was thirteen. "According to the story, the black sheep wrote to his mother when he married, but when he and his bride were not welcomed home with open arms, he was never heard from directly again. A trickle of news came in from travellers.

4

Rumour reported that he had a large family living on the edge of respectability."

"Who were not listed in the family bible, I take it."

"I can't say I ever looked, but I suppose not, or Edgar wouldn't be having so much trouble now. My—let's see—my grandfather also had a lot of children, a typical Victorian family, so they must have assumed the direct line was well assured. Geraldine says Tommy started the search by hiring someone to go through all the musty old papers in the muniments room. Oh, I think this says—"

"Is there an end to this story, Daisy?"

"Aren't you itching to make the acquaintance of all the skeletons in my family's cupboards?"

" 'Fraid not."

"Geraldine does go on a bit. Six pages! Let me see if I can find . . ." She skimmed through the rest, picking out phrases here and there. "Advertised in newspapers throughout the Empire. . . . Three claimants responded already—Good heavens! They'll be at each other's throats—Tommy thinks—No! She can't be serious. Or am I misreading? . . ." She went back to the beginning of the sentence and pored over it word by word.

" 'No' what?" Alec's attention was caught.

"I don't believe it! She wants me to be present when Tommy interviews the would-be heirs. Tommy wanted Edgar, as head of the family, but Geraldine says he'd be completely useless."

"I'd agree with her there. Unless one of them turns out to be a fellow lepidopterist, in which case he'd be biased in his favour."

"And Geraldine herself is not a member of the family by birth."

"What about your mother—No, the same applies. Though I hardly think she'd appreciate anyone reminding her of the fact."

Daisy giggled. "Darling, can you imagine either of them in attendance? The poor heirs would turn tail and decide the game wasn't worth the candle."

"Your sister? No, I suppose not."

"I doubt if she's ever spoken to a solicitor in her life. If Tommy really considers it necessary, I'll do it."

"Come off it, love. Don't try to tell me you're not dying to listen in."

"It might be interesting. And, you never know," she added persuasively, "I might spot something proving one of the claimants is a fake."

"I presume that's why Pearson would like a family member present. Don't worry, I shan't try to stop you, if he's agreeable. In fact, I'd bet he approached Edgar first only as a matter of etiquette and he was really angling for you all along."

Such a vote of confidence deserved a kiss, which Daisy duly bestowed. The rest of Geraldine's screed and the dowager's letter did not get read that evening.

TWO

A fresh crop of envelopes, the first post, was waiting beside Daisy's place at breakfast next morning.

"Heavens, what a pile!" she exclaimed, sitting down.

"There's some of yesterday afternoon's post, too, madam," said Elsie, the Fletchers' parlourmaid, "that you didn't open last night. You left it in the sitting room. I put it on your desk. Tea or coffee, madam? And how would you like your eggs?"

"Just tea and toast today, thank you." Daisy was beginning to fear that bosoms and hips had gone out of fashion forever. She tried, she really did, but her curves just would not go away.

As Alec and Belinda decided what kind of eggs they wanted, she flipped through the post. Mostly tradesmen's bills and circulars— she'd deal with those later. As Alec disappeared behind his *Daily Chronicle*, she slit open an envelope addressed in her Indian friend Sakari's beautiful and beautifully legible hand.

"Bel, Mrs. Prasad's invited you to go to the zoo with Deva today. She's invited Lizzie as well, and two other girls. Brenda and Erica, Do you know them?"

"Oh yes, Mummy, don't you remember? They were at school with us before we went away to school. May I go? Please?"

"Anyone would think you'd never been to the zoo before," said Alec.

"Darling, it's as much about seeing her friends as seeing the animals. Yes, of course you may go, Bel. Eleven o'clock, she says. Do you want to bike down or would you like a lift?"

"I'll bike. It's fun going downhill, and I expect Mrs. Prasad will have Kesin put my bike in their car and drive me home."

"All right, but if she doesn't think to offer, make sure you set out in time to get home before dark. You'd better ring up right after breakfast to accept."

Daisy had three postcards and a couple of letters from friends, which she read as she absentmindedly consumed several slices of buttered toast. When Alec left for the Yard, she and Belinda went up to the nursery to play with the twins.

At two and a bit, Oliver and Miranda were very active. Their stepsister was very good about letting them climb all over her, even when the dog, Nana, joined in. When they quieted down, Miranda liked looking at picture books and listening to stories, her dark head resting warmly on Daisy's shoulder. Oliver's rusty-brown head was more often bent over his wooden blocks. Belinda helped him build, fending off Nana and straightening his towers before they tumbled.

Belinda departed at ten. Daisy went to the kitchen for her daily consultation with the cook-housekeeper, Mrs. Dobson, then settled in her office to tackle the bills. As always, when she set about this task, she was grateful to Alec's estranged great-uncle for the legacy that made it unnecessary to juggle creditors.

Business dealt with, she finished reading Cousin Geraldine's letter. However, just looking at the envelope from her mother made her feel craven. She put off opening it till the evening. In Alec's presence, she didn't care a farthing for the Dowager Lady Dalrymple's inevitable disapproval of her younger daughter's every action.

Besides, she had to translate from shorthand to typescript the notes she had taken yesterday at Westminster Abbey, before she forgot what the squiggles meant. When she had sorted them out, she got down to writing the article for her American editor. She decided she had plenty of information to make two articles, one on famous people buried in the Abbey, from Oliver Cromwell and Henry Purcell to Charles Darwin and Alfred Lord Tennyson, and one on kings and queens. Americans, having rid themselves of the monarchy, apparently found it fascinating.

After lunch, she went for a walk on Hampstead Heath with the twins, the dog, and the nurserymaid. On their return a message was waiting for Daisy. Mr. Pearson had rung up and would like her to ring back, at her convenience.

Had he, too, received Geraldine's suggestion? Was he about to squash any notion Daisy had of attending the interviews with the claimants to her father's title? Surely not. He wouldn't have telephoned to tell her in person that she was unwanted; he'd have written a polite, discouraging note.

Elsie had carefully written down his telephone number. Daisy sat down on the chair by the hall table, took the receiver from the hook, and dialled.

"Pearson, Pearson, Pearson, and Brown," said a crisp secretarial voice.

Daisy knew that the first Pearson had retired, but she wasn't sure about the second. "Mr. Tommy—Thomas Pearson, please. This is Mrs. Fletcher, Mrs. Alec Fletcher. He rang me while I was out."

"Oh yes, Mrs. Fletcher, would you mind holding the line a moment while I see if Mr. Pearson's free?"

She didn't wait for an answer. Daisy wondered what would have happened had she been given time to say yes, she'd mind, and Tommy could jolly well call her back. However, she wasn't given much time for pique, either.

"Daisy? Tommy speaking. Thanks for ringing back so quickly."

"Hello, darling. I—"

"Daisy, not 'darling' in business hours, please!"

"Sorry. Is 'Tommy' all right?"

"I suppose so, as I find myself addressing you as Daisy," he said ruefully.

"No, let's start again. I take it, Mr. Pearson, that you've heard from Cousin . . . from Lady Dalrymple?"

"Several times. And her latest suggestion is actually quite sensible.

9

We can't discuss it over the phone, though. Do you mind coming in to Lincoln's Inn, or would you rather dine with us and talk afterwards? The invitation has Madge's blessing, of course, and includes Alec."

"Which suits you better?"

"You coming to chambers." Tommy, a daring, much-decorated soldier in the war, had become rather staid and proper since joining the family firm, but Daisy heard the grin in his voice. "That way our meeting can be billed to the estate with a good conscience. Difficult to explain away a dinner party on the account. . . ."

"Besides, much as I love Madge and Alec, it will be easier without them putting in their two pennyworth."

He laughed. "True, though I hope you'll consult Alec before coming to a decision."

"Assuming this is about what I assume it's about, he's already granted his approval."

The cautious lawyer came to the fore. "Oh? I wouldn't have expected . . . But that's not my affair. Let's set a date and time, and Madge will get in touch about a business-free date for dinner."

Daisy checked her diary and suggested the following afternoon. Tommy was going to be in court all day.

"There's no hurry," he assured her. "This is going to drag on for months."

"Jarndyce and Jarndyce?" she asked forebodingly.

"No, no. There's no question about the will, or rather the letters patent."

"Letters . . . ? No, don't tell me!"

"It's just a matter of carrying on until we're as certain as possible that we've heard from all claimants and discovered the proper heir."

"More like the Tichbourne claimant, then. That dragged on for years, didn't it?"

"We'll just have to hope it won't come to that."

They made an appointment for the following week. Daisy returned to her office. Having decided to give famous people precedence over monarchs, she now had to write about Mrs. Aphra Behn, who died in 1689 and whose monument, according to Daisy's notes, read *Here lies a Proof that Wit can never be Defence enough against Mortality.* She didn't remember learning about Aphra Behn at school. She turned to *Nelson's Encyclopædia*, Volume 3, B-Ble.

A spy for Charles II and a successful professional playwright, making her living by her writing in the seventeenth century! Daisy wanted to know more, but the encyclopædia entry was quite short. Reminding herself that all she needed was a snippet for a travel article, she moved on to Sir Isaac Newton.

His monument was much grander, with a much longer inscription, which unfortunately was in Latin. Her school had considered the study of Latin to be too much of a strain for the brains of young ladies. Science, also, and higher mathematics, so she didn't understand Newton's work any better than she understood his epitaph, but good old Nelson—the encyclopædic one, not the sailor—came to the rescue.

Elsie brought in tea and biscuits. "Lemon jumbles, madam. Mrs. Dobson made 'em because Miss Belinda does like 'em so. Only she rang up just now, Miss Belinda did, and said not to disturb you, madam, but Mrs. Prasad's invited her to stay the night and could you please ring back."

Daisy rang and talked to Sakari, who was dying to know all about Lord Dalrymple's search for his heir. She'd picked up hints from Belinda, of course.

"I'd better not talk about it, darling," Daisy apologised. "One never knows when legal business might turn out to be confidential. Don't let Bel be a nuisance or overstay her welcome."

"Belinda is never a nuisance, Daisy. But the zoological gardens are utterly exhausting! I confess, after half an hour I retired to the tearoom with a book and let the girls escort themselves."

"I don't blame you," Daisy said, laughing. "Though I'm looking forward to taking the twins when they're a little older."

That evening, for once, Alec escaped from the Yard on time. He had spent a boring day on paperwork and meetings, with no interesting new cases on the horizon. Looking forward to spending some time with his children, he was disappointed to find Belinda away from home for the night.

A visit to the nursery and a romp with the twins cheered him up a bit. Having changed out of his suit, he played horsie and they took turns riding on his back.

Mrs. Gilpin was scandalised. "Fathers ought to command awe," she told him, not for the first time. "How can they respect you, sir, when you let them—"

"They're only babies. Down you get, Manda. Your turn, Oliver."

At dinner, over Lancashire hotpot and broad beans, Daisy reported the second part of Cousin Geraldine's letter. "Edgar wants the whole family to turn out to celebrate his birthday and to meet the three heirs—or rather, I presume, as many as haven't been debunked by then."

"Sounds like a jolly party," Alec grunted. "More Geraldine's idea than Edgar's, I'll be bound."

"Oh yes, she loves playing Lady Bountiful, whereas August must be a prime season for moths and butterflies, don't you think? Edgar will want to be out in the fields with his nets and jars."

"If that's where he wants to be, that's where he'll be, after gently agreeing with his wife that his place is with his guests. So this grand gathering is to be at Fairacres in August?"

"Yes, the first week. From the thirtieth of July, actually. His birthday is the sixth of August, but the first is August bank holiday and the village fête. There's plenty of time for you to arrange to take a few days off."

"Me! I'm not family, and I don't want anything to do with games of 'debunk the heirs.'"

"Darling, of course you're family. Geraldine specifically says you're expected, and the children, too. Johnny and Vi will be taking all three of theirs."

"You mean they've already accepted? They were invited before us?" Alec pretended outrage.

"Idiot! As though you cared. No, Geraldine just says she's inviting them. But Violet's bound to accept. She'll see it as a family obligation. And I have to agree, actually."

"*Your* family. No, sorry! I didn't mean that the way it sounded."

"I should hope not," Daisy said severely. "Edgar may be obsessed with lepidoptera but he's a sweetie, and I wouldn't dream of spoiling his birthday by refusing, even if the celebration is really Geraldine's idea."

"You're right. You know I can't guarantee anything, but I'll try to get a few days off for it." With any luck, he'd be unsuccessful, he thought. He'd much prefer to go to the New Forest with Daisy and the children.

"They owe you a holiday. You're so often late for dinner that Mrs. Dobson never makes anything that can't be eaten cold, unless it wouldn't suffer from being kept hot or reheated! Not to mention last summer: We were supposed to have a week on the Isle of Wight and they called you back after three days."

"It was an emergency."

"It always is. Anyone would think you were the only detective chief inspector in the CID. Not that I'm not proud of you for being indispensable, but there ought to be a limit. I don't suppose Mr. Crane would be impressed by Edgar's title?"

"I've no intention of using it to impress him. On the other hand," Alec went on thoughtfully, "if I told him my mother-in-law insists on my presence and I'm terrified of her . . ."

Daisy laughed. "What bilge, darling!"

"Not at all. Your mother can be very intimidating. Besides, can you think of any words more likely to strike fear into the average male breast than 'mother-in-law' and 'dowager'? The Super would credit it."

"I'm not at all sure whether Mother is planning to take any part in the affair. She still hasn't forgiven Edgar for inheriting Fairacres, though he had no choice about it. One couldn't describe her as being on neighbourly terms with them, even if the Dower House is all of half a mile away."

"But she's bound to want to vet the next heir, or claimants to heirdom, don't you think?"

"*I* certainly do. It's an intriguing situation. But you never can tell with Mother." Daisy grimaced. "I'd better see if she has anything to say on the subject. I'll open her letter after dinner."

"You haven't read it yet? Coward!"

Daisy wrinkled her nose at him. "I am," she acknowledged, "when it comes to Mother. You deal with her much better than I do."

"So that's why you're so determined to get me down to Fairacres?"

"She's going to be breathing fire at these poor people Tommy's digging up. Not that I'm too keen on them myself."

"I don't know why you want to go," Alec grumbled, "when you're already prejudiced against them."

"I'm not!"

He merely raised his eyebrows, well aware that the simple change of expression always had the devastating effect of making her examine her conscience. It had much the same effect on suspects and recalcitrant witnesses, though for them he put enough ice in his stare to intimidate; some claimed he froze the marrow of their bones. With Daisy, he was laughing at her—usually.

"I can't dislike them when I haven't even met them yet. But I resent them," she admitted. "I resent anyone who might take Father's and Gervaise's place. When it happened before, I didn't have a chance to think about it beforehand so . . . it came as a shock but I didn't have to participate. I expect it sounds silly, but I feel disloyal."

"Not silly at all, love. Very natural." Reluctantly he resigned himself to doing his best to be there to support her. "But if we're committing ourselves to staying for several days, I hope you'll try not to show your dislike."

"I don't dislike them, truly. I'm just a bit disgruntled."

"Well, gruntle yourself, love, or I'll conjure up an emergency at the Yard and go back to work."

"You wouldn't!"

"I might."

"You will come, then?"

"If I can wangle the time off, yes. I take it you've decided not to participate in Pearson's interviews with the claimants."

"Of course I shall. I've already made an appointment with him to talk about it. It'll be easier to cope with meeting them one at a time, rather than facing a horde of strangers at Fairacres, don't you think? And I might be able to help weed them out so there isn't a horde by then."

"'A consummation devoutly to be wished,'" said Alec.

After dinner, when they were settled with coffee in the sitting room, Daisy picked up the Benares brass letter opener and attacked the dowager's cream linen paper envelope.

"At least it's short," Alec remarked, as she took out a single sheet.

"Mother can pack a lot into a few pithy sentences when she tries. Ah, I might have guessed. It's all Edgar's fault. He was unforgivably remiss not to ascertain the identity of his heir as soon as he had appropriated the title."

"Appropriated? Is that the word she uses?"

"I told you she's by no means resigned to dowagerdom. Dowagership? Dowagerhood?"

"All the same, she has a point about his being remiss."

"Remember, the poor man wasn't brought up to the business of being a lord."

"Lordhood, as it might be."

"To do him justice, though he must be glad not to be surviving on a schoolmaster's pension, he doesn't care two hoots about the title. So, not having any children, why should he care who gets it next? Mother does, however. Wouldn't you think she'd have learnt that she has no say in the matter?"

"Your mother considers herself a law unto herself." And her younger daughter occasionally followed her example, as he'd discovered the very first time Daisy had interfered in one of his investigations.

"Anyway, she intends to keep a close eye on things, since Edgar has neither the common sense nor the breeding to. . . . Yes, well, we'll skip the invective. Aha, here we are. She expects me to bring you down to Fairacres, because if a policeman can't sort out the impostors from the real heir, what's the use of having one in the family? She'll be very disappointed in me if—As if that was an inducement! She's disappointed in me whatever I do."

"Whereas," Alec smugly pointed out, "she has at least acknowledged the value of having a policeman in the family. Although she seems a little confused about the function of the various branches of the law. Pearson would have every right to resent my poking my nose into his business, supposing I were inclined to interfere, which I'm not."

"But you must admit it's an intriguing situation. Gruntled or not, I wouldn't miss it for anything. Besides, Bel and the twins will enjoy seeing their cousins, and you'll have time to spend with them, darling."

"I can't say intriguing is the word I'd use." The word he'd use was not to be pronounced in feminine company. "Still, I expect you and Pearson will sort them out before we get there. How difficult can it be to tell the fake heirs from the real one?"

THREE

On a warm, damp morning in early May, Daisy took the number 63 bus from Hampstead to the City. She disliked driving in central London, especially in the rain.

Not that it was exactly raining. The air was heavy with lilac-scented moisture. It was neither falling in droplets nor visible as mist, but she knew from experience that as it settled on the wind-screen it would obscure her vision even worse than actual rain.

Though Alec kept telling her she ought to take taxis, the years of penny-pinching between her father's death and her marriage had taken their toll. Why waste money on a cab when the bus would take her within ten minutes' walk of Lincoln's Inn? Besides, she needed to think; in a taxi the inexorable tick of the meter always distracted her with worry about whether she had enough change in her purse.

She had to marshal her arguments. A chat with Madge had dispelled her impression that Tommy was enthusiastic about including her in his initial interviews with the claimants. Apparently he'd had second thoughts about Geraldine's sensible suggestion and would have to be persuaded.

Daisy had put on her navy costume, the plain one she wore for calling on editors. The skirt reached below the knee, which had been a businesslike length when she bought it, though now it was fashionable. A silk blouse in a blue paisley pattern and a speedwell-blue cloche brightened it up. She didn't want to look like an ordinary shorthand typist.

Come to think of it, though, looking like a secretary for the interviews wasn't such a bad idea. She would put it to Tommy.

The bus duly deposited her at Ludgate Circus. She always enjoyed walking along Fleet Street, feeling herself a small part of the great machinery of news gathering and disbursement, even if "news" wasn't quite the word for her largely historical articles. Like the reporters dashing in all directions around her, she dealt in words and information. The offices of *Town and Country* magazine, her English publishers, were tucked away in the labyrinth of alleys, courts, and lanes to the north of the bustling street.

Fleet Street became the Strand. Rising ahead was a Victorian Gothic building holding a different kind of court, the Royal Courts of Justice. Just before reaching it, Daisy turned right into Bell Yard. Now the figures passing her were barristers in black gowns and white wigs, and solicitors in dark suits and bowlers or—among the elderly—frock coats and top hats.

In these surroundings, no wonder Tommy had grown staid. Had he become too old-fashioned to let a woman have her say in legal matters?

As he had advised, she entered the precincts of Lincoln's Inn by the Carey Street gate, an elaborate archway with two coats of arms above and fanciful wrought ironwork supporting a gas lamp below. She confirmed his directions with the porter.

"Number 12, New Square, madam? Pearson, Solicitors? Straight on. You'll pass two passages with a bit of a garden between them, then it's the second door on your right."

Daisy thanked him and went on into New Square. On three sides of a wide stretch of lawn and trees stood terraces of four-storied brick buildings. Most had regular rows of sash windows, with the symmetry beloved of the Georgians. As she approached numbers twelve and thirteen, Daisy saw they were obviously older, their windows odd sizes and misaligned, very likely replacements for the original mullioned casements.

The interior matched, Daisy found when she entered after ringing the bell, as instructed by a small sign. The entrance hall boasted centuries-old carved oak panelling and stairs—and electric lights.

The rattle of typewriters halved in volume and a girl came out of a room to one side. She escorted Daisy up to the second floor, to a small room gloomily lined with shelves of black deed boxes, where she presented her to Tommy's secretary. Miss Watt had steel-grey hair set in steely marcel waves. Her plain costume was steel-grey, the skirt four inches below the knee, worn with a severely plain white blouse. Her eyes, examining Daisy over half-spectacles, were also steel-grey. Daisy suspected they could be as cold and sharp as steel if required to guard her employer from unwanted intruders.

However, Daisy met with Miss Watt's approval. "You're a few minutes early, Mrs. Fletcher, but I believe Mr. Pearson can see you immediately. I'll let him know you're here."

Tommy appeared at once to usher her into his office, and she remembered to address him as Mr. Pearson. She had met him and Madge at the military hospital in Malvern where Madge had been a VAD nurse and Tommy a patient after one of his more perilous exploits. Daisy herself had squeamishly stuck to working in the hospital's office, but she'd become good friends with the older girl, a friendship that had continued after both she and Madge married.

"Will you be needing me, Mr. Pearson?"

"No, thank you, Miss Watt. No interruptions."

The office was a further example of mixed eras. The panelling, especially the ornately carved mantelpiece, was certainly older than the large Victorian rosewood desk, with its silver inkwell, and the leather chairs. Shelves bore row after row of legal books, the older bound in calf, the newer merely clothbound. The window, open at the top, looked out over New Square.

Daisy sat down in front of the desk, Tommy behind it. "I've been reconsidering," he said, steepling his fingers.

Though she had been expecting this, Daisy was annoyed. "I do think you might have let me know. I needn't have—"

19

"Reconsidering," he repeated, "not decided against. But it would be most irregular to allow anyone other than the head of the family to attend the interviews."

"The head of the family would be worse than useless. Apart from his lack of interest in anything other than moths and butterflies, Edgar didn't grow up as part of the family and never heard the stories—"

"Ah, the stories! Those are what you expect to trip up any false claimant? You do realise it's close to a hundred years since Julian Dalrymple ran off to Jamaica?"

"Julian? I'd forgotten his name, if I ever heard it. I realise he wouldn't have known anything that happened since he left, but there's plenty of family history—the sort that doesn't get into *Burke's Peerage*—dating from much earlier."

"The sort that he might have told his children and grandchildren?"

"How can I know? Was he the strong, silent sort, or a tale spinner? Did he ramble on about the past in his old age? He must at least have told them his father was a lord, or his descendants wouldn't be turning up hoping to be recognised as heir to the viscountcy, would they?"

"You'd be surprised. I've had two letters from men whose surname is Dalrymple, as attested by a clergyman and a judge respectively, but who admit to having no reason to suppose they might be related. Also several from people who claim to be Dalrymples but adduce no evidence; and one from a person living in the village of Dalrymple, in Scotland, who considers his abode to be proof of a relationship to the family, albeit his name is McDorran."

Daisy laughed. "Heavens above! You can dismiss those at once, though."

"The last, yes. The rest will have to be investigated. Those who can provide proof of their surname, I'll have to interview. If I can't debunk them at once, I'll have to send a clerk to Somerset House to trace their ancestry. The records there go back to 1837 and Julian left England in 1831, so there's a gap. Besides, those are records from England and Wales. We have no reason to suppose he or his descendants ever returned to Britain."

"Gosh, it does sound like a complicated job."

"I assume you're not interested in the preliminaries."

"Not really," she admitted. "Once you've whittled it down to those who are serious contenders, I do think I might be able to help to separate the sheep from the goats."

"You do realise your opinion of them will carry no weight. Only primogeniture and legitimacy count with the College of Arms, who are the final arbiters."

"Give me a little credit, Tommy, I do know that much! I won't be able to prove anything, but I might manage to disprove someone's story, or part of it."

"Hmm." Tommy sounded sceptical. "What sort of family history are you thinking of?"

"Well, going right back to the beginning, for a start. Back to the fifteenth century, the Wars of the Roses, and how the Dalrymples rose to the nobility."

"Good lord! I've seen the original patent, as it happens, but it doesn't provide reasons for the ennoblement. It was talked about in the family when you were growing up?"

"Not exactly talked about, but Father told Gervaise. He told Violet—my sister—and me. I should think even younger sons would be bound to have heard about it, and it's not the sort of thing they'd forget. I don't suppose anyone else knows, except a few fusty old historians in ivory towers."

"Probably not. How did it come about?"

Daisy shook her head. "If I tell you, then you won't need my help."

"Daisy, you can't possibly tell me everything that happened in four centuries!"

"So you *will* need my help!"

"Let's say I still have an open mind on the subject. Let's hear about the Wars of the Roses. The short version."

"If there's a long version, I can't remember it. I can never keep Lancaster and York straight, either, nor remember which is red rose and which is white. Anyway, legend has it Sir Roger Dalrymple was an obscure knight who fought for the wrong side. However, at the

Battle of Bosworth he managed to switch sides just in time, taking his men with him. Henry Tudor was duly grateful and made him a baron. The story is that he'd promised a monetary award, but handing out titles was cheaper."

"Henry VII was a notorious penny-pincher."

"The funny bit is that the Petries, our neighbours, fought for Henry all along and were also rewarded with a barony."

Tommy grinned. "That can't have pleased them. And I see what you mean. It's not the sort of story the Dalrymples would be keen on broadcasting to the world."

"I don't suppose anyone would care two hoots nowadays. Or be in the least bit interested, come to that."

"Except those ivory-tower historians of yours. The Petries—I met your friend Phillip Petrie at Fairacres, but I didn't make the connection. It was the Petries' governess Julian Dalrymple ran off with."

"Propinquity," said Daisy. "The two families have always been friendly in spite of inauspicious beginnings. There was probably lots of visiting back and forth. She—What was her name, by the way? I can't keep calling her 'she.'"

"Marie-Claire."

"Julian and Marie-Claire. I can't help thinking of her as Jane Eyre. I picture her looking like Mabel Ballin. Have you seen the film?"

"Madge dragged me to the 1915 version, with Louise Vale," Tommy said impatiently. "To return to business. We know that Julian and Jane—Louise—Marie-Claire, that is, you've got me thoroughly confused. They were married in Bristol and the marriage properly registered, so the legitimacy question doesn't arise that far back. The letter from Julian found in the muniments room declared his intention of taking ship for Jamaica if his wife wasn't welcomed into the family."

"Which she wasn't? I gather that's another family legend come true."

"So it seems."

"What about the travellers' tales of their having a large, barely respectable family?"

"Just that: travellers' tales. Rumours, hints, but no details, and certainly nothing that could be described as evidence. Even if it's true, my correspondent in Kingston hasn't been able to discover records of the births of Julian's children. There was a halfhearted attempt to set up a national registry in 1843—"

"Twelve years after they left England. Time enough to have any number of children."

"Exactly. And in any case, that law was pretty much neglected. It wasn't till 1880 that the civil registration of births, marriages, and deaths was really put into effect. Besides, the islands had all sorts of upheavals: earthquakes, tidal waves, slave revolts and the freeing of slaves, sugar tariffs—"

"I don't want to hear about sugar tariffs," Daisy said firmly. "Just tell me about the earliest records of the family you've discovered. If any. Just a minute, I want to write this down." She took out her notebook.

"The earliest official record is a ship's crew list of 1882: James Dalrymple, aged seventeen; then his marriage in Kingston in 1891; James, aged twenty-six, son of Alfred Dalrymple, who may have been Julian's son. Alfred died in 1900, age unknown. James was lost at sea in 1917, his ship sunk. Torpedoed. His son—" A knock on the door interrupted. "Come in. Yes, what is it, Miss Watt?"

"It's twelve o'clock, Mr. Pearson. You have an appointment with Mr. and Mrs. Liston and they have arrived."

"Thank you. I'll be with them in just a moment," said Tommy. Miss Watt withdrew.

The sound of church clocks far and near chiming the hour wafted in through the window, a multitude of different tones, unsynchronised so that the ringing seemed to go on and on.

Daisy asked, "James's son?"

"Samuel. Also a sailor." Tommy looked and sounded evasive. "He's at sea, his present whereabouts uncertain. Sorry, I can't give you any further information now, but I'll be in touch." He stood up.

Daisy wrote down *Samuel* and regarded with dissatisfaction her very sketchy family tree:

Julian Dalrymple m. Marie-Claire Vallier
  ?
    Alfred d. 1900
    James d. 1917
    Samuel

Putting away her notebook and gathering her gloves and handbag, she said, "Just one more thing, Tommy. Geraldine's house party. She said—or implied, I can't remember exactly—that she's going to invite all the claimants. She's not thinking of gathering them together and then revealing the heir, is she?"

"Good lord no. If we have an heir by then, prospective guests will be told who he is beforehand. Then they can attend or not, as they choose. If we still haven't confirmed the heir, it'll be a further opportunity to sound them out." As he spoke, he came round the desk and opened the door.

"And about . . . ?"

"I'll let you know in due course, Mrs. Fletcher."

Too well brought up to stay put and insist on an answer when people were waiting, Daisy meekly let herself be shepherded through to the outer office.

Miss Watt gave her a cool, professional smile and a nod that could have meant anything. "The Liston file, Mr. Pearson?" Laden with a deed box, efficiently ready to hand on her desk, she followed the elderly, expensively dressed Mr. and Mrs. Liston and Tommy into his office. The door closed.

Daisy, thwarted, thought furiously. Tommy said it would be "most irregular" for any member of the family other than its head to be present at his interviews. What if she posed as his secretary, sitting in a corner taking notes? She had done it often enough for Alec, when the men he had available were needed elsewhere. Unorthodox and not according to police procedure, but he couldn't deny that she had been useful. She might as well at least propose it to Tommy.

24

Was taking notes at interviews part of Miss Watt's duties? Daisy decided to wait a few minutes to see if the secretary reappeared and was willing to chat.

She glanced about the room, looking for something that could conceivably have held her attention enough to delay her departure. A couple of chairs were provided for clients forced to wait, and on a table between them was a selection of magazines, including an issue of *Town and Country* containing one of her articles. It might provide a subject of conversation but she could hardly pretend to be reading it. Studying the names on the shelved deed boxes would just look nosy. The desk . . . Aha! On the desk was a shiny new typewriter.

Daisy stared at it with genuine envy. She didn't like to go closer to examine it properly lest Miss Watt should pop out and assume she was inquisitive about the document protruding from the roller. How long would be reasonable to linger to ask a few questions about it?

Luckily, Miss Watt appeared after only a few moments. Seeing Daisy still there, she raised her eyebrows. "Is there something I can help you with, Mrs. Fletcher?"

"I was wondering . . . I see you have a new typewriter. I'm thinking of buying one—mine is ancient and rather creaky—but I can't decide which model to get. The salesmen are all so very persuasive. May I ask, are you satisfied with this one?"

"Very. It's the new Imperial 50. You're a writer, aren't you? I've read some of your articles, and enjoyed them. I didn't realise you type them yourself."

"Oh yes. Some writers prefer longhand, but having learnt to type I find it much faster, and publishers like it better, of course. Do you do a lot of typing? I noticed two typists downstairs."

"They deal mostly with correspondence, for all our partners. One of them deals with the telephones, as well, and the other acts as receptionist. Each partner has his own secretary. I type Mr. Pearson's legal documents and any of his letters that include confidential information."

"I should think the legal terminology must get pretty complicated."

"Much of it is standard wording, conveyances and wills and trusts, sometimes partnership agreements, though we don't touch company law, let alone criminal, I'm glad to say. Most of our clients are professionals and businessmen. In any case, I don't have to understand it, just get it right. No mistakes permitted in legal documents! One misplaced comma can ruin everything."

"Goodness, I'm glad I don't have to worry about every comma. I write shorthand, too, when I interview people."

"I take shorthand dictation sometimes, but generally I work from Mr. Pearson's notes. Most clients don't much like a secretary listening to their business, even though it's obvious I'm going to deal with the results of their consultations."

Blast! thought Daisy. Not much chance that Tommy would be willing to try to pass her off as an unremarkable part of his office routine.

The last post brought a brief letter from Tommy.

Full of misgivings, Alec watched Daisy as she read it. "Well?"

"He's decided to ask each claimant whether he'd have any objection to the presence of a representative member of the family, without mentioning beforehand that said representative will be a junior female member. Junior female! What a revolting description!"

Alec couldn't help laughing. "Accurate, love, you must admit. It sounds like a reasonable compromise."

"And he says their responses could be revealing. True; what reason could a legitimate claimant have for refusing?"

"None that I can think of," he said obligingly.

"So, unless they're too stupid to realise it would look suspicious, I'll be there."

He grinned at her. "I never doubted it for a moment."

26

FOUR

Ten days passed before Daisy next heard from Tommy. He had an appointment with a Mr. Vincent Dalrymple, who was willing to allow a representative of the family to be present at the interview. He hoped the date and time were convenient, though, Daisy noted, he didn't offer to change them if not.

She gladly rescheduled a visit to the dentist.

Vincent Dalrymple was fortyish, of medium height, slender, and sleek, with fair hair receding at the temples. He wore a formal dark suit, well cut, with a white shirt and a green-and-white striped bow tie. Daisy thought he looked like either a Harley Street consultant or a high-class maître d'hôtel. He displayed a professional charm that would be of service to either. "Smarmy" was the word that sprang to mind.

"How do you do, Mrs. Fletcher." With a smile, he bowed slightly over her hand. "May I say how pleased I am to meet a relative on my father's side, however distant."

Tommy invited them to sit down. Vincent held Daisy's chair for her, then took his seat, careful to preserve the creases in his trousers. They both looked expectantly at Tommy.

"Mrs. Fletcher, Mr. Vincent Dalrymple has provided me with

certain documents and information which indicate, though they do not prove, that he may well be descended from your great-great-grandfather."

"That's a start," said Daisy, smiling encouragingly at Vincent.

"I suggest," Tommy continued, "that he himself tell you his story."

"What a good idea." Daisy turned towards her presumed distant cousin.

"Should I start from the present and work back, or start with my grandfather? Which would you prefer, Mrs. Fletcher?"

"Why don't you try chronological order. But don't worry if you get sidetracked, or skip about a bit." She knew from experience how difficult it was to recount a straightforward narrative. Whenever she found herself mixed up in one of Alec's cases, he was forever chiding her for wandering or for missing out important details. She took out her notebook.

"Thank you. Well, let's see." Vincent frowned in concentration. "My grandfather told us—"

"You knew him? Sorry, I shouldn't interrupt."

"No, please do, if anything isn't clear. I was sixteen when he died. Mr. Pearson has a copy of his death certificate."

Tommy consulted one of the documents on his desk. "February 1901, in Scarborough, North Riding. Timothy George Dalrymple. Unfortunately, his age at time of death was omitted."

"Because my father didn't know it. The family never did much in the way of celebrating the birthdays of adults, and my grandmother died before him."

"What about his marriage certificate? I remember ours has my husband's age and mine."

"Dai—Mrs. Fletcher, could we leave the question of legal papers till the end? I'll show you what I have then, with Mr. Dalrymple's permission, of course."

"Granted." Vincent glanced from Tommy to Daisy and back, his eyes sharp. He'd obviously caught Tommy's slip of the tongue and was wondering what, if anything, it portended for him. However, he continued smoothly, "Maybe I'd better start again. My grandfather was born in Jamaica, date unknown. He knew his father was the younger son of a lord, though if my grandfather was aware of the precise rank he never mentioned it, as far as I recall."

"What was his name?" Daisy asked. Unlike some noble lineages, her family had never gone in for repeating christian names generation after generation, but she was creating another family tree, probably as partial as the first.

"My grandfather was Timothy. His father—I have a vague impression he was Julius, or Julian. I may have dreamt that."

"Julian," Tommy said drily. "Son of Julius, Viscount Dalrymple. It's easily checked in *Burke's Peerage*. An unsatisfactory offspring can be struck out in the family bible but not in Burke, though his descendants can be lost track of."

"*Burke's Peerage*, did you say?" He took out a pocket diary and a gold fountain pen. "I'll make a note of that. I'd better look up my illustrious ancestry, eh?"

Daisy couldn't tell whether he was being disingenuous or had genuinely never heard of Burke before. "Do go on," she urged. "I'm dying to hear why Timothy Dalrymple left Jamaica and went to Paris."

"He left to escape the cholera. There was an epidemic in the island around the middle of the last century. Several of the family fell ill. For safety, he was sent to his mother's family in France."

"Oh, that's right, I keep forgetting she was French. Timothy was the only one sent to France?"

"Yes, I'm pretty sure of that."

"Eldest? Youngest? Favourite? Only one not ill?"

"I don't know. He didn't talk about it. Not to me, at least. I wasn't particularly interested in my grandfather's early life. Not till now."

"Did any of the others survive?"

Vincent spread his hands and shrugged, a very French gesture. "By the time I was old enough to wonder, the old man had lost touch. His mother died of the cholera, that much I know."

"So there must have been some correspondence, at least to inform her family."

"Presumably. Even before the epidemic, times were hard in Jamaica, he told us. I suppose they had other priorities than writing

29

letters. My grandfather settled in with the Vallier family, worked in the family business—"

"What was that? I beg your pardon, I'm insatiably curious. You don't have to answer."

"It's no secret. They're hoteliers, as I am."

Tommy ostentatiously consulted his wristwatch. "Mrs. Fletcher, if you want time to look at the papers . . ."

"Not another word, I promise."

Vincent gave her a look of sympathy. "To make a long story short, my grandfather married. My father, George, was born in 1861. In 1870 the Germans invaded and when their army approached Paris, my grandfather brought his wife and children to England. He still had a British passport, you see. The Valliers had friends in the business, in Scarborough, who helped him find work. In fact . . ." He hesitated. "This may not please you, Mrs. Fletcher. He changed his name to Vallier. Not legally, but in everyday use."

Daisy pondered. "I can't see why I should have any objection. Because of his mother being rejected by the Dalrymples? Wait a bit." She glanced at her notes. "This is Timothy we're talking about, not George?"

Tommy cleared his throat meaningly.

"He asked me!" said Daisy, indignant. By implication, at least.

"Indeed I did." Vincent sounded like a maître d'hôtel discreetly smoothing over a minor dispute between guests. "Yes, Timothy, my grandfather, Mrs. Fletcher. Exactly what was in his mind I can't say, but a French name can be an advantage in the trade. Besides, he'd been well taught by the Valliers. He obtained a position as undermanager of one of the finest hotels in Scarborough, rose quickly to manager, and then became a partner. My father married his partner's daughter, his only child, and eventually they inherited both shares of the Castle Cliff Hotel. My parents left it to me, so I'm now the sole owner, with a hired manager responsible for day-to-day business."

Daisy was touched by his obvious pride in being not merely manager but proprietor of a good hotel in a seaside resort. It was, indeed, a notable accomplishment on the part of his immediate forebears.

Timothy had presumably arrived in Paris with little more than the clothes on his back. Then the refugee from cholera had become a refugee from war, yet he had built a prosperous life for his family.

There was something admirable about this branch of the Dalrymples. What was more, if Vincent was the heir, the ownership of the hotel could be useful when it came to death duties. He could sell it and pay with the proceeds, rather than depleting the estate. And whether he turned out to be the next viscount or not, his son might find himself in a position to call himself a gentleman.

"Have you any children?" she asked.

"A boy and two girls. My son is at a prep school. My daughters have a French governess. Speaking several languages is useful in the business. Not that my girls will need to work," he added hurriedly.

As Tommy didn't make any ominous noises, Daisy ventured to comment, "Of course! Your . . ." She paused to work it out. "Your great-grandmother must have taken the post with the Petries to learn English."

Vincent hesitated, darting a quick glance at Tommy. "The Petries . . . Yes, of course."

Tommy glared at her, then turned to Vincent. "As you've so kindly brought us up to the present, Mr. Dalrymple, I don't believe we need keep you any longer. You have other business in London, I gather."

"Nothing more important than this." Vincent rose reluctantly. "If you have any more questions, Mrs. Fletcher—"

"They can wait until you meet at Fairacres in August," Tommy interrupted. "Should you receive further documents from your relatives in France, Mr. Dalrymple, no doubt you'll be in touch, and naturally I'll let you know of any developments that affect your position. Thank you for sparing the time for this meeting."

"Oh, my time's mostly my own these days. Good-bye, Mrs. Fletcher."

Daisy smiled at him and offered her hand. "Good-bye, Cousin Vincent. I look forward to seeing you at Fairacres."

He flushed—with gratification, she hoped—but before he could speak, Tommy bustled him out.

Returning, Tommy closed the door firmly behind him and hissed, "'Cousin Vincent'! There's no proof that he's descended from Julian Dalrymple."

"I can always uncousin him," said Daisy, unrepentant. "Anyway, if he turns out to be a fraud, I won't be seeing him again."

"It's going to be that much harder to prove fraud now that he can trot out the Petries! He'd obviously never heard of them."

"I'm sorry about that. It slipped out before I realised it might give him information he didn't already have. Do you think he's a fraud?"

"At this stage, I'd need a crystal ball—"

"I think he's real, though he may turn out not to be the eldest. I mean, his grandfather may not have been Julian's eldest son. Show me his papers. Perhaps they'll spark an idea."

"Heaven preserve me from your ideas," Tommy muttered.

Daisy pretended not to hear. She pulled up her chair to the desk and Tommy set the documents before her. There were four: three certified copies of entries in the national registry at Somerset House, and a letter in French, in crabbed, elderly handwriting.

The first was the notice of Vincent's birth, at the Castle Cliff Hotel in Scarborough in 1885. His baptismal names were Vincent Vallier. His father was George (also known as Georges) Vallier Dalrymple, his mother Amanda Rosemary Dalrymple, formerly White. George's profession was given as hotelier.

"So far, so good," Daisy observed, picking up the second paper.

It was George and Amanda's marriage certificate, Scarborough, 1883. George had been twenty-two, Amanda twenty-seven at the time, assistant hotel manager and hotel housekeeper respectively. George's father was Timothy Dalrymple; Amanda's, Frederick White, both hoteliers.

"Gosh, all the family are really dedicated to the hotel business! What's this? Timothy's death notice. 1901, age: 'elderly'! I wonder why he wouldn't tell his son how old he was, or do you think he genuinely forgot? It must have been fearfully disorientating being sent away from home, from Jamaica to France. I wonder whether he even spoke French when he arrived. He could have learnt from his mother. Perhaps the Valliers didn't care about his age, just put him to work."

"We're unlikely ever to know the attitude to birthdays of the Valliers of the time, though we may eventually find out his date of birth. Here's Vincent's marriage certificate."

"1912, to Laurette Vallier. Some sort of cousin presumably, keeping the business in the family. What's this?" She peered at the last document. Her knowledge of French wasn't bad but the handwriting looked a bit like her own shorthand hieroglyphics. It had an impressive seal, though.

"A notarised affidavit from the present clergyman of the church where Timothy Dalrymple married Jeanette Desrochers, and George was baptised. It's a small Protestant church that was badly damaged in 1870. Vincent got the present Valliers to dig through the remains of the old records. They were pretty well scorched, but books don't burn easily. Enough of it is readable, apparently, to be certain that they actually were married, but that's about all. The rest is gone. George's legitimacy is proven, at least."

"Aren't there civil records?"

"A large part of the Paris civil registry was destroyed when the Jerries invaded."

At least the family tree for this branch was slightly less sketchy:

Julian m. Marie-Claire Vallier
Timothy George Dalrymple (d. 1901) m. Jeanette Desrochers
George Vallier Dalrymple m. (1883) Amanda Rosemary White
Vincent Vallier Dalrymple (b. 1885) m. Laurette Vallier
Two girls, one boy.

"How will you ever find out for sure? About Timothy being Julian's legitimate son? Or not, as the case may be."

"The best chance is Jamaica, obviously. But the chap I had checking the registry in Spanish Town, the old capital, didn't find any records of Dalrymples before 1882, as I told you before."

"So, in fact, we may never know for sure who's the rightful heir? What if we can't?"

"That's another bridge to be crossed if we come to it. It's possible," the lawyer admitted grudgingly. "I *told* you, Daisy, conditions were chaotic at times: slave revolts, tidal waves, plantations abandoned, much of Kingston burnt to the ground. If Julian and Marie-Claire lived in an out-of-the way corner of the island, communications would have been difficult."

"But it's not a very big island, is it? As big as Ireland?"

"About a third the size. That's the comparison that occurred to me, and I looked it up. But much of Jamaica is mountainous jungle. Before I get in touch with the Dalrymples of Kingston and raise their hopes, perhaps for nothing, I'm hoping to discover a solid connection with Julian. It can't wait much longer, though."

"I wonder what sort of a viscount Vincent would make. It sounds as if he must be a competent manager, capable of running the estate, unless the title goes to his head and he and his wife go gadding about. Mother's bound to have forty fits anyway. A teacher's bad enough. An innkeeper would be the last straw!"

"Don't cross your bridges. Even if he does turn out to be the heir, he'll be heir presumptive, not heir apparent. If Edgar were to have a child—"

"Come off it, you've met Geraldine."

"Should Lady Dalrymple die, Lord Dalrymple might remarry, a younger woman."

"Only butterflies interest him, and I don't mean the social kind." Daisy suddenly stopped. "Tommy, I've had a perfectly frightful thought. You don't think Vincent will want to turn Fairacres into a grand country hotel, do you? Horrors! Could he, legally?"

"I don't propose to investigate the legal ramifications unless the contingency arises. But I suspect the act of 1925 would make it possible."

"What act?"

"The Administration of Estates Act."

"Why, what does it say?"

Tommy went over to his bookshelves and selected a volume. "Let

34

me read you a selection. '(1) With regard to the real estate and personal inheritance of every person dying after the commencement of this Act, there shall be abolished—' "

"That seems clear enough."

He continued as though she had not interrupted, " '(a) All existing modes rules and canons of descent, and of devolution by special occupancy or otherwise, of real estate, or of a personal inheritance, whether operating by the general law or by the custom of gavelkind or borough english or by any other custom of any county, locality, or manor, or otherwise howsoever; and (b) Tenancy by the curtesy and every other estate and interest of a husband in real estate as to which his wife dies intestate, whether arising under the general law and (c) Dower and freebench and—' "

"Stop! All right, I concede. Forget about it unless it turns out to be necessary."

"Thank you." He returned the volume to its place. "If and when, I shan't lift a finger without taking the advice of counsel. Speaking of which—"

Tap tap. Miss Watt appeared. "Mr. Pearson, sorry to interrupt but you're due in court in quarter of an hour."

"I'm on my way." He picked up his briefcase and ushered Daisy to the door, grabbing his hat from the hatstand on the way. As they walked down the stairs together, he said, "I must warn you, less acceptable claimants than Vincent may appear."

Daisy sighed. "No doubt. Just keep them from Mother as long as you can. But you will let me know what's going on, won't you? And let me talk to them before they go to Fairacres?"

"I don't know, Daisy. If you're going to make them a present of information that could bolster their claims—"

"Must you harp on that? It was a mistake. I've apologised. And I promise to be more careful."

It was Tommy's turn to sigh. "I suppose it will be all right. You have given me one or two ideas."

"That," said Daisy, "is what Alec always has to admit."

FIVE

"*You're just* in time for tea, darling." Daisy gladly abandoned her battle with the recalcitrant household accounts. She always tried to cope with them herself but, as usual, she would have to ask for Mrs. Dobson's help. "I'll join you. Or would you rather have breakfast?"

"Mrs. Dobson's making me a combination breakfast-high tea, bless her." Alec had just got up. After leaving for work at the usual time yesterday, he hadn't come home until the birds were breaking into their dawn chorus. "Then it's back to work."

"What's going on?"

"Just one thing after another, culminating in a nightclub stabbing just as we thought we were done for the day. All the witnesses and suspects are night owls, so we are, too, perforce."

In the dining room, Elsie was setting the table with an eclectic selection of tableware. "You'll take your tea in here, madam?"

"Yes, please, Elsie." Daisy waited till the ever-efficient parlour-maid finished her task and whisked out. "Alec, I simply must tell you the latest from Tommy."

"You've heard from him again? It's been a couple of weeks since you made the acquaintance of your Cousin Vincent, hasn't it? But it's your family's business, not mine, thank goodness."

"I was hoping for your advice, but if you'd rather tell me all about the nightclub stabbing—"

"Great Scott, no. I'll be getting back to that soon enough. All right, go ahead. Has Pearson turned up an heir, or just another new cousin?"

"Another cousin, Raymond. He's already on his way from South Africa."

"South Africa!"

"When Tommy got the letter saying he was coming, he wired back immediately to tell him it might well be a waste of time and money, but by then he'd sailed from Cape Town. He'll arrive in Southampton at the end of next week."

"That doesn't seem to call for my advice."

"No, it's the letter Tommy enclosed. The copy of a letter, rather. He wants to consult me before replying to it."

"What on earth makes you think I have anything helpful to contribute?"

"You probably don't. Talking about it may help me to work out whether I do."

Sighing, he nodded acquiescence, but he cheered up when his meal arrived. Mrs. Dobson had cooked for Alec's mother before he and Daisy were married. She was well aware of the needs of a hungry policeman and the tastes of her employer. A ham omelette with fried potatoes was flanked with bread and butter, salad, and a plate of cold roast beef. Rhubarb-and-strawberry tartlets, almond biscuits, and dark, moist gingerbread completed the spread, with a pot of coffee for Alec and tea for Daisy.

"Aaah!" breathed Alec and dug in.

Pouring herself a cup of tea, Daisy surveyed the offerings. It would be much easier to drop a few pounds if Mrs. Dobson wasn't so good at baking as well as accounts. She took a thin slice of gingerbread and, to make it last, started talking.

"The letter is from a Mrs. Samuel Dalrymple in Jamaica. Her husband is a first officer in the Merchant Navy."

Alec swallowed a mouthful and translated: "Mate of a freighter, since the war at least. He's not illiterate, then, if he got his mate's papers."

"Illiterate? Why should he be?"

"I just wondered why she's writing for him."

"Because he's off on a voyage, according to Tommy, and she doesn't know when he'll be back."

"Must be a tramp steamer. No wireless? A small, elderly tramp steamer."

"Pure speculation," Daisy teased. Tit for tat: He had said it to her often enough.

"Not at all. Pure deduction."

Daisy considered. "Oh yes, I suppose it's reasonable."

"What's worrying Pearson?"

"Not really worrying. You see, Mrs. Samuel—Martha's her name—wrote as soon as the advert was brought to her attention, because she wonders whether her husband is descended from Julian and Marie-Claire."

"Obviously."

"Yes, but the thing is, *she* was worrying that another man might be coroneted before anyone was aware of Samuel's existence. She wrote because she didn't dare wait for him to come home before notifying Tommy. And she asked him whether she ought to come to England right away. That's what's got him fussing. He doesn't think she should travel on her own—he's rather old-fashioned that way—and he doesn't know what to do with her when she arrives. Given Samuel's occupation, Tommy's pretty sure she hasn't got enough money for what he'd consider a suitable hotel for a lady on her own."

"Given Samuel's occupation, is she a lady?"

"Whatever she is now, she'll be a lady if her husband turns out to be the heir presumptive. In the meantime, she must be treated as such."

"Why doesn't he just tell her to stay in Jamaica and wait for Samuel's return?"

"He probably will. The thing is, he'd like to get his hands on whatever information she can provide, as soon as possible."

"Didn't you say he's had someone in Jamaica looking into the family history? Can't he talk to her?"

"That's a good point, darling. I'll suggest it, though I'd be surprised if Tommy missed it. Perhaps the man is good at searching records but isn't the type who'd be any good at interviewing."

"Could be. We have plenty of those at the Yard."

"So what should he do?"

"He could try to employ someone more appropriate—not easy at such a distance, I imagine. Or he could wait for his information until Samuel arrives. Or he could write to her asking for details, which might or might not produce useful results. Does her letter give any reason other than his name to believe her husband is a legitimate descendant of whatsisname—the black sheep?"

"Julian. No, the letter's very short."

"Well, that's about all I have to contribute." Alec finished off a tart, gulped the last of a second cup of coffee, and stood up. "I must be gone. Reports to be written and read before we go off in search of the creatures of the night. I'll see you when I see you, love."

Daisy went out to the hall with him to see him off, then returned to the office to reread Martha Dalrymple's letter—or rather the copy typed by Miss Watt—in the light of Alec's comments.

It was written in perfectly correct English, but not the formal language people usually use when addressing a solicitor. Either she had worded it herself, or with the help of someone equally unsophisticated. It was very short, conveying no more information than Daisy had passed on to Alec.

She found the appropriate family tree in her notebook and added Martha:

Julian Dalrymple m. Marie-Claire Vallier
?
    Alfred d. 1900
    James d. 1917
     Samuel m. Martha

It was still more of a branch than a tree.

Turning to Tommy's letter, Daisy considered its content from the point of view of Martha, rather than the lawyer's convenience. He was very likely right that she wouldn't be comfortable staying alone at a London hotel, even if she could afford it. Come to that, could she afford the passage? Would the estate pay the fare without a better reason than his residence in Jamaica for believing Samuel might be directly and legitimately descended from Julian?

Had Martha failed to provide information about her husband's ancestry because she hadn't thought of it, because she didn't know of any, or because there was none? If there was none, if Samuel was not a legitimate descendant of Julian and Martha was aware of the fact, why would she have responded to Tommy's agony column notice?

The only answer Daisy could think of was that she—or they—contemplated an attempt at fraud.

What nonsense! The possibility would never have dawned on her if she hadn't spent so much time associating with policemen. All the same, she had a lot of questions, and she really wanted to see the original letter from Martha. Though she thought the more esoteric claims of graphology were akin to spiritualism, she did believe handwriting could sometimes provide a clue to character.

She dashed off a quick note to Tommy, saying she would like to talk to him. Having wrested the twins from Mrs. Gilpin's custody, she took them and Nana to post it, along with a couple of other letters. With Bertha, the nurserymaid, pushing the double pushchair, they went down through the garden in the centre of Constable Crescent and by the footpath to Well Walk. When they reached the pillar-box, Oliver had to be lifted up to push the envelopes through the slot.

Then Miranda had to be lifted to touch the beasts in the crest above the slot. "Look, Mama. Lion, 'corn, King George."

"*Uni*corn, darling."

"I *not* 'corn. I Manda!"

"So you are, Miss Miranda," said Bertha, "and don't you let anyone—not even your mum—tell you other. You're not a nasty old unicorn, which from what I hear ain't even a real animal! Begging your pardon, madam. Now then, Master Oliver, you naughty boy, you climb right back in this instant!"

Words failing to do the trick, Bertha picked up the child, put him in his seat, and strapped him in.

Daisy knew she was lucky to have such admirably competent servants, and all good-natured except Nurse Gilpin. Even Nurse, while always ready to thwart her employers, was firm but fair with the children. Other people seemed constantly to complain about their inability to find good servants. Years ago, Daisy had started writing an article on the "servant problem" from the servants' point of view, but what with one thing and another it hadn't progressed very far.

She was glad she didn't have to cope with a staff the size necessary to run a place like Fairacres. Why, she wondered, would anyone be eager to take on the job, unless the alternative was penury?

Such might be the case for Samuel and Martha, but Vincent seemed to be comfortably off. What was more, he knew the difficulties of dealing with a large staff, if his hotel was as superior as he claimed. Then there was the mysterious South African, so keen to be the missing heir that he sailed for England without waiting to hear from Tommy.

While Daisy mused, they had strolled back along Gayton Road and Well Walk. When they reached the garden, Nana was released from her lead and the twins from the pushchair. Naturally they all headed straight for the fountain in the middle. A quarter of an hour later, Daisy cravenly let the nurserymaid take the damp twins upstairs to face Mrs. Gilpin's wrath.

"Tell her it's my fault, Bertha. It's such a warm afternoon, they can't possibly come to any harm."

She took Nana round to the alley at the side of the house and let her through the gate into the garden. The dog would soon dry off there. She was good about staying out of flower beds and not digging, though the thrice-weekly gardener had had to fence off the vegetable plot to keep her from eating his prized tomatoes as soon as they ripened.

As Daisy entered the house, her thoughts returned to Edgar's heir. Edgar, she was sure, wouldn't care who it was as long as he was left in peace to pursue his lepidoptera. Geraldine would fuss whoever it was, but probably wouldn't make a great to-do about it unless he and his family chose to take up residence at Fairacres. Would he be legally entitled to move in? Another question for Tommy.

The one who was absolutely certain to cut up rough, no matter what the result, was the dowager viscountess. Daisy sighed. A hotelier or a freighter's officer—it made no odds. Her mother would find something to complain about if the angel Gabriel himself came down to Worcestershire to take over Fairacres.

SIX

The following morning, Miss Watt rang up to ask if it would be convenient for Mr. Pearson to drop in that afternoon after calling on a client in Highgate.

"Yes, certainly," Daisy assured her. "Do make sure he brings Mrs. Samuel Dalrymple's letter, will you, please, Miss Watt?"

"I'll remind him that you'd like to see the original, Mrs. Dalrymple. In fact, I'll slip it into his despatch case, so that he can't possibly forget it." Her tone was conspiratorial.

"Thank you, that's very kind of you." Daisy felt she had gained an ally—not against Tommy, exactly, but against the sort of footling obstacles men tend to raise against any mild unorthodoxy when proposed by a female.

If some professional nicety made him reluctant to show her Martha's letter, the secretary's ploy made it difficult for him to claim to have accidentally left it at the office.

No sooner had Daisy hung the receiver on its hook than she remembered Sakari Prasad was coming to tea. She nearly rang back, but there was no knowing when Tommy's busy schedule would allow him to save her the trouble of going to Lincoln's Inn. Besides,

Sakari was a close friend who wouldn't take offence if Daisy deserted her for a few minutes to speak to Tommy.

An inveterate attender of lectures and classes, Sakari had written an essay encouraging others to do likewise. She wanted Daisy's opinion as to whether it was worth submitting to *Time and Tide*, the liberal, feminist, literary magazine.

Comfortably settled in the small sitting room at the back of the house, Daisy read the article while Sakari poured tea and started to make inroads into the supply of watercress sandwiches, three kinds of biscuits, and a sponge filled with whipped cream and strawberries. Mrs. Dobson thoroughly approved of Sakari, who appreciated good food. Saris—such as the gold-embroidered scarlet she was wearing—were forgiving as to fit, Sakari said, so she had no inhibitions when it came to her waistline. Besides, her chauffeur, Kesin, had become a welcome visitor in the kitchen.

Sakari's article, with a subject that could have been as dry as dust, was delightful. Daisy should have known that her friend's forthright sense of humour would shine through. She found herself chuckling, and a most unladylike snort escaped her just as she took a sip of tea.

"Oh dear, I've sprayed the page. I'll type the whole thing for you, darling. It's wonderful, and it may have a better chance if it's typed. You must definitely send it in."

"I am glad you like it, Daisy. Do you think I should use a pen name?"

"No, definitely not. I'm sure Lady Rhondda, the proprietor, will be tickled pink to have an international contributor. Now I'll finish my tea before I finish reading." She picked up her cup.

"Eat a sandwich also. You will fade away!"

"Not I, alas." But she ate one of the small crustless triangles, then emptied her cup and went back to the article. Turning to the next page, she exclaimed, "You went to a lecture on graphology? I don't remember you talking about it."

"A great deal of nonsense was spoken," Sakari said severely.

"You didn't believe any of it?"

"A little, perhaps, but to read a person's entire history in a few scribbled words—balderdash." The last word she pronounced with the relish she always took in her infrequent use of colloquialisms.

"All the same, I'd like you to look at the letter Tommy Pearson's bringing to show me."

"The lawyer? What letter is this?"

Daisy explained. "He already sent me a copy, but I want to look at the handwriting, just in case it can tell me something about the writer. There's the doorbell now. That will be Tommy."

A few moments later, Elsie came in to announce Mr. Pearson's arrival. "He'd like a word with you, madam."

"Ask him to join us, will you, Elsie?"

Tommy came in wearing his lawyer face. He greeted Sakari politely but unenthusiastically, and turned to Daisy. "Could we go to your office? I'm sorry to interrupt your revels but this won't take a minute."

"There's been a change of plan." Daisy smiled at his irritated expression. "Elsie, another cup, please. Do sit down, Tommy."

"Daisy, I haven't got time for a tea party."

"But darling, I've just discovered that Sakari is an expert graphologist. She's going to take a look at Martha's letter and tell us her entire history."

Sakari shook her head, laughing. "Nothing of the sort, Mr. Pearson. However, the handwriting may tell us a little about the character. May I propose that you show the letter to Daisy while I powder my nose? She will give you her opinion and then I will give you mine. Should they coincide—"

"Coincidence, Mrs. Prasad, sheer coincidence!"

"Possibly. It can do no harm to try, can it? I need to see only one line, so the letter will remain confidential." Seeing him unconvinced, she heaved herself out of her armchair. "I will go, and you may decide when I return."

Reluctantly, Tommy produced the letter from his briefcase. "I wondered why you wanted to see it. Surely you don't buy that superstitious nonsense?"

"No more than Sakari does."

"It's no better than astrology!"

"Darling, I have friends who are quite convinced that their fate is written in the stars. I suspect there's a bit more substance to graphology. Let me see the letter."

He passed it to her and turned with obvious relief to the cup of tea Sakari had poured him before departing for the cloakroom.

The handwriting was round and schoolgirlish, suggesting that Martha didn't write often enough to have formed her own style. She was probably young, not well-off, facing an unprecedented situation in her husband's absence, not knowing when he would return to deal with it or what he would want her to do.

Daisy sympathised.

"She's young, and probably naïve. Unsure of herself."

"And so she should be, providing not the slightest hint of what her husband's claim may rest on, apart from the name."

"And he lives in Jamaica. We know Julian went there."

"His offspring seems to have spread all over the world," Tommy grumbled.

"You must admit this Samuel is very likely one of them who stayed put. Your investigator in Kingston is still investigating?"

"Yes, but he's not getting any further."

Daisy found the family branch in her notebook. "Samuel's father, James, he was the one lost at sea?"

"That's right. His ship was sunk by a U-boat. Samuel's ship was torpedoed, too, but he survived. He even turns out to have been something of a hero; he saved the lives of several of the crew. In fact, he was decorated after the war, when they got round to the Merchant Navy."

"Tommy, you can't just ignore them and hope they'll go away!"

"I've no intention of doing so," he retorted looking, harassed, "but what am I supposed to do when the man seems to have vanished? He sailed from Kingston weeks ago."

Sakari appeared in the doorway, winked at Daisy, and advanced into the room in her stately way. "Have you decided, Mr. Pearson, whether I am to be trusted to see the letter?"

Tommy stood up, slightly flustered, turning towards her. "Of course I don't distrust you, Mrs. Prasad. However, I have a duty to my client, who, in this case, is Lord Dalrymple—or the estate, rather—not Daisy."

"As if Cousin Edgar would care!"

Sakari sank majestically into her chair. "Daisy, will you be so kind as to cut me another slice of this delicious-looking cake? I adore strawberries and cream."

"Of course. Will you have some, Tommy?"

"I beg your pardon?" Apparently lost in thought, the lawyer had absentmindedly demolished the rest of the sandwiches.

"Cake?"

"Oh, yes, please. Our present cook isn't much of a baker. Thank you."

Daisy gave him a big piece, and cut a smaller one for herself. For a few minutes the only sounds were contented murmurs and the song of a blackbird in the garden.

Mellowed by the cake, Tommy showed Sakari a couple of lines of the letter, comprising *Dear Sir, A friend has shown me your . . .* , the rest carefully covered with a sheet of paper.

She took one glance and said, "Young, unsophisticated, lacking self-confidence."

"Exactly what I said."

Tommy snorted—luckily not with a mouthful of tea. Daisy thought she heard a mutter of "Piffle!"

"She is a simple person."

"Simple-minded?" Tommy exclaimed, aghast.

"No, no, that is not what I said, Mr. Pearson. Uncomplicated. Without guile. And this is cheap paper   She is not well off."

"That much I had worked out for myself."

"Well taught, but not well educated." Sakari handed the letter back to him.

"What do you mean?"

"I am sure you understand me. Her writing is clear and her English is good—as far as I, a mere foreigner, am able to judge. Nonetheless, she has no notion of the formal language a lawyer surely expects."

"Believe me, we get letters in all sorts of language."

"But you judge the writer thereby."

"Touché. You are a shrewd woman, Mrs. Prasad. I grant you all you have said of her education and her means, if not necessarily of her character. Have you thought that perhaps she might be illiterate and have had someone else write it for her?"

"It is, of course, possible. However, is not the usual practice to mark an X for the signature in such cases? Is the letter signed with an X?"

"No, with her name in full. Possibly her signature is the only thing she's able to write."

"Is it in the same handwriting as the rest of the letter?"

"Yes," Daisy intervened. Listening to Tommy and Sakari matching wits was entertaining, but enough was enough. "Tommy, argument may be your métier but you're not going to best Sakari, not in a million years."

Sakari laughed.

Tommy protested, "I'm a solicitor, not an advocate. I deal in facts, not in arguments."

"There you go again, darling. We're agreed—aren't we?—that Martha is not strikingly knowledgeable or accomplished, and that she's short of money. And we know her husband, who may be the missing heir, is away from home and apparently out of touch for the foreseeable future."

"Mrs. Prasad didn't know that until you just told her."

"She does now. The question is, should you ask her to come here right away—"

"Heaven forbid!"

"Or should you request any information she has about Samuel's family, to be sent to you or given to your representative there. Or should you just advise her to do nothing till Samuel turns up, which for all we know could be after Geraldine's house party. Being late wouldn't invalidate his claim, would it?"

"No—unless, in the meantime, the College of Arms had declared someone else to be the rightful heir. But they're never in a hurry. No, more likely, to my mind, is that he won't turn up at all."

"What would happen in such a case?" Sakari asked.

"Nothing, if one of the others proved his claim. But if it turns out that Samuel is descended through eldest sons from Julian, we might have to wait until he's presumed dead."

"Why shouldn't he turn up?" Daisy demanded.

"I just think it's odd that he's been completely out of touch for so long. His grandfather's death certificate gives the cause of death as cirrhosis of the liver. Perhaps Samuel is subject to the same weakness. He may be down-and-out in some Caribbean port, with no means or no intention of going home."

"Facts," Sakari reminded him tartly. "Lawyers are not supposed to have premonitions."

"You're quite right, Mrs. Prasad. Nor should I have mentioned Alfred Dalrymple's unfortunate disorder in your presence. I trust you will disregard it."

"My lips are sealed."

"He seems to have been employed by a rum distillery in Kingston." Tommy shrugged, as if to say cirrhosis was a natural, if not inevitable, result of the job. "Unfortunately, my informant is unable to trace the family before 1882. I expect no better of Mr. Raymond Dalrymple, due to arrive shortly from South Africa. Julian's branch of your family, Daisy, had an unfortunate penchant for settling in turbulent regions of the world."

SEVEN

On his arrival from South Africa, Mr. Raymond Dalrymple went to stay at the Savoy. Rather than writing to request an appointment with Tommy, he sent for him to come to the hotel.

Somewhat miffed because, after all, his client was the estate, not Mr. Raymond Dalrymple, Tommy had nonetheless heeded the call. Because he was miffed, he afterwards told Daisy all about the interview. He took her to lunch at the Old Cheshire Cheese.

"Raymond's a businessman," he told her. "A partner in Pritchard and Dalrymple, a member of the De Beers cartel."

"Diamonds!"

"Buying and selling diamonds," Tommy confirmed. "He was coming to Europe on business anyway, leaving his cousin and his son to run things in South Africa."

"How old is he? I don't know why I assumed he was a young man."

"He's in his early sixties and the son, Stanley, is in his late thirties. He presented me with their birth and marriage certificates right away, very businesslike. His credentials, he called them."

"Early sixties . . ." Daisy attempted the mental maths while she started scribbling down a family branch. "His father must have been Julian's son, then?"

"Yes, Henry by name."

"Surely Raymond must know whether Henry was Julian's eldest."

"He didn't even know his grandfather's name, just that he was the son of an English lord. His father, Henry, was born in Jamaica, quarrelled with *his* father, possibly Julian, and emigrated to Cape Colony, as it was then. Henry married the daughter of a settler, Alice Pritchard. He and his brother-in-law went prospecting together, and he was killed in a brawl—"

"He told you that? I'm surprised that he'd reveal such a discreditable blot on the would-be escutcheon."

" 'Brawl' is my interpretation. He sounds like a thoroughly quarrelsome chap. To be precise, Raymond said the two were attacked by rival prospectors."

"Claim jumpers. It sounds like the Wild West."

"They were out in the wilds somewhere. No death certificate."

"How old was Raymond when Henry died?"

"Just five. He was brought up by his mother's family."

"So he hardly knew his father, and if he was told anything about his grandfather he could well have forgotten."

"His mother used to say his great-grandfather was an English lord. That's really all he knows. Raymond's baptismal certificate names his father as Henry Herbert Dalrymple of Jamaica, giving no age, no profession."

"It sounds as if he was in search of a profession when he died."

"You could put it that way. Once again, the earlier certificates aren't what they might be. The church where Henry married Alice and Raymond was baptised, by an itinerant preacher, burned down in one of their wars or uprisings, and bureaucracy didn't hold much sway in the wilds in those days."

"So once again there's no proof. Most unsatisfactory." Daisy frowned at the family branch:

?Julian
Henry Herbert Dalrymple m. Alice Pritchard
Raymond m. ?
Stanley

"Raymond's beginning to sound a lot like Vincent," she said.

"Oh, far superior. In his own estimation, at least. The brother-in-law struck a vein of diamonds, or a pipe, or whatever they call it. The family went into the diamond business and prospered mightily, including Raymond, whom his mother's family more or less adopted. He's not here in hope of becoming viscount, he's here to find out whether the estate is worth his while bothering to enter the lists. He wanted me to describe Fairacres and provide information about income and expenses."

"What cheek! Did you tell him about the other claimants?"

"Only that there are others. When I refused to give him the financial details he asked for, he said he would motor down to Worcestershire and call on Lord Dalrymple, so as to see Fairacres for himself. I've written to warn them."

Somewhat to Daisy's surprise, she received a letter from Lady Dalrymple begging her to go and stay at Fairacres for the weekend.

Raymond Dalrymple had written to announce that he would call on Saturday afternoon. Cousin Geraldine wanted Daisy's advice and support in meeting him.

If Geraldine had simply summoned Daisy, she might have refused in spite of her curiosity about Raymond. She couldn't resist a plea for help, however, especially as she was dying to meet Raymond. He had already managed to annoy her by not giving permission for her to attend his meeting with Tommy.

Besides, June was her favourite month in the country, when trees and fields still wore their fresh spring green.

The weather was beautiful, so she decided to drive rather than be stuck in a stuffy train. It was a pretty route, through the Chilterns and the Cotswolds, though negotiating the streets of Oxford in between could be tricky.

She set out on Friday morning. The A-40 from London to Oxford was quite busy but all went smoothly. She managed not to run over any undergraduates—or dons, come to that—in the streets of Oxford. Beyond the city the traffic thinned out, and she was able to enjoy sailing through the countryside in her sky blue Gwynne Eight.

After stopping for a picnic lunch, she came in midafternoon to a high point with a view over the Vale of Evesham. Just over the crest, a convenient gateway in the drystone wall offered a place to pull over. She got out and, shading her eyes, gazed over the fruitful valley of the Severn to the Malvern Hills and the distant, hazy-blue line of the Brecon Beacons beyond.

Once that sight had meant she was nearly home. Now she was a visitor.

"Brace up," she told herself firmly. If it weren't for the war, if Gervaise had not been killed, he would have married, perhaps someone she disliked. She would have married Michael. . . . Best not to dwell on that. One way or another, Fairacres would have ceased to be her home.

Sighing, she turned back towards the car. The right front tyre was flat.

"Blast!" Hands on hips, she glared at it.

Alec had made her learn how to change a wheel, but she had far rather not. She belonged to the RAC, and this was a main road; perhaps a patrolman would come by soon. Or if she sat on the running board looking disconsolate, perhaps a helpful motorist would stop to give her a hand. If she took the spare wheel off the back of the boot and leant it against the car, it would be obvious what the trouble was.

She glanced at her watch. She had written to Geraldine that she'd arrive at teatime, so there was no hurry. On this glorious day, to sit hopefully in the sun for half an hour, listening to the song of larks and the bleat of sheep, would be no hardship.

Besides, trying to do it herself and making a mess of it might take far longer than waiting for an expert to come along.

With a bit of a struggle, Daisy managed to unbuckle the spare wheel. She was examining with dismay the black marks on her driving gloves when a vast, gleaming car purred over the hill and down towards her.

It slowed as it came alongside. The smartly uniformed chauffeur, in the open front, turned towards her. "Trouble, miss? Puncture, is it?"

In the enclosed rear, a khaki-clad figure leant forward and rapped on the dividing glass with the handle of a stick or umbrella. "Get on, get on!" snapped the passenger impatiently, his voice muffled by the closed windows.

Her would-be gallant rescuer rolled his eyes, shrugged, and mouthed, "Sorry!" as he changed into first gear. With a soft, expensive hum, the bronze Daimler slid away down the steep hill.

"Brute!" Daisy exclaimed indignantly. Khaki—a high-ranking army officer? But the chauffeur's uniform was not military. Whoever the passenger was, he was a rotten cad.

Contemplating the wheel without enthusiasm, she reminded herself that she was a modern, competent woman. It didn't help. She just plain didn't want to tackle the job.

However, the trickle of vehicles she had encountered before seemed to have dried up entirely. She could at least show willing and make a start by getting out the jack from the tool chest. That was easy. Alas, having accomplished it, she realised she had forgotten how to use the blasted thing.

This bar obviously fitted into that hole, but what next?

The drone of a motor caught her ear. Something was coming up the hill, so it couldn't be going fast. Daisy decided she was jolly well going to stand in the middle of the road and force it to stop.

As she stepped forward, a blue motorcycle came round the bend. Beholding the blue and white RAC insignia, Daisy breathed a sigh of relief.

The blue-liveried patrolman pulled up and saluted. "Puncture, ma'am? A chap in a Daimler told me you needed help."

"The passenger?" she asked, surprised.

"No, the shover."

"That sounds more likely. Yes, a puncture."

"You've got the spare all ready, and the jack, I see. Won't take a jiffy."

And it didn't. Which made the Daimler passenger's refusal to stop all the more egregious.

"Don't forget to get the tyre repaired before you go much farther, ma'am." Her saviour pocketed a tip, saluted again, hopped onto his bike and buzzed off.

Daisy drove on, passing north of Bredon Hill. Soon the pepperpot bell tower at Upton-upon-Severn came into view. Reaching the drawbridge just as it opened, she watched a brightly painted narrowboat chug through the gap. She refrained from the childish pleasure of waving to the boatman and his wife.

Miranda and Oliver were old enough to enjoy waving to the colourful boats and watching the bridge open and close, she thought. When they all came in August, she would bring them here one day, even if it meant a battle with Nurse Gilpin.

Her own nanny had disapproved, saying it was unladylike. That had stopped Violet, though not Daisy nor, of course, Gervaise. How much fun one could miss through fear of not being considered ladylike!

Daisy got out of the car and, as the bridge closed, waved vigorously at the receding boat. She was gratified when the boatman took off his hat and saluted.

The bridge clunked into place. Daisy drove across and turned right, past the old church. A few hundred yards farther on, she turned into a narrow lane and wound about for a bit, between hedges adorned with sweet-scented dog roses and honeysuckle. She came to the village of Little Baswell and there she stopped at the smithy.

The smith, Ted Barnard, had married a favourite Fairacres nurserymaid. With the decline of the blacksmith's trade, he had turned his hand to doing minor repairs for motorists, and he was more than willing to repair Daisy's tyre.

"Won't take but a few minutes, Miss Daisy. I know the wife'd take it kindly was you to pop in to say hello while ye're waiting."

"Of course." She walked over to the neat whitewashed cottage next door. The garden was full of sweet peas and sweet william, as fragrant as the hedgerow flowers. The dog, a shaggy, tousled creature called Tuffet, greeted her with rapture. Mrs. Barnard was delighted to see her and at once set the kettle to boil. Daisy regretfully declined a cuppa. "Lady Dalrymple is expecting me for tea, you see.

55

We'll all be here in August, the whole family. I'll bring the children to see you."

Chatting about children made the wait pass quickly, and Daisy was soon on the road again. Fifteen minutes later, she turned in between the gates of Fairacres. Just beyond the lodge, she stopped under the shade of the first elm of the avenue and walked back to have a word with the lodge keeper, Mrs. Truscott, wife of the chauffeur.

They were all family, in a sense, the old servants. Their continued presence at Fairacres increased Daisy's feeling of dislocation, of the world being slightly askew, when she visited. In spite of Edgar's sincere and Geraldine's consciously gracious assurances that she was always welcome, she hadn't spent enough time there since Edgar's accession to adjust to the changes and the many things that had not changed.

She was glad that almost all the old servants had been kept on. Apart from maids and garden boys, who tended to come and go, and the aged butler who had been pensioned off, the staff had barely changed.

Having assured herself that the Truscotts were all well, Daisy continued along the avenue to the house. She stopped in front of the impressive portico. Its marble pillars, pediment, and cupolas had been superimposed by an eighteenth-century ancestor to add consequence to an otherwise sprawling, multiperiod mansion. Brick built, it was clad in whatever stone happened to be convenient at the time, pinkish sandstone, amber Cotswold limestone, pale grey Portland stone, a patchwork mellowed by time.

Daisy had scarcely time to powder her nose before the footman ran down the steps to open the door for her.

"Hello, Ernest."

"Good afternoon, madam. We've been expecting you. If you don't mind me saying so, madam, her ladyship will be very happy to see you."

Daisy laughed. "No, why should I mind?" She was on informal terms with the young man that would have horrified her mother, ever since he had helped her and Alec—and Tommy, come to think of it—to foil a dastardly plot. "Now if you'd told me the opposite . . ."

"As though I would, madam!"

"But I bet you'd manage to warn me."

"A hint, maybe, madam. His lordship, of course, will be delighted." He raised his voice for the benefit of the butler, who was waiting at the open front door. "Mr. Truscott will take your car round to the stables, madam, unless you was wanting it again this afternoon?"

"No, thank you. I may go down to the Dower House later, but I'll walk. Good afternoon, Lowecroft."

He gave a slight but stately bow. "Good afternoon, madam. May I say that your arrival is particularly welcome at this time."

"Thank you." Goodness, Geraldine must really be in a state!

"Her ladyship is in her sitting room, madam, not being at home to unexpected visitors." He took the light coat she had worn for driving and handed it on to Ernest.

"I'll pop in to say hello, but I must wash off the road dust before tea."

"Certainly, madam. Your usual room has been prepared."

"Thank you. You needn't announce me."

She crossed the hall, still hung with centuries' worth of family portraits—of course, they were Edgar's family as well as her own. Several of the oldest had obviously been professionally cleaned, revealing the long obscured features of Tudor and Stuart Dalrymples. The passage she turned into was also adorned with pictures she remembered: her grandmother's collection of Quattrocento martyrdoms, from which she averted her eyes. In Daisy's childhood, St. Sebastian had given her nightmares.

The new chatelaine respected the claims of history and had changed very little in the house. Unlike the grounds, Daisy thought with a smile, where Edgar fought an obstinate battle against his gardener and his bailiff to provide wild areas for the sustenance of his beloved lepidoptera.

What their successors would choose to do with the place remained to be seen.

The door of Geraldine's sitting room, which had been Daisy's mother's, was ajar. Daisy tapped and went in.

"Daisy!" The letter Geraldine was reading dropped to the floor—uncharacteristic untidyness—as she stood up and came to meet Daisy, both hands held out in a warm greeting. She kissed Daisy on each cheek, also uncharacteristic.

In her late forties, Lady Dalrymple was a rather bony woman who moved without grace, though almost a decade of being a viscountess had imparted a somewhat self-conscious graciousness to her usual manner. She was always smartly and appropriately dressed, yet never looked quite at ease in her clothes. Her long-sleeved, shin-length linen frock was an unfortunate shade of mauve that did nothing for a pale complexion, unaided by cosmetics, beneath carefully waved iron grey hair. She wore a modest pearl necklace and a gold cloisonné brooch in the form of a butterfly, accurate to the last detail, Daisy was sure.

"Hello, Geraldine."

"I'm so glad you're here."

"I hope I'll be able to help you, Geraldine, though I'm not sure how. But I've only just arrived. I must go up and wash my face."

"Of course, dear. I'll ring for tea."

Daisy went up to the bedroom she had slept in all through the years between the night nursery and leaving Fairacres after her father's death. It, too, had changed little, though Geraldine had asked her permission a couple of years ago to have it spruced up. The curtains were still blue chintz with a pattern of wildflowers, though not quite the same; there was a new blue bedspread, and the two easy chairs by the fireplace had been reupholstered in the same shade of blue. The dark oak floorboards shone. The bedside and hearth rugs were the old ones but they had obviously been thoroughly cleaned.

Daisy was touched by Geraldine's obvious care in making sure she still felt at home, especially as she usually stayed with her mother at the Dower House when she came down, unless Violet and her family visited at the same time.

In the miraculous way of well-run households, her bags had already been brought up and a maid was unpacking them. She promised to get the black marks out of Daisy's driving gloves as well as the dust from her hat.

A few minutes later, cleaner and tidier, Daisy went downstairs. Tea had arrived in Geraldine's sitting room, and so had Edgar. His pince-nez and baggy tweeds made him look the epitome of the absentminded professor.

"Look!" he greeted her, presenting a jar with a few leaves in it for her inspection.

"Hello, Edgar. What have you caught now?" She took the jar and peered through the glass. Among the hawthorn leaves was a brownish caterpillar with bumps on its back. "A country bumpkin butterfly?" she suggested, quite wittily in her own opinion.

"No, no, a moth, a Brimstone moth. More colourful than most, a vivid yellow."

"Edgar, do let Daisy sit down and have her tea. Are you going to join us?"

"Tea? Is it teatime? Not now, my dear, thank you. I must see this little fellow settled in his case first. He's quite large and may be almost ready to pupate. You see, if he—"

"I'm sure Daisy will excuse you, dear," Geraldine said firmly.

"My dear Daisy, how kind of you to pay us a visit. We're always happy to see you, you know." Retrieving his jar, he patted her on the shoulder and trotted out.

"The White Knight," said Daisy. "Oh, sorry, it just slipped out. I didn't mean it unkindly. Cousin Edgar's such a sweetie."

"I know exactly what you mean," said Geraldine with fond exasperation, handing over a cup of tea and waving at the selection of edibles on the tea table. "Believe it or not, he was a good teacher and very competent with the boys. But you understand why I've taken it upon myself to deal with this business of finding his heir."

"Absolutely. And I'm perfectly willing to . . . um . . . stand in for him in London, to the best of my ability. I'm not sure what I can do here, though, as Raymond has already refused to accept my 'credentials,' so to speak." She bit into a watercress sandwich. The cress was crisp and green, quite unlike the limp, yellowish substance sold by that name at the greengrocer's in Hampstead.

"He can hardly ban you from any room here into which I invite you, even if he is a millionaire!"

"A millionaire? Is he? Tommy told me only that he's a businessman in the diamond trade."

"Mr. Pearson's last letter said he'd been making enquiries. All the diamond people know all about each other, it seems. Mr. Raymond Dalrymple is an extremely wealthy magnate."

"If he's filthy rich, it explains his expecting to have it all his own way."

"The truth is, I have no idea how to handle the man. I get on comfortably enough with the local gentry—I've been a viscountess long enough to learn how, though sometimes it still seems like a dream. I have no ambition to scale the heights of London society."

"I don't blame you!"

"And I can handle a large staff with a degree of success; that is to say, the servants are not constantly leaving for greener pastures."

"I noticed you still have Ernest. Footmen are hard to keep, or so I've heard."

Geraldine flushed. "I confess I have a soft spot for Ernest, though I trust he's unaware of it. He hasn't the sedate temperament of the ideal footman, but he reminds me of the boys at school."

"Do you miss them?"

"Not the school, but the best of the boys. And their liveliness. You might not think it, but I got on well enough with most of them, and with their parents when they visited. They were mostly professional people and successful business people. No millionaires, though! I have no experience with millionaires."

"You're forgetting Mr. Arbuckle, Geraldine. The American whose daughter was kidnapped? He was charming when he wasn't worried half to death."

"You got on well with him, I remember. I didn't see much of him. And I daresay the Americans are quite unlike the South Africans in character. You're at ease with everyone, without even trying. I don't know how you do it."

"I don't exactly *do* it. It just happens. And not absolutely everyone. I must admit I'm a bit fed up with Cousin Raymond—assuming he's really a cousin—before I've even met him. But who knows, perhaps he'll turn out to be charming in person."

"Perhaps. More likely he won't care to take tea with a couple of women."

"Won't Edgar join us?"

"Who knows? I never venture to predict or dictate Edgar's movements. After twenty years ruled by bells, from rising to lights-out, he deserves his freedom."

Politely agreeing, Daisy privately wondered whether it might be more a matter of Geraldine recognising the limits of her ability to control her husband. "If Raymond wants to ask nosy questions about your finances, as I gathered from Mr. Pearson, it might be an idea to sic him on to Cousin Edgar."

"Edgar knows next to nothing about . . . Ah yes, an excellent idea. Perhaps a lecture on British lepidoptera will send him quickly back to South Africa, or at least to London, where he can pursue his claim through the proper channels." Geraldine sighed. "It would be so much easier just to refuse to see him, but I suppose that would be unthinkably discourteous."

"Probably not wise," Daisy agreed. "You won't want to deliberately alienate him. He may, after all, turn out to be Cousin Edgar's heir."

EIGHT

"*A jeweller*, an innkeeper, and a seaman." The Dowager Lady Dalrymple's lip curled. "Each worse than the one before. And descended from a black sheep! Wasn't it bad enough when a mad schoolmaster set himself up in your father's place?"

"Cousin Edgar is not mad, Mother." Daisy's protest came automatically, having been repeated many times over the past nine years. She didn't know why she bothered. "Nor did he 'set himself up.'"

"At least he wasn't in trade, I'll allow him that much. But he could have chosen an acceptable heir. Tradesmen!"

"A millionaire, the owner of a luxury hotel, and an officer of the Merchant Navy. They're our relatives as much as they're his."

"Had your father lived, he would never have permitted such a disgraceful state of affairs."

Daisy thought it wiser, as well as kinder, not to point out that her father had left a mess of a different kind. Shattered by the death of Gervaise, he had failed to alter his will to provide for Daisy, having earlier assumed that her brother would take care of her. Though, when the flu pandemic bore him off in his turn, Edgar had been willing to correct his omission, Daisy had not been willing to sponge on her then newly discovered relative.

Choosing to work for her living had led to her meeting Alec, so all had turned out for the best—in her eyes, if not the dowager's.

Avoiding her mother's outraged look, Daisy took a sip of sherry, which she didn't really care for, and glanced round the sitting room. It was somewhat larger than Geraldine's, but the Dower House didn't have a separate drawing room, another source of continual complaint. The furnishings were equally elegant, however, since the dowager had bagged the best of the smaller pieces when forced to move— "forced" by her own refusal to reside with the usurper, as he had proposed.

Having done likewise, Daisy didn't blame her for refusing. It was about time she stopped complaining, though.

A bowl of glorious pink and yellow roses caught Daisy's eye. Eager to change the subject, she got up and went to smell their fragrance. "Gorgeous!"

"That little Welsh gardener you recommended to me is still with me, surprisingly. Of course, my little plot is nothing like the Fairacres gardens. It's so tiny, Morgan doesn't have a great deal to do. He has no excuse for anything short of perfection."

"Mother, no garden can ever be perfect, what with insects and diseases and weeds and the vagaries of the weather." Not to mention that the Dower House boasted a sizable vegetable plot and orchard, not just a lawn surrounded by flowering shrubs and borders.

"Don't change the subject. It's a bad habit I have had to reprimand you for since you were a child. You say this jewellery pedlar is calling tomorrow afternoon? I'm free until six, I believe. It's time I paid that woman a visit."

"I didn't know you and Cousin Geraldine were on visiting terms."

"*I* know my duty." Drawing herself up, the dowager spoke frostily. "I'm aware that my accommodations are vastly inferior to Fairacres, but when my daughter prefers to stay with Edgar and Geraldine—" Her tone suggested that though it pained her to use their christian names, she simply could not bring herself to refer to them as Lord and Lady Dalrymple. "However, it's not for me to complain."

"They invited me."

"Only because Edgar is unfit to evaluate the claimants and Geraldine is unwilling. That lawyer friend of yours should have requested my assistance. I can't think how you came to take it upon yourself—"

"I didn't, Mother. Geraldine asked me because I'm a Dalrymple by birth, which neither she nor you are."

"Well, I must say . . . !"

For once Daisy had left her mother speechless. She took her leave with all possible celerity.

Walking back across the park to the big house, she looked forward with dismay to the morrow. Bad enough that Cousin Raymond had not so far shown himself a sympathetic person; the prospect of the dowager viscountess and the present viscountess crossing swords over the teacups made Daisy cringe.

Saturday morning promised another sunny day and Daisy's spirits rose. After breakfast, she went for a walk along the riverside path. Edgar's spaniel, Pepper, went with her, as Wharton, the bailiff, had cornered his lordship and driven him into his study to accomplish several overdue tasks.

The Severn slid by, reflecting the blue of the sky and the green of the willows leaning over it. A dark red butterfly with white edges to its wings flitted past. Swallows darted and swooped over the water. Daisy hoped they would confine their diet to midges and not go for the butterfly.

The water level was about eight feet below the path, but Pepper, undeterred, scrambled down to go for a dip. Presuming he knew what he was doing, Daisy didn't call him back until he started to paddle determinedly after a pair of crested grebes. He took no notice, giving up only when the birds submerged and swam off underwater. Then he turned downstream on a diagonal towards the bank.

By the time Daisy caught up with him, he had climbed out onto a dilapidated floating landing stage. After shaking vigorously, he scampered up the equally dilapidated wooden steps and greeted her with more enthusiasm than she quite cared for.

"Down, boy! I'd better ask your master if he wouldn't mind having the steps and dock repaired. I bet Derek and Belinda are getting too old to be satisfied with puttering about the backwater. The boat probably could do with an overhaul, too."

A little farther on, they crossed a wooden footbridge over the backwater. Surrounded by willows and alders, it was overgrown with reeds and scummed with pondweed. Watching scarlet dragonflies dart and hover, Daisy realised Pepper's intention too late. She grabbed for his collar but she missed. He took a flying leap from the bridge into the stagnant water, so he was both soggy and mucky when she left him—with apologies—with Bill Truscott in the stables.

By that time, the day was growing hot and humid. The sky was hazy, with the feel of thunder in the air. After lunch, Geraldine told Lowecroft they would take coffee on the terrace. Ernest moved the wicker chairs and table into the wedge of shade provided by the house. Daisy, Geraldine, and Edgar settled there, looking out over the crazy paving and the low parapet to the lawn, with its huge chestnut, and the gardens, gently sloping down towards the river, marked by the willows on the bank. Daisy broached the subject of refurbishing boat, steps, and dock before the children came to stay in August.

"Of course, my dear. I'll write it down immediately." He took out his fountain pen and his lepidopteran notebook.

"And it might be a good idea to have the backwater cleaned up a bit, dredged perhaps. Though the dragonflies seem to like it as it is. Which reminds me, I saw a very pretty butterfly by the river. Dark reddish brown, with white edges. I think there were spots, too."

"Blue spots? Among the willows? Camberwell Beauty!" He jumped up and glanced about him. "Where's Pepper?"

"He got wet and dirty this morning. I left him in the stables for Truscott to deal with. Sorry."

"No matter, no matter. I'll have Ernest fetch him." He dashed off towards the conservatory, a Victorian excrescence that disfigured the south façade of the original Tudor house. There he kept his collections. Lord Dalrymple was not among those lepidopterists who slaughter their prey and pin it to a board. He liked to collect eggs and caterpillars and observe their transformation into moths or butterflies, then free them to fly off and produce another generation.

A few minutes later, he came round the corner of the house, binoculars round his neck and his collecting satchel slung over his shoulder. He'd had no need to change his clothes as he was wearing a faded blazer, a barely discernable school crest on the breast pocket, over ancient cricket whites. They watched his broad-brimmed straw hat recede between two marble fauns, beneath the dangling seed-pods of the pleached wisteria alley. Pepper trotted after him.

Enervated by the heat, Daisy and Geraldine stayed on the terrace, chatting in a desultory way about Edgar's birthday house party and wondering how best to entertain such a disparate group as it seemed destined to be.

"But will all of them be coming if the heir has been identified by then?" Daisy asked.

"I'm afraid so. Edgar says they're all family and must all be invited, however many 'all' turns out to be. He doesn't often put his foot down, but when he does, he can be extremely obstinate."

"And is everyone invited for the whole week—ten days, really, with both weekends—as we are?"

"He wants the family to have a chance to get to know one another. Of course, some of them may not be able to come, for the entire time or at all. I shan't send invitations until Mr. Pearson is able to tell me who are the actual relatives."

"Everything seems a bit vague so far. I hope he finds out in time for Cousin Edgar's birthday celebration, at least."

"It might be better not to know who the heir is until afterwards. Otherwise the majority are going to be resentful the entire time. Yes, Lowecroft? What is it?"

"The dowager viscountess has called, my lady."

"Oh dear!" Geraldine ineffectually patted her hair, which was as always perfectly neat. "You'd better show her into the drawing room.

I'll be with her in a minute." She waited as the butler bowed and left. "Daisy . . . ?"

"I won't desert you. Don't worry, Mother just wants to meet Cousin Raymond. Like the rest of us, she's dying of curiosity."

"Oh dear! This interview is going to be difficult enough without— Sorry, dear, I don't mean to imply . . . But it *is* awkward! I wonder whether Edgar will put in an appearance?"

Daisy had no answer. "I'm sorry I mentioned the Camberwell Beauty."

"For pity's sake don't mention it to your mother! I'd hate her to get the impression that Edgar is chasing after a lady of doubtful virtue from South London!"

They went into the house through a door in the north wing, a Regency addition with Strawberry Hill Gothic pretensions, including a hexagonal turret. It was much cooler inside. Geraldine hurried to the cloakroom to check her appearance. Daisy couldn't decide whether it was more proper to wait for her or to go straight in to greet her mother—the minutiae of etiquette had always bemused and bored her, one reason she was the "unsatisfactory" daughter. Violet had always been the good girl.

Before she made up her mind, Geraldine reappeared. Daisy let her lead the way into the drawing room.

The Dowager Lady Dalrymple was standing at the French window on the far side, silhouetted against the comparative brightness, looking over the terrace, the lawn, and the gardens. Daisy hoped she hadn't got there soon enough to see them sneaking round by the side door.

The dowager turned on hearing their footsteps. "Good afternoon, Geraldine."

"Good afternoon, Maud."

"Hello, Mother."

"Won't you sit down? To what do I owe the pleasure?" Geraldine enquired, as if she didn't know.

"Isn't it obvious?" the dowager declaimed, her voice throbbing. "You cannot suppose I have no interest in the man who is to take the place of my husband and my son?"

67

"Cousin Edgar succeeded Father," Daisy objected. "Besides, this chap who's coming this afternoon may not be the one."

"A shopkeeper! A hawker of baubles! At least a schoolmaster *may* be a gentleman. Of sorts."

Geraldine bridled. "Edgar is a gentleman in the best sense of the word," she said with some heat.

"Precisely." She paused to let her meaning sink in. "When do you expect this . . . this *person* to call?"

"Mr. Raymond Dalrymple did not give a precise time, just mid-afternoon."

"*Not* a gentleman. In any sense of the word."

"He must be driving down," said Daisy. "One never knows when a puncture will strike."

"For a writer," said her mother, "you use words rather inaccurately. A puncture cannot strike."

"You will take tea, won't you, Maud?" Geraldine said hastily. "Daisy, would you mind ringing?"

Lowecroft, arriving in response to the bell, seemed more deferential than usual towards Geraldine. Daisy got the impression that he was, in his dignified way, cocking a snook at her mother. Clearly conscious of his altered demeanour, Geraldine perked up. The dowager, no fool, missed nothing of the byplay. Her lips tightened.

Daisy wondered whether the butler had been listening at the door and heard her mother's snide remarks. He wouldn't take kindly to denigration of his master, whatever his own opinion of that eccentric peer.

"Tea, Lowecroft. Unless you'd prefer lemonade, Maud?"

"Lemonade would be pleasant," the dowager acknowledged reluctantly.

"Good idea," said Daisy.

Supplied with lemonade and crisp, sweet, light-as-air wafers, Daisy's mother got round to asking after her grandchildren. As she had completely ignored their existence the previous day, Daisy took this sudden solicitude with a pinch of salt. A wayward impulse made her begin with Belinda, in whom the dowager had even less interest than in the twins.

"Belinda's doing very well at school. She's even thinking she might like to go on to university, though it's much too early to make a decision, of course."

"Belinda . . . ? Oh, your stepdaughter. I cannot approve of excessive education for young ladies . . . but of course, the child doesn't quite—"

"Mother!"

"I'm very fond of Belinda," Geraldine put in hastily. "A nice child, and bright. And having seen many decidedly unintelligent boys going on to fritter away everyone's time at Oxford and Cambridge, I don't believe it can be right to waste a good brain just because it's female."

"If Bel wants to continue her studies when she's seventeen or eighteen, she shall. Miranda, too. She loves picture books and she knows most of her ABCs. Oliver is more interested in trains at present. Not content with his wooden train, he builds his own with his blocks."

"Not what I would describe as a useful accomplishment. Still, you did at least produce an heir." The dowager gave Geraldine a disparaging look, then transferred it to Daisy. "Though it hardly matters, since there is no title to inherit."

Daisy's mother was the only person who invariably succeeded in bringing her to the boiling point. It must have been obvious because Geraldine, with an alarmed glance at Daisy, said, "Will you have another wafer, Maud?" and thrust the plate towards the dowager, as if to stop her mouth. "And may I pour you some more lemonade? Daisy, let me refill your glass."

They both accepted. The social amenities restored, the dowager took a sip and said graciously, "An excellent notion. June is seldom so hot. I believe we shall have a storm."

As if to confirm her prediction, a distant mutter of thunder made itself heard. Though they were sitting by the open window, not a breath of a breeze relieved the stifling heat. Heavy clouds darkened the sky, but no rain fell. Conversation languished.

Daisy roused herself from her lethargy to say, "I hope Cousin Edgar won't get caught in the storm." She also hoped her mother would decide to leave before it broke. To spare Geraldine another mother-daughter squabble, she didn't say so. It was dismaying to realise that though naturally she loved her mother, she liked Geraldine better.

NINE

Sunk in heat-induced torpor, Daisy, her mother, and Geraldine were all startled when Lowecroft came in and announced, "My lady, a Mr. Raymond Dalrymple has called—by appointment, he says—to see his lordship. I put him in the anteroom. I fear I have been unable to ascertain his lordship's whereabouts."

"That's quite all right, Lowecroft. Please show the gentleman into the library. I'll come and see him, if you'll kindly excuse me, Maud. Daisy—"

"My dear Geraldine, I have every intention of observing this . . . this *person* for myself." The dowager rose with a celerity that belied her sixty-odd years.

"Lowecroft, tell Mr. . . . ." Geraldine began, but the butler had softly and silently vanished away, discretion being the better part of valour.

"I shall be with you directly," said the dowager, sweeping out after him.

"Daisy . . ."

"*I* can't stop her."

"Oh dear!" Geraldine popped up out of her seat almost as briskly as had her guest. "Do you think she's going straight to the library?"

"To the cloakroom, I expect," Daisy reassured her. "But all the same, we'd better get a move on or she'll be stealing a march on us."

They met Lowecroft coming away from the library. "Did you wish me to offer Mr. Raymond Dalrymple any refreshment, my lady?" he asked.

"No, no. I'll ring if we want anything. All I want," Geraldine continued, her voice lowered, as the butler bowed and went on his way, "is to keep his visit as short as possible. Without discourtesy, of course."

"It seems to me he's already been discourteous, turning up without so much as a 'by your leave'. But I suppose we shouldn't sink to his level. If he has to be routed, I dare say we can rely on Mother for that," Daisy added thoughtfully.

The library was a long room lined with glass-fronted bookcases containing, for the most part, calf-bound books that no one had read and very probably no one ever would read. One section, however, held novels, travellers' tales, and light biographies suitable for house-party guests. Another had books of scientific interest belonging to Daisy's grandfather, who had had an unaccountable interest in natural philosophy—a reaction, perhaps, against his wife's fascination with martyred saints. It was he who had replaced the customary busts of Greek philosophers with British scientists such as Darwin, Lyell, Stephenson, and Faraday.

Gloomy at the best of times, the library was now positively stygian. Daisy flicked on the overhead electric lights.

On hearing Daisy and Geraldine enter the room, a tall, bulky man turned from contemplation of Lyell's whiskers. He himself was clean shaven and thinning on top. He looked about sixty, perhaps a few years older. He frowned.

Geraldine bade him "good afternoon," and introduced herself and Daisy. He returned a brusque greeting, scarcely sparing Daisy a cursory glance. He spoke with the clipped, flat, slightly nasal accent of British South Africa.

"I'm happy to meet you, Lady Dalrymple." His voice was that of the man in the car who had ordered his chauffeur not to stop and help Daisy. "But it's Lord Dalrymple I've come to see."

"I'm afraid you've had a wasted journey. Today is not at all convenient for my husband."

"Not convenient? I wrote to make an appointment!"

"But I don't believe you waited for a reply?"

"I'm sure he'll see me now I'm here."

"As a matter of fact, I don't know where Edgar is just now."

Bravo, Daisy cheered silently.

"Well, I'm staying in Worcester, at the Diglis House Hotel. I can come back tomorrow if it suits him better."

"On *Sunday?*" The dowager viscountess made a grand entrance. "Is he speaking of transacting business on a Sunday? Geraldine, who is this person?"

"Mr. Raymond Dalrymple, Maud."

"Indeed." She looked him up and down, and Daisy became aware that his well-tailored tweed suit was much too new, the colour a trifle too green—especially as his complexion was florid. Worse, he wore a large diamond pin in his tie. "Well! A Dalrymple? What does he want?"

"Madam, my business is with Lord Dalrymple."

"To be frank, I can't see why he should see you just because you claim your name is Dalrymple. My late husband would not have countenanced your visit without a letter of recommendation."

"Oh, you must be the old lady."

Freezingly, the dowager said to Geraldine, "Has this person presented such a letter? No? I wonder at your admitting him as far as the library! The least he can do is explain his presence."

"Didn't that lawyer fellow let you know I was coming?"

"Me? I have nothing to do with the matter."

Raymond blinked. For the first time the dowager had shaken his assurance. He took out a gold cigarette case, then hurriedly returned it to his pocket, as if realising it was not the moment to light up. Daisy glimpsed a monogram formed from inset diamonds; she could hardly believe her eyes.

"Mr. Pearson wrote to my husband," said Geraldine, "to tell him you intended to call. He didn't say at what time, and I dare say he felt it wasn't his place to disclose your business. Lord Dalrymple is a busy man." Her voice quivered the tiniest bit and Daisy had to bite her lip to keep herself from laughing.

"I think we should all sit down," Daisy said pacifically, "and let Mr. Dalrymple tell us what he wants. Then we can decide whether it's worth Lord Dalrymple's precious time."

Her mother and Raymond regarded her as if she were a wolf that had unexpectedly cast off its sheepskin. Daisy suspected Raymond had assumed her to be a hired companion or poor relation or something of the sort.

Geraldine said, "Good idea, Daisy, and perhaps you wouldn't mind taking notes."

"Ah, your secretary," Raymond said, enlightened.

"Nothing of the sort," snapped her mother. "Mrs. Fletcher is my daughter."

By then, Daisy had settled herself behind the big walnut desk—a position of some authority, as she had learnt from Alec—and produced a notebook. Geraldine sat down, and the other two reluctantly followed her example.

"Now look here," Raymond protested, "I—"

"I'm ready." Daisy dipped a pen in the ornate eighteenth-century inkwell. "Do tell us what has brought you to Fairacres."

For a moment, she thought he was going to stand firm. Then he sighed and capitulated.

"My branch of the family has done well in diamonds. My son and his cousin run the firm now and I'm more or less retired, though I do still have a finger in the pie. I had to come to Europe on business, but I have the leisure to look into this affair." He didn't sound particularly interested in the possibility of inheriting a viscountcy and Fairacres. Daisy, bristling, wondered whether he could conceivably be as indifferent as he appeared.

" 'This affair'?" the dowager enquired coldly.

"The inheritance. The title and estate. I gathered from the lawyer that it's going to take quite a while to sort out who is the heir. I don't want to waste time here in England if it's not worth the trouble."

Daisy saw her own aghastness mirrored in the faces of the

Ladies Dalrymple. Before any of them had recovered enough to speak, Raymond went on.

"The house is quite something, and it looks like a prosperous little farm, but—"

"Geraldine!" Edgar appeared on the threshold. He was soaked to the skin and thoroughly muddied to the knees. "The Odonata! Daisy, I can't thank you enough for drawing my attention. The Red-veined Darter . . . Oh, hello, Maud, you here? Nice to see you. Hello," he added doubtfully to Raymond, "don't believe I have the honour of your acquaintance. I'm disgracefully ignorant about the Odonata. It might be merely a Common Darter. However, if it isn't the Red-veined, a rare visitor to Britain, I'll eat my hat. And I found a nymph!"

Daisy and Geraldine exchanged glances. Though Daisy couldn't be sure what Geraldine was thinking, she, too, might well have been wondering whether a nymph was preferable to a Camberwell Beauty.

"Yes, dear," said Geraldine. "How nice. This is Mr. Raymond Dalrymple."

Edgar nodded at the visitor, who had been stunned into silence by his appearance. "How do, my dear chap. I can't be sure about the identification of the nymph but I'm sure I have a book on the Odonata." He made for the appropriate bookcase. "Now let me see . . ."

"Lord Dalrymple," Raymond said loudly, standing up, "I've come to you for information about—"

"Yes, yes, my dear chap, but not just now. Here it is." He drew a large volume from the shelf. "Daisy, my dear, do you mind if I utilise a corner of the desk?"

"Not at all, Cousin Edgar. But mind you don't get your book wet."

"Wet?" The book thudded onto the desk. Edgar looked down at himself. "Goodness me, you're quite right. I'd better go and change."

"Lord Dalrymple, just a moment. I want to talk to you—when you've changed, of course—about the income and expenses of the estate."

"Good heavens, I don't concern myself with that sort of stuff. Rely on my lawyer and my agent, don't you know."

"Then I'll speak to your agent."

Edgar drew himself up and fixed Raymond with a commanding eye. "No, you won't. Not unless and until you are legally declared to be my heir. Excuse me, please, ladies." He turned and squelched out of the library.

The silence he left behind was broken by another distant mutter of thunder. A wave of cool air came in through the window. The sky had darkened. Raymond seized the excuse to take his hurried, discomfited leave.

"I hope we'll be seeing you again," said Geraldine untruthfully, offering her hand.

He took it and shook it gingerly, muttering something Daisy didn't hear. He gave the dowager a half bow, Daisy a nod, and stalked out, not waiting for butler or footman to be summoned to conduct him.

The dowager rose. "This has been quite an instructive afternoon," she said to Geraldine. "I trust your husband will not take a chill."

"I doubt it. Edgar is quite accustomed to being out in all weathers. Won't you stay for tea?"

"Thank you, no. Daisy, I shall doubtless see you in church tomorrow."

"I'm afraid not, Mother. I'm leaving early. I promised Alec."

"Indeed!"

Without further words, Daisy and Geraldine escorted the dowager to the front door. A bronze Daimler was just starting off down the elm avenue. Daisy recognised it. Now she knew for certain that it was Raymond Dalrymple who had abandoned her by the roadside.

Having seen her mother off in her far more modest car, Daisy and Geraldine retired to the latter's sitting room and subsided, exhausted, into the comfortable chairs.

"Geraldine, I confess I didn't altogether believe you when you told me Edgar was a good teacher. But after seeing him put Raymond in his place . . . And when he was dripping all over the carpet, too!" Daisy giggled. "Well, I'm sure he used to handle a classroom full of adolescent boys with the greatest of ease."

"'Instructive,' your mother said. I can't help wondering what she learnt."

"It's a bit of a poser, isn't it?"

Ernest's arrival with tea saved her from having to speculate aloud on whether Geraldine's spirited defence, Edgar's bedraggled appearance, or Raymond's unmitigated presumption weighed more heavily in the dowager's scales.

"Shall I close the windows, your ladyship?" the footman asked, having deposited the tray. "Looks like the rain won't hold off much longer."

"Yes, do."

The clouds hanging above Fairacres had darkened to near black. Somewhere to the west there must have been a break, though, because the landscape was illuminated by a lurid, eerie, ominous light. Every tree and bush stood out distinctly. Thunder rumbled not far off, and a few seconds later lightning briefly blazed. Still not a drop of rain fell.

Geraldine shivered. "Someone's walking across my grave," she said.

TEN

A month passed before Daisy heard any more from Tommy about the heirs. Then came a cry for help.

Miss Watt rang up at half past ten that morning. "Mrs. Fletcher, Mr. Pearson wondered whether you could possibly come in to chambers right away. We have . . . ah . . . something of a situation here." She sounded uncharacteristically flustered.

"What on earth . . . ? Can't you tell me what's going on?"

"It's a bit complicated. But if—"

"Never mind. I'll come. About an hour?"

"*Thank* you, Mrs. Fletcher. I've had to clear Mr. Pearsons schedule. He'll be very relieved."

Daisy was rather annoyed. She was in the middle of drafting a proposal for an article about Hampton Court for Mr. Thorwald, her American editor. The result was always smoother if she did the whole thing in one sitting. If she drove into the City, she'd just have time to finish the section she was working on. It wasn't raining, and now that she had seen Lincoln's Inn she knew where she would be able to park the car.

Perhaps Mr. Thorwald would be interested in an article on the Inns of Court, too, she thought.

End of paragraph, full stop: Leaving the paper and carbons in the typewriter, she hurried upstairs to change her summer frock for a more sober costume. Half an hour later, she left the car in Lincoln's Inn Fields and walked under the impressive arch of the early Tudor main gate, into New Square. Tommy's chambers were on the opposite side. As she approached, she wondered what sort of emergency Tommy imagined she might be able to help with.

Miss Watt came out of her room to meet Daisy on the landing, closing the door behind her.

"I'm so glad you came, Mrs. Fletcher. Mr. Pearson asked me to apologise and to explain."

"He doesn't need me after all?" Daisy asked indignantly.

"Oh yes." She lowered her voice. "But there's a person—a young woman—in my office."

"Not the one from Jamaica?"

"Yes. Mrs. Samuel Dalrymple."

"Didn't he advise her not to come?"

"Yes, but she's come anyway."

"And Tommy doesn't know what to do with her?"

"Exactly. Mr. Pearson would like to consult you. Unfortunately, it's necessary to pass through my room to get to his, so he asked me to warn you of her presence. After you have talked to him, he'll introduce her to you if appropriate, depending on what's decided. Will you see him?"

"Since he's haled me down here . . ." Not that she wasn't dying to meet Mrs. Samuel Dalrymple. Martha, she remembered.

Martha Dalrymple sat in a chair against the wall of shelved deed boxes. She wore a cheap cotton frock, flowered, a bit shabby, with a light cardigan. Her bowed head let Daisy see pale blond hair—natural blond, Daisy thought enviously, her own shingled locks being light brown. Martha's was pulled back into a knot at her nape. The style was severe, but when she raised her head, she revealed a round, youthful face, woebegone, with a hint of tears in her blue eyes.

She looked little more than a child. Daisy smiled at her, and she gave a tentative, rather wobbly smile in return.

Miss Watt swept Daisy onward into Tommy's office, then returned to her own, closing the door with a firm click.

"Well?" said Daisy.

"Er, hm . . . What do you think of her?"

"Honestly, Tommy, I've just had the briefest glimpse of her. Miss Watt didn't give me time even to say good morning. She's the one who wrote from Jamaica, isn't she?"

"That's right."

"Why did she come, when you advised her not to?"

"She still doesn't know when her husband will return to Jamaica," Tommy said crossly, "and she was still afraid of missing a great opportunity for him and the family if no one turned up in person to advance his claim. Frankly, I suspect there's more to the story—something she isn't telling me."

"And you expect me to ferret it out for you? She looks just as naïve and innocent as Sakari and I guessed from her letter and even younger."

"I knew you'd have formed an impression, at a glance. Can it be true, or could it be a clever pose?"

"You really think it might be, that she's another false claimant?"

"I never said so!"

"The rest were living in England, weren't they? Oh, and that Scottish chap from the village called Dalrymple. Britain, anyway. Jamaica's a long way to come on the strength of a remote possibility. Especially as her clothes suggest the fare must have been a strain on her budget."

"Anyone can buy cheap clothes."

"True. And didn't you say the estate would pay the fare?"

"Only if Samuel's claim has a valid basis."

"Jamaica is suggestive, isn't it? Since we know Julian went there. Hasn't she brought any sort of proof with her?"

"Various documents, good enough as far as they go, but none leading directly back to Julian. At least, unlike the others, she doesn't claim to have heard a family story about descent from an English lord. As for what her husband would have to say of the entire business . . . According to her he's entirely unaware of it, having sailed off before my advertisement was brought to her attention. He's the principal, and nothing can be decided without him. You must admit, it's put me in a difficult position."

"Aren't difficulties what lawyers thrive on?"

"An impossible position!"

"What do you want me to do, then? Have a good long heart-to-heart with her?"

"Er, hmm . . ." Tommy was not in general the kind of lawyer who prefaces every remark with a premonitory cough. "Well, yes. She may well speak more freely to you. But also . . . You see the thing is . . ."

"Spit it out, Tommy."

"I don't know what to do with her. I can't very well send her back to Jamaica. A young girl like her, married or not, shouldn't have undertaken such a voyage all by herself in the first place. She can't stay alone at an hotel, even if she could afford it or the estate could legitimately pay her expenses. A cheap women's hostel doesn't seem right when she may be the next viscountess. On the other hand, I can't send her down to Fairacres for several weeks, not knowing whether she has any actual connection with the family! I'm sure Madge would be willing to put her up, but it could lead to a perception of favouritism among the other possible heirs."

"I thought I saw it coming." Daisy sighed. "You're hoping we'll put her up. Of all the cheek!"

Tommy looked abashed. "Sorry. It seemed like a solution. Grasping at straws."

"I'll have to ask Alec. . . ."

"You mean you'll do it? It's an awful lot to ask, particularly as we know so little about her. But if there's anything fishy about her, you've got a copper in the house."

"One night. We'll see how it goes. I'm not promising anything, even if Alec consents."

"Of course. Perhaps I'll come up with a better idea by tomorrow." He pushed his phone across the desk. "Here, ring up Alec."

"At the Yard? Not likely! This doesn't exactly qualify as a life or death emergency."

"Oh, is that the criterion? You won't be able to take her home with you right away, then. What on earth am I to do with her in the meantime?"

Daisy pictured the dejected face of the blond girl, her brave, pathetic attempt to smile. "Let me talk to her. In private."

With a harassed air, Tommy glanced round his sanctum. "I don't—"

"You must have somewhere. Miss Watt's room? Can't you call her in here to take dictation or something? Or a partner who's presently in court? A garret? A cellar?"

"Really, Daisy! The basement is full of archived files, all still confidential, and the garrets are full of clerks. . . ."

"I'll take her out for a cup of coffee."

The cautious lawyer examined this proposition from all sides. "I suppose that would be all right."

"For pity's sake, I promise I won't lose her!"

That made him laugh. "Come on, then." They went through to Miss Watt's office.

As they turned towards Martha Dalrymple, she stood up. She was small and her figure would normally have been slight; five months pregnant, Daisy guessed. Hadn't Tommy noticed? Apparently not, or he'd have been in even more of a flap. And Miss Watt—a spinster dedicated to her job, she might not have realised either, or might not think it proper to notice.

"Mrs. Fletcher—Mrs. Samuel Dalrymple. Mrs. Fletcher is the daughter of the late Viscount Dalrymple."

"How do you do?" Daisy said in her friendliest manner, holding out her hand.

Martha took it tentatively, but she did not—thank goodness—have a hand like a dead fish. Equally tentatively, she said, "How do you do?" as if she wasn't at all sure it was the correct thing to say. Unsurprisingly, she looked tired and worried.

"If it's all right with you, Mrs. Dalrymple, I'm taking you out for morning coffee."

"Th-that's very kind of you." She gave Tommy an anxious glance.

"Mrs. Fletcher will bring you back here," he assured her, before retreating back into his office.

Recalling the discomforts of pregnancy and taking into account the girl's shyness, Daisy said to Miss Watt, "I'd like to powder my nose before we go out."

"There's a cloakroom at the rear, Mrs. Fletcher. Just turn right outside this door."

"Thank you. Shall we go, Mrs. Dalrymple?" Leading the way along the narrow, dimly lit passage, she said, "When I was expecting the twins, I was always hunting for the nearest lav. Would you like to go first?"

Martha gratefully accepted. Her voice was soft, her accent—presumably Jamaican—a lilting cadence with a touch of almost jazzy syncopation. Daisy found it pleasant.

A few minutes later, as they walked slowly towards the Strand, Daisy asked, "Is it your first baby?"

"Oh no." She blinked back tears. "I left my two little girls at home, with my sister. You've got twins?"

"A girl and a boy. It was very brave of you to cross the ocean alone."

"I didn't dare wait any longer," she explained, patting her burgeoning abdomen. "Another month and I couldn't have done it."

The gesture drew Daisy's attention to her frock. Not Fuller's, she decided. Martha would feel more at home in an ABC or Express Dairy tearoom. Also, if she wanted something more nourishing than the fancy cakes that were Fuller's speciality, neither ABC nor Express Dairy would refuse because they were serving only morning coffee at this hour.

"Besides," Martha continued, "I had to travel when a passage was available. The people who helped me . . . You know my husband is a sailor?"

"Yes. Mr. Pearson told me. Let's go in here."

Martha was awed by the hurrying waitresses in black uniforms with white aprons, and the chattering crowd. It was late for elevenses, though, and early for lunch, so they easily found an empty table in a comparatively quiet corner. Discovering that the girl had had nothing that morning but a cup of tea—station tea at that— Daisy persuaded her to eat a couple of boiled eggs with lots of buttered toast, and to drink a glass of milk, or at least milky coffee. She was reluctant to accept, but Daisy pointed out that it was for the baby's sake—true—and claimed that Tommy would reimburse her— a white lie.

While they waited, Daisy asked, "Who were the people who helped you with the passage?"

"Sam's friends. My husband's. He knows just about everyone who ships out of Kingston. They found me a freighter with a few passenger cabins that was going to sail with one empty. The purser didn't charge me for it. Everyone was so very kind." Her eyes filled again.

Daisy hoped she wasn't going to turn out to be a deplorably weepy young woman. With any luck, a good meal would cure her. "It sounds as if your Sam is pretty popular," she said, as a waitress arrived with a tray. Daisy had intended to have only coffee, but she'd ordered a scone just to keep Martha company.

Though Martha ate hungrily, her table manners were acceptable, thank goodness. The food brought a touch of colour to her cheeks.

When she paused before tackling the second egg, Daisy said, "You came to town by train this morning?"

"Yes, from Southampton. I didn't know what to do when we landed last night, but some of the fellows took me to a YWCA hostel. And this morning, the purser and the third officer turned up to take me to the station. They'd even had a whip-round for my ticket! The hostel was quite cheap," she said doubtfully, "but noisy. Is there one in London?"

"Lots." Daisy didn't want to pursue that subject for the moment. "Have you absolutely no idea where your husband is or when he's likely to return to Kingston?"

She blushed vividly. "N-not exactly."

"Well, finish your meal and you can tell me. As much as you choose."

Daisy's scone had somehow disappeared. She really hadn't meant to eat more than half. She sipped her coffee. "Doesn't Jamaica produce coffee, as well as rum?"

In response to this apparently innocent question, Martha's face suffused with pink again. She nodded, her mouth full.

Though Daisy was dying of curiosity, she kept quiet till the last scrap of toast was gone.

"Would you like more? Or something else?"

"No, thank you. I feel much better." She looked much better, too, her cheeks retaining some of the colour of her flush. "If I tell you about Sam, do you have to tell Mr. Pearson?"

"Not unless it's somehow related to the viscountcy, to Sam's descent from Julian Dalrymple. That's his only concern."

"Nothing like that. He didn't even know about that when he left. I didn't find out about the advert till much later. He signed on as mate on a ship taking a cargo of rum to the Bahamas."

"For sale in America?" Daisy had considerable knowledge of the rumrunners and bootleggers who defied Prohibition to bring alcoholic beverages to the thirsty hordes. The Fletchers' next-door neighbours, the Jessups, were wine merchants involved in the business.

"It's not illegal," Martha said defensively. "The trouble is, instead of staying with the ship, he decided to go with some smugglers to Florida. His captain brought me a letter when he got back to Kingston. Sam hoped to make enough money to quit the sea and start a business at home. He missed me and the girls, you see. He didn't think there was much danger. The runners are hardly ever caught, and if they are, the judges and juries in Florida hardly ever convict them."

"But Sam was caught and convicted?"

"I don't *know*! I haven't heard a word from him since he left Nassau, more than three months ago."

"You must be horridly worried."

"I try not to think about it. Whatever's happened, I can't let this chance slip without doing what I can. Not only for Sammy." She patted her belly. "I might have a boy this time."

"That being so, I think we'd better enlighten Tommy—Mr. Pearson. He doesn't seem to have noticed that you're expecting."

"I thought he was just too polite to mention it."

"He would have mentioned it to me." As an added inducement to take the girl under her wing.

Daisy paid the bill and they left. Walking back along the Strand, Daisy decided Martha's frock, though just about acceptable for the country, simply would not do in town. Besides, she'd need new clothes as her pregnancy advanced. Lucy, Daisy's closest friend, was the person to consult. A devotee of haute couture, Lucy was always trying to persuade Daisy to dress with more attention to fashion, but surely she'd lower her sights for Martha and suggest what styles were suitable, flattering, and inexpensive.

That was when Daisy realised she had made up her mind. No matter what Alec might think of it, she was taking Martha home with her.

ELEVEN

Martha had never ridden in a motorcar before. However, as was to be expected of an intrepid young woman who had crossed the ocean alone, pregnant, and with very little money in her purse, she was not at all nervous. The weepiness that had dismayed Daisy had been dispelled by food and the end of uncertainty about her immediate future.

"I might as well enjoy today," she said to Daisy. "The bridge between laughing and crying's not long."

Daisy, on the other hand, was more than a little anxious about how Alec would take her foisting a long-lost and very distant relative by marriage on the household. No doubt he would harp on her propensity for taking people at face value. He'd point out that even if Martha really was a Dalrymple (by marriage), they knew next to nothing about her or her husband—except that her husband had recently embarked upon an illegal enterprise, at least as far as American law was concerned. To a policeman, it was not the best of recommendations. Daisy wondered whether she could get away with not telling him.

Better not, she decided with a sigh. He'd find out sooner or later and then he'd be furious at her lack of candour.

She parked in front of the house. "I hope you can manage the steps," she said. "If it looks too much, we can go round through the garden. There's a door on the level there, because of the slope."

"Easy, compared to the companionways on the ship! I'll just get my suitcase." Martha reached back for the cardboard suitcase they had picked up from the station left luggage.

"Leave it. Elsie will bring it in. Our parlourmaid."

Turning, Martha looked up at the house. Her eyes widened. "Is it all yours?"

"Yes. We inherited it from a great-uncle. My husband's, not the Dalrymple side. I expect I ought to tell you, Alec's a policeman, a detective."

"Oh!"

"An *English* policeman. Prohibition is none of his business. He does know some people over there, though. Perhaps he could put out some careful feelers and see whether he can discover any news of your Sam."

"I suppose you have to tell him. . . ."

"Well, I do think he's due an explanation, don't you?" They reached the top of the steps. Daisy crossed the porch and opened the front door. "Do come in."

They had barely crossed the threshold when Elsie appeared at the back of the entrance hall. "Madam—" She stopped when she saw Martha.

"Mrs. Dalrymple is going to be staying with us for a while, Elsie. Please fetch her case from my car." Daisy could rely on her parlourmaid and Mrs. Dobson to have the bed in the best spare room ready made up and aired regularly.

"Right away, madam." She gave Martha a curious glance, but she was too well trained to stare. A treasure, Daisy thought warmly. "Madam, Mr. Fletcher telephoned to say he's going out of town. He'll be gone tonight and maybe several nights, he said."

Martha looked relieved. She wouldn't have to face the bogey-man for a day or two.

That afternoon, when Martha was taking a nap, Daisy rang up Lucy and explained the situation. "So I wondered whether you could help me buy her suitable clothes."

Lady Gerald was not interested. "Darling," she protested in her high, clear soprano, "you know I'm always ready to advise you—"

"Keen is the word."

"All right, 'keen' to advise you on your wardrobe, for all the notice you take. But you really can't expect me to dress a pregnant poor relation."

"Who might be the next Lady Dalrymple."

"*Might.* Besides, if your first impressions are correct, she won't want to be beholden to you for the latest modes, which, unless expensive, are invariably vulgar. I haven't a clue about preggy clothes, in any case." Lucy had no children and, as far as Daisy knew, no intention of ever having any. "Take her to Selfridge's Bargain Basement and buy her something practical."

"I'd like her to look pretty when her husband arrives."

"If he does."

"Of course he will, darling, don't be such a pessimist. In any case, she'll have to be decently dressed when we go to Fairacres and she meets the other would-bes."

"Talking of that gathering, I think your cousin must have run mad to invite them all. They'll be at one another's throats. There'll probably be murder done."

"What rot! You're only saying that because I've been involved in one or two murder investigations."

"One or two!" Lucy was the only person other than Alec who knew exactly how many bodies Daisy had somehow managed to stumble upon.

"A few. All right, several. It's no reason to expect more. These are all respectable people, after all."

But when Lucy had rung off, Daisy thought, what did she really know about them? Raymond and Vincent were undoubtedly prosperous and respectable, if not likeable. Martha was likeable, though not prosperous; Samuel's present escapade could hardly be described as respectable. Suppose he turned out to be a ruffian, willing to kill for the inheritance?

And others might yet turn up.

That evening, Martha retired to bed right after dinner, exhausted despite her afternoon nap. Daisy put a soothing record on the gramophone, Paderewski playing Mendelsohn's *Songs Without Words*. Half listening, she read through the list she and Martha had compiled of everything unpacked from the suitcase brought from Jamaica. It wasn't long. And most of the things were unsuitable either for English weather, or for London and Fairacres, or both.

Daisy started to make a list of everything they would need to buy.

The telephone rang. Daisy hurried out to the hall to answer it before Elsie started up from the basement kitchen to get it.

"Daisy, it's Madge."

"Hold on just half a mo. I've got a record on. I'd better stop it or the needle will carve a groove." When she returned, she asked, "I assume Tommy has told you about the latest applicant?"

"Martha Dalrymple. It was unconscionable for him to land you with the poor girl."

"I don't really mind. The children have taken to her already— she has two of her own that she had to leave with her parents, did Tommy tell you? And with a third on the way—"

"What!? He didn't tell me she's expecting."

"Darling, I suspect he didn't notice. About five months. He probably assumed she was a trifle stout. Her frock wasn't exactly flattering."

"She's bursting out of her clothes?"

"Not quite that bad, though she will be. It's just that what's suitable for a Caribbean island is hardly appropriate for London, nor practical for the climate."

"Tommy didn't mention that either. Really, men can be so blind. Daisy, I'd love to take her shopping. I have plenty of experience of dressing for pregnancy." Madge had produced three little Pearsons in four years.

"Would you really? That would be simply marvellous. I hate shopping for clothes and I have a due date creeping up on me. An article due, not a baby! I'll pay, of course."

"Oh, that's right, she hasn't a penny. I don't see why you should be out of pocket. Tommy will just have to work out how to charge the estate."

"I don't mind. She's a relative, after all, however distant. If Tommy can pay me back from the estate at some point, well and good. Just don't go overboard, Madge. Nothing too extravagant."

Madge laughed, the frothy bubbling laugh that matched her frothy bubbles of blond hair. "I'll pinch your pennies, don't worry. Everything?"

"Head to foot, and from the skin out. Cheap cotton undies are all very well here, but I don't want the maids at Fairacres sneering at her."

"Heaven forbid, especially if she turns out to be the next viscountess."

With that load off her mind, Daisy felt much less apprehensive about explaining the situation to Alec—though, considering the matter dispassionately, there was no real reason for her relief.

When Alec came home at last, four days later, Martha had settled nicely into the household, with the beginnings of a new wardrobe for which she promised Sam would reimburse Daisy. He would have plenty of money, from his venture into rum-running.

On that score, Daisy was not sanguine.

Alec arrived just in time for dinner, tired and hungry. He accepted a brief explanation of Martha's presence without much visible reaction, merely saying he hoped she would enjoy her stay. Martha retired to bed shortly after dinner, as had become her habit. In the sitting room, Alec listened, though apparently more interested in getting his pipe going, as Daisy expanded upon the story. She finished it with: "So you see, Samuel may be in jail or dead."

"In jail! Daisy, honestly, how do you get into these situations?"

"What situations?" she demanded indignantly. "I've never had a relative in jail before. And he may not be now. It's just odd that he hasn't been heard from in several months. Darling, you know people in the American police—FBI, is it?—and there's whatsisname, too, Lambert, our pet Prohibition agent. Couldn't you find out if Sam was caught?"

"It would be a very good way to draw the wrong kind of attention to him." Alec puffed contentedly, his annoyance diminished by the accomplishment of his aim. "I'll think about it," he conceded.

"Or there's the Jessups. They have connections among the bootleggers."

"You may remember Mr. Jessup said the firm was no longer going to ship to America. You'd only embarrass them. Don't ask the Jessups, please, and, Daisy, *don't* mention their past connection with the illegal trade to Martha."

"You read my mind. Oh, all right! I've already advised her not to talk to anyone about her husband's situation. But I shall certainly introduce her to the Jessups. They'd think it very odd if I didn't, living next door. They've already heard she's come to stay, what with our Elsie being their Enid's sister. Besides, Audrey's children must be about the same age as the two Martha left in Jamaica."

Daisy had run out of ideas for helping Martha. They would just have to wait and see what happened.

Only a few weeks remained before Edgar's birthday and as yet the succession was very much in doubt. Nor was there any indication that any of the claimants would be able to come up with proof of his descent from Julian Dalrymple by way of eldest son to eldest son.

With no heir declared, the birthday celebration was going to be an uneasy event at best—unless, in the meantime, someone else turned up bearing an impeccable lineage.

Time passed and Tommy Pearson didn't get in touch with Daisy, though both Miss Watt and Madge rang up every couple of days to make sure Martha was all right and not becoming a burden.

Daisy assured them she was not, which was mostly true. Martha had became quite friendly with Audrey Jessup. She missed her little girls badly and spent much of her time with the twins, in the nursery and on their daily walks, come rain or shine. But if she had any more weepy fits, she didn't impose them on Daisy, and she continued to retire after dinner, leaving Alec and Daisy in connubial peace.

A brief note came from Tommy just a week before everyone was due to arrive at Fairacres. He had received an even shorter note from Trinidad, from someone signing himself Frank Crowley. All Crowley said was that he was bringing Benjamin Dalrymple to London. The letter had taken quite a while to travel from Port-of-Spain to Lincoln's Inn. How far behind it Crowley and the latest Dalrymple claimant were following was anyone's guess.

Would Mrs. Prasad care to analyse the handwriting?

Before telephoning Sakari, Daisy got out the atlas and looked up Trinidad. It turned out to be a tiny island in the Caribbean—not very far from Jamaica, she noted. The map suggested that Benjamin Dalrymple, who could apparently neither write for himself nor travel alone, might just possibly be a legitimate descendant of Julian Dalrymple.

Sakari was delighted to be consulted. She pronounced Frank Crowley to be careless, cheerful, and of an optimistic nature.

"Overoptimistic," said Tommy gloomily, "if he thinks to pass off some illiterate goodness-knows-whom as the rightful heir to a viscountcy."

TWELVE

"*I'm afraid* you have just missed the Hebrew Character." Lord Dalrymple came down the steps and shook Alec's hand warmly as he got out of the big green Vauxhall that had met the Fletchers, Martha Dalrymple, and Nurse Gilpin at Malvern station. "Never mind, quite common and not particularly attractive."

"One of the claimants is Jewish?" Alec asked, startled. Unlikely— but possible, he supposed, as Jews were matrilineal.

The viscount looked equally startled. He pushed his pince-nez lower on his nose and peered at Alec over the top.

Daisy stepped down from the car with a hand from the chauffeur. "Thank you, Truscott. A butterfly, darling," she advised Alec, not that he hadn't already realised, given his host's obsession. "Or a moth. Or even a dragonfly."

"Moth. Setaceous Hebrew Character, *Xestia c-nigrum*. Ah," said Lord Dalrymple triumphantly, "you're the Large Copper, Daisy's young man. Butterfly," he added in parentheses. It was the first time Alec had known him to crack a deliberate joke about his passion.

Laughing, he clarified: "Her husband, sir. Alec Fletcher."

"Yes, indeed. I believe I attended your wedding? Some time ago, was it not? I had forgotten."

Alec forbore to remind him that he had given Daisy away and provided a grand reception.

Daisy kissed his cheek, as Belinda appeared from the car with Oliver in her arms, followed by Mrs. Gilpin carrying a wiggling Miranda.

"You remember Belinda, Cousin Edgar."

"Of course, my dear." He patted Bel's cheek. "Small Red Damsel."

"I'm not small anymore, Uncle Edgar, and my hair isn't as red as it used to be. It's getting fairer. Or is that a butterfly?"

"Damselfly. *Ceriagrion tenellum.*" He smiled at her, then peered at Oliver as Alec set him down.

"My brother, Oliver. He was only a baby when we came last year. He can almost talk now. Oliver, say hello."

"Dada," said Oliver firmly, reaching out to Alec.

Miranda was more obliging: "Heyo," she said with a beam.

Lord Dalrymple beamed back. "Heyo, Miranda. Would you like to see some butterflies?"

"Buf'eyes?"

"*I'd* like to," said Belinda. "I'll bring them both to your conservatory later, all right, Uncle Edgar?"

"Certainly, certainly. You can help me release the Migrant Hawker."

"I take it, sir," said Alec dryly, "that you haven't imprisoned a wandering pedlar?"

"Butterfly," said Daisy, "or moth."

"No, no, dragonfly. It hatched this morning. Pretty dragonfly," he said to Miranda.

"Dagfwy? Manda pitty."

"So you are, my dear, so you are."

"What nonsense, Miss Miranda," Nurse Gilpin intervened. "Vain as a peacock, that's what you'll be. If your lordship'll excuse us, I'd like to get them settled in the nursery."

"I have several Peacocks that will probably hatch in a few days."

"Bird or butterfly?" Alec asked, laughing.

"Oh, butterfly, my dear fellow, butterfly. *Inachis io*, don't you know.

Geraldine was talking about acquiring some peacocks for the terrace, but I can't abide their screeching. For my taste, it's too like a rabbit's scream when a fox or stoat gets it." On this gruesome note, he stepped forward to greet Martha, whom Truscott was solicitously handing down from the Vauxhall. She looked apprehensive, unsure of her welcome. "And here is the Beautiful Demoiselle."

"Mrs. Samuel Dalrymple," Daisy introduced her. "Demoiselle" was hardly appropriate for the by-now distinctly pregnant young woman!

However, perhaps Edgar was not so oblivious as his choice of words suggested. He offered Martha his arm, patted her hand, and said, "I'm very happy to meet you, my dear. Don't worry, we'll take good care of you until your husband arrives."

At last the butler succeeded in ushering everyone out of the heat and glare of the July afternoon into the cool dimness of the hall, lit only by the clerestory and lantern of the cupola high above.

"Her ladyship is in the drawing room," Lowecroft announced. "Tea will be served shortly. Perhaps the ladies would like to go to their rooms first?"

"I'll go up too," Alec said firmly.

Ernest was waiting by the stairs to escort them, and upstairs a maid was in attendance. Belinda was thrilled to find she had risen to the dignity of a guest room of her own, instead of one of the nursery bedrooms. In fact, she was in Daisy's old room, as Daisy and Alec had the second-best bedroom.

"Mummy, do you think that means I'm supposed to have tea with the grown-ups, not with the babies?" she asked anxiously.

"I expect so, darling. You can come down with us to say hello to Aunt Geraldine, and if it looks as if you're not expected you can quietly fade out, all right?" Daisy turned to the maid. "Are the other . . . guests already here?"

"Lord and Lady John will be staying at the Dower House, madam. There's others as came yesterday," she added in an ominous tone, "but who they may be, I'm sure it's not my place to say."

She made sure they had everything they needed, then departed.

"It sounds as if the servants don't approve of the heirs of the body," said Alec.

"Darling, it sounds to me as if they strongly *dis*approve."

"They're your relatives." He was determined not to be drawn into Daisy's family affairs. "I'm not going to get involved. I'd rather face a gang of thugs than massed Dalrymples, unless you're by my side to protect me."

Daisy giggled. "Then hurry up, do. I'm dying to see how Vincent and Raymond get on with each other."

They washed off the inevitable grime of a train journey. When Belinda tapped on the door, Daisy sent her to see if Martha was ready.

Meeting on the landing, Alec saw that Martha was wide-eyed with apprehension, daunted by the prospect of facing a roomful of strangers. He was not a little apprehensive himself—of a week of boredom or, alternatively, of hordes of squabbling relatives whose ruffled feathers Daisy would expect him to help to smooth. With a certain fellow feeling, he gave Martha his arm and escorted her down the wide stairs to the hall.

Daisy followed with Belinda, doing her best not to act as if Fairacres were still her home. She wondered whether Martha found the mansion any more intimidating than she had—at first sight— the Hampstead house.

"I wish Derek was here," Bel whispered to her.

As they reached the foot of the staircase Lowecroft, adept in the magical art of butlerdom, appeared from nowhere and ushered them into the drawing room.

Geraldine came to greet them. Behind her, three men stood up: Raymond, Vincent, and a stranger. Belatedly Edgar followed suit. With him rose a boy he had been chatting to, a dark lad of about Belinda's age. An unknown lady remained seated.

Daisy presented Martha to Geraldine, who welcomed her kindly though with a distracted air. General introductions followed, not without some difficulty, as many of those present had the same surname.

Raymond Dalrymple favoured Daisy with a half bow, shook

hands with Alec, gave Martha a nod and a hard stare, and ignored Belinda.

Vincent Dalrymple was all smiles and complaisance. The unknown woman turned out to be his wife. Mrs. Vincent Dalrymple was a handsome woman who spoke excellent English with a slight French accent and was dressed and made up with the Parisian chic attained without effort by so many Frenchwomen. Her manner was graciously condescending to Daisy, as if she already knew her husband to be the true heir. She couldn't—could she?

To Martha, Mrs. Vincent didn't bother to be gracious. She was coldly polite, after a glance with narrowed eyes at the younger woman's obvious pregnancy. After an appraising look at Belinda, she bent enough to say, "My elder daughter must be about your age."

"What's her name? Is she here?" Bel asked eagerly.

"Certainly not. The children are *en vacances* on the Continent with their governess."

Geraldine swept onwards. "Daisy, this is Mr. Crowley."

So the stranger was the one who had told Tommy he was escorting a Dalrymple scion to England. In his late thirties, Mr. Crowley was dark haired, extremely good-looking, with green eyes and an engaging smile that displayed very white teeth. Altogether too much of a good thing, Daisy thought. What was his association with the unknown Dalrymple and why was his attendance necessary?

He grinned at Daisy and, as if reading her mind, said, "I've brought my stepson over to take his chances in the Dalrymple stakes."

Doubtless he had had to answer the same question, spoken or implied, over and over again, she realised crossly.

He turned to the boy beside him, between him and Edgar. "Benjamin Dalrymple, son of my late wife and her first husband, Lucas Dalrymple, of Port-of-Spain, Trinidad."

An orphan, then. Benjamin, a lanky lad about Bel's age, was as dark skinned as Daisy's Indian friend Sakari. Though his features were more European than African, his short-cropped hair was crow-black and tightly curled. Daisy had been vaguely aware of these facts since her first glance at the assembled company, but she hadn't paid much attention, concentrating on the adults. It hadn't crossed her mind that he was one of the would-be heirs.

He bowed slightly, looking apprehensive.

"Hello," said Belinda, eschewing the formal "how do you do" with which she had addressed the grown-ups. She went straight to the question that most interested her: "How old are you?"

"Twelve, miss."

"I'm thirteen. So's Derek. My name is Belinda but you can call me Bel."

He beamed. "You can call me Ben. Or Benjie, but I like Ben better." His voice had an attractive lilt, rather like Martha's, though less strong and with a mixture of other elements. It sounded almost Welsh to Daisy's ears.

"Bel and Ben. I bet people will get confused."

"Who's Derek?"

"My cousin. My stepcousin, really. And my friend. You're a sort of stepcousin too, I expect. You came from Trinidad?"

Daisy heard no more, as Ernest bore in the tea tray and Geraldine bustled her and Martha away to sit down. However, she was glad to see the two heads, ginger and black, remaining close together. Belinda's coeducational school had made her quite at ease with boys, unlike many girls her age, and Sakari's daughter was one of her best friends, so dark skin was no impediment.

However, it didn't seem remotely possible that a half-caste child could be a legitimate "heir of the body." That was not the boy's fault. Crowley was responsible for his claim. Daisy wondered whether he really was Benjamin's stepfather.

The ramifications were so complex she soon stopped wondering, in favour of answering Geraldine's polite enquiries about the rigours of the train journey and the health of the twins. Geraldine was always meticulous about asking after the babies, though Daisy was pretty certain she really preferred older children, in spite of—or perhaps because of—having spent years as unpaid housemother to a horde of adolescent boys.

Mr. Crowley came over to have his teacup refilled, and stayed to talk to Daisy. "Let me get this straight," he said with his charming smile, "you're the daughter of our illustrious host's predecessor?"

Ingratiating, Daisy thought. Was he a bit of a bounder, out to make something from his stepson's possible good fortune? Perhaps even something of a con man? However, presumably he'd satisfied Tommy Pearson that Ben really was a Dalrymple, though, like the others, without proof that his was the eldest line.

"That's right. Lord Dalrymple is my cousin." Daisy looked round the room. "One of my cousins, I should say."

"Oughtn't you to be Lady something, then?"

"No." She didn't bother to explain the ramifications of her honorary "honourable" title. "Benjamin is an orphan, I gather?"

"Yes. His father was Lucas Dalrymple, son of John Dalrymple, who came to Port-of-Spain from Jamaica when he was a child, it seems, with his father Josiah. John married Dolores—I brought their marriage cert so that part's all legit. That's why I thought there's half a chance . . ." He glanced round the room, with a wry face, while Daisy tried to memorise the names so as to create Ben's family branch. "Quarter of a chance for the lad. Besides, I've always wanted to see the old country, though I didn't expect to do it in such luxury!"

"How did you come to be responsible for Ben?"

"Luke was a pal of mine. He volunteered for the West India Regiment and before he left I promised to look out for Susanna and the kids if he didn't come back."

"Kids?"

"Ben has two older sisters and a younger brother."

"Luke Dalrymple was killed in the war, I assume."

"The Palestine Campaign. Your brother, too, I heard?"

"In Flanders." Ten years later, Gervaise seemed to belong to another world. "Hence the search for an heir. A legitimate heir," Daisy added.

Crowley grinned. "Don't worry, Susanna and Luke were properly married, I assure you. In church. I was Luke's best man. Susanna was a mulatto, a beauty. Her father was a Frenchman. We've got all sorts at home. I won't say mixed marriages are common, but matches between white men and black women aren't as uncommon as you may think."

"You married Susanna, after Luke died?"

"A couple of years later. She was going to have my baby. They both died." After a sombre pause, he went on, "I don't know why I'm boring you with all this."

"You're not boring me, I'm interested. I'm so sorry about Susanna and your child. How on earth have you managed with the children?"

"My brother's wife's sister, Carlotta, has been helping, taking care of them after school and so on, and I've paid her what I can. But now . . . Look here, if I tell you something, you won't pass it on? It's personal, nothing that will change Ben's prospects."

Why people insisted on confiding in Daisy she had no idea. Alec blamed her deceptively guileless blue eyes, which she considered very unfair. More likely it was because her insatiable curiosity, her besetting sin, made her interested in whatever people told her, and in turn her interest made them want to confide. Was that circular reasoning, such as Alec had been known to reproach her for? She was still never quite certain.

"Tell me," she invited. "I won't gossip."

"I want to marry Carlotta. I'm fond of Susanna's brood, and we've done our best for them, but we want to settle down and have a family of our own. Carlotta won't marry me if it means becoming mama to four kids from eleven to fifteen."

"It's quite a lot to take on," Daisy said doubtfully.

"Carlotta thinks Anita, the eldest, is old enough to take responsibility for them all—with a hand from the family. But Anita won a scholarship to Bishop Anstey High School and she wants to get her School Certificate, even the Higher Cert. The rest are bright, too. I promised Luke . . . To cut a long story short, when I heard about the lawyer looking for a Dalrymple heir, I decided it was worth a gamble. I reckoned that if Ben turns out to be a lord, or an honourable or whatever, they'll all be taken care of."

"I'm sure they would be, if . . ."

"If." Crowley nodded ruefully. "I didn't count on so much

competition. I don't like the odds. What happens if the lawyer man can't find the proof he needs?"

"I can't imagine." Daisy looked up as Belinda came towards her, Ben trailing behind. "What is it, darling?"

"Mummy, Uncle Edgar wants to go and look at the butterflies right now because Ben's been telling him about the giant butterflies in Trinidad, so may I go and fetch the twins and then afterwards is it all right if Ben and I go to the Dower House to see Derek? Ben hasn't met him yet. I wish Derek was staying here. Do you think Aunt Violet would let him? We—"

"Slow down! You may do all that *provided* you get permission from Aunt Geraldine to leave the room and to invite Derek; and from Nurse Gilpin to take the twins; and from Grandmama Dalrymple as well as Aunt Violet to ask Derek to move up here. I take it you've already consulted Benjamin, not dragged him along in your wake?"

"Oh yes, ma'am. If I may go with Miss Belinda, Uncle Frank?" Crowley gave his permission.

"Bel, let me know when you're going to the Dower House. I'll go with you. I want to see your Aunt Violet. And I must say hello to Mother." She hoped Belinda hadn't noticed her priorities.

From what little she'd seen of him, Benjamin's manner and manners appeared to be excellent, perhaps due to the influence of the male equivalent of Bishop Whatsit's High School. All the same, if he was Edgar's heir, a black viscount would be a real turnup for the books!

Crowley watched Bel and Ben cross the room to Geraldine, who was now engaged in laborious conversation with Mrs. Vincent Dalrymple. Daisy thought Crowley looked part speculative, part calculating, and part satisfied. She wasn't sure how much of his story she believed. Was he a plausible rogue, or a man in a difficult position trying to do his best for his wards? Or a bit of both? Though his relationship with Benjamin seemed to be good, at best his motives were decidedly mixed.

She couldn't make up her mind whether she liked him or not, far less whether she'd trust him an inch further than she could see him.

THIRTEEN

The Vincent Dalrymples decided it behooved them to make their bows to the dowager viscountess and so proposed to join the walk to the Dower House. Daisy didn't particularly want their company, but their presence might deflect attention from herself, always a good thing. What her mother's reaction to Ben's dark face might be she resolutely put out of her mind.

"Should I come along?" Alec asked her, when she told him of the expedition. "I ought to make my bow to your mother, too."

"Do, darling. You know how it is. She has to complain about something, and given a choice of your negligence or too many people invading her tiny house, I'd prefer the latter. Especially as the house is quite big enough to absorb all of us. Besides, she does have some respect for you. Perhaps you can prevent her being rude to the Vincents and poor Ben."

"Don't count on it, love."

"All right, then, you can protect me from the Vincents en route. I can't go on calling them that. We're going to have to come to an agreement on christian names all round. After all, we're all family."

"*Your* family," Alec reminded her.

"Don't rub it in!"

"Martha's not coming?"

"It's a bit far for her to walk, with the hill to climb, and she's tired from the journey. She's going to lie down till dinnertime."

"And Raymond?"

"He's already met Mother, remember, and got rather the worst of that encounter. I expect the longer he can put off seeing her again, the happier he'll be. It's different with Edgar, who completely routed him. He can't very well avoid his host, and refusing the invitation would have looked like turning tail. Did you talk to him at all?"

"Yes. Very full of himself, as you said, and disparaging about the viscountcy. I'd argue that his presence suggests he's less indifferent than he wants to appear. He was disparaging about my supposed profession, too, when I told him I'm a civil servant. Too much red tape in this country. They won't stand for it in South Africa."

"You've been known to complain about red tape."

Alec grinned. "True. And I have no desire to be a lord."

"You should be best chums. I like Vincent better than Raymond, but his wife is a bit hard to take."

However, Mrs. Vincent Dalrymple seemed to have worked out, or had pointed out to her, Daisy's position in the family. Not that Daisy had a high opinion of her own importance, but she did dislike being condescended to. On the other hand, she was no keener on fulsome flattery. As they walked across the park, Laurette—she'd instantly agreed to first names—gushed about how wonderful it was, and the house as well, and how envious she was of Daisy for growing up there.

"I mean to get to know every corner this week," she said, with an arch laugh, "because, considering the *tohu-bohu* of his lordship's affairs, I may not get another chance. I can't imagine why the lawyer hasn't sorted it out yet."

"Mr. Pearson is doing his best," Daisy defended him. "It's not his fault no one has yet provided the needed documents."

Warned by her tone, Laurette reversed course. "*Ça se voit.* Of course not. I'm afraid he's having a difficult time. Vincent is still hoping his relatives in France may be able to find proof that his grandfather was the eldest son. I don't know what Vincent's father was thinking of, to throw away the old man's passport when he died."

"Luckily no family papers ever get thrown away at Fairacres. Otherwise we wouldn't have known about Julian Dalrymple going to Jamaica, and none of you would be here."

"I suppose Mr. Pearson has checked that *everyone* is descended from Julian?" She nodded significantly at Benjamin, walking just ahead with Belinda. "I wouldn't have thought—"

"Ben has French blood, I understand," said Daisy, "like your husband."

Irrelevant, perhaps, but it shut Laurette up on that subject. She chose instead to say how happy she would be to meet the dowager. "Because, though Lord and Lady Dalrymple are very worthy people, they were not, after all, brought up to the position, as your mama was. And you, of course, and Lady Violet."

"My sister is known as Lady John, Laurette. Like me, she has no title of her own. She married Lord John, who is the younger son of a marquis."

"How kind of you to explain. That's exactly what I mean—you grew up knowing that sort of detail. I'm sure you and Lady John and the dear dowager will be able to give me and Vincent any number of hints when he . . . *if* he is acknowledged to be the heir."

The "dear dowager" was most unlikely to do anything of the sort, Daisy reflected. Nor could she imagine herself or Vi ever becoming mentors to Laurette and Vincent. One of the things she liked best about Edgar and Geraldine was that on the whole they set their own style—Edgar especially—and didn't fuss about the county's opinion, still less that of London society.

Laurette chatted on. Daisy listened with half her attention, answering occasional questions automatically. Alec and Vincent had walked on ahead. She couldn't hear what they were talking about, if they were talking. Alec would probably prefer silence, but she doubted Vincent was capable of keeping his mouth shut. She hoped Alec's policemanly restraint was not under too great a strain.

Bel and Ben were closer to her. Bel was telling Ben about all the fun to be had at Fairacres. She pointed down the hill at a stretch of mixed woodland a few hundred yards away, on the far side of the drive.

"That's a ripping place for hide-and-seek and building forts. The stream goes through the middle, too, the one I told you about that flows into the river, where we can go boating. Uncle Edgar lets the woods grow wild, mostly, instead of having the undergrowth and fallen trees cleared. He says it's better for butterflies. Did you know butterflies like stinging nettles? Some caterpillars won't eat anything else."

"What are stinging nettles?" Ben asked with trepidation. "Are they snakes?"

"No, plants. Don't worry, if you touch them it smarts like blazes but only for a little while, 'specially if you rub it with dock leaves. We'll show you."

"Are there snakes in the woods? Poison snakes?"

"Not *really* poisonous. Adders won't kill you and I've never seen one anyway. Are there poisonous snakes in Trinidad? Deadly ones?"

"Oh yes."

"Gosh!"

Laurette had also listened to them, apparently, with both disapproval and amazement. "You let your daughter go off to play in the woods with her cousin?"

"They're both sensible children and they stay on the estate. I suspect this is the last year Derek will care for hide-and-seek, though. He's just passed his Common Entrance. Once he gets to Harrow, he won't want to play with girls any longer. I remember how my brother changed at that age."

They came to the top of a rise. Away off to the north, Worcester was visible, the square tower of the cathedral dominating the city. Down to their left, in the corner where the drive met the lane, an outcrop of booths and marquees studded the meadow set aside for the fête. Shouts and hammering indicated that preparations were still in full swing, tomorrow being the sabbath, when any remaining work would have to be hushed.

"Look!" cried Belinda. "I can't wait for Monday." She explained to Ben the delights of a village fête.

"It sounds a bit like our Carnival," he said doubtfully. Judging by his description of Carnival, as overheard by Daisy, the fête was a far more staid affair.

To the right, towards the village, the Dower House lay near the foot of the gentle downward slope, a red-brick Georgian house surrounded by its own gardens and orchard. Though small in comparison with Fairacres, the house easily accommodated Violet and John and their children, together with their nanny and Vi's personal maid, in addition to the dowager and her servants. Daisy's mother complained bitterly of overcrowding, but she would have complained equally bitterly of being neglected had her elder and favourite daughter and family accepted Geraldine's invitation to stay at Fairacres.

Daisy hoped she wouldn't be too set against Derek moving up to the big house. After all, she was always complaining about noisy boys, and Derek was the noisy one, his younger brother being of a quiet and contemplative nature.

"I'll race you," said Belinda, and she and Ben dashed off down the hill.

Laurette tut-tutted, but sotto voce.

The visit went better than Daisy had feared. Both the dowager viscountess and Lord and Lady John Frobisher were accustomed to deference and found no fault in the Vincent Dalrymples' manners. Belinda and Benjamin were on their best behaviour, and Bel's request for Derek to join them at Fairacres was met with "If he'd like to, we'll see."

Lady Dalrymple appeared to be blind to Ben's colour. As she later confided to Daisy, "Obviously Edgar's lawyer has made some stupid error over the boy; no doubt he'll soon sort it out. I'm not at all prejudiced against black people, the civilised sort. You will recall that I was of some assistance to the Indian person at Brockdene, when we mistakenly spent Christmas there. But naturally it's quite impossible that a black could be a member of *our* family."

Daisy didn't argue. In the first place, arguing with her mother was entirely pointless. In the second place, she had her own doubts of Crowley's veracity.

Her brother-in-law also drew her aside. "To tell the truth, Daisy, I'll be very happy if Derek wants to go up to the house. Violet isn't well. The journey exhausted her."

"I thought she was looking a bit pale and wan. She hasn't really been well since the baby was born, has she?"

"I'm afraid not," John said wryly. "The doctor says no more children. I'll be glad to see Derek off her hands this week, especially as I'm going to have to go home for a couple of days. The hop harvest is just getting going and it's the one thing my bailiff isn't comfortable handling on his own, with all the pickers coming down from the East End."

"You'll be back for Edgar's birthday?"

"Of course. But if you could keep an eye on Violet while I'm away, and make sure she doesn't overexert herself. . . . You know how she likes to spend time with the children."

"I'll keep an eye on her, and Derek can bring his things over tomorrow after church." Daisy went to talk to her sister.

"Has John been telling you I'm at death's door?" Violet asked resignedly, in a soft voice. "Don't go spreading it about, will you, Daisy?"

"Of course not, darling. Is it true?"

"Just a bit done up from the journey. You know how I hate to travel, and John gets in a fuss. I just need a couple of days of peace and quiet and I'll be perfectly all right for Edgar's birthday 'spree,' as Derek insists on calling it."

"You'll have much more peace and quiet if Derek comes to the house."

"Y-yes. I suppose, if you and Alec think the . . . that boy is an acceptable friend for Belinda. . . ." She glanced at the three children, who had their heads together as if they'd known each other for years. "Much as I love him, he's at that awkward age—active and noisy, but too old to be sent to the nursery. All right," she conceded with a sigh. "And I won't even ask you to try to keep him out of mischief. It's impossible."

Daisy briefly wondered whether she had bitten off more than she could chew. She took comfort in the thought that Edgar and Geraldine were both accustomed to dealing with large numbers of children at that "awkward" age. Derek, Bel, and Ben must be encouraged to work off their excess energy in insect-hunting expeditions.

As usual, as the party from Fairacres was leaving, Lady Dalrymple had the last word. "You didn't bring the twins, Daisy. Belinda is a nice enough child, but after all, she's only a stepgranddaughter. . . ."

"Mother, it's past their bedtime! You'll see them tomorrow. I nearly forgot, Geraldine's invited everyone to lunch."

"Nearly forgot to pass on an invitation? Well, I must say, modern manners are quite extraordinary! I suppose we shall have to go, though I don't know how the woman has the nerve to ask *me* to be a guest in what should be my own home!"

Daisy dutifully kissed her cheek, rounded up the flock, and left the Dower House with all possible speed.

On the way home, they met Frank Crowley coming along the footpath from the village, which joined their path. "I've always wanted to see an English country pub," he explained. "That young chap Ernest—the vice-butler?"

"Footman," Alec told him.

"I asked his advice and he told me how to get to the Wedge and Beetle in Morton Green. Nice place. Good beer."

"I'll come with you one evening," said Alec. "I stayed there a few years ago and found it friendlier to strangers than some I could name." He hesitated. "Perhaps you'd like to go too . . . er . . . Vincent?"

"Certainly, certainly," Vincent agreed insincerely.

Catching Alec's eye, Daisy was fairly certain the invitation would not have been extended if he had thought for a moment that a country pub held any attraction for Vincent.

When they reached the house, it was time to change for dinner. Ernest met them in the hall with instructions from Geraldine that black ties would not be worn. Daisy was not surprised. Edgar loathed evening dress as much as Alec did, and the chance of Mr. Crowley owning a dinner jacket seemed slim.

Belinda pulled at her sleeve. "Mummy!" she whispered urgently.

"Ernest, did her ladyship mention whether Miss Belinda and Master Benjamin are to join us?"

"Oh yes, madam. My lady expects the young people to dine with the company." He gave a slight bow towards said young people, who exchanged a happy smile and made for the stairs. Ernest said to Daisy in a lowered voice, "Mr. Crowley asked for Master Benjamin to be seated tonight with the rest of the—er—cousins, so as not to make an exception of him. My lady expects the young people, given a choice, to choose *not* to dine with the grown-ups after the first time."

"My lady is experienced in the ways of young people," Daisy agreed, laughing, remembering the excruciating boredom of grown-up dinner parties.

Daisy and Alec followed the Vincent Dalrymples and the children upstairs. Belinda was waiting at their bedroom door.

"Should I wear my best frock, Mummy?"

"Second best, pet. Save the best for Uncle Edgar's birthday. And come and see me before you go down. I'll help you with your hair."

"Oh yes, I want to go down with you and Daddy."

"Of course. Would you go and ask Aunt Martha whether she needs any help? Let me know if it's something you can't do for her. You know which is her room?"

"Yes. Did you know Aunt Geraldine put Ben in the turret room? She says it's perfect for boys." It had been Gervaise's room in the all-too-short years between nursery and war. "It's not really fair, because *I* think it's perfect for girls, too, but it's nice of Aunt Geraldine, and Ben's happy."

"You like Ben?"

"Oh yes. He was telling Derek and me all sorts of interesting stuff about Trinidad. We're going to go and visit him there when we're grown-up, unless he's the next Lord Dalrymple."

Pondering this possibility, Daisy took a moment to write down Ben's family branch:

Julian?
Josiah m.?
John m. Dolores
Lucas m. Susanna (m. 2 Frank Crowley)
Anita Benjamin ++

Benjamin, Viscount Dalrymple? No more improbable, really, than Raymond, Vincent, or Martha's Sam.

FOURTEEN

What with one thing and another, Daisy felt as if she scarcely had time to draw breath until after Sunday's lunch party. Everything had gone remarkably smoothly, considering the possible causes for antagonism. Even Daisy's mother was on her best behaviour, perhaps mindful that if Edgar predeceased her, one of those present might become her nearest neighbour.

Not that she'd ever shown the least desire to conciliate Edgar and Geraldine. But, to be fair, when they arrived at Fairacres she was still suffering from the shock of losing her husband and her son.

She and Vi and John had gone back to the Dower House. Martha went upstairs for a rest. Edgar took Pepper and the children to hunt for dragonfly nymphs. Geraldine and Crowley—unlikely companions—went out together to sit on the terrace, discussing Benjamin's education. Raymond and the Vincent Dalrymples had vanished, Daisy cared not whither.

The afternoon was warm, with a cooling breeze and huge white cumulus floating in a summer-blue sky. Daisy and Alec took the twins and Nana out in the park, where they could run and roll on the grass and make as much noise as they wanted, until Nurse Gilpin whisked the babies away for their afternoon nap; then they took the dog for a walk along the river, in the opposite direction to that taken by Edgar. Reaching the boundary of the park, they turned away from the Severn, through fields and orchards.

A Sunday afternoon hush embraced the countryside. Even the birds were silent, except for the distant cawing of rooks. Daisy and Alec saw no one but a pair of hikers until, climbing a stile and turning along a hedge to circle a field of onions, they came face to face with Raymond.

He was wearing a safari suit, such as Daisy had seen in photographs of big-game hunters: a khaki linen jacket with a multiplicity of pockets, breeches, calf-high boots, and a broad-brimmed hat that he raised in greeting. He had binoculars hung around his neck and carried a walking stick propped on his shoulder, as if it were an elephant gun.

"A beautiful afternoon. Does this farm belong to Fairacres, Mrs. Fletcher?"

"Daisy, please. Yes, this is part of the home farm."

"*Home* farm?"

"It's run by Edgar's bailiff, not leased to a tenant." She hoped she was not providing more information than Tommy would approve of—but it was information easily come by elsewhere.

"Good, rich land," Raymond commented.

"You're a judge of farmland?" Alec asked. "I took you for a city dweller."

"We kept the family farm—my mother's family—when we went into business. One of my cousins runs it, but I grew up there and I visit when I can. I know good soil when I see it." He raised his hat again and stood aside to let them pass.

As soon as he had lumbered over the stile and out of sight, Daisy said, "He's totting up whether it's worth his while to inherit Fairacres."

"But nothing he does or doesn't do will make any difference," Alec reminded her.

"Unless he's plotting to get rid of the others."

"Daisy, honestly, do try to curb your imagination!"

"Don't you think Fairacres is worth killing for?"

"That's got nothing to do with it. Besides, they all have sons, or brothers."

"Not Martha's Sam."

"He's not here. In any case, he may have a brother or two, for all you know. Or has Martha told you he's an only child?"

"No. She may have told Tommy. I'll ask her."

"You're talking about international assassination!" Alec protested.

"It doesn't sound very likely," Daisy said with a touch of regret, "but you never know. The diamond business is pretty cutthroat, isn't it? Raymond may know an international assassin or two."

Alec laughed. "Better not say that in anyone else's hearing or you'll be sued for slander. He seems to me the litigious sort."

"Definitely."

"Look, a caterpillar."

"Pretty." Daisy allowed him to distract her from her train of thought. "We'd better take it home to Edgar."

By the time the black-and-yellow striped creature had been removed from a ragwort plant, along with several leaves, and tied up in Alec's handkerchief, he regretted having mentioned it.

They returned to the house in plenty of time for tea. Alec took his specimen to the conservatory/insectarium while Daisy and Nana went out to the terrace. Geraldine and Martha were there already, Martha looking much refreshed.

The dog curled up in the shade of Daisy's chair. They were left in peace for a while, before Belinda, Derek, and Ben arrived. The children looked recently well-scrubbed—Daisy wondered just how much filth they had picked up while "helping" Edgar. Bel was wearing her new yellow sundress; Daisy hadn't been sure of the colour for her, but Lucy said the only thing to do if one was cursed with red hair was to carry it off with flair.

"We found some Brilliant Emeralds," Derek said enthusiastically.

"Emeralds?" Frank Crowley came out of the house. "Buried treasure?"

"Emeralds?" echoed Raymond, following him.

"Dragonflies, Uncle Frank," said Ben.

Both men lost interest.

"Ruddy Darters, too," Derek persevered, somewhat deflated.

"Oh là là !" exclaimed Laurette, appearing in her turn. "This word I do not let my children speak."

"But that's what it's called, Aunt Laurette," Belinda enlightened her. "Uncle Edgar told us."

Laurette pursed her lips. "*Alors*, if Lord Dalrymple . . ."

Geraldine said kindly to Derek, "Not in company, dear."

Lowecroft chose that moment to escort Ernest and a parlour-maid with tea trays out to the terrace. As teapot, cups and saucers, plates, and cake stands were transferred to a table, Derek forgot his momentary pique.

"Golly, what a smashing spread!" Cucumber sandwiches, water-cress sandwiches, bread and butter, five different biscuits, and four kinds of cake.

His grandmother, the dowager, fell short in catering to the appetite of a growing boy, a mistake Geraldine was unlikely to make.

"Is Mr . . . Is Vincent joining us?" Geraldine asked Laurette.

"He said he intended to be back for tea." Laurette looked at her watch. "He went for a short walk an hour or so ago."

"I expect he'll be along any minute." She started pouring tea.

The children—Ben taking his cue from Derek and Belinda—handed round cups and plates and then took their own milky tea and heaped plates and sat on the wide, shallow terrace steps. Nana joined them.

Martha watched them wistfully. "They're very good kids," she said to Daisy. "I hope Millie and Rosie will be as well-behaved at that age."

"Well behaved in company," Daisy agreed, "and Ben seems well schooled. I hope the other two don't lead him into mischief. Derek is very inventive when it comes to finding things to do that haven't been absolutely forbidden because no one imagined the possibility."

"Oh, I know! My sister's children are just the same."

"You have just the one sister? The one your girls are staying with?"

"She's the only one."

"Any brothers?"

"I had a brother. He was killed in the earthquake."

"Earthquake?"

"In 1907. The school fell down and ninety children were killed. My other sister, and Sam's brothers, as well."

"I'm so sorry," Daisy said inadequately.

"It's a long time ago, but I still have nightmares sometimes. There was a big fire after the quake and most of Kingston was destroyed. Sometimes when I smell smoke in the evening, I dream about it. Otherwise, I don't think about it much."

Ernest brought out a fresh pot of tea and jug of hot water, and removed the old ones.

"More tea, Martha?" Geraldine offered, in a bright voice that suggested she had overheard and wanted to distract Martha from sad memories—or perhaps hoped merely for a momentary relief from Raymond's interrogation.

Daisy had been distantly aware of his nosy questions about the Fairacres farms, and Geraldine's polite, adroit answers lacking any specifics. Laurette, on her other side, seemed to be distracted. She kept glancing at her wristwatch. Alec was talking to Crowley.

Ben had heard Geraldine. He popped up from his seat on the steps and came to fetch Martha's teacup, taking Daisy's for a refill, too. As Geraldine poured, Edgar came onto the terrace, looking reasonably presentable though somewhat less thoroughly scrubbed than his young acolytes. Pepper, as usual, was at his heels.

"An excellent collecting day," he announced. "I haven't yet identified the nymphs. . . ."

"Nymphs!" Laurette exclaimed, staring at him as if he was even pottier than she already suspected.

Edgar's eyes twinkled. "My dear lady, not the kind commonly depicted as being chased by fauns or satyrs. These are the larvae of damsel- and dragon—"

"Damsel! Dragon!" Her eyes popped.

"Oh dear," sighed Geraldine. "Laurette, you haven't stepped into a mediaeval romance. Edgar's talking about insects."

"Unlike the Lepidoptera," Edgar informed them, "the Anisoptera and Zygoptera do not pupate."

"No chrysalis," said Ben.

"That's right, my boy." Edgar beamed.

"How can you talk about insects," Laurette cried, "when Vincent is missing?" She jumped up and hurried over to the low parapet to scan the gardens.

"Vincent missing? Bless my soul!"

"I'd hardly go so far," said Geraldine dryly, handing Edgar a cup of tea. "Apparently he went for a stroll. I expect he walked farther than he intended. I see no cause for alarm."

Edgar picked up the plate he had absentmindedly loaded with tidbits. "I'll go and talk to her."

He crossed the terrace. Daisy couldn't hear what he said to Laurette, but she shook her head, checked the time again, and went back to staring out over the gardens. Edgar sat on the wall. Setting down his cup and his plate on either side of him, he proceeded to enjoy his tea. Pepper sat facing him, his hopeful gaze on the plate.

Laurette screamed. Edgar's plate crashed to the crazy-paving, scattering shards and crumbs.

"We *never* use the best china on the terrace," said Geraldine, but she, like everyone else, rose to her feet and gazed in the direction Laurette was pointing.

Vincent had lost his hat and acquired a limp. He hobbled along the gravel path from the south corner of the house towards the steps, leaning heavily on a walking stick.

Alec and Crowley ran to help him. As they reached him, he staggered. Each seized an arm to support him. Slowly they came up the steps, Vincent stumbling between the two larger men. He was dishevelled, his clothes soiled with leaf mould all down one side; it was even stuck in his brilliantined hair.

"Hop it, you three," Alec said to the children.

"Oh, Daddy!"

"Go along."

The trio, plus dog, reluctantly took themselves off.

Vincent slumped into a chair. Laurette hovered over him, bleating with dismay and flapping ineffectually with a napkin at the dirt on his jacket.

"My dear fellow!" said Edgar. "My dear fellow!"

"Tea," said Geraldine, pouring a cup. "With plenty of sugar for shock. And you must send for the doctor, Edgar."

"No," Vincent gasped. "I don't need a . . . doctor. I'll be all right in a minute."

Martha, distressed, said to Daisy, "Ought we to . . . ?"

"No," Daisy said firmly. "We'd only be in the way."

Lowecroft appeared with a silver tray holding two decanters, a soda siphon, and a glass. He moved at his usual stately pace but was visibly out of breath. Ernest, now hovering on the threshold of the French windows, must have witnessed the scene and notified the butler. "Brandy, sir?" he enquired of Vincent. "Or whisky if you prefer."

"Brandy . . . yes . . . neat." The brandy chased down the sweet tea, already dispatched, and Vincent held out his glass for more.

Daisy wondered whether to suggest some bread and butter to sop up the resulting cocktail in his insides.

Alec sat down beside him, while Frank helped himself to a slice of cake and went to sit on the parapet, where he had a dress-circle view.

"What happened?" Alec asked.

"I went for a stroll in the park and into the woods. I was walking among the trees when a branch . . . fell. I saw it from the corner of my eye and was able to dodge, so it didn't hit me. It made me lose my balance and I tripped over something."

"A branch fell? You don't sound very certain of that."

"It must have, mustn't it? A limb broke off a tree. . . ."

"But . . . ?"

Vincent frowned. "But I have a sort of vague impression that it actually came whizzing at me out of the bushes. It was quite overgrown along the path I was following."

"Edgar," said Geraldine severely, "you really must allow some clearing in the woods. I know your caterpillars like undergrowth but when it comes to a guest being injured—Enough is enough."

"Yes, dear. I'll speak to Wharton."

"See that you do!"

Raymond, who had remained silent and apparently uninterested since Vincent's arrival, suddenly put in a truculent oar. "What do you mean, *whizzed* at you?"

"We-ell, I must have imagined it. I was taken by surprise, pretty shaken up, in shock really."

Geraldine frowned. "Are you sure you oughtn't to see a doctor?"

"Oh yes, *chéri*, do!" Laurette urged.

"No, I don't need a doctor. I'm just a bit bruised." He patted his left hip. "Nothing to it. I'll be right as rain in no time."

"Lowecroft, a hot bath with Epsom salts for Mr. Vincent, in a quarter of an hour."

"Certainly, my lady." Lowecroft took the decanters with him, apparently thinking Vincent had had quite as much restorative brandy as he needed.

"How long ago did this happen?" Alec asked.

"I don't know. I lay half-stunned for some time—"

"You didn't lose consciousness completely, however."

"No."

"That's good. No concussion. Sorry, go on."

"Then I sat awhile till I felt able to move. And I couldn't move very fast."

"Did you notice what tripped you?"

"I can't say I paid any particular attention. Another branch, I suppose, or a stone. Just something lying there on the path."

"Perhaps I'd better go and have a look, to make sure whatever it was isn't going to trip some other unsuspecting stroller. Could you describe the spot? Tell me how to get there?"

"I'm afraid not. I started out wandering at random. Coming back, I was still a bit dazed. I took the nearest path that seemed to go in the right direction, until I was out of the wood. Then I saw the house and followed the path that brought me here."

"My dear fellow," said Edgar again, "I will certainly make sure all the paths in the woods are cleared and all dead branches trimmed off. I must apologise for my hobby having led to your accident."

"A hot bath will prevent any stiffness," said Geraldine firmly. "Alec, would you be so kind—"

"I'll give him a hand up the stairs," offered Crowley, sauntering across the terrace from his seat on the parapet. "Come along, old chap."

Alec looked at him with narrowed eyes, but made no comment.

Crowley hauled Vincent out of his chair and gave him an arm to lean on into the house, with Laurette fussing over him all the way. He was already moving more easily.

"I think I'll take a stroll," said Alec, "to work off that magnificent tea, of which I ate far too much. Coming, Daisy?"

"Darling, I was going to go and see the twins before they're put to bed."

"I'll come with you, Alec," said Edgar.

The two of them tramped off and the tea party broke up.

Daisy next saw Alec when she went to their room to change for dinner. Plumping down on the bed she said, "You think there's something fishy about it, don't you?"

"About what? Thank heaven Geraldine's said no starched shirts and stiff collars."

"Don't change the subject. About Vincent's 'accident.' You don't think it was an accident."

"Rubbish."

"Then why did you march off to view the scene of the crime?"

"Nonsense. We didn't find it. There are fallen branches all over the place. Not that I believe for a moment that there was any crime."

"Then why did you interrogate Vincent?"

"Interrogate? I didn't. Dammit, I'm a DCI, can I help it if my manner suggests . . ." He was silent for a moment, then said in a voice intended to quell his own doubts, "It's nonsense. It's your speculations making me imagine things. A branch fell. Vincent dodged it and tripped. That's the end of the matter."

Daisy wasn't convinced. She didn't believe Alec was either.

FIFTEEN

Belinda and the boys, offered a choice of joining the adults for dinner or supping *á trois* in the breakfast room, had unanimously chosen the latter. Daisy still felt responsible for Martha though. She was shy with everyone else, and they tended to ignore her. So, on their way down to dinner, Daisy and Alec collected her.

She was looking very pretty in a lilac crêpe frock, and very pregnant in spite of the slimming effect of diagonal trimming—the latest thing, according to Madge. A mother-of-pearl necklace and earrings were her only ornaments. She had refused to buy even the simplest of jewelry, though Tommy had agreed that charging the estate for dress expenses was permissible, as long as they were modest.

Sammy wouldn't like it. They had always paid their own way.

They had just settled in the drawing room, and Edgar was asking what they would like to drink, when Lowecroft came in. He came over to Alec and leant down to say in a hushed voice, "A trunk call, sir. From London. Will you take it in his lordship's study?"

"Alec, they *can't*—!"

"I hope it's just some information I've been waiting for." He stood up. "Yes, the study, please, Lowecroft."

"I shall switch the instrument through immediately, sir."

Alec excused himself and went out, leaving Daisy fuming. Though she had said, "They can't," she knew very well that "they" could call him back to the Yard if they were shorthanded. It was all very well hoping the call was to provide information he expected, but she had had too many holidays interrupted by the call of duty to have much faith.

"What's wrong?" Martha was dismayed.

"Oh, sorry, was I scowling? Nothing, probably." An idea had struck Daisy: The only information she was aware of that Alec might expect was news from his American acquaintances about Martha's Sam.

Which might be good news or might—from what she knew of rumrunners—be very bad indeed.

She was glad of the distraction when Frank Crowley brought her Dubonnet and Martha's gin and lime with water instead of gin. Deserting Raymond, next to whom he had been seated, he sat down beside Martha and started chatting with her about their respective Caribbean island homes.

Laurette came in, followed by Vincent, limping along supported by Ernest. Alec returned a moment later.

Daisy raised her eyebrows at him. Flashing a glance towards Martha, he shook his head. He went over to get the whisky Edgar had poured him, then joined Raymond, leaving Daisy to wonder what he meant. Official business he couldn't tell her about till they were alone? Or bad news he didn't want to break to Martha in public?

She didn't find out till bedtime. "Well?" she asked, as Alec closed the door.

"He still hasn't made up his mind."

"Samuel? About what? How do you—?"

"Not Samuel, Raymond. I must say I'm impressed by Geraldine and Edgar's ability to dodge his questions. He's remarkably persistent. Though why he thinks *I* know—"

"Darling, you know that's not what I meant. The phone call—What was that about? News of Martha's Sam? You said you'd ask someone in America to make enquiries."

"I said I'd consider doing so. But yes, I did, and I asked Mackinnon to keep an eye out for a response, whether cable or letter, while we're away. Strictly unofficially. The Yard has no conceivable official interest."

"It arrived today? Sunday—it must have been a cable."

"A long one. But there's a limit to how much one can cram into a cable, and," he added ruefully, "a limit to how well I can interpret American telegramese."

"News of Sam, though."

"Sort of. Possibly. I can't be sure."

"Why on earth not?"

"Because when rumrunners are caught they don't give their real names if they can possibly help it."

"He was caught? Oh no!"

"Let me tell you the story as I understand it. A black ship, the *Sunny Susie*, was taken off Florida after an exchange of shots. She was escorted into Key West. On arrival, the crew reported that the captain had been wounded and fallen overboard, whereupon the mate, a Jamaican known as Samson Dalloway—"

"Who *must* be Sam Dalrymple!"

"People who use false names do frequently choose the same initials."

"The same nickname, too. And Martha was told he shipped on the *Saucy Sally*."

"Easy to change one to t'other with a spot of paint."

"Oh, Alec, I'm sure it was him. I bet he jumped overboard to try to save the captain. Did you know he got a medal after the war for saving several lives when his ship was torpedoed? He can't have drowned now, in peacetime!" She studied his expression. "No, you'd be looking grim."

"The crew claimed they both drowned. The captain being a local man and Key West being on the whole anti-Prohibition, there was talk of lynching the coast guard who ordered the shots fired. At least, that's what I think my informant's cryptic abbreviations are saying. The ship was confiscated, but most of the cargo had already been sold. Yet they found no money."

"Sam and the captain must have taken it with them. What happened to them?"

"The captain was found a couple of weeks later, at home with his wife. He had plenty of witnesses to swear he'd never been away."

"And Sam?"

"Nothing certain. Rumours that a stranger had been staying at the captain's house. That's all."

"Blast, what are we going to tell Martha?"

"That's up to you. I've done my part."

"Very much above and beyond the call of duty. Thank you, darling."

Some time passed before she was able to consider the question, being otherwise happily engaged, but once Alec had fallen asleep it nagged at her. On the one hand, she didn't have any real news of Sam, even if Samson Dalloway was indeed Samuel Dalrymple. On the other, if Martha found out some day that she had not passed on even such vague information, she might be very upset. She still hadn't decided when she, too, fell asleep.

The morning was misty with a promise of warmth by afternoon, perfect for the fête, as forecast last night on the wireless. By the time Daisy went downstairs, the children had all dashed off to see what was going on at the site, taking rolls and hard-boiled eggs to sustain them.

After breakfast, Edgar considered it his duty as lord of the manor to see that all was well with the preparations. Alec decided to go with him, to stretch his legs and to make sure the children weren't getting in the way. Daisy and Martha went up to the nursery to play with Oliver and Miranda. Daisy wasn't looking forward to informing Nurse Gilpin that she intended to take the twins to the fête.

Mrs. Gilpin, as expected, was not pleased. "There'll be all sorts there," she objected. "Nasty ragamuffins from the village, full of germs, and dirty farm workers, maybe even a wise woman who'll put a spell on my babies."

"Don't talk nonsense," Daisy said sharply. "I won't have you putting such silly ideas into their heads."

"And poachers and tinkers, like as not," the nurse muttered, sulking.

"You needn't worry about them. Mr. Fletcher and I, and Miss Belinda, will take care of them so that you can enjoy the fête."

"I wouldn't set foot near the place, madam, and that's the truth."

"Manda go?" Miranda asked anxiously. "Manda an' O'ver?"

"O-li-ver," Daisy corrected her.

"Oyiver."

"Me!" said Oliver, looking up briefly from his blocks.

"An' Auntie Marfa, an' Ben?"

"All of us, pet."

"An' Nana, an' Nurse?"

"Nurse can go if she wants to see the fun."

"No thank you, madam."

"As you wish. I think Nana had better stay here. There will be lots of people and she might get stepped on."

"Fun," Oliver said firmly, picking out the only word that mattered.

"Not if it's still foggy," said Mrs. Gilpin, equally firmly.

Daisy didn't argue, but nor did she intend to keep the children indoors if the mist didn't clear. It was nothing like a coal-smoky London fog, and neither of the twins had a weak chest, thank goodness.

By lunchtime the sun was breaking through. Lunch was served early, a cold buffet, to allow all the servants a chance to attend the fête. Most of them were local, so their friends and relatives would be there, as Geraldine explained to her guests in apologising for the informal meal.

"It's just simple country merrymaking," she added, "but I hope you'll enjoy yourselves."

"I'll enjoy it, for sure," said Frank Crowley. "I've already met half the population of the district at the Beetle." He laughed. "The male half."

"I think I'll give it a miss," Raymond said.

"Not my cup of tea," said Vincent, stroking his moustache. Laurette nodded.

Edgar leant forward and addressed them earnestly. "It's up to you, of course. But if one of you ends up as proprietor of Fairacres, people won't forget that you didn't participate. It's an event of some importance for the villagers, raising funds to rebuild the village hall. I hope you'll reconsider. Geraldine will be opening the festivities at two o'clock."

"Oh, in that case . . . Of course we will be there, *n'est pas*, Vincent? I must not miss the chance to learn how one addresses a crowd of peasants."

"If everyone else is going," Raymond conceded ungraciously, "I might as well." In a more conciliatory tone, he added, "I look forward to hearing you speak in public, Lady Dalrymple."

"It's nothing much, no more than a welcome and encouragement to spend freely for a good cause."

Daisy knew the "nothing much" had caused a huge hullabaloo the summer after her father's death. The village committee had invited Geraldine to open the fête, both because the dowager was assumed to be in mourning and because, after all, Geraldine was now viscountess. Daisy's mother was furious, considering herself slighted. Geraldine willingly abdicated the task.

However, the widow then took offence at being introduced as "the Dowager Lady Dalrymple." Henceforth, Geraldine opened the fête. After Geraldine's speech was safely over and she had finished her obligatory tour of the flower and vegetable exhibits, Daisy's mother would put in a brief appearance.

As star of the show, Geraldine was expected to arrive in state in the Vauxhall, driven by Truscott.

She took Martha with her. The rest walked down the half mile of drive, Raymond stalking ahead, Vincent and Laurette lagging behind, Alec in between in charge of the twin's double pushchair. Frank walked with him. The twins hadn't seen much of him, but took to him at once. Miranda chatted away, with Oliver interpolating his occasional monosyllable.

Daisy was right behind them with the older children. They had lunched with the adults but sat together, quietly minding their manners, so she hadn't talked to Belinda since their return to the house after the morning's exploratory expedition.

All three were excited about the fête. They had helped unpack china in the tea tent, filled vases for the flowers as villagers brought in their prime dahlias and gladioli, and best of all, fed the donkeys.

"They'll be giving rides," said Belinda. "But we're too old for that."

"And having races later," Ben added.

"We're going to race each other," Derek said.

"If that's all right, Mummy."

"I don't see why not."

"Daddy gave us each half a crown."

"And so did Uncle Edgar, even when we told him Uncle Alec already had."

"And I expect my father will, too," Derek said hopefully. "So we can do *everything*. Coconut shies, fortune-teller, test your strength, shove-ha'penny, archery—"

"Egg-and-spoon race."

"Three-legged race. It's almost like Carnival at home, only different."

"Ben told us about Carnival in Port-of-Spain, Mummy. They all dress up in fancy costumes and play music in the streets and dance."

"Dance!" Derek was scornful. "I'd rather race a donkey. Father's going to buy me a proper horse next birthday. I'm too big for my pony."

"You'll squash the poor little donkey," said Belinda, and they all went off into gales of laughter.

As they quieted, Daisy overheard a censorious mutter from Laurette, behind her. She wondered whether the French in general disapproved of children having fun, or was it just Laurette? She hoped Laurette's own children, on holiday with their governess, were enjoying themselves more than if their mama had gone with them.

They reached the gate and paid their sixpence apiece admission. Daisy knew most of the villagers—the population hadn't changed much—so she was quickly surrounded by old acquaintances eager to admire the twins. Oliver and Miranda revelled in the attention, but inevitably they wanted to get out of the pushchair. Miranda ended up riding on Alec's shoulders, and Frank obligingly hoisted Oliver to his. Along with the slow drift of the crowd, they made for the makeshift dais where Geraldine was to make her introductory speech.

Geraldine kept her remarks admirably brief. The vicar whisked her away to admire the winners of the various displays; during the lunch hour his wife had whipped round affixing blue rosettes to the longest runner beans, the biggest vegetable marrow, the most perfect rose, the greatest variety of wildflowers stuffed into a jam jar by some enterprising schoolchild.

Daisy found Martha and went with her to have her fortune told. As the fortune-teller was the district nurse, nicely got up in a black-and-red robe of shiny artificial silk, the fortune was vague but optimistic. Martha was happy to be told that someone dear to her would soon appear.

Coming out of the tent, she said, "She must mean Sam, don't you think?"

Or the baby, Daisy thought, murmuring a sound that could be taken for agreement.

"Does she really know?"

"Darling, I haven't the foggiest. I've heard her mother was a wise woman."

"Wise woman?"

"A sort of village witch, regarded by many people as having uncanny powers, and often very knowledgeable about herbal medicines." That might be why she had gone into nursing.

"Oh, a Myal-woman."

Whatever a Myal-woman was, Martha was content with her acceptance of the perceived similarity, so Daisy didn't upset the applecart by asking for an explanation.

They went to look at some of the stalls. One was selling knitted baby clothes: caps, jackets, leggings, mittens, and socks.

"Oh, Daisy," Martha cried, "I haven't started sewing for the baby! Do you think Mr. Pearson would let me buy some material?"

"Of course, or whatever clothes it'll need."

"I'd rather make them. But I don't know how to make things like these, for cold weather."

"It's happy I'd be to teach you, madam." The woman minding the stall, almost as pregnant as Martha, was the Welsh wife of a village shopkeeper. Her knitting needles clicked away busily as she spoke. "This very minute, if you like. I've spare needles and wool in my bag and a spare chair right here beside me."

Martha looked at Daisy. "Would that be all right? Would anyone mind?"

"It sounds like an excellent idea. I'll come back in a bit and see if you want to have a look at anything else, or go straight to have a cup of tea."

Daisy went in search of her children. Miranda and Oliver were sitting on Alec's and Frank's laps, mouths agape at a Punch and Judy show. They didn't even notice their mother's arrival. Frank said he was quite happy to continue to help Alec with them, and Alec said if they got fretful, he'd take them back to Mrs. Gilpin. So Daisy went to find Belinda and the boys.

She came across Raymond. He was staring gloomily at a white elephant stall as though trying to decide whether there was anything among the bits and pieces he could conceivably bring himself to buy.

"Hunting for bargains, Raymond?"

He gave her a look that spoke volumes. Taking out his gleaming gold cigarette case with the diamond initials, he opened it and started to offer it to her. "Oh, you don't, do you?" He lit one for himself and slid the case back into his breast pocket. Then he pointed at the display and said, "I'll take that. Please."

"Er, which was that, sir?"

"It really doesn't matter."

A joyful light came into the eyes of the stall minder. "Right you are." Quickly, before he could change his mind, she picked up a pewter hand mirror, tarnished and dented, with blurry glass, optimistically marked at ten shillings. Among china dogs with chipped ears for fourpence, raffia napkin rings at a penny apiece, and a three-volume set of Victorian sermons (rejected by the book stall) for one-and-six, it was quite the most expensive item. "D'you want it wrapped, sir?"

Declining the sheet of newspaper she offered, he handed over a ten-shilling note and unenthusiastically took possession of the looking glass. He waited while Daisy spent half a crown on a travelling chess set with one bishop missing.

"The twins will invent games for it," she said as they turned away.

"I suppose they've provided barrels somewhere for rubbish?"

"Don't throw it away! That looking glass has provided increasing sums for good causes at least since I was a child. If you give it to the vicar's wife, she'll see that it goes back among the white elephants at the next jumble sale."

Raymond shook his head in wonderment. "If you say so!"

"Mummy!" Belinda hurried up to them. "Hello, Uncle Raymond. Mummy, I'm glad I found you. Derek and Ben are having a go at the archery. They say girls aren't allowed. Will you come and make them let me?"

"I've done some bow hunting," Raymond said unexpectedly. "I'll go with you. On the veldt, most women know how to shoot in case of necessity. I don't see why you shouldn't try your skill with a bow and arrows."

"All right, pet?"

"Oh yes, Mummy. They're bound to listen to Uncle Raymond."

They left Daisy to contemplate Bel's lack of confidence in her stepmama's persuasive ability. She also gave some thought to Raymond's sudden show of an amiable side to his nature, hitherto invisible. She couldn't believe he'd been concealing a liking for young people. Perhaps he just wanted to show off, though she would have thought he considered himself too superior in every way to need to demonstrate the fact.

SIXTEEN

After chatting with several people, Daisy decided she'd better go and check on Martha.

Martha was knitting. "A scarf to start with," she said proudly, holding up a pale blue square. "Purl as well as plain. Mrs. Latchett says I can keep the needles and this ball of wool."

"Very nice." Knitting was another skill Daisy had never attempted. "Are you ready for a cup of tea?"

"Yes, please. Mrs. Latchett, I can't thank you enough for teaching me."

"Anytime you want another lesson, *bach*, just you have Bill Truscott run you down to the shop—Latchett's, in the main street."

"It's very kind of you, Mrs. Latchett," said Daisy. "I'll have someone bring you a cup of tea."

"That's all right, thank you, madam. Someone'll soon be taking over for me here." She chuckled. "And thank you for making Mr. Raymond buy the looking glass! It's all over the fair."

They made their way to the tea tent. Daisy was pleased to see her sister sitting at a table to one side.

"Vi, you remember Martha. Mrs. Samuel." They had met at lunch the day before.

"Yes, of course." Violet smiled her gentle smile. "Do come and sit down, Mrs. Samuel—"

"Martha, please, Lady John!"

"As you wish. We'll make Daisy fetch your tea. John's getting mine."

"Is Mother here?"

"Come and gone, like a whirlwind. The gardener was sent to spy for her, to let her know as soon as Geraldine left. She had a word with Edgar. I don't know what was said. Then she departed, in case Geraldine should come back. Martha, you're one of the family, so I know you'll be discreet."

Martha blushed with pleasure. "Oh yes, Lady John."

"Violet," Vi told her, smiling, just as her husband arrived with a tray of tea and pastries.

"Hello, Daisy. Hello, Cousin Martha. Just let me empty this tray and I'll go back—Oh, here's Owen. Be a good chap, and fetch tea for Mrs. Fletcher and me, will you?" He gave the dowager's gardener a handful of coins. "And keep the change."

Owen grinned. "Right away, m'lord."

"Milk and sugar not optional, I'm afraid," John said, passing a thick white cup of muddy liquid to Martha and one to his wife. "Have you seen Derek about, Daisy?"

"Belinda told me he and Ben are taking a turn at archery."

"Bows and arrows?" Violet exclaimed. "Oh no! John, remember what happened last time Derek got his hands on bows and arrows? Will you go and—?"

"Darling, he was only seven when he put an arrow through the butler's best bowler. Jolly good shot, too, and Mitchell wasn't wearing it at the time. But I'll track him down and see what he's up to as soon as I've had my tea. Here it comes."

Seeing that Vi was really worried, he drank his tea quickly, excused himself, and departed. Violet and Martha started talking about their children, subjects that had been thoroughly covered with each of them separately by Daisy. She was happy to see them getting on well together, but she had little to add.

Violet's concern had to some extent infected her. She doubted that Derek was not by now to be trusted with a bow and arrows, but what about Ben? Was Frank keeping an eye on him or still helping Alec with the twins? He seemed to have a genuine liking for children. No doubt he would make as excellent a father as he was step-father if Ben was the sought-after "heir of the body" and Frank was able to marry his Carlotta when he returned to Trinidad.

Ben as viscount—had there ever been a black peer? If so, no doubt Lucy would have the details at her fingertips. Daisy knew only of Lord Sinha, who was Indian, not of African descent.

Across the crowded marquee, Daisy saw Vincent standing in the line at the tea urns. He still favoured his left leg, leaning heavily on his walking stick.

Reminded of his accident, Daisy wondered again how accidental it had been. Had someone attacked him? A disgruntled hotel employee? Or someone who wanted to put Vincent out of the running as heir? Raymond? Frank—surely not! One thing was certain, not Martha. Unless her Sam was actually in England, known or unbeknownst to her. . . .

Because she liked Martha, Daisy had been assuming that Samuel Dalrymple was a pleasant man, but he was—at least in American terms—a criminal. Though rumrunning and bootlegging had a touch of the romantic allure of Robin Hood, some of those engaged in the illegal trade were violent ruffians. She must not forget that.

She watched as Vincent shifted uncomfortably from foot to foot. Then he limped past the queue to speak to the women dispensing the tea and cakes and collecting payment sixpences. Daisy couldn't hear what he said over the general chatter and clatter, but she saw him making authoritative gestures, like a bobby on point duty.

Vincent got results. The three volunteers and a couple of people from the queue started moving cups and saucers and plates and trays around. In no time the table was set up in a much more practical way, more like what Mr. Arbuckle, the American automobile magnate, would call an assembly line.

Balancing his own tray with the skill of a practised waiter, Vincent went to join Laurette. In no time, the queue was down to four people. One might not like the man, but his efficiency was undeniable.

On the other hand, everything now moved so smoothly that people were standing about waiting for somewhere to sit down, and the more considerate among those already seated were eating and drinking hastily to make room. Though Vincent had doubtless created the ideal conditions for a restaurant that wanted to keep its patrons moving so as to seat and feed as many as possible, the result was less satisfactory for leisurely country folk.

However, the ladies in charge were also leisurely country folk. By the time Vincent and Laurette left, a few minutes later, the usual muddle was restored.

"Don't you think so, Daisy?" asked Violet.

"What? Sorry, my mind was wandering."

Vi and Martha burst out laughing. "I told you so," Vi said to Martha.

"She hasn't heard a word we've said."

"And ate and drank without tasting a morsel."

Daisy was pleased to see them so much in sympathy. She had no qualms about leaving them together. She was feeling a bit anxious about Belinda having taken Raymond to the archery. John had gone to make sure Derek was being sensible and careful. No doubt he'd do the same for Ben—and for Belinda, come to that—but he wouldn't be watching for an attack on Ben.

A surreptitious attack, made to look like an accident. The archery range seemed like an ideal spot. A demonstration shot from Raymond, going astray? Or someone concealed nearby and shooting from hiding. . . .

Suddenly Daisy was in a great hurry to inspect the setup, to make sure it was not a convenient spot for an ambush.

"If you'll excuse me, I think I'll go and see what Belinda's up to."

"Do," said Vi. "If you happen to see my younger ones, tell Nanny she can come and leave them with Martha and me for a few minutes while she has a cup of tea."

On her way out of the marquee, Daisy crossed paths with the local GP coming in. Dr. Hopcroft was a slight, rather shy man. She had met him and his tubby wife two or three times as dinner guests at Fairacres, though she had never had cause to call for his medical advice.

"Hello, Doctor," she greeted him. "Are you here in your professional capacity?"

"Strictly speaking, no."

"And leniently speaking? Your services have been called upon?"

"Just a broken toe. A young fellow won a coconut, tossed it in the air, and failed to catch it."

"Good gracious, I never thought of the coconut shies as dangerous. I'm just on my way to the archery butts to find my daughter. Do you happen to know where it is?"

"Over at the foot of the hill. They have straw targets set up with the slope behind them, so that if anyone overshoots the arrows hit the ground rather than supplying me with patients."

He looked mildly pleased when Daisy laughed at his little joke. He obviously missed the note of uneasiness in her laughter, but she heard it herself and was anxious to be on her way. "Then I hope your enjoyment of the fête won't be spoilt by any further accidents," she said fervently.

"We medical men must always be prepared. You'd be surprised how many people fall over guy ropes at these affairs. I keep my bag in the fortune-teller's tent."

"And the fortune-teller is the district nurse. Most appropriate. I must be going. Please give my regards to Mrs. Hopcroft in case I don't come across her today."

"I'm supposed to meet her in here." He scanned the still-crowded marquee.

Daisy hurried on her way. The hill, so-called, was the low, shallow ridge between Fairacres and the Dower House. The drive from the lane to the mansion curved around the southern end. Some quirk of geology had created on the west side a short stretch of steep slope which was ideal as a backing for the targets. However, the slope was not too steep to support a fair number of hazel and hawthorn bushes, ideal for an ambush.

She passed several acquaintances with a smile and a wave. When she reached the butts, Belinda was fitting an arrow to the bow under the guidance of Raymond. The boys were nowhere to be seen. As Daisy watched, he helped her pull back the string, aim, and loose the arrow. It hit the edge of her target.

"I did it! *We* did it. Thank you, Uncle Raymond." Turning towards him, she saw Daisy. "Mummy, did you see? My first five arrows didn't even reach the target. Derek said I should do press-ups to make my arms stronger. He has to do them at school. But at least I got one arrow in the target."

"Well done, and thank you, Raymond." Did the diamond magnate have a soft side after all? "Where are Derek and Ben, pet?"

"They'd nearly finished when I got here. You get six arrows for sixpence and they didn't want to do it again. Besides, it was time for the three-legged race. Come on, if we hurry maybe we can see them finish."

The three-legged race—behind schedule as events at the fête always were—was just about to begin in the meadow by the lane. Unlike the other children's races, which were mostly watched by parents of participants, it garnered a crowd of spectators. Belinda wormed through to the front. The people she passed, glancing back, parted to let Daisy follow her.

Kneeling on the grass behind a row of cross-legged small children, Bel pointed. "There they are, Mummy."

The starting pistol cracked. Eight pairs of boys, aged from about eight to fifteen, started to stagger down the fifty-yard course. Cheers, jeers, laughter, and cries of encouragement emanated from the crowd.

Derek's right leg was bound with a scarf to Ben's left. They were better matched than most, about the same height and weight, and fiercely determined. They only fell three times, while some gave up after a few feet and others fell with practically every step. However, an older pair had obviously been practising. They stumbled but caught themselves up and won by twenty yards.

Derek and Ben made it across the line in second place, to shouts of "Well done, Master Derek! Well done, Blackie!"

Oh dear, Daisy thought. She had noticed the curious glances at Ben, the people who stopped talking when they saw him and muttered together after he passed. No one had spoken to her openly about his colour. Most of the villagers must have known by then that he might conceivably be the next viscount and owner of Fairacres. She'd hoped the possibility would protect him against slights.

Afraid that he must be upset, Daisy made her way through the throng as quickly as she could, trailing Belinda by the hand.

The contestants had been separated from their partners. The winners already sported blue ribbons, and a half-crown first prize was tucked safely in each youth's pocket. Edgar was pinning red rosettes on Derek's and Ben's lapels. He shook their hands, said, "First next year, eh?" and turned to the third place pair, the only others who had completed the course.

Alec was there. While Belinda commiserated with the boys on not winning—it turned out that she had come in second in the egg-and-spoon race, so they were even—Daisy said to Alec, "You took the babies back to the house?"

"They were getting a bit fractious. But as it happened, Mrs. Gilpin ran us down and insisted on removing them for their nap. You're looking a bit frazzled, love?"

"I was worrying about the potential for accidents with bows and arrows. But they seem to have come through unscathed. Bel says they're racing donkeys in half an hour or so."

Alec laughed. "The poor beasts are far too small to cause any serious accidents. I would have said they're too small to carry kids the size of Bel and the boys. The owner claims they're quite capable of bearing an adult, only people don't like to see them with such a load. A Gypsyish chap, unless he dresses up à la Gypsy for the occasion."

"He's probably the same man who brought donkeys to the fête when I was a child. His son, perhaps. Not, I trust, the same donkeys! He takes them round the country fairs to give rides, but his chief business is, or used to be, hiring them out to farmers. That business is probably not doing very well. Most farmers seem to have tractors these days."

"Let's go and look them over. You grew up with horses. You'll be able to tell whether they're likely to collapse under the weight of our three."

"Darling, I always avoided riding as much as I possibly could. Father and Gervaise were neck-or-nothing hunters, of course, and Vi enjoyed going to a meet on horseback, in a ladylike way, though she never followed the hounds. Mother never went near horses if she could help it. They're so big! Come to think of it, not riding is probably the only thing she did support me in. Although I did used to enjoy my pony, which, I suppose, was about the size of a donkey."

"Small but sturdy. Yon donkeys have a lean and hungry look."

"Well, the Ides of March are long past."

"My concern is for the donkeys, not the children! Come and see them. They're over that way."

Daisy slipped her arm through his. They walked back past the starting post of the racetrack, where a group of hefty young men were about to run a hundred yards with their sweethearts—some almost equally hefty—on their shoulders.

The half-dozen donkeys were trudging round a well-worn circle with children on their backs, the first led by an olive-skinned, sharp-featured man in a colourful shirt and a leather jerkin. They were scrawny beasts, but one was ridden by an extremely fat child who couldn't possibly weigh less than skinny Belinda. It didn't appear any more overburdened than the rest.

"They look all right," Daisy said dubiously. "They must be sturdier than they look, though I can't picture any of them actually racing."

"Derek might get his moving. He's done some riding, hasn't he? Bel's only been on a similar creature at the seaside."

"She's been on a pony a couple of times, staying with Violet and John. I don't know about Ben, but it doesn't seem likely he's had riding lessons."

"Oh well, it's not far to fall if they slide off. We'll come back to watch. Let's go and get a cup of tea. I haven't had a chance yet, with the twins on my hands."

"I've had mine, but I'll come with you."

At the entrance to the tea marquee, they met Bill Truscott. "Her ladyship sent me to see if Mrs. Samuel would like a lift back to the house," he said. "Someone told me she's in here."

"She was last time I saw her, and she didn't look as if she was thinking of going anywhere. Yes, there she is, with Lady John. Alec, I'll go and have a word while you get your cuppa."

Violet decided to go with Martha back to the house, to call on Geraldine without the dowager's oppressive presence. Truscott escorted them out.

Alec had barely time to gulp his tea before they had to hurry back to the donkey track. Of course, the race was nowhere near beginning. The donkeys were no longer patiently plodding round the circle, but their owner was fiddling with saddles and bridles and lengthening stirrup leathers.

Belinda and the boys were there, gazing at the donkeys and apparently discussing them, with Derek posing as the expert to judge from his gestures. Nearby were another three youngsters of about the same size and age. Two looked like lads from the farms. The third was a sulky-faced girl in newish jodhpurs and a hard hat, carrying a whip. A man in good tweeds was talking earnestly to her. Daisy, with a pang of sympathy, suspected the girl was getting a lecture just like the ones she herself used to get from her father when she balked at mounting a horse. Perhaps he thought riding a donkey would accustom her to the idea.

The donkey man went over to them. Daisy heard him say loudly and firmly, "No whips."

The father started to argue.

As soon as the donkey man moved away from his animals, Bel, Ben, and Derek closed in. Each went to a particular mount, stroked its nose, and fed it something produced from a pocket.

"I hope they've somehow got hold of carrots or apples," said Daisy. "I don't know how a donkey's insides would react to toffees or cake."

"Aren't they omnivorous, like goats?"

"I don't think so. Let's pretend we didn't see. There's Edgar at the end of the course, ready to present the prizes."

"He must shell out a pretty penny. I must say I'm impressed by his lord-of-the-manor persona. He seems to know everyone by name."

"Easy names compared to his moths and butterflies. And drag-onflies. He likes people. He just isn't interested in running the es-tate except when it comes to leaving parts au naturel."

Quite a few spectators had gathered by now. The donkey man returned to his beasts and led them to their starting places. They seemed puzzled to be lined up side by side instead of nose to tail. Ears twitched and one brayed.

Derek mounted his donkey in style. The farm boys clambered aboard with less style but equal confidence. The father helped his angry daughter with detailed instructions for every move. The don-key man gave Bel and Ben a hand. When everyone was settled, he stepped aside, raised a whistle to his lips, and blew.

The riders dug in their heels, shook the bridles, and added their cries of encouragement to those of the spectators. The donkeys, used to being led, paid little heed. After a few indecisive moments, Derek's superior technique got his mount to start walking. The oth-ers followed, except the one ridden by the girl in jodhpurs. Perhaps it caught her sulkiness. It stood unmoving, and when her father went to its head and pulled on the bridle, it dug in its heels.

Meanwhile Derek had coaxed his donkey to a trot. Before the others made up their minds to copy it, he had opened a fair lead. Then the beast remembered the circles it had been doing for several hours and veered off course into an arc that took it into the path of both the farm lads. Derek hauled on the reins, but it was determined. The nearer of its blocked competitors made a slight detour to get past its rear end, speeding up. The second joined Derek's mount. Scattering spectators, they circled back towards the start.

The crowd was in an uproar, laughing and yelling advice. Ben was in the lead, with Belinda at his heels, and the remaining farm-er's boy fast closing the gap.

"Go, Blackie!"

"You can do it, Miss!"

"Get a move on, our Jim!"

Suddenly Ben raised one hand as if to shade his eyes. He must have pulled on the reins reflexively, because his steed slowed. Be-linda caught up.

The noise from the crowd redoubled.

Without warning, Belinda's donkey bucked. Her head swung forward and thumped against its neck. Blood streaming from her face, she slid to the ground.

SEVENTEEN

Ben, abandoning his donkey, was the first to reach Belinda. She lay flat on her back on the grass. He knelt at her side and leaned over her. Their donkeys calmly strolled off, nibbling the short turf.

Inevitably people quickly gathered round, so Daisy, running, couldn't see Bel. At her side, Alec rapped out in his policeman voice: "Let us through. And clear a space, please."

"Find Dr. Hopcroft," Daisy begged, charging onward.

Bel's eyes were open, thank goodness. She was clasping to her face a large cotton handkerchief, sodden with blood.

"I think I've got another one somewhere," said Ben, searching feverishly through his pockets.

Daisy knelt down beside Belinda, who promptly burst into tears. "Bubby, it hurts!"

"What hurts, darling? A pain in your back? Arms, legs? Do try not to cry, sweetheart, it'll make your nose worse. Does your head ache?"

"By *dose* hurts. Daddy, ab I goi'g to bleed to death?"

"Of course not, pet." Alec squeezed the hand she held out to him, then put a clean hankie in it. "Here, press as hard as you can bear to. But try not to move otherwise in case you've hurt your back."

Dr. Hopcroft and Derek arrived.

"I thought I'd better find the doctor first," Derek panted. "Is Bel all right? Gosh, that's quite a nosebleed!"

"Let's just make sure it's all that's wrong," said the doctor as Daisy and Alec moved aside to give him room.

A couple of minutes of "Move this," and "Can you feel that?" sufficed to indicate no serious damage.

"Whed will by dose stop bleedi'g?"

"That I can't tell you. But put the hankie aside and take this cotton wool instead. Let's see if the flow is diminishing."

Belinda cautiously obeyed. The cotton wool showed seepage rather than the previous flood of blood.

With the doctor's arrival, most of the gawkers had scattered to find something else to gawk at. The donkey man had rounded up his animals and was tethering them. Edgar, having presented the winner of the race with his five bob, came over with anxious queries.

Reassured, he said, "Given the alternative attraction, the lad had to make do without public acclaim. You'll be a nine days' wonder, Belinda."

"I do't want to be a wonder," Bel said crossly, starting to sit up.

Dr. Hopcroft pushed her down. "Flat on your back for quarter of an hour," he ordered.

"But it's trickling down my throat! It tastes disgusting."

"I've set my stopwatch for fifteen minutes, Bel." Derek held up his watch for her to see.

"Not a minute longer!"

The doctor smiled down at her. "That should do it. Stuff a bit of cotton wool up each nostril. That will absorb some. And when you get up, if it starts bleeding seriously again, back down on your back at once."

Bel sighed. "I hope my nose won't be swollen."

"Cold compresses, and send for me if it starts bleeding freely again."

"Have I lost a lot of blood?"

"Good gracious, no! You could spare a pint or two yet. I'm off." He strode away towards the fortune-teller's tent.

Ben examined Belinda's nose gravely. "It looks all right. Apart from the blood."

"I'll send someone with water and cloths to clean you up a bit," said Edgar. "I have to go and present some more prizes. Good heavens, look, there's a Scarlet Tiger!"

They all looked round nervously, before reminding themselves who was speaking, and spotting the bright-coloured butterfly.

"I don't have my net with me," Edgar lamented. "What's it doing in this crowd? It should be by the water."

"It was attracted by your blood, Bel," said Derek. "It looks as if it dipped its wings in it."

"Does not!"

Attention was diverted by the arrival of the donkey man. Scowling, he demanded, "What did the young miss do to my Bonnie to make her behave so?"

Alec said sharply, "My daughter did nothing. You shouldn't be letting kids ride on such a dangerous animal."

"Ho, dangerous is it? I'd have you know Bonnie's never done aught like it in her life before! Gentle as a lamb and calm as a dove, saving she don't like flashing lights. I don't never take her out at night, but 'tis broad daylight here and now. No one using 'lectric torches or them motor lamps, stands to reason."

Derek suggested, "Maybe some village brat in the crowd hit her with a peashooter."

"A pea wouldn't bother her none," the man said contemptuously. He narrowed his eyes. "Mind, I'm not saying a stone from a catapult wouldn't make her shy."

Ben raised a tentative voice. "About flashing lights. That's what happened to me. A light flashed in my eyes, and I put up my hand to block it."

"And that's when Bel pulled ahead," Daisy recalled.

"I bet the same light flashed in the donkey's eyes," said Derek. "Don't you think so, Uncle Alec?"

"Could be." He turned back to the donkey man. "Well, we'll say no more about the beast's manners."

"I'm not doing no more races. Talked me into it, they did. Rides for little kids, that's what my donkeys do. And a good day to you, sir." He stalked back towards his patient beasts.

The district nurse bustled up in her witchy costume, bearing a flask of water and a roll of lint. "His lordship sent me, Mrs. Fletcher. Well, now, Miss Belinda, looks like your poor nose copped it good and proper. Let's get you cleaned up a bit. I never saw an accident like this in your future, I must admit."

Daisy and Alec and the boys stepped back to let her get at her patient.

An accident? Daisy was beginning to wonder. "Alec, don't you think it's rather too much of a coincidence—"

He gave her slight shake of the head, his lips compressed. She abandoned the subject for the present.

A couple of minutes of scrubbing and one loud "Ow!" from Belinda left her face more or less normal, apart from the lint sticking out of her nose. Her yellow frock was a disaster, fit only for the rubbish bin. Admittedly, even before the nosebleed, after her various pastimes of the afternoon, culminating in riding the donkey, it hadn't been fit for much but the rag bag.

The nurse went back to more esoteric activities.

"Derek, is it quarter of an hour yet? I want to get up."

"The alarm hasn't rung yet. Three minutes." He and Ben amused themselves with counting down the seconds until the watch chimed.

Alec helped Belinda up. Ben picked up her hat, dusted it off, and handed it to her.

"Thanks." She put it on and pulled the brim down at the front. "I ache."

"I bet you'll have whacking great bruises." Derek's tone suggested admiration.

"Daddy, have you got an extra hankie, just in case?"

"I always have an extra hankie." Alec was usually well supplied, as his work often involved a lot of weepy people: witnesses, suspects, the friends and relatives of murder victims. . . .

Relatives and murder. Daisy tried to find something else to occupy her mind.

She and Ben followed Alec, Belinda, and Derek towards the gate. Frank caught up with them.

"I just heard the news." His breath smelled slightly of beer. The fête was supposed to be nonalcoholic but someone always managed to smuggle in a crate or two of bottles, all in a good cause. "No serious injuries, I take it." He gestured at Belinda who was walking unaided.

"Just a bloody nose, Uncle Frank," Ben assured him. "And bruises. I might have won the race but I stopped when she fell off."

"Good for you, young 'un. Rotten luck for both of you!"

The mention of Ben's near win reminded Daisy of the crowd cheering him on. "Ben, do you mind them calling you Blackie? I can put a stop to it in the village."

"Not much point in minding, is there? At home there's plenty more like me." He glanced at his stepfather. "Uncle Frank says there's some in London. But round about here—Well, I looked and looked and never another black face did I see."

Frank nodded.

Daisy regarded Ben thoughtfully. "It's not actually black, is it. A rather nice brown. Would Brownie be better?"

"Six of one, half a dozen of the other. Don't let it worry you, Aunt Daisy. I'll be all right."

"Are you too old to be hugged and kissed? Because I'm going to hug and kiss you." She suited action to the words. "I'm happy to have you as a nephew, or cousin, or whatever exactly you are."

Shyly he kissed her cheek. "Me too. And Belinda and Derek are bricks!"

"I see you're picking up Derek's school slang," said Daisy, laughing.

"They sounded friendly to me," Frank said thoughtfully. "Encouraging, not heckling. Wouldn't you agree, Daisy?"

"Absolutely." Daisy refrained from elaborating. At present Ben had a certain novelty value. Many of the villagers had probably never seen a black—or brown—face before. Should Ben turn out to be heir to the viscountcy, the local people might be less receptive, and he'd have the wider world to face.

Bill Truscott was waiting with the Vauxhall just outside the gate, in case anyone wanted to be driven back to the house. He had already been told about Belinda's mishap. He swooped upon her and lifted her into the car. Alec handed Daisy in after her.

"May we stay here a bit longer, Aunt Daisy?" Derek asked. "Ben and I have a couple of shillings left." He put his hand in the pocket of his shorts and jingled his change.

Daisy looked to Alec, who nodded.

"All right. But please stay away from donkeys and bows and arrows!"

"I'll keep an eye on them," said Frank.

"Would you like me to go back with you?" Alec asked Daisy and Belinda.

"No thank you, Daddy."

"We just have to get her cleaned up and changed, darling. Frankly, you'd be in the way. Truscott, does Mrs. Warden still make that wonderful salve for bruises?"

"Yes indeed, Miss Daisy. Madam, I should say."

"It smells funny," Bel complained. She had had cause to be annointed with the salve on previous visits.

Daisy assumed she couldn't be feeling too sore if she was concerned about the smell.

By the time Daisy, the housekeeper, and Geraldine's maid had between them dealt with Belinda's woes, the boys had come back from the fête. They were ravenous because, Derek explained, instead of spending their last sixpence on a couple of buns, they had bought Belinda a necklace.

Inside the silver-gilt locket was a tiny, black-bordered photograph of a young man with a great deal of whisker about his face. Opposite, protected by a watch glass, was a braided coil of hair, the creation of which, Daisy thought, must have cost someone her eyesight. Privately she considered it rather morbid. At least it was oval, not heart shaped. Belinda was thrilled.

"You can tell people it's a picture of your sweetheart," Ben suggested. "Well, not now, but when you're old."

"It's time for supper," Derek intervened, and the three went off together.

Daisy paid a visit to the nursery. After reading a story to the twins, she said goodnight and, feeling a bit limp after the events of the past few hours, she went downstairs to see if Alec had returned from the fête. In the entrance hall, Raymond was handing his hat to Ernest. He looked round at the sound of Daisy's footsteps.

"Ah, Mrs. Fletcher—Daisy. I'm told your daughter is not seriously hurt?"

"Just a nosebleed and a bruise or two." Where had he been when Belinda fell?

"Happy to hear it. Could I have a word with you?"

"Yes, of course." Did he still have hopes of her providing financial information about Fairacres?

"No one in the morning room at present, madam."

Daisy and Raymond made their way to the morning room. Daisy chose an armchair near the open window, glad of the cooler air wafting off the river, for the late afternoon was sultry. Raymond sat down nearby and took out his cigarette case, the ostentatious diamond monogram glittering coldly against the gleam of the gold. With an automatic gesture, he started to offer the open case to Daisy, then remembered she didn't smoke. He took a cigarette and lit it, slipping the case back into his breast pocket.

"What can I do for you?" she asked.

He seemed uncharacteristically uncertain. "Nothing, really. It's just . . . I was watching Lord Dalrymple this afternoon. I hadn't realised there was so much to this 'lord of the manor' business. I'm coming to have considerable respect for Cousin Edgar."

"You thought he was just a crackpot would-be entomologist—"

"A typical useless sort of aristocrat. We get them visiting South Africa. All they want to do is kill the biggest, fiercest animals, not

148

even for food, just so that they can boast about it. But it's obvious the villagers respect Edgar."

"You didn't know Edgar had a useful career before he inherited the viscountcy? He was a schoolmaster for twenty years or so."

"A teacher? No, I had no idea. No one told me."

"Anyone capable of controlling a classroom, let alone a school house, full of adolescent boys is worthy of respect. The lord of the manor stuff is smooth sailing in comparison. Schoolboys and tenants both require the same friendliness and consideration combined with a firm hand and a certain distance, yet without condescension." Not that Daisy's father had viewed his position quite like that. "If you see what I mean," she added.

"Yes." Raymond's voice held a note of doubt. "It's different from the blacks on the farms at home, I suppose."

"I daresay." She did not want to get involved in a discussion of colonialism, still less to hear his opinion of the discovery that he had a coloured cousin who might be the heir. "Edgar manages to be on good terms with everyone, as far as I can see. And although he's not interested in the running of the estate, he's a good judge of character and employs an excellent bailiff."

"I gather he owns the village as well as the farms."

"Edgar doesn't own it, Fairacres does. The estate. Most of the estate is in some sort of trust that can't be broken without the agreement of both Edgar and his heir." Too late, she wondered whether she had told him more than she ought. Were trusts a matter of public record? They were not uncommon, at least, so Raymond could have guessed.

Or perhaps the new law Tommy had told her about had abolished the trust? In any case, it wasn't worth worrying about.

Raymond, momentarily silenced, started to say something when Edgar came in. "Pretty good show, eh?" he said jauntily. "Apart from poor little Belinda, but I went to see her just now and she's eating like a horse, so not much harm done, I'd say. It's a good job she gets on so well with the lads. I'm pleased with the lot of them, very pleased. Hope you enjoyed our little country festivity, Raymond?"

149

"I found it interesting, sir."

"Sir? Sir? What's this? Edgar to you, my dear chap. After all, you can give me ten years or more, what?" The twinkle in his eye was slightly malicious. "I say, has either of you seen my butterfly net? I seem to have mislaid it." He pottered about the room, looking behind chairs. Having decisively put Raymond in his place at their first meeting, he now seemed to be playing the part of a vague, unworldly aristocrat straight out of a Criterion farce.

"Sorry, no," said Daisy, "but I haven't been looking out for it. I'll keep my eyes open."

"Oh well, no rush you know. It'll turn up. Must be about time to dress for dinner. No dressing gong in this house," he said to Raymond. "I did away with it. Had enough of being summoned by bells in my life. So, no dressing gongs or bells. 'Changing,' I mean. Crowley chappie doesn't own a dinner jacket, I understand. Different customs in Trinidad, of course."

"We dress for dinner in Cape Town. Must keep the side up, don't you know." Raymond sounded sarcastic.

What was he up to? One minute he was professing respect for Edgar, the next mocking him. Daisy couldn't make him out.

EIGHTEEN

"*It was* strange," said Daisy, describing to Alec the encounter between Edgar and Raymond as they changed into slightly more formal clothes for dinner. "They don't like each other, that was obvious. But I had the impression that Raymond has decided Fairacres is worth having, and even worth sucking up to Edgar."

"Being on good terms with Edgar won't make any difference to the likelihood of his being heir," Alec pointed out.

"No, but he might think it would be best to be on the right side of the present viscount if he *is* the heir."

"Daisy, stop beating about the bush. You suspect Raymond now wants Fairacres badly enough to try to get rid of his rivals?"

"It's just that he took out that hideous gold cigarette case and I noticed how it caught the light from the window. The sun would reflect brilliantly from it. He could have deliberately flashed it into Ben's eyes, hoping to cause an accident. No one would notice. They'd only see him taking out a cigarette. It would certainly be less conspicuous than using the hand mirror he bought at the white-elephant stall."

"He did? Odd!"

"Not really," Daisy said regretfully. "It was more or less by accident."

"How can one accidentally buy a mirror?"

"He didn't want to buy anything, but I persuaded him it would be the diplomatic thing to do. He told the woman minding the stall he'd take anything, so of course she picked out the most optimistically priced object. So, at least at that point, he wasn't intending to use it to cause an accident. Perhaps it gave him the idea, though. Of course, Laurette carries a pocket mirror at all times. She's always touching up her makeup. She or Vincent could have used that. Frank—"

"It's not difficult to come by something with a reflective surface," said Alec, impatient. "The question is, why do it at all? A fall from a trotting donkey is about as likely to be lethal as jumping off a mounting block. Not to mention that Ben has a little brother at home, so what would be the point?"

"That's true," Daisy conceded. "They all seem to have sons and/or brothers waiting in the wings."

"They do? There you are, then."

"I doubt they're all aware of one another's closer relatives. Martha chats to me and you seem quite pally with Frank; otherwise they hardly speak to each other, though, beyond polite nothings. But do you realise how it widens the field of suspects? Any of the sons and brothers could be lurking hereabouts—Well, not Ben's little brother."

"So could Martha's husband. We seem to have lost track of him."

"He wouldn't know who was who."

"Unless he's been in touch with Martha. Did she write or receive any letters in London?"

"Only a couple to and from the sister who's looking after her little girls. She showed me the ones with news of the kids."

"But not the ones she wrote?"

"Of course not. In any case, she didn't meet the others till we came here."

"But you told her about them?"

"Well, yes. Vincent and Raymond, not Frank and Ben."

"Then she could have described Vincent and Raymond to her sister. Even if Sam Dalrymple actually was the mysterious Jamaican who avoided arrest in Florida, we have no idea when or whether he returned to Jamaica. The sister could have told him what she knew, and he came straight here and is, as you suggested, 'lurking hereabouts.' It wouldn't be so very hard to have a word with Martha in secret, if he was determined. I've seen her strolling alone in the gardens."

"Darling, I don't believe it. I'm supposed to be the one who indulges in wild speculation! You're the copper who has to have facts."

"Touché! Really, the question is, what are we suspecting them of? Yes, Vincent could have been killed by the branch, but it probably just fell off a tree, given Edgar's lack of interest in keeping up his woodland. In any case, it was just as likely merely to injure him."

"Or to knock him out and make it easy to murder him." Daisy laughed. "All right, I know, wild speculation, and there isn't anything you can do about it anyway."

"Nothing. I can't keep an eye on all of them and I have no grounds for requesting help."

"So let's assume none of my relatives have plans to kill one another."

"All the same, I hope Pearson brings the answer when he comes on Friday. Once everyone knows who's the heir, it'll clear the air a bit."

"Yes. Now if you'll just fasten my necklace, I'll go and check up on Belinda and see if Martha needs any help. See you downstairs."

Bel wasn't in her room or the nursery. Daisy decided to check the turret room. One of the enticing things about it was the access by way of a narrow spiral staircase of openwork wrought iron, leading up to a trapdoor in the high ceiling at the end of the corridor below. The room had not been intended as a habitable room. In fact, it had had no windows until Gervaise took a liking to it and Daisy's father had it done up for him. It now had windows in five walls, with the trapdoor opening right next to the sixth.

Daisy stood at the bottom of the staircase looking up. She heard no voices. For the benefit of adults unwilling to climb halfway up

153

and knock on the underside of the trapdoor above their heads, a bell rope dangled beside the steps. She gave it a tug and heard the jangle.

There was no response.

If they had all gone off together, Belinda must feel better, Daisy deduced. She went down to Martha's room.

Martha was sitting with her feet up on a chaise longue, sipping tea. "It's peppermint tea," she told Daisy. "I had an attack of indigestion and Mrs. Warden said peppermint will help. I do feel better."

"That's good. Would you prefer to have dinner on a tray up here?"

"Oh no, I'll come down." She set down her cup on the small table beside her. "I didn't realise it's time. . . ."

"No hurry. Finish your tea." Daisy sat down. "I had terrible indigestion with the twins. I sucked peppermint drops but I wish I'd known about peppermint tea."

"Mrs. Warden says it grows like a weed in the kitchen garden, so I can have as much as I want. It even tastes nice! Medicine the Myalwomen give you almost always tastes nasty. There." She set down her cup. "I'm ready."

Down in the entrance hall they crossed paths with Ernest.

"Miss Belinda said to tell you, madam, they've gone down to the river. They promised to be back before dark."

"Did she mention whether they were going to go boating?"

"She didn't say, madam."

"Let me know when they come in, please."

"Certainly, madam."

Daisy wasn't really worried. Derek and Belinda had learnt to swim at school and, given the irresistible proximity of the river, she had made sure that Ben was also competent in the water. Both he and, more important, Frank said he was.

Besides, the backwater wasn't very deep, even if Edgar had kept his promise and had it dredged. On the other hand, she remembered thinking that Derek and Bel wouldn't be satisfied with puttering about on the backwater much longer. What if they went out on the river? Had the boat been refurbished, as she had requested?

How easy would it be to sabotage a rowing skiff in a way that wouldn't be obvious until it sank beneath its load?

"What's wrong, Daisy?" Martha asked anxiously.

"Oh, nothing, really. I was just hoping the children are being sensible."

"I hope they'll come in before the storm arrives."

"Storm?" Daisy glanced at the west-facing window. The lower edge of the sun had disappeared behind dark cumulus clouds towering far off, probably over the Welsh mountains. The air was hot and still. "It may not come this far. Not for quite some time, if at all."

"Do you get hurricanes in England?"

"Good gracious no. Nothing so dramatic." She decided not to mention the occasional cloudburst that could send water racing down the Severn to inundate flood-prone Upton. "Just a bit of thunder and lightning. Would that bother you?"

"Not really. I should think this house is solid enough to survive a hurricane, anyway. What if lightning strikes it?"

"I know of at least two lightning conductors. There's one on the cupola over the main hall and one on the turret. It's perfectly safe. I only asked because some people are afraid of thunderstorms, even though there's no danger." Violet for one. Daisy didn't give her away.

She and Martha went down to the drawing room. Geraldine and Frank were already there. Vincent and Laurette came in shortly after, full of solicitude about Belinda.

"The child was lucky to avoid severe injury," said Laurette. "I cannot think it advisable to allow young ladies to ride. Girls are fragile creatures, not like boys."

"It's to be hoped she won't suffer any delayed consequences," Vincent put in. "The symptoms of a concussion sometimes develop later, and I once knew a man to break his neck in an accident and go about his usual business for three days before he collapsed."

"Nonsense," said Geraldine briskly. "Dr. Hopcroft examined her at once and he's quite satisfied that there's nothing seriously amiss. We have always found him most reliable. In fact, Vincent, I wish you would see him. When you came in, I noticed you're still limping badly."

Vincent waved this away. "Bruises, merely. I've been applying your housekeeper's herbal ointment, as you suggested, and it's working wonders. Laurette has obtained the recipe from her. You're using it for Belinda?" he asked Daisy.

"Yes. Apparently it eased her aches enough for her to go off to the river with the boys." Daisy wondered whether she had been a negligent mother, not for letting Bel ride the donkey but for not keeping a closer eye on her since the fall.

"Edgar had the skiff thoroughly overhauled," said Geraldine. "Have they taken it out?"

"I expect so."

"Ben said the others promised to teach him to row." Frank had been pouring drinks. He handed Daisy and Martha theirs. "What's your tipple?" he asked Vincent and Laurette.

"I hardly think it's your place to act as host," said Vincent sniffily.

"Just helping out." Frank's geniality was unimpaired.

"At my request," Geraldine said. "But by all means take your turn, unless you'd rather wait for Edgar. He's hunting for his butterfly net and may be late."

"No doubt those naughty children have borrowed it to go fishing," said Laurette with a thin smile as her husband went a trifle sulkily to get their drinks.

"They wouldn't," Daisy said. "Bel and Derek know how much he prizes it."

"The other boy . . ." Laurette left the phrase hanging.

"If you're implying that Ben would," Frank sprang to his stepson's defence, "I can tell you he's not going to do anything the others wouldn't. We know we're out of our depth here, and I've made sure he understands he's to follow their example. He's a good lad."

"Which is not to say they won't ever lead him into mischief," Daisy warned, "but not that particular mischief."

"Boys will be boys," said Geraldine tolerantly. "Besides, Derek knows perfectly well where the fishing equipment is kept. Do help yourselves to a drink," she added as Alec and Raymond came in, thus putting an end to that particular cause for offence.

Edgar appeared at last, Lowecroft arriving moments later to announce dinner. Halfway through the meal, Ernest murmured to Daisy, as he offered her a dish of runner beans, "The young people have come in, madam."

Much relieved, Daisy nodded and smiled her thanks. One less worry.

The storm broke in the middle of the night, with a huge, booming crash that sounded as if it were right overhead. Daisy sat bolt upright.

"Thunder," Alec said sleepily.

"Oh, of course. For a moment I couldn't think . . . I'd better close the window."

The evening had been so hot that they were sleeping under just a sheet. The air coming in now was comparatively chilly. A few drops of rain spattered against the windowpanes, then it came suddenly slashing down, as if released by the thunderbolt. Having shut the window, Daisy returned to bed, pulled up the blankets, and settled in cosily under them. A drumroll of thunder sounded, but nothing like the crash that had wakened her. Alec was already fast asleep again. Policemen learnt to sleep through practically anything.

Anything other than an emergency. A battering at the door took Alec halfway across the room before Derek's desperate cry made Daisy realise it was not just more thunder.

"Aunt Daisy! Aunt Daisy!"

NINETEEN

Daisy clicked on the bedside lamp and reached for her dressing gown as Alec opened the door.

"Calm down, Derek," he said. "Come in. What's the trouble?"

"It's Ben, Uncle Alec. He tripped on the stairs and he's knocked himself out. The stairs from the turret. His eyes are closed and he doesn't answer or move and I think there's blood in his hair. A tremendous bolt of lightning hit the turret and then there was a huge explosion and we thought we'd better get out."

"Very wise, though the explosion was thunder, I expect." Alec returned to the bed for his dressing gown and slippers. "I'll come at once."

Derek was shivering in cotton pyjamas and bare feet. "I let him go first, but I had the torch. I shone it down the stairs for him. I should have given it to him."

"Don't second-guess yourself, darling," said Daisy, now sufficiently clad to give him a hug.

Alec had stripped a couple of blankets off their bed. "Here, put this one round you, Derek. No point in risking a chill. Come on."

Before following, Daisy went to the chest of drawers for a cardigan, a pullover, two pairs of Alec's socks, and three of his handkerchiefs. Though the lightning conductor had almost certainly averted damage to the turret, there was always a chance the boys' things in the room might be inaccessible.

Apart from the turret's winding steps, electric lights were kept on all night at the head and foot of every staircase. Daisy hurried after Alec and Derek, along the passages and up the stairs. As she turned into the last corridor, the others reached the far end.

Ben was sitting on the bottom step, his head in his hands. He looked up groggily as Alec knelt beside him and draped a blanket about his shoulders.

"How are you feeling, Ben?"

"My head hurts." He raised a hand to feel the side of his head. "It's sticky."

"Derek, the torch, please."

The torch was still turned on. As Derek handed it to Alec, the beam flashed across something on the floor beside the steps. Daisy put down the stuff she'd brought and went to look.

"I'm going to shine this in your eyes. Try to keep them open."

"All right."

Daisy picked up a length of bamboo, broken at one end.

"Both pupils dilated and the same size," Alec said with satisfaction. "You're probably not concussed. Let me see that head wound now."

"I brought some hankies," said Daisy, putting back the cane as nearly as possible in the exact position she had found it. "Here. And Derek, put on this pullover. It won't get in your way like the blanket. Socks. Alec, may I put socks on Ben's feet while you check his head?"

Alec shifted a bit to let her get at the small, brown pink-soled feet. The socks were much too big, of course. He wouldn't be able to walk in them, but the important thing was to warm the boy quickly.

"You've got quite a gash there, but it's already just about stopped bleeding. I don't think it'll need stitches. Derek, would you go and soak this handkerchief in cold water, please. Don't wring it out. Sodden, not dripping too much."

"Yes, sir." Derek set out at a run, nearly tripped on the overlarge socks, impatiently tore them from his feet, and sped onward.

Daisy glanced up at the trap door. It was open, a square of darkness. No signs of destruction—fire, smoke, ashes—wafted through. She could fetch the boys' own clothes in a minute.

"I suppose you hit it on the railing." Alec turned the torch on the curlicued banisters. The fractured beam paused for a long moment on the piece of bamboo on the floor beyond, then moved on. "Yes, here. Quite near the bottom."

"I didn't slip. It felt as if my ankle caught on something."

Derek raced back, panting, clutching a soggy hankie.

"Give it to your aunt. There's electric light up there? Can you manage to turn it on without taking the torch?"

"Yes, of course." He stepped past Ben and tramped up, clutching the rail on both sides.

A moment later, light flooded down through the trap. Gently, Daisy set about cleaning up the wound on Ben's head.

"Ouch!"

"Sorry. Try to keep still, darling."

Meanwhile Alec directed the torch at the floor on the far side of the stair. "Ah."

Though Daisy couldn't see what he was looking at, she could guess. "Don't make cryptic Tom noises," she said. "Ah" was the favourite monosyllable of his sergeant, Tom Tring, who managed to infuse it with a wide variety of meanings. "Is it what I think it is?"

Alec laughed. "Who's being cryptic now? Hold on a tick." He examined the iron coils of the banisters a few steps up. "Yes, it looks as if . . . Hmm."

Derek, coming back down in his own socks with a pair for Ben, said, "That's Uncle Edgar's butterfly net! We didn't take it, Uncle Alec," he added defensively. "Even if we had we wouldn't be so stupid as to leave it on the stairs."

Ben jerked his head round to see what they were talking about. "Ouch! Is that what I fell over?"

"Must be," said Derek. "How on earth did it get there?"

Alec caught Daisy's eye. "Someone must have thought it was yours and put it there for you. Perhaps it was leaning, and fell over across the step."

Daisy didn't venture to mention that absolutely no one in the household could possibly have thought the butterfly net belonged to anyone other than his lordship.

Instead, she said, "Do you two want to find somewhere else to spend the rest of the night? Or are you all right with going back to your own beds?"

Ben looked up at Derek, who assured him, "Everything looks fine. No damage."

"I don't mind, then."

"I'd better put a dressing on your head first. Derek, do you know where the first-aid kit is kept?"

"No, Aunt Daisy."

Daisy sighed. "I'll fetch it myself. Go on up to bed, but don't lie down till I've bandaged you, Ben."

She was halfway along the corridor when Belinda and Frank Crowley came round the corner from the landing. Bel ran towards her.

"Mummy, has something happened? I couldn't go to sleep after that big thunder crash, and I started worrying about the boys, because lightning strikes the highest place, doesn't it?"

"Yes, darling. The lightning conductor was the highest point. It gave them a shock—a surprise, I mean—and Ben had a bit of a tumble, but no worse than yours this afternoon."

"He's all right?" Frank asked.

"Yes," Daisy said patiently, hoping the rest of the household wasn't going to appear with the same questions on their lips. Geraldine, her housekeeper, a housemaid, Frank as Ben's guardian—No one else had any reason to know where the boys slept. No *good* reason. "I'm just going to get a dressing for Ben's head. Daddy's with him and Derek. Go back to bed, darling, and don't worry."

Frank grinned. "I'll take that advice as meant for me, too. Thanks for taking care of him."

She went down to the second floor with them. They headed for their beds and Daisy continued down to the housekeeper's room, where the first-aid box had been kept in the same cupboard since time immemorial. Lint, Germolene ointment to keep it from sticking and to kill germs, and a bandage; sticking plaster might come in handy. She had a vague feeling that aspirin was not a good idea after a concussion, however slight. Oh, and the famous bruise ointment, if any was left after the heavy use it had undergone recently. Too many accidents. . . .

A branch, some kind of reflector, the butterfly net—It was fortunate that Edgar wasn't the irascible sort. He wasn't at all likely to blame the boys for breaking his net. He was more likely to blame himself because it was responsible for Ben's injury.

When she plodded up the circular stairs, she was careful not to brush against the banisters or touch the rail more than was absolutely necessary to keep her balance. For one thing, she didn't want blood on her dressing gown. For another, she wasn't sure whether Alec would be interested in looking for the fingerprints of whoever had set the trap, though it was probably too late by now anyway.

It must have been a trap. The odd thing, one of the odd things . . . But she'd consider that later.

She could hear voices—Alec's, and Ben's distinctive lilt—but not what they were saying, the floor effectively blurring their words until her head emerged through the trapdoor.

The boys were both in bed, Ben sitting up, Derek already nearly asleep. Alec sat in a chair where he could watch Ben.

"No signs of trouble so far," Alec assured her.

"Thank goodness." Daisy neatly bandaged Ben's head, about the limit of her nursing ability. He looked as if he were wearing a turban. "Do you feel sleepy?"

"Not very."

"Hop out of bed and stand up for just a minute, Ben," said Alec. "Do you feel at all dizzy?"

"No, sir."

"Roll your head a bit. All right? It looks as if you've been lucky. Back into bed and try to sleep. Don't be alarmed if one of us comes and wakes you up in a couple of hours just to check."

Daisy tucked him in and dropped a kiss on what was visible of his forehead below the bandage. "Sleep well, Ben."

"Good night, Aunt Daisy, Uncle Alec. Thank you."

Despite his words, when Daisy glanced back before turning off the light and following Alec down the stairs, he was fast asleep.

"One of us . . . ?" she said, joining him in the corridor.

"I'll set the alarm clock and you—"

"Oh no, you've much more idea of what symptoms you're looking for. Alec, the net on the stairs, and everything else that's happened—I don't understand it. What on earth do you think is going on?"

"We'll talk about it tomorrow."

Daisy yawned. "You agree that it's strange."

"In the morning," he said firmly. "I need to sleep on it."

In spite of distant rumblings of thunder, he slept on it so soundly that the alarm clock didn't rouse him and it was Daisy who went to check on Ben. He was less difficult to wake. He seemed perfectly normal to Daisy, but when she returned to her own bed she reset the alarm for another two hours, just in case.

By then the sun was rising. The sky was as clear as if the storm had been a dream. When Daisy looked out of the window, a faint mist hazed the grass but everything higher was fresh and bright, leaves washed clean by the downpour, and lingering raindrops sparkling.

As Alec again slept through the alarm's bell, Daisy decided it wouldn't hurt to put him under an obligation by letting him sleep. If he was reluctant to discuss his theories with her, she'd be able to point out that he owed her.

When she reached the turret, the boys were already getting up, although it was not yet six o'clock.

"It's such a ripping day," Derek explained. "We can sleep in some day when it's raining. We're going to the river."

"*To*, not *on*," said Daisy. "It'll be in full spate after the rain."

"That's half the fun," he protested.

"Not the boat. And not swimming, either."

"Oh, all right."

"Did you go out in the boat yesterday?"

"Yes," Ben chimed in enthusiastically. "They let me have a go at rowing."

So the boat hadn't been sabotaged. Or at least not effectively. Daisy would make sure Edgar had it examined thoroughly before it was used again.

"On the backwater?" Derek bargained.

"Also out of bounds. The storm will have swelled the stream, as well." She interpreted with ease the look Derek and Ben exchanged. "If you must. As long as you stay upstream, in the woods or farther."

"Thanks, Aunt Daisy!"

"But let me look at Ben's head first."

Since she stood on the steps protruding into the room from the waist up, Ben came and knelt in front of her. "I feel fine. It hardly hurts at all, only when I touch it. Can I take the bandage off? It looks silly."

"Let me have a look." She undid the safety pin and unwrapped the bandage. The wound had stopped bleeding and was not inflamed, though there was some swelling around it.

"Sorry, Ben, it still needs something to keep it clean and protect against bumps. I could try to make it less obtrusive, but if I use sticking plaster, it's going to hurt like the dickens when it comes off."

"And pull out your hair," Derek added. "I'd keep the bandage if I were you. We can pretend you're a wounded soldier or something."

Daisy had left supplies in the turret, so Ben's turban was soon restored.

"There. Do try not to bump it!"

"Aunt Daisy, if you're going back to your room, could you possibly stop at Bel's and tell her we'll meet her in the kitchen in five minutes?"

"I'm glad you're including Belinda in your plans."

"Oh, she's not a bad sort, for a girl."

Daisy couldn't reach to box his ears for the last part of that remark. She let it pass. "Don't leave a mess in the kitchen."

"We won't," they promised in chorus.

"And don't expect Bel to clear it up because she's a girl."

She went to give Belinda their message. Bel was already awake.

"Five minutes!" She scrambled out of bed. "Is Ben all right, Mummy?"

"I think so, but keep an eye on him for me. And stop the boys from doing anything too harebrained if you can."

Alec woke up when Daisy slipped back into bed beside him. She interpreted his grunt as an enquiry as to Ben's well-being.

"He seems to have been lucky. I've said they can go out, Bel and the boys."

"Out?" he mumbled.

"On one of their expeditions. No boating."

"An expedition?" Alec was now thoroughly awake. "At this time in the morning?"

"They're young, and the sun is shining." In spite of which she was quite chilled after her expedition to the turret. She snuggled up to him.

Quite some time later, Alec said, "No boating?"

"Because the river will be dangerous. If it rained heavily here, you can bet it bucketed down in the hills where the Severn rises. But also, I'm awfully afraid the boat may have been sabotaged. I don't want them going out in it until it's been thoroughly checked. Tell me that's nonsense."

"It's a reasonable precaution. Even though I can't work out what's going on, nor who's responsible, I'm pretty sure there is something going on."

"It must be Raymond! Or is it just the thunder that makes me suspect him?"

"The thunder?" Alec asked, astonished.

"I'm not serious. It's ridiculous. Just because there was thunder when I came to Fairacres to meet him the first time, and then again last night. . . . It gives me a sort of uneasy feeling. Superstition, I suppose. Nonsense, of course, but when nothing makes sense . . . Raymond *is* the most likely. Vincent was attacked."

"He has a vague impression that he may have been attacked."

"Ben twice," Daisy continued.

"I've come up with a sort of motive for Frank, though."

"A motive for wanting his stepson out of the way? It's not as if Frank can possibly inherit."

"I said 'sort of.' Assuming he hopes to get his hands on some of the loot, a younger child, Ben's brother, would be more pliable, more easily persuaded, or cheated."

"Not with Tommy looking out for him. Besides, though it wouldn't surprise me in the least if Frank Crowley is out to feather his nest, I don't believe for a moment that he'd harm Ben."

"You've probably seen more of the two of them together," Alec conceded. "It's worth bearing in mind, though."

"So after sleeping on it, you believe there's a plot to do with the inheritance? Although it could well have been Derek who fell? And although the fall was not very likely to be fatal?"

"I don't know what to believe. What I do know is that I can't guard all of Edgar's blasted heirs. If one of them is killed at Fairacres and I've done nothing to prevent it, I'm going to be well and truly persona non grata at the Yard, with the county police, and at Fair-acres, not to mention your mother."

"No, please don't." Daisy shuddered. "Clearly you need to be seen to be doing something. What?"

"First, I'm going to have a chat with the chief constable."

"Is it still Sir Nigel?"

"Colonel Sir Nigel Wookleigh himself. Or was, last time I had occasion to lend a hand in Worcestershire."

"He was very cooperative that time when—"

"Don't remind me! All the same, that's why I'm going to tackle him first."

"You're going to ask him to send in bobbies to watch everyone? That wouldn't go down very well."

"Great Scott, no! The most I can do is advise him that we may have trouble on our hands and ask for prior permission to request aid from the Yard if necessary. What I'd really like is to get Tom and Ernie down here, but the AC would never go for it without far more evidence of wrongdoing than I've got. I wouldn't myself, if I wasn't in the middle of the situation. All it amounts to as yet is a broken butterfly net. Dammit!" He flung back the covers and swung his feet to the floor. "I should have secured it last night. Was it still there this morning?"

Daisy pulled the covers back up. "Yes. I nearly brought it back with me, but I thought you might want to make a note of the position of the pieces. And splinters on the banisters—that's what you spotted last night, wasn't it?"

"Will the housemaids have done that corridor already?" Alec retrieved his notebook from a drawer and shoved it in his dressing-gown pocket.

"Shouldn't think so. They start on the ground floor and work up, and it's still quite early."

"I hope to heaven the boys haven't mucked about with it," he flung back at her from the doorway.

"*They* won't have dusted the banisters," she assured the door.

TWENTY

Alec collared his hostess on her way to breakfast. They disappeared into Geraldine's sitting room. Daisy had just started on her fresh-cooked scrambled eggs when Ernest came in to convey her ladyship's request that she join them as soon as convenient.

Daisy looked sadly at the steaming, sunshine-yellow eggs.

"I'll bring you more when you get back," Ernest promised.

When Daisy entered the sitting room, Geraldine burst into speech. "Daisy, my dear, I want to ask you about this extraordinary story of Alec's. He's reminded me more than once that he's a police officer and therefore inclined to be suspicious of untoward occurrences, so I'd like to hear what your common sense has to say about the subject."

Daisy was about to point out that she was just as likely to harbour suspicions. Just in time she remembered that Geraldine was unaware of her occasional involvement in criminal matters, other than the goings-on at Fairacres four years ago. "I thought Alec was just going to request the use of the car to go into Worcester," she temporised.

"I was," Alec said dryly. "Geraldine decided to make a party of it, to invite all her guests to visit the town and the cathedral. So I explained that I merely hoped to speak to the chief constable."

"Who is—I think I may claim—a friend of mine." Geraldine blushed; she actually blushed. Surely she couldn't be carrying on a flirtation with Sir Nigel? "You'll be surprised, I don't doubt, to hear that I've applied to become a justice of the peace."

"Goodness!"

"I have such an excellent staff here at Fairacres that I simply haven't enough to occupy me. I really don't care for bridge, I'm afraid. And a number of women have become magistrates in recent years. One doesn't have to have to be trained in the law, you know. I approached Sir Nigel. I was already acquainted with him socially, of course. He has agreed to support my application."

"Geraldine, what a wonderful idea!" Daisy went over and kissed the blushing cheek. "I'm sure your years of nailing schoolboy culprits will stand you in good stead." She sat down. "Naturally you were interested in why Alec wanted to see Sir Nigel."

"I hope I'm not nosy, but yes, I was curious. Now I'm horrified, to think one of my guests, one of Edgar's *relatives*, may be attempting to kill the others!"

"*May* be," Daisy stressed. "That's the trouble. Alec can't ignore what's happened, but nor can he do anything official about it."

"Yes, I understand the situation. You, too, are convinced there's something to worry about?"

"I'm convinced Alec ought to report his suspicions to someone. Sir Nigel is the logical person."

"All right." Geraldine sighed. "I must tell Edgar. You won't mind that."

"All to the good," said Alec. "He'll be another pair of eyes on the lookout for trouble."

"Since his net is involved in the latest incident, he may take an interest in the matter, especially as he'd be very upset if harm came to the boy. He's taken quite a liking to Benjamin. Very well. If you have no objection, I should like to be present when you speak to Sir Nigel."

"As you wish."

"Would you like me to ring him up and make an appointment?"

Alec looked decidedly taken aback. "No, thank you. I'd better do that myself."

Geraldine inclined her head. "I believe it will be best if I go ahead and invite everyone to come to Worcester. 'Camouflage' is the word the forces used in the war, I understand. Many of the boys are—were—very keen on the notion. Especially the Boy Scouts."

Grinning, Alec said, "Camouflage let it be."

"I'll tell them I have business in town and give them a map of historical sites, so that they won't expect me to dance attendance. No doubt you are an expert, Alec, at simply fading away."

"By far the most useful weapon in the detective's arsenal."

"And I," Daisy said mournfully, "shall undoubtedly be stuck touring the shops with Laurette." She would have liked to be present at the interview with the chief constable, but being ninety-nine percent sure Alec would say no, she didn't bother to ask.

Sure enough, as soon as Raymond, Frank, and the Vincents had agreed that a day in Worcester sounded like a pleasant outing, Laurette said to Daisy, "You and I, we will look at the shops while the men see the sights."

Daisy politely agreed, though she couldn't bring herself to enthuse.

Martha was in no shape for sightseeing or window shopping. She asked Geraldine's permission to invite Violet to spend the morning with her, and permission was gladly given. "If Lady John is busy, I'll get on with sewing for the baby," Martha said without regret. She really was a most placid person.

Daisy remembered their first meeting, with Martha in floods of tears. Was her change of spirits attributable to the progressing pregnancy, or could she, as Alec suggested, have heard from her Sammy?

Edgar, unsurprisingly, declined to accompany the party. The children, turning up for breakfast in spite of their earlier raid on the kitchen, decided they'd rather hunt insects with him than waste a beautiful morning in viewing fusty old buildings.

"I'll keep an eye on them," Edgar promised.

Ben, who had lost his bandage already, looked disappointed. Obviously the decision was Derek and Belinda's. They had both seen more than once what Worcester had to offer, but Ben might never have another chance to visit an ancient cathedral city. Daisy resolved to arrange a visit later, with a promise of ice cream and buns to lure the others.

Sir Nigel having set an appointment at noon, Geraldine suggested that after their various wanderings they should meet for lunch at one at the Talbot, just opposite the cathedral. "Alec, if you wouldn't mind driving the Vauxhall, there will be plenty of room for everyone."

"I'll take my hire car," said Raymond brusquely. "Smethwick, the driver, has been sitting about for three days doing nothing at my expense. And that's just since I came here. I've had the same man since I arrived in England. A cushy job he's had of it."

As no one else seemed about to volunteer, Frank offered to go with him. Alec frowned. Daisy wondered if he was worried that they might kill each other en route. If so, she didn't know what she could do to stop them, but she was about to suggest keeping them company when Geraldine said, "In that case, Truscott can drive the Vauxhall. So why don't you go with Raymond, Alec?"

She thus relieved Daisy of the responsibility of keeping the men from one another's throats as far as Worcester. Though Daisy still couldn't see the cheerful, easygoing Frank Crowley as a murderer, his having brought Ben all the way to England at considerable expense showed him to have more determination than was apparent.

The Vauxhall and the Daimler duly came round to the portico to pick everyone up. Geraldine told the chauffeurs to take them to the Edgar Tower, the fourteenth-century gatehouse to the cathedral close.

When they arrived, she instructed her guests to visit the cathedral first, in the school matron voice that was as effective as the dowager's grande dame voice, as Daisy was amused to note. Even Laurette trailed through the gate with the group.

The ancient building inspired awe in Raymond and Frank, and even in Vincent and Laurette, though they were more accustomed to historical surroundings. In Daisy, familiarity inspired not contempt, but comfort. She had grown up visiting the cathedral quite frequently, for christenings, weddings, and funerals, and for the Three Choirs Festival. Her favourite spot was the sepulchre of Bad King John, whose sinister reputation had fascinated her as a child.

She had a job to do now. She had to spread people out so that the others wouldn't notice when Alec went off to see the chief constable. Though Geraldine having an appointment in Worcester would arouse no curiosity, the same could not be said of Alec.

If someone was up to something—which wasn't entirely clear—their suspicions might be awakened. Before they left Hampstead, Martha had been asked not to mention that Alec was a copper. However, the Fairacres servants knew, so the chances were that all the guests knew by now.

In which case, they had a pretty poor opinion of his competence, or they wouldn't be trying whatever they were trying.

Having thoroughly confused herself, Daisy suggested that the men might like to climb the tower or visit the eleventh-century crypt.

"I'm afraid I'm avoiding steps when I can," said Vincent, waving the walking stick he was still dependent on.

"Oh yes. You might like to inspect the effigy of King John."

"King John!" Laurette muttered scornfully.

"I thought you and I would go and admire the stained glass in the lady chapel—Victorian but beautiful—so that we can tell Geraldine we did," she whispered to the disgruntled woman. "Then we'll go shopping, I promise."

The sun shone in through the delicately colourful east window of the lady chapel. Laurette made it plain that she'd much rather be looking through the windows of the best department store in town. She took out her compact and, peering into the small round mirror, powdered her nose.

Daisy delayed her as long as was humanly possible. When they returned to the nave, none of the men was in sight. Hoping Alec had managed to slip away unnoticed, Daisy wished she could, too.

An hour or so later, she and Laurette were walking briskly back along The Tything amidst a crowd of bustling shoppers, many bearing baskets, some pushing prams or accompanied by small children. Laurette complained about the Worcester shops' lack of any clothes worthy of purchase.

Shopping with her had been a revelation to Daisy. Lucy always dressed in the height of fashion; attaining it was a long drawn-out process that bored Daisy to tears, involving models and seamstresses and milliners and much discussion of everything but cost. Laurette, on the other hand, swept through the ready-to-wear racks with an inerrant eye for what would both suit her and fit her, at a reasonable price. Her aim was not fashion but a businesslike chic.

That was the way to do it, Daisy thought. Now all she needed was the inerrant eye. . . .

Not that she had any way to judge Laurette's claim of inerrancy, as she hadn't actually bought any clothes, just sighed for the shops of London and Paris.

They crossed Castle Street and went straight on along The Foregate. A tram passed them as they walked under the railway bridge. Ahead was the busy intersection known as The Cross. Some traffic, including trams and an occasional horse dray, continued along the High Street, some turned left into St. Swithin's Street, and some turned right to go down Broad Street to the bridge over the Severn. A white-sleeved policeman on point duty managed the flow with an almost balletic grace.

As Daisy and Laurette approached, he held up his hand to stop the tram that had passed them to allow another, coming up Broad Street, to turn left. Suddenly he waved his arms frantically and blew several piercing blasts on his whistle.

People started screaming and shouting. The trams both came to a halt, as did cars, vans, lorries, motorbicycles, and everything else on the road except for errand boys on pedal bikes. They weaved through the rest, necks craned to see what was going on. Some pedestrians on the pavements held back, others ghoulishly pressed forward.

"Run over by a tram!" said a woman pushing past Daisy and Laurette. She sounded hopeful.

Daisy was relieved that Laurette wasn't one of the gawkers. It would have been too frightful to have a relative—even if just by marriage—who gaped at accidents.

Accidents. Another accident. Sheer coincidence of course. In the middle of the busy city, the odds against one of the party from Fairacres being involved were enormous.

All the same, she was not displeased when the press of people moving forward forced them to go along with the flow. Not that she wanted to see what had happened, but she did want reassurance that no one she knew was involved. A gruesome rhyme Gervaise used to chant to tease Violet circled in her mind:

"Oh look, Mama, pray what is that,
"That looks like strawberry jam?"
"Hush, hush, my dear, 'tis poor papa,
"Run over by a tram."

Several more bobbies came running from all directions. Some started to clear away the throng.

"Nothing to see, ladies and gentlemen. Keep moving, please. Move along there."

In any case, as Daisy and Laurette approached, people started to disperse, talking and shaking their heads. To Daisy they seemed disappointed or relieved, not shocked.

Then two policemen came round the end of the nearer tram, supporting between them a large, hatless man. . . .

"Raymond! Let me through, please. He's my cousin!"

A youth came out of the nearest shop carrying a chair, which he placed on the pavement against the wall. "Here, set the gentleman down to catch his breath."

Looking dizzy and disoriented, Raymond slumped onto the chair. As Daisy reached him, he dropped his head into his hands.

"He's my cousin," she repeated to the bobby who stepped forward to stop her. "Is he badly hurt?"

"Not a scratch, madam, saving on his hands from the cobbles. Gentleman stumbled but summun shoved him aside from the tram tracks. Could o' bin nasty, else."

174

"He didn't get a knock on the head?"

"Don't b'lieve so, madam, but you better arst him yoursel'. The lady's the gemmun's cousin, Jerry," he introduced her to his colleague, who was bending solicitously over Raymond, notebook in hand, asking his name.

"He's Raymond Dalrymple, officer. He's a guest of Lord and Lady Dalrymple at Fairacres, as I am. I'm Mrs. Fletcher, if you want it for your report."

"No need for that, thank you, madam."

"We're going to meet the rest of the party at the Talbot. Mr. Raymond's car is there, and his chauffeur. Perhaps someone could—"

"Here, you!" the constable called to the boy, who lingered in the shop door. "Run over to the Talbot, lad, and have them send Mr. Raymond Dalrymple's car for him."

The trams had already clanged away and the flow of traffic resumed. Most of the police had returned to their beats, but one brought Raymond his hat and his cane, broken in half.

" 'Ere you go, sir. I 'opes you don't need the stick for walking."

Raymond raised his head. "No no." He reached for his felt hat and settled it on his head, then snatched it off again. "It hurts. Someone pushed . . ."

"Yes, sir, someone pushed you out of the way and lucky for you it was."

"Raymond, did you bang your head?" Daisy leant over him, examining his balding scalp for bruising.

He looked at her vacantly, apparently finding it difficult to focus. "Daisy? No, I didn't. . . . Someone pushed . . ."

Though she couldn't find any marks suggestive of a blow, she was worried. "We'd better get you to a doctor."

A shake of his head turned into a wince. He dropped the hat and clutched his head. "No. Home. Go to bed."

Arguing seemed inadvisable. Daisy decided to go with him, and if he was no better by the time they reached Fairacres, she would ring up Dr. Hopcroft.

The bronze Daimler arrived at last, the shop boy lounging happily in the seat beside the chauffeur. He bounced out and he, the chauffeur, and the one remaining bobby vied to help Raymond into the car. Daisy tipped him, as Raymond showed no sign of doing so, and he handed her in next.

Laurette, who had been hanging back from what she appeared to consider a disgraceful scene, came up to the car. The bobby looked at her askance.

"Another cousin," Daisy told him. To Laurette she said, "I'm going to go back to Fairacres with Raymond."

"You can take me to the Talbot, *n'est-ce pas?*" Laurette joined them in the car. "I will explain to the others what has happened."

"Good idea."

They dropped her off. Raymond remained slumped in the corner, eyes closed. Before they were halfway back to Fairacres, he started to breathe stertorously, an unpleasant cross between a snort and a gasp. Alarmed, Daisy spoke to him. He didn't respond.

She listened for a few minutes, then reached for the speaking tube. "Smethwick?"

"Yes, madam?"

"Mr. Raymond seems to be very ill. I think we'd better take him straight to the doctor, in Upton-upon-Severn. Just stay on this road."

"Yes, madam."

"I don't know his address."

"We'll just have to ask, madam. You're all right, are you?"

"So far, thank you." After all, having hysterics or fainting would hardly alter the situation for the better. "Oh, by the way, I've been wanting to thank you for trying to help me when I had that puncture a few weeks ago, and for sending the RAC man to the rescue. The blue Gwynne Eight?"

"I thought it was you, madam. My pleasure, I'm sure."

Daisy sat back. The horrible sound had stopped and Raymond's chest no longer heaved at each breath. Perhaps he'd be all right just going to bed? Should she take his pulse?

Reluctantly she slid across the leather seat. His breathing was so quiet she couldn't hear it at all. She couldn't see his chest rising and falling. When she lifted his wrist, his hand flopped downward. His skin felt clammy.

No pulse. The blank stare wasn't a stare because those fixed eyes were seeing nothing.

TWENTY-ONE

Daisy's heart stood still. For a moment she couldn't speak, then she cried out, "Stop!" so loud that Smethwick heard her, although she didn't use the tube.

He glanced back, his expression startled. A hundred yards farther on, he pulled into a farm gateway. "Madam?"

She opened the door and jumped out, her one thought was to escape from the immediate vicinity of Raymond's body. "I can't find a pulse," she blurted out as Smethwick, alarmed, also sprang out of the Daimler. "I think he's dead."

"Let me check," he said in a businesslike way. "I drove an ambulance in the war. Flat feet."

He climbed into the back of the car, leaving Daisy thinking sad thoughts of her fiancé, Michael, who had likewise been an ambulance driver during the war but had not returned.

"You're right, he's gone." The chauffeur emerged from the interior. "Had an accident in Worcester, did he?"

"Yes, but the police seem to think he just fell, and he himself said he hadn't hit his head."

"Heart attack. Or stroke. He's the age and figure for it."

"He seemed so vigorous!"

"Oh well, you never can tell. I s'pose I better lay him out on the seat. Otherwise he's going to slide off when we start moving. If you don't mind sitting in front with me, madam."

"Yes, please!" said Daisy.

Once the Raymond's body was in a decently recumbent position, Smethwick fetched a car rug from the boot to spread over him. The cheerful red-and-yellow tartan was altogether inappropriate, but as the chauffeur said, "Beggars and corpses can't be choosers." He returned to his seat behind the steering wheel. "I haven't driven around with a stiff behind me—if you'll pardon the expression—since the Armistice. Where to now, madam?"

"Oh dear, I expect we ought to take him to Dr. Hopcroft, even though it's too late. He'll know what to do."

"Right you are. I've got to find a post office and send a wire to my company, too. The boss isn't going to be happy."

"If he didn't pay in advance, I daresay Lord Dalrymple will cover the expense." She only half listened to Smethwick's response. She was wondering whether Raymond's death fitted into the pattern of accidents—assuming there was in fact a pattern—and if so, how.

From what the copper had said, it sounded as if someone had pushed him aside at the last minute, possibly saving his life. It was slightly odd that the Good Samaritan hadn't stayed to make sure he was all right and to enjoy the kudos. Perhaps he'd been in a tearing hurry, or perhaps just shy.

He might yet be found. Daisy had learnt from experience the sequence of events that Raymond's death would lead to. As he had not, to her knowledge, been under the care of a doctor, and no medical practitioner had been present, an inquest would be necessary. In the circumstances, after Alec's hobnob with the CC, the coroner would surely require an autopsy. If there was anything fishy about Raymond's death, a police investigation would follow.

The police—

"Hell!" Smethwick jammed his feet on the brake and clutch. The car slithered to a halt in a few inches of brown water. Ahead, the lane was under water as far as they could see, ripples spreading round the next curve. "Begging your pardon, madam. I was took by surprise."

"Never mind that. Upton must be flooded again."

"It's not just a big puddle, or a water-splash?"

"No, it'll be deeper farther on. We can't drive into the village. Blast! I wonder what we should do? I don't want to dash about trying to find another doctor."

"Go back to Fairacres and use the telephone."

"I dare say we ought to take him back to Worcester, to the hospital or the police station. But I must say, I don't feel like spending any more time in the car with the poor man than I must." She shuddered.

"Back to Fairacres and telephone."

"I expect you're right." She brightened. "I'll ring up the Talbot and speak to Alec. My husband," she elucidated.

Smethwick grinned. "Detective Chief Inspector Fletcher of Scotland Yard."

So even the visiting hire car driver knew! Daisy wondered why Alec bothered to try to keep quiet about his profession. Not that she was really in any doubt: A policeman's wife was almost equally subject to the phenomenon of people falling silent when she entered a room. Except when he was working, life was simpler if he vaguely introduced himself as a civil servant.

His being a copper didn't seem to bother Smethwick, and the chauffeur's awareness didn't necessarily mean all the heirs knew, Daisy assured herself.

He put the car into reverse gear and they motored backwards up the lane. Hedged and without verges, it was too narrow for the big Daimler to do a three-point turn. They soon came to a cart track, where Smethwick, muttering about mud, backed in and drove out forwards. Ten minutes later they reached Fairacres.

Daisy was so anxious to talk to Alec, she didn't wait for the chauffeur to open the car door for her. Getting out, she said, "I may want you to fetch—Oh no, I suppose not."

"No, madam. In fact, I was thinking I better get the car out of the sun."

"Oh dear, isn't it awful. . . ." Suddenly Daisy was on the edge of tears. Poor Raymond had been a relative, after all, even if she hadn't liked him much. She swallowed. "You wanted to send your employers a telegram. I'll have Ernest let you know when I'm finished on the phone."

"I could walk over to the post office in Morton Green, madam."

"No, I'm sure Lord Dalrymple would want you to use his telephone. I'd . . . I'd rather you stayed nearby, please. But please don't tell anyone. . . ."

"Of course, madam," Smethwick said soothingly.

He really was a very nice man, Daisy thought, going up the steps.

Ernest appeared as she entered the house. "The chief in—I mean, Mr. Fletcher telephoned, madam, from the Talbot Hotel in Worcester."

"Thanks. I'm just about to ring him, anyway."

"He said he's coming back right away."

"Good. Is his lordship in?"

"No, madam. He took the young 'uns bicycling. Off to Cooper's Wood, they was, dogs and all, hunting a Wood Tiger. Sounds dangerous, don't it?"

"Butterfly or moth?"

"Moth, I believe, madam. Cook packed lunches for them, so they won't be back for a while."

"And Mrs. Samuel?"

"Lady John didn't feel well enough to come here, madam, so she sent the car to fetch Mrs. Samuel over to the Dower House. Mrs. Samuel telephoned later to say she would stay there for lunch."

Daisy was relieved. The fewer people about while Raymond's body remained in the Daimler in the garage, the better. She hoped Alec would arrange to have it removed before the children and the pregnant Martha came back. And she hoped Martha would not suffer for going without her usual cup of mint tea before the meal.

"I'll wait for Alec in Lord Dalrymple's den, Ernest. Would you go and tell Smethwick the telephone is available for his use?"

Too agitated to sit in one of the huge leather armchairs, Daisy stood at the window in the study, gazing out but seeing only the scene at The Cross—the trams, cars, lorries at a standstill, and people crowding forwards. If only she had been closer, had been able to see exactly what had happened. The point-duty policeman hadn't noticed anything more than a stumble, though, and he surely would have noticed anything suspicious. Perhaps not; he had to keep an eye on the movements of all those vehicles and people.

She should have taken Raymond straight to a hospital.

Not more than five minutes passed before Alec strode into the room. "Daisy, what's this garbled story of Laurette's? Raymond's had an accident?"

"Oh darling, he's dead!" Daisy burst into tears and flung herself on Alec's chest.

He gave her a handkerchief and put his arms round her. "Dead! Laurette seemed to think he just had a fright."

"That's what I thought. He said he wanted to come back here and go to bed, so I decided I'd better go with him, and if only I'd taken him to a doctor right away he might still be alive. But he died in the car. Alec, it was simply frightful!"

"Come and sit down and tell me all about it. Does Edgar keep any booze in here?" After scanning the room in vain, he unceremoniously yanked open the kneehole desk's two bottom drawers. "Damn." He rang the bell, then went impatiently to the door.

It opened as he reached it, revealing Ernest with a silver tray. On it stood a decanter, a bottle, and a soda syphon.

"You've read my mind," said Alec.

"Mr. Lowecroft did, sir. Brandy for madam. He thought you'd prefer whisky."

"Perfect." He took the tray from Ernest and closed the door.

"I don't want brandy," Daisy said crossly.

"Whisky, then. You've had a shock."

"I don't like whisky." She accepted the B and S—more B than S—that he handed to her, and took a sip. "Alec, could Raymond have died of shock?"

"That's for a doctor to say." He frowned. "I'd have thought it would be instant or not at all. You've sent for a doctor? The man who was at the fête?"

182

"I was going to, but then he died, so I thought I ought to—"

"Better start at the beginning, Daisy, if I'm to have a hope of sorting this out."

She described the scene in Worcester and her recognition of Raymond. "He was obviously dizzy and he said his head hurt. He denied he'd hit it, though. He wanted to come home so I sent for his car. Then he suddenly got worse. I thought he ought to see the doctor right away, but he died. . . . And then we couldn't get through. The road's flooded."

"So you came back here. I take it Dr. Hopcroft couldn't get here, either."

"I haven't talked to him. I didn't know who to tell, so I was going to phone you at the Talbot, but you were already on your way. Thank you for rushing to the rescue! Did they all come back with you?"

"No, no one. I sent Truscott back to pick them up when they're ready to leave."

"Thank goodness, and the children and Martha are all still out. Edgar, too, so I couldn't ask his advice. Should I try to get hold of Dr. Hopcroft? Or report Raymond's death to the local bobby?"

"You were quite right to ring me first, love. I'm going to go straight to the top." He went over to the telephone on the desk.

"Sir Nigel?"

"Sir Nigel. He was quite chummy, and sent you his best regards. I'll try the main police station first, but if he's not there, I'll call him at home." He picked up the receiver and the daffodil base and sat on the corner of the desk.

"Smethwick was sending a telegram to his employer."

"He's not on now. Hello? Put me through to the main police station in Worcester, please. I'll stay on the line."

"What did Sir Nigel think of the string of accidents?"

"He was inclined to pooh-pooh the whole thing. Not that he doubts the incidents occurred, but that they might have any sinister significance. I have a feeling he sees my profession as making me apt to see crime where none exists."

"Darling!" Daisy said indignantly.

"However, Geraldine—Hello, this is Detective Chief Inspector

Fletcher of the Metropolitan Police. Is the chief constable still there? Put me through, please. Yes, I'll hold."

" 'However, Geraldine' . . . ?"

"He seems to have considerable respect for her. I shouldn't be surprised if—Yes, Fletcher speaking, sir."

Abandoning the remains of her brandy, Daisy hurried over to perch on the desk beside him, her ear as close to the receiver as possible.

She heard Sir Nigel say, ". . . another already?"

"Another 'accident.' " Alec managed to put quotation marks in his voice. "And a fatality. The same person, though the two may not be connected."

"Some unfortunate person suffered an accident and died within . . . what . . . an hour or so? It's not much more than that since you left my office. And you say they may not be connected!"

"Sir, only a doctor can pronounce on that question. And a coroner's jury."

"No doctor present?"

"No, sir. The local man's surgery is in Upton, which is flooded, so he's out of reach. In any case, with your permission, I would prefer to call in your police surgeon."

"Of course. You'd better talk to my superintendent. He'll be in charge of the investigation, if there is one. No, by damn! You're on the spot and up to the neck in things already. If there's a case, I'll get on to your AC right away. No sense in wasting time fumbling about."

"Er . . . I'm not sure the Assistant Commissioner will think it's appropriate to put me in charge in the circumstances. My wife's family, I mean. . . ."

"Bosh, my dear chap. Who better? That's settled. Now, just where is the deceased?"

"Here at Fairacres, sir. In his car—"

"He died at the wheel? By gad, how the devil did he—?"

"No, no, his chauffeur was driving. I gather the body is laid out on the rear seat. In the garage."

"You gather? You haven't seen it?"

"No, sir, it seemed more important to get in touch with you at once when I was told—"

"Who told you?"

"My wife," Alec admitted reluctantly, glowering at Daisy.

"Indeed! And just how did Mrs. Fletcher come to be—"

Interrupting in his turn, Alec explained Daisy's involvement.

"And she's quite certain he's dead," Sir Nigel asked plaintively, "not merely unconscious?"

"The driver was an ambulance man in the war, as it turns out. He was quite certain."

"Oh, good enough, I suppose. You've sent for the local bobby?"

Alec looked at Daisy, who shook her head and pointed at him. "You were already on your way," she mouthed.

"Not yet, sir. It seemed more important to notify you immediately."

"Yes, yes, of course, quite right."

"As soon as I've finished reporting to you," Alec hinted, "I'll get on to the local chap."

"Anything else to report? Still no idea who's responsible, eh? If anyone."

"No, sir, no idea. The dead man was at the top of my list."

TWENTY-TWO

"*I was* just about convinced it was Raymond," said Daisy, return-ing to her chair. She picked up her glass, then put it down again. She no longer felt in need of a stimulant.

"Is there a bobby in Morton Green?"

"No, the nearest is Upton. Which is flooded."

"Damnation!"

"Two constables and a sergeant, so one or more might have been outside the village, doing his bicycle beat, when the water rose. Isn't there a chance someone would know whereabouts he might be?"

"You're right, someone *ought* to know his whereabouts. Country bobbies can't be expected to keep as strict time as in town, but they have schedules." Alec clicked the telephone hook twice to get the operator's attention. "Upton police, please. . . . Engaged? Please ring back as soon as it's open. Official business."

"I can't see," said Daisy, "even if one of them can get here, what use he's going to be."

"None. It's a matter of professional courtesy. As far as I'm con-cerned, that is. As far as you're concerned, it's the duty of every citizen to report an unexpected death to the police." He was halfway to the door. "And that being so, I'm going to go and inspect the deceased, and leave you to do your undoubted duty."

Daisy's indignant "Hi!" followed him out. She had done her duty in reporting to him.

Still, she could cope with a local sergeant on the phone, especially if he was stuck in flooded Upton and not likely to turn up on the doorstep.

The telephone rang. She jumped up and hurried to the desk to grab the receiver before anyone else could answer the call and be alarmed at hearing a policeman on the other end.

"Telegram for G. Smethwick," said the operator. "Are you ready?"

"No! Half a mo." Daisy found a pencil in the middle desk drawer and the blotter was handy to write on. "All right, operator, go ahead."

"Sender: Cox's Motorcar Hire Co." The brief message told Smethwick to bring the car back to London at once. No hurry to pass it on, Daisy thought. The Daimler would not be leaving Fairacres until the police had had their way with it. Daisy was about to hang up when the operator said, "Hold on, please. There's another call coming through for your number."

This time it was the Upton police sergeant. He had just heard about Raymond's death from his superintendent in Worcester, and he was very much offended that he hadn't been the first notified. She soothed him as best she could, and got him to admit that he was hemmed in by floodwaters and unable to act anyway.

"I can send one of my constables, when the dolts get round to reporting in by telephone."

Alec was unlikely to appreciate the arrival of a dolt, but it wasn't Daisy's place to dissuade him. She murmured assenting noises and said goodbye.

Should she go and warn Alec? No, the last thing she wanted was to be anywhere near poor Raymond's remains. She needed cheering up. A visit to the nursery would be the perfect antidote to the unpleasant events of the morning.

She glanced at the brass clock on the mantelpiece. Nearly three o'clock! Morning was long gone and she hadn't had any lunch, unless one counted half a glass of B and S. No wonder she had a hollow, sinking sensation in her middle. Food before fun, she decided. She would just pop down to the kitchen and beg Cook for some bread and cheese.

She was making for the door when Ernest reappeared. "Beg pardon, madam, I didn't know you was still in here." He held out an envelope. "Letter came for his lordship this morning marked *personal*, that got into Mr. Wharton's pile by mistake. My fault, and I've copped it proper from Mr. Wharton *and* Mr. Lowecroft. It says URGENT in big letters, see, in red ink and all, and *personal*'s writ small, so I didn't notice. I was going to leave it on the desk and mention it to his lordship when he comes in."

"He's not home yet?"

"No, madam."

"Oh dear, I wonder how urgent it is?" Daisy put out her hand and the footman passed over the letter. URGENT was indeed large and red and eye-catching. The postmark showed it had caught the last post. "I see what you mean. Thank you."

Ernest bowed and departed.

The handwriting was vaguely familiar. As she turned to put it on the desk, she glanced at the back of the envelope. The embossed address was the Pearsons'. "From Tommy!"

"Did you say something, madam?"

"Oh! No, thank you."

Daisy put the letter in the centre of the blotter, where it couldn't possibly be missed. She stared at it, and it stared back, pleadingly shouting, "*Urgent!*"

She picked it up again and studied the postmark. It had caught the last London post, long after Tommy's office was closed; addressed in Tommy's own writing, not his secretary's. Urgent.

Tommy was not accustomed to sealing his own letters. The flap was barely stuck down.

Daisy fought temptation, but not for long. After all, Edgar would undoubtedly hand over the letter to Geraldine, and Geraldine had involved Daisy in the business of finding the heir, right from the start. Tommy hadn't objected very strenuously, either. A letter from

188

the lawyer was undoubtedly business, not personal. Edgar wasn't at home. Geraldine hadn't yet returned from Worcester. It was really Daisy's duty to find out just what was so urgent, in case there was something she could do about it.

She checked to make sure one of the desk drawers contained a bottle of LePage glue, in case circumstances made it advisable to reseal the flap rather than confess her misdeed.

The letter was handwritten, like the envelope, on Tommy's personal stationery with the engraved address.

> *My dear Lord Dalrymple,*
>
> *I write in haste to inform you and her ladyship that a gentleman purporting to be Mr. Samuel Dalrymple of Kingston, Jamaica, called at my house this evening. The documents he carried appeared to support his claim to descent from Julius, Lord Dalrymple, by way of Julian Dalrymple of Jamaica, with further details about the family. However, due to an unavoidable engagement, I was unable to examine them thoroughly and Mr. Samuel declined to entrust them to me.*
>
> *He declared his intent of taking the early train to Worcester next day, namely Tuesday, and proceeding thence to Fairacres. I asked whether he would like to be met at the station, but he prefers to make his own way. I therefore cannot tell you at what time to expect him.*
>
> *As for his wife, allow me to suggest that you show Mrs. Fletcher this letter and ask her to break the news of her husband's coming to Mrs. Samuel.*
>
> *I have no appointments in the next two days that cannot easily be postponed. Should you wish me to come to Fairacres before Friday in order to enquire more closely into Mr. Samuel's claim, I shall be happy to oblige.*
>
> *Signed, Thomas Pearson, Solicitor.*

Breathing a sigh of relief, Daisy slipped the letter back into the envelope and laid it on the blotter. Though to read someone else's correspondence was a shocking breach of good manners, in view of the self-proclaimed urgency and the fact that the writer suggested showing it to her, she felt it was forgivable. She intended to confess, so she didn't bother to gum down the flap.

Besides, there was no hope of concealment of her sin, as she had to act on the information received.

What to do first? Her impulse was to go at once to tell Alec. Samuel had been in Worcester that very morning. Who was to say he hadn't attempted to push Raymond under a tram? However, Alec couldn't act on the possibility without some sort of evidence of foul play. No hurry.

She must break the news to Martha, in person, not on the telephone. No doubt Martha would return from the Dower House any minute for her afternoon nap. If Daisy walked over, she would probably miss her.

The butler and the housekeeper must be notified that another guest was expected. That could be done at once. Daisy rang the bell.

And now that Tommy Pearson had reminded her of his existence and involvement, she realised that he ought to know about the death of one of the prospective heirs. Apart from other considerations, he was the proper person to get in touch with Raymond's family in South Africa. Raymond's eldest son was now a candidate. . . .

"You rang, madam?"

"Ernest, I must speak to Mr. Lowecroft immediately. Also, please let me know at once when Mrs. Samuel comes in. And, come to think of it, her ladyship."

"Certainly, madam."

"And his lordship." She had to give Edgar his letter and confess that she had read it. "And if you see my husband, tell him I have news for him."

"I believe Mr. Fletcher is in the stables, madam. I can go and—"

"On no account! Just wait until he puts in an appearance."

"Very well, madam."

"That's all. Oh, Ernest," she added as the footman bowed and turned to leave, "would you bring me something to eat? I seem to have missed lunch and I'm ravenous. Bread and cheese will do."

He grinned at her. "Right away, madam."

Daisy contemplated the telephone. She had to send a wire to Tommy, worded discreetly, because no matter what the Post Office said, operators in country districts could not be relied on not to wag their tongues. The news of Raymond's death would be common knowledge soon enough without such assistance.

In the end, she kept it simple: *RAYMOND DIED TODAY CAUSE UNKNOWN*. She wasn't getting her—or rather, Edgar's— shillingsworth, but there really wasn't anything more to be said without telling the whole complicated story. After all, it didn't matter much if the villagers knew he was dead. The devil was in the details.

Lowecroft came in while she was dictating the telegram. Though he must have heard the message, he preserved the myth that a butler hears what is spoken by his betters only when it is directed to his ears.

As Daisy hung up, he said, "You wished to speak to me, madam?"

"We're expecting another guest, Lowecroft." She could have had Ernest tell him, but he would have been deeply offended. Hierarchy must be observed. "I understand Mr. Samuel Dalrymple is on his way. I'm afraid I don't know when he'll get here."

"No matter, madam. Everything will be set in readiness to receive Mr. Samuel. If I may mention it, madam, I believe I saw Lady John's car arriving. No doubt Mrs. Samuel has returned from her visit."

"Good! I expect she'll want to go upstairs for a rest. Please tell her I'd like a word with her and I'll come up to her room if she prefers."

"Very good, madam."

"Don't let anyone tell her about Mr. Samuel before I do."

"Certainly not, madam. There is no reason," he said austerely, "for anyone other than Mrs. Warden to know whose arrival we are preparing for." He paused for a perfectly judged moment to see whether she had anything else to say, then bowed and made his stately way out.

He crossed paths with Ernest bringing a tray. On it were home-farm cheese, home-farm butter, home-baked bread, a couple of ripe plums, and a glass of local cider, made from a mixture of apple and pear juice.

"Perfect," said Daisy.

She had her mouth full when Lowecroft returned to say that Mrs. Samuel would be happy to see her upstairs in ten minutes. "Also, madam, the Vauxhall has just returned with, I presume, her ladyship and the rest of the party."

"Blast!" She managed not to spray crumbs at the butler, but one went down the wrong way. Spluttering, she wondered why everything had to happen at once.

"May I suggest, madam, that I should draw her ladyship aside and apprise her privately of Mr. Samuel's expected appearance?"

Daisy brought her cough under control. "Yes, please, Lowecroft. And ask her if I can see her in—" How long would it take to break the news to Martha? Would she weep and have to be soothed? Daisy could hardly tell her and immediately rush off. "In half an hour."

What would irritate Alec more, further delay in getting the information or a servant with a note looking for him in the stables with the body in the car? He'd better wait.

She finished her late lunch and went up to Martha's room.

Martha was reclining on the chaise longue in the negligée they had picked out together at Selfridge's, sipping a cup of mint tea. She put down the cup on the small table at her side. "It tastes a bit funny. Not nasty, still sort of minty, but not very nice."

"Perhaps it's a different kind of mint. Laurette was saying the French make tisanes from other kinds of mint, and all sorts of herbs. Or it might just be that your taste buds have changed. I found I liked things I'd always disliked and vice versa."

"Oh yes, I've noticed that. What did you want to see me about?"

"Good news, Martha."

"Sammy?" Her face lit up and she clasped her hands. "He's safe?"

"Not merely safe, darling, he's on his way to Fairacres."

"He's in England already?"

"He saw Mr. Pearson yesterday in London and told him he was taking the train to Worcester. I don't know why Worcester. Malvern's closer to Fairacres."

"I expect he wanted to see Worcester. He's always been interested in travelling and seeing foreign places. That's why he enjoys being a sailor. His friends think he's a bit odd because when they're in port he doesn't head for the nearest tavern, he goes strolling about the town. Which is good, because he brings most of his pay home!"

Daisy smiled. "Very good. So he probably wandered about Worcester this morning and will turn up any minute."

"He may decide to walk, to see the countryside. It's such a lovely day. Violet and I had lunch in the garden. Lady Dalrymple—your mother—was out for lunch."

They exchanged a glance of understanding. The dowager's icy politeness would be enough to put anyone off accepting an invitation to lunch—which would probably not have been extended in the first place.

"Well, I'll leave you to take your nap. You'll want to be rested when he comes. I'm very happy for you that he escaped from Florida intact and that he's nearly here."

"Oh Daisy, I'm so relieved! All I need now is my girls."

"One way or another, I expect it won't be long before you're reunited. Sleep well."

With a few minutes to spare, she went to change from her cathedral-visiting outfit into a summer frock, wash her face, tidy her hair, and powder her nose, armouring herself against Geraldine's righteous wrath. All this she accomplished automatically, while ruminating on Martha's reaction. She had been surprised and relieved to hear that Sam was on his way. Daisy didn't believe she could have convincingly acted the part. She was a simple, straightforward person.

She returned to Edgar's study to retrieve Tommy's letter. Waiting for Geraldine to join her or to summon her was as nerve-wracking as waiting to confess some misdeed to her old headmistress.

When the phone rang, she was glad to be distracted—until she picked up the receiver and heard the operator announce, "I have a person-to-person trunk call from Mr. Crane in London. Is Mr. Fletcher available?"

The Super! Alec would undoubtedly be happier not knowing

about the call, but his superior couldn't be avoided forever. "I can go and look for him. It may take a little while."

"Is that Mrs. Fletcher?" Superintendent Crane's voice boomed along the line, unimpeded by the usual crackles and hisses.

"Speaking," Daisy said reluctantly.

"Caller, do you wish to be connected?"

"Yes! She'll do, for the moment."

Thanks very much! Daisy said silently, leaning against the desk. "What can I do for you, Mr. Crane?"

"Tell me what's going on," he snapped. "The Worcestershire chief constable wired some cock and bull story about a series of accidents, which hardly seems enough to call for our services."

"It probably isn't. But now, one of the accidents has proved fatal, and Alec can hardly ignore it. He went to examine the body. Given how long he's been gone, I shouldn't be surprised if the local police surgeon is with him by now."

"Who is the deceased?"

"A distant c-cousin of mine." Daisy was annoyed to hear her voice wobble. She hadn't even liked Raymond!

"My condolences, Mrs. Fletcher. I'm sorry, I didn't realise your family were personally involved. Have all the accidents—"

"Yes. It's a family gathering." She started to explain the search for an heir.

"Your time is up, caller. Do you want another three minutes?"

"Yes, yes, as long as it takes. Go on, Mrs. Fletcher."

Daisy tried to be brief. "So you see," she finished, "they may be accidents or they may be . . . something else."

"Hmmmm, yes. It does sound a bit much for the county force to handle. And since Fletcher is on the spot . . . Yes, if he's willing to do a bit of investigating on his own time, I'll talk to the AC about acceding to the CC's request."

"Could you send DS Tring and DS Piper?" Daisy knew Alec had wanted Ernie Piper, newly elevated to sergeant, and Tom Tring to lend a hand, even before Raymond's death.

"Mrs. Fletcher, you're not even sure whether a crime has been committed. We're shorthanded, as usual. I can't authorise seconding busy officers to sort out your family's machinations. I'll tell you what, though. If and when Fletcher has proof that a serious crime has been committed, I'll see that he gets those two men."

"Thank you, Mr. Crane."

"I know they're both accustomed to coping with your interfere . . . ah . . . presence in an investigation."

"They're both friends of mine," Daisy said with dignity.

"Hmm. And don't go putting yourself in danger."

"Don't worry, I won't. It's sweet of you to care."

The superintendent made gargling noises. She could practically hear him blush. He mumbled something, then continued in a more characteristic sarcastic tone, "Thank you for casting a little light on what seems to be a thoroughly obscure situation. Perhaps you'd have the goodness to ask your husband to get in touch if he can find a spare moment."

Daisy promised she would and they rang off.

What next? Oh yes, Geraldine and grovelling apologies.

TWENTY-THREE

Picking up Edgar's letter from Tommy, Daisy glanced at the clock. Forty minutes since she had told Lowecroft half an hour. She hoped Geraldine wasn't waiting for her somewhere else, adding tardiness to her causes for complaint.

But Geraldine came in, looking a bit frayed at the edges. She sank wearily into a chair by the desk. "I vow, if Vincent is Edgar's heir and Laurette wants to move into Fairacres, I'm moving out! What was it you wanted to tell me, Daisy? Thank you, by the way, for coming home with Raymond."

"I imagine Laurette told you about his fall."

"Never stopped talking about it! How is he? I've been too busy since I got home to—Daisy! What is it?"

"Raymond. He . . . he died on the way home."

"Oh, my dear!" Geraldine sprang up and swooped on Daisy to enfold her in her arms. It was a somewhat bony embrace, but for the first time Daisy could imagine her mothering Edgar's pupils, not just disciplining them. "You shouldn't have had to cope with that. I'm glad Alec came back to see what was going on. I presume he's . . . dealing with things now?"

"Yes. I'm afraid he's having to deal with it as a police matter."

"As I anticipated. Sir Nigel said he was going to talk to the Assistant Commissioner at Scotland Yard about what's been going on here. I would have expected the local police to manage, with Alec's help. After all, what we described to him was just a string of odd accidents. Now that a death is involved, I'm glad he took that step."

"I've just taken a call from Superintendent Crane, at the Yard. Alec's officially on the case. I must go and tell him, but first . . . Geraldine, I'm most frightfully sorry." She handed over the opened envelope. "I read Tommy's letter to Edgar. Apparently it went to the bailiff by mistake so it was delayed, and it's marked *urgent*, and neither you nor Edgar was here, and considering everything that's happened, I decided . . . Shockingly bad form, but it seemed like a good idea at the time."

"In the circumstances . . ." Geraldine took out the letter and quickly read it. "Ah, the missing Samuel. In the circumstances, I consider your action entirely justified. After all, Mr. Pearson might have written to tell us Frank Crowley's been unmasked as a kidnapper and forger—"

"What! You don't like Frank, I gather."

"I like him very well. He's an amiable, obliging sort."

"You don't trust him?"

"Not as far as I could throw him. It wouldn't surprise me in the least if he were a forger. However, I'm certain Derek and Belinda would know by now, and have told us, if Ben had been kidnapped, so we can acquit Frank of that. In any case, that was not what Mr. Pearson wrote about."

"I can't help feeling he would have sent a cable!"

"Very likely. You've broken the news of Samuel's coming to Martha?"

"Yes indeed. She's tickled pink. And now, if you're not going to haul me over the coals for reading the letter, I must go and tell Alec."

"Tell him if there's anything I, or Edgar, or the household can do to help, it shall be done."

"Thank you for being so understanding."

"Believe me, Daisy, the thought of going through all this without you and Alec to support us is . . . inconceivable!"

197

"All the same, it won't hurt to have Tommy here too. If I were you, I'd wire him to come at once." She pushed the telephone towards Geraldine.

"You're right. I think I will."

Daisy went to find Alec. Ernest, never the most wooden of footmen, told her with obvious curiosity that Smethwick had brought a message from Mr. Fletcher: He was going into Morton Green to send some cables from the post office.

"Mr. Fletcher got a lift with a gentleman that came about the same time as the ambulance. They was round at the stables. Smethwick wouldn't say what was going on. Said the Chief Inspector—Mr. Fletcher, I should say—swore him to silence. But I cou'n't help noticing, madam, Mr. Raymond didn't come home with the rest. He's not been took ill, I hope?"

"Sorry, Ernest. I've been sworn to silence as well. Did Mr. Fletcher intend to walk back from the village? I think I'll go to meet him."

It was a beautiful afternoon, sunny and warm but not humid and oppressive. Daisy started out across the park on the path that led to the Dower House, then took the right-hand branch towards the village. The beige Jersey cows lay chewing the cud under the scattered oaks and chestnuts or paced slowly across the slope, bright green after the rain, cropping the grass short as they went.

The distant crack of a rook rifle, familiar from childhood, reminded Daisy that all was not as peaceful as it seemed. In the orchards, birds were gorging on ripe fruit. She hoped the shooter had scared them off without killing any.

Before she reached the top of the hill, Alec came over the crest. She waved but, lost in thought, he didn't respond.

"Alec!"

He looked up and his pace quickened. The only spectators being bovine, they met with a kiss before walking down towards the house, arm in arm.

"Who did you send cables to, darling? Let me rephrase that: To whom did you send cables?"

"Haven't you left something off the second version?"

"To whom did you send cables, *darling*?"

"That's better. First I rang up Sir Nigel to make sure the county force would pay for them, because I wired South Africa and Jamaica and Trinidad, as well as Scarborough. Pearson investigated their ancestry. I want more information about their present-day families, their backgrounds, their way of life."

"Raymond's as well?"

"*If* his death was no accident, it was not necessarily associated with the inheritance."

"Diamonds!"

Alec reached into his inside breast pocket and produced a small wash-leather pouch, closed with a tightly tied drawstring. "Diamonds."

"Let me see."

He opened the bag and showed her a handful of grey and yellowish pebbles. Some looked like lumps of glass or quartz, some just like bits of gravel. "Not very spectacular." He retied the string and returned them to his pocket.

"Have you any idea what they're worth? Where did you find them?"

"Not a clue. He had a secret pocket sewn into the lining of his jacket—all his jackets, I expect. Dealers in gemstones often choose to carry their merchandise on their persons when travelling, rather than trust an unknown safe. I assume Edgar has a safe I can lock these in?"

"Father did. I doubt he's got rid of it. Do you think Raymond could have been the target of a thief? It was rather a public place for robbery."

"Lots of people and general confusion, perfect place for an expert pickpocket. One to push him at the tram—the police surgeon, Pardoe, found a suspicious bruise on his back."

"He said 'Someone pushed . . .' The bobby assumed he meant someone pushed him out of the way of the tram."

"One to push him towards the tram; one to save him and abstract the loot at the same time, then scarper with it."

"Only he was foiled by the secret pocket."

"At any rate, it's not a possibility I can dismiss, though the chances of identifying the putative culprits are dim. The local coppers are working on it, but not exactly enthusiastically."

"Was his wallet pinched?"

"No. Either the whole theory is bosh, or they were after bigger game and not interested in the few pounds it contained."

"Someone who knew he had diamonds on him. Someone at Fairacres?"

"They might have found out about the diamonds. They'd have a hard time summoning up an expert pickpocket, though, in the few days they've been here."

"Unless one of them is already a pickpocket. Frank? We don't know anything about how he makes a living—at least, I don't."

"One to push and one to pick. In collusion with . . . ?"

"Martha's Sammy. I hate to say it but . . . They both come from the West Indies. Sammy travels a lot. He could well know that one of the family emigrated to Trinidad and go looking for descendants. Oh, wait, Frank isn't a descendant."

Alec laughed. "No. Much more likely to be someone Raymond had business dealings with in London, or on the Continent, or someone from South Africa."

"Hence the cable? To the Cape Town police?"

"To them, and to the business. He had business cards in the wallet, so I thought I'd better inform them of his death."

"I sent a wire to Tommy, telling him. I expect he'll notify Raymond's immediate family. Alec, I've just thought: Could he have been stabbed with something very thin, like the Empress Elizabeth? She walked on and then collapsed and died, just like Raymond. If I'm remembering it right, the wound hardly bled at all."

"Dr. Pardoe would probably have seen it, presumably in the centre of the bruise. He'd certainly find out when he does the autopsy."

"I suppose so." Daisy didn't care to think about the autopsy. She changed the subject. "Darling, there was a letter from Tommy to Edgar, but as he's still out with the children, Geraldine read it." The truth, if not quite the whole truth. "He says Martha's Sammy has turned up! That's really what I was coming to tell you. Sammy was supposed to reach Worcester this morning and should arrive at Fairacres this afternoon."

"Hmm. I'll take another look at a possible connection between Frank and Sammy. Pearson's satisfied with his credentials?"

"To a degree. He's apparently sure enough of his descent from Julian, but he wanted more time to study the papers he brought, which he wouldn't leave with him. Sammy wouldn't leave with Tommy, that is. I think Geraldine's inviting Tommy to come down as soon as possible."

"Good idea."

"The other thing I have to tell you is that the Super rang and gave me an earful."

"The local man, or Crane?"

"Crane. As you weren't immediately available, he said I'd 'do.' He just wanted someone to rant at. He said you can assist the locals, but you won't get days off to make up for it."

"What cheek!" said Alec. "Worcestershire will pay the Met for my services, but they'll take it off my holiday!"

"Perhaps he'll relent. He refused to send Tom and Ernie, though, till you're certain it's murder. In that case, he'll make sure you get the two of them. Because they're accustomed to my . . . assistance in your cases, he said, rather snarkily. All the same, he actually sounded almost genial in the end. Do you suppose he's getting resigned?"

"Resigned?"

"To me."

"I doubt it, love. He's been told blowing up is bad for his blood pressure. Blood pressure—Great Scott! I wonder whether . . ."

Daisy waited a moment for him to finish, then asked, "Whether what?"

"Never mind. The autopsy will tell us. As for the Super," Alec added sourly, "no doubt he's enjoying ruining another holiday for me."

"Come on, darling, you know you're dying to get your teeth into it."

"Always supposing there's actually something to get them into.

And you keep your teeth out of it! I wish you could take the children home, but you'll have to appear at the inquest."

"We could send Bel and the twins home with Mrs. Gilpin. But what about Derek? Vi really isn't well enough to handle him. And more to the point, what about Ben? He's a target, if anyone is. We can't leave him here on his own."

"Nor send him with the others. He'd carry the risk, if any, along with him. To tell the truth, I have a 'hunch,' as the Americans say, that he's safe here, and the others as well. If that damn butterfly net had been intended to kill, it would have been placed at the top of the stairs, not so near the foot. It was a feint, and I don't know why. I just can't work out what's going on."

"It *is* strange. The butterfly net is the only actual clue, and Edgar was always leaving it all over the place. Anyone could have got it. He's already sent for a new one, by the way. His old spare is full of holes. Bigger holes than it's supposed to have."

"Moth holes?"

Daisy laughed. "Holes big enough for moths to get through, at least."

"Just like this case. If there is one."

TWENTY-FOUR

"*Ahoy there!*" From behind them came the voice of a sailor used to hailing nearby ships through the roar of wind and wave.

Daisy and Alec swung round. Down the hill, his tread jaunty yet as firm as if beneath his feet was an ever shifting deck, strode a hatless man in a blue jacket, duck trousers, and seaman's boots. His hair was dark gold and curly, on the long side, dishevelled by the breeze. Over his shoulder, he carried a large kit bag.

"Martha's Sammy, I presume," said Daisy, waving.

"Who but?"

They waited for him to catch up.

"This is Fairacres? I'm Samuel Dalrymple, out of Kingston, Jamaica," he introduced himself. He spoke with only a slight trace of the melodic Jamaican accent, smoothed by constant contact with the people of many lands, no doubt.

"How do you do." Daisy shook hands. "I'm Daisy Fletcher, née Dalrymple. You and I are some sort of cousins. And this is my husband. . . ." She glanced at Alec, who gave a slight nod. Anyone who didn't know yet who he was soon would. "Detective Chief Inspector Alec Fletcher."

Samuel took the announcement without a blink. Alec shook hands, which he generally avoided with suspects, but as yet he had little reason for suspicion. Besides, it was impossible not to respond to that cheerful grin and the twinkle in the blue eyes.

He turned back to Daisy. "Martha's here? My wife?"

"She came down with us. I've grown very fond of her. She stayed with us in London for several weeks."

"With you? Mr. Pearson told me a relative of mine had taken her in. I can't thank you enough, Mrs. Fletcher. Who could have guessed that my quiet little sweetheart would embark on such an adventure? You can't imagine how I felt when I got home and found she'd left for England! But I'm proud of her."

"She must have caught the spirit of adventure from her husband," Alec said drily.

"Ah, you've heard about my latest voyage, Mr. Policeman." Samuel grinned. "I'm glad you're not an American cop. It got a bit exciting at times, but I don't regret it. If this business hadn't come up—" His expansive gesture took in the mansion and all its surroundings "—I'd still have enough to be able to provide a decent living for my family without being away so much of the time."

"Well done," said Daisy, who had no moral objection to a little lawbreaking in a good cause. "Did you manage to see your daughters on your way here from America?"

"Yes. I wish I could have brought them with me, but I worked my way over. No sense in wasting good money. I'll go fetch 'em when everything's settled. In the meantime, there'll be a little brother or sister for them, as you'll surely have noticed by now. I can't thank you enough for taking care of my Martha. How is she doing, Mrs. Fletcher?"

"Very well, apart from a bit of indigestion. Come in and I'll take you to see her before we go through all the introductions. By the way, we're all rather on christian name terms here, as there are swarms of Dalrymples staying here."

"You're welcome to call me Sam."

The front door stood open to the afternoon warmth. Nonetheless, as they stepped into the hall, Ernest appeared.

"Footman," Daisy explained in an undertone. "Ernest, this is Mr. Samuel."

Ernest bowed slightly, and Samuel nodded, to the manner born. "The carrier will be delivering my chest, if it hasn't yet arrived."

"Not to my knowledge, sir. I shall enquire."

"Is Mrs. Samuel still upstairs?"

"Yes, madam."

"I'll take Mr. Samuel up. Tell her ladyship he's arrived, please."

"Lord Dalrymple's not back yet?" Alec asked. "I'd better see Lady Dalrymple."

"Her ladyship is in her sitting room, I believe, sir."

During this exchange, Samuel glanced about the spacious hall. As he and Daisy made for the stairs, he said, "Plenty of room for a swarm of Dalrymples in here all right." He didn't sound overawed, just reflective. "It'll be interesting to meet my long-lost relatives."

"I'll be happy to introduce you to all the portraits, too."

He laughed. "I'm happy to postpone that pleasure. Did you grow up here?"

"Yes, my father was the last—the previous—viscount, before Cousin Edgar. My mother resides at the Dower House, but you don't have to deal with that yet. My sister's staying with her. She and Martha are quite friendly. Here we are." She knocked on Martha's door. "It's Daisy."

"Come in."

Daisy stuck her head round the door. "There's someone to see you." She stood back and let Samuel past.

"Sammy! Oh Sammy!"

Daisy quietly closed the door behind him and went back downstairs.

As she trudged along the passage towards Geraldine's sitting room, the door at the end opened. Edgar came in, followed by his three acolytes. All four were grubby, in stockinged feet, carrying muddy boots.

"Mummy!" cried Bel, "we found so much stuff for Uncle Edgar." She dropped her boots and started to take off her knapsack—Edgar's solution to the perennial problem of the lack of decent-sized pockets in girls' clothes. "You should see—"

"Not now, darling! You three go right back out and round the house to the conservatory. Unload your collections, then upstairs and clean up. Nursery tea today."

Derek protested, "Uncle Edgar said—"

"Out!"

Muttering apologies, the three filed back out. Edgar started to follow, saying, "Sorry! You're quite right. Not the thing to traipse through the house like this but we left the bicycles and the dogs in the stables—"

"Not you, Edgar." Daisy tugged his sleeve, urging him towards Geraldine's sitting room.

He glanced down at himself. "Not like this, my dear. Geraldine won't care for—"

"Never mind that. You're needed."

Bewildered, he padded after her. She knocked but didn't wait for a response. He set down his boots neatly to one side of the door and followed her in.

Alec stood up. Geraldine looked round, blinked, and said, "Edgar, really! I could wish you hadn't transferred your affections from the Lepidoptera to the Odonata. Hunting butterflies involved a good deal less mud."

"My fault," said Daisy. "And I practically dragged him in here."

"No, no, my dear." He patted her hand, leaving a smear of mud.

"I'm glad you've come, sir," said Alec. "We have a great deal to tell you, and the sooner the better."

Daisy sat down beside Geraldine, and Edgar made for a nearby brocade-covered seat.

"Not there, Edgar!"

Alec placed a cane-bottom chair for the beleaguered peer.

"Thank you, my dear fellow."

"Thank *you* for keeping Belinda and the boys out of the way all day. It was a relief not to have to worry about what they were up to."

"Delightful children, high-spirited but always polite and obliging. It was my pleasure."

"Alec, please tell him what's happened," Geraldine said impatiently.

"Bad news, I'm afraid, sir. Raymond was involved in an accident in Worcester and has since died."

"Died!" Edgar was horrified. "I was under the impression that the mishaps we've been suffering were simply coincidental accidents, or perhaps a series of practical jokes."

"I daresay Alec's profession makes him more suspicious than most," Geraldine allowed. "Sir Nigel intimated as much. But Raymond's death alters the picture."

"I can see that, my dear."

"Unfortunately," said Alec, "it doesn't make the picture any clearer. We can't be sure whether the accident was, in fact, sheer bad luck, or if not, whether the attack had any connection with what's been going on here, or even whether the incident caused his death."

Edgar took off his pince-nez and blinked earnestly at Alec as he polished a few daubs of mud off the lenses. "I see your difficulty. Is Wookleigh taking the matter seriously? Willing to provide aid and assistance in such dubious circumstances?"

"Lady Dalrymple put it to him most forcefully, sir," Alec said dryly. "After initial scepticism, he became most cooperative, even before Raymond's death, and now he's bending over backwards to pass the whole thing on to Scotland Yard."

"And your superior at Scotland Yard? Do you wish me, or better Geraldine, to speak to him?"

"I appreciate the offer." His voice had become, if possible, even dryer. "But the chief constable's request for help should be sufficient. With any luck, my sergeants will be on their way in the morning. Meanwhile, the local police surgeon is preparing to conduct a post mortem examination—"

"Surely that's not necessary!" Edgar exclaimed in distress.

"Of course it is, Edgar," said Geraldine. "If we don't know *what* killed Raymond, how can we possible discover *who* killed him?"

"There's also the question of *why*," Alec added.

"Not for the inheritance?"

"Could be. Or could be these." He took out the little bag he had found in Raymond's secret pocket. "Diamonds. At least, so I assume."

"Good gracious! Apparently they weren't taken, though."

"He had them well hidden. You have a safe, sir? The sooner they're locked away, the happier I'll be."

"Certainly. In my den." Edgar started to get up.

"Just a minute," said Daisy. "Don't go before you hear the good news. Martha's Samuel has arrived."

"Oh dear!" Geraldine jumped up in her turn. "And neither of us there to greet him. Why on earth didn't Lowecroft announce him?"

"My fault. I took him straight up to Martha."

Edgar beamed. "Quite right, my dear."

Geraldine, more conscious of the proprieties, said with a touch of austerity, "I trust they were happy to see each other." Thawing a bit, she added, "They've been separated for a long time, and Martha anxious about his well-being, as well. Do they mean to come down for tea?"

"I expect so. Sam walked from Worcester so he must be hungry."

"Walked!"

"Martha says he enjoys exploring new places."

"Ten or twelve miles is nothing to a healthy young man, my dear. In fact, I daresay I walk as far on some of my little expeditions." Edgar scratched absently at a smear of drying mud on his cheek. A blob crumbled and dropped to the carpet. "Alec, Samuel must be warned about the possibility of an attack. I don't wish to sound melodramatic, but here he is, newly arrived in England, newly arrived at Fairacres, quite unaware that he may be in danger."

"You're right. I'll explain the situation to him. Daisy, does Martha know what's going on? Or rather, what we fear may be going on?"

"Not really. I mean, she knows Belinda and Ben both had falls, but considering the way they all racket about, she doesn't think anything of it. She was there on the terrace when Vincent came back limping. She hasn't put them together. And I haven't told her about

Raymond. Of course, she'll have to know about that, but I don't think she ought to have the rest spelt out for her."

"Definitely not," said Geraldine.

"I rather doubt she's as fragile as you suppose. I seem to remember Daisy surviving an adventure or two in the same condition! But I bow to your judgment, ladies. However, I must remind you that we have no evidence other than his own word that Samuel has only just arrived in England, nor that he and Martha have not been in touch."

"True, alas," Edgar admitted with a heavy sigh. "I hate to say it of my own kin, but there's not one of them we can trust, except—"

"Remember the diamonds, Edgar," Geraldine interrupted. "If Raymond was killed for those, he still might have been responsible for the rest."

"I realise that, my dear. I was going to say, except for Ben. I cannot and will not believe the boy responsible, whatever the failings of his guardian."

"Cheer up, Cousin Edgar," said Daisy. "Frank Crowley is no kin of yours and mine."

"But not therefore beyond suspicion," Alec reminded them.

Edgar shook his head sadly. "Ben looks up to him. He might reasonably expect to control the estate, or at least to profit from it, if the boy inherited. What I don't understand is how anyone profits from Raymond's death. He has a son in Cape Town, does he not, my dear?"

"So Mr. Pearson told me," Geraldine agreed. "It makes one suppose the diamonds were indeed the motive, if it wasn't pure accident."

"Vincent has a son," said Daisy. "Benjamin has a brother."

"It's all very puzzling."

"It is indeed, sir," said Alec. "I hope the queries I've put out will bring some clarity. At best, we'll find it's just a fortuitous series of accidents, though what Sir Nigel and Superintendent Crane will have to say in that case, I hate to think!"

"You let me worry about Sir Nigel," Geraldine said staunchly.

"As far as the Super's concerned," said Daisy, "you can blame it all on me. He probably will, anyway."

Alec gave an ironic bow. "Thank you for your protection, ladies!"

"That's all very well," said Edgar, "but it seems to me we ought to be thinking about how to protect young Benjamin. Little though I want to send him away, God knows, perhaps it would be safest."

"Alec and I have discussed that. We didn't really come to any conclusion, did we, darling? But on the whole I think he'll be safer here, where we can all keep an eye on him. I'm going to talk to Belinda and Derek—"

"Edgar should talk to Derek," Geraldine said, "and Benjamin, come to that. Unless he's lost his touch—"

"Really, my dear, I trust not!"

"—he's extremely good with boys that age and I'm sure can make them see it as an adventure."

"Then I wish you'd include Bel, Edgar. She enjoys expeditions with you just as much as the boys do."

"By all means, Daisy. She's a very sensible young lady."

Alec nodded in agreement and consent. "I wonder whether it's worth trying to get Frank Crowley to take a hand. His sense of responsibility towards Ben has limits I have yet to fathom."

"He spends a good deal of time at the Wedge and Beetle," Geraldine said austerely.

"He feels more at home there," said Alec. "I can understand that. Perhaps he'll find a fellow spirit in Sam—"

"And they'll go off carousing together! Though I must admit, Mr. Crowley has never come back visibly intoxicated."

"I was going to say, who'll keep him closer to home. Unless, of course, they're trying to kill each other."

TWENTY-FIVE

Martha came down on Sam's arm to tea on the terrace. She was radiant as, with obvious pride, she introduced him to everyone. Daisy felt happier just looking at her. Geraldine was every inch the gracious hostess. She invited him to sit beside her and plied him with tea and questions.

"I hope you had good weather for your voyage. When did you arrive in England?"

"Just a couple of days ago," he said cheerfully, without hesitation. "I've been in America."

"So I heard."

Sam grinned. "Yes, well, a successful trip, though not without a bit of excitement. Then I had a fair amount of business to be done in Jamaica. I was lucky to get a first mate's berth for an Atlantic crossing when I did. Sometimes you have to wait quite a while, or settle for second officer, but my friends were looking out for a place for me."

Frank joined in the conversation. Vincent and Laurette listened, but they kept looked round, as if wondering where Raymond was. Martha, her fond gaze on her Sammy, sipped her tea and pulled a face, then drank it at a gulp, as if it were medicine. Either it was the wrong kind of mint again or her taste buds were still out of order, Daisy guessed.

Alec had asked Daisy, Edgar, and Geraldine not to announce Raymond's death to the others. He wanted to see who would ask after him first, and how each would react to the news. Geraldine was to keep a close watch on Sam and Martha, Daisy on Vincent and Laurette, and Edgar on Frank Crowley, while Alec had a good view of everyone from his seat on the wall.

Laurette grew more and more disturbed and at last said, "Daisy, do you know how Raymond goes? It seemed to me that he was *à peine*—not much—shaken by his fall, but he hasn't come to tea. Does he find himself unwell?"

"I'm afraid there's bad news, Laurette. Edgar was going to tell everyone after tea, so as not to spoil Sam's welcome, but since you ask . . ." She glanced at Edgar who, well-primed by Alec, nodded assent. "Raymond died on the way home."

Laurette was aghast. "*Mais, ma foi, c'est inouï!* Impossible! A small fall, it does not cause the death."

"Did you see him fall?" Alec asked.

"*Non, non.* I was with Daisy. We were not close and the tramway blocked our view. We saw that something happens. The policeman blows the whistle. All vehicles cease to move. But Raymond we did not see until a policeman helps him to the pavement. He felt himself weak from shock. This is natural. But to die . . . impossible."

"Impossible," Vincent echoed. His face was very pale. Daisy wondered if he was thinking of his own "accident" in the wood and whether it could have proved fatal.

"Nonetheless, he is dead."

"Poor old chap!" said Frank, without much concern. "I'm sorry to hear it."

Alec looked round. "You were all in Worcester this morning except for Martha and Lord Dalrymple. Did anyone see Raymond fall?"

Daisy kept her gaze on Vincent and Laurette as instructed, but from the corners of her eyes she saw the others shake their heads, as did Vincent.

"This whistle-blowing policeman," said Frank, "he must have seen the whole thing."

"Not clearly," Alec said. "It's a busy corner and directing traffic is his job. He glimpsed a pedestrian stumbling into the path of a tram. Thereafter he concentrated on stopping the traffic in every direction. He couldn't provide any useful description of the person who saved Raymond from the wheels. All we know is that it was a man in a hat, an ordinary sort of bloke."

"'*We* know?'" Frank asked with lively interest. He made no effort to put on a show of mourning for Raymond.

"Mr. Fletcher is a copper," Sam revealed. "A detective."

"What?" Frank immediately looked shifty, casting a sidelong glance at Alec. "How do you know?"

"Martha stayed with the Fletchers in London for several weeks. She wrote to her sister at home, so I found out when I returned to Kingston. I'm a sailor by profession, if you didn't know."

"Someone mentioned it. Ever been to Trinidad?"

Sam had. The two young men were soon caught up in a comparison of Port of Spain and Kingston, Raymond's death for the moment forgotten.

Vincent and Laurette, upon whom Daisy was supposed to be concentrating, talked to each other in undertones, looking decidedly glum. In fact, Laurette looked distraught. Daisy moved to sit beside her.

"I'm sorry," she said. "It's a horrid thing to have happened. I wish I'd realised sooner how badly hurt he was. I'd have taken him straight to a doctor instead of bringing him back to Fairacres."

"He didn't tell you he felt really ill?" Vincent asked anxiously. "Did he say anything about the accident, how it happened?"

"No, he didn't speak after the bobbies helped him into the car."

"Then I don't see how you can blame yourself," he said with relief.

Daisy was touched by his concern. "Still, I can't help hoping the postmortem will show even immediate medical care couldn't have saved him."

"Postmortem!" Laurette exclaimed in horror. "*L'autopsie?*"

"It's required, as he didn't have a doctor in attendance to give a death certificate. They have to find out what he died of so that they can report to the coroner."

"You mean there will be an inquest?" Vincent was outraged. "Surely they can't expect a viscount and his family to attend an inquest."

"I can't see any reason you would be expected to, unless you know something pertinent about his health."

"Of course I don't."

"Laurette might be called," said Daisy, "as we were both with him waiting for his car, and in the car for a couple of minutes. I doubt it, though, as she won't be able to tell them anything I can't. I'm sure to have to give evidence, as I was with him when he died. Not necessarily right away, though, if the police ask for an adjournment to give them time to investigate."

"I can't see that there's anything for the police to investigate."

"Vincent, *je ne puis supporter ça encore un instant.*"

"*Bien, chérie.* If you'll excuse us, Daisy, Laurette is very distressed, as you can see. She'll be the better for a stroll in the garden." He presented their excuses to Geraldine; the couple went down the terrace steps and headed for the shade of the pleached alley.

Daisy watched. Vincent hadn't brought his stick. He was walking normally without it, even with Laurette leaning on his arm. He, at least, had recovered from his "accident." She noticed that Alec, also, was watching them, with narrowed eyes. She went to sit beside him on the wall.

"What's bitten those two?"

"It was rather insensitive of me, I suppose, when Laurette was obviously upset by what happened to Raymond. I mentioned the autopsy and the inquest, and she said she couldn't stand it any longer."

"Would you say she was genuinely upset?"

"Oh yes, and Vincent too. Not suffering from grief, I would say, but shocked and horrified. I wondered whether they were thinking that *his* accident could have been a serious attempt on his life."

"I see he's not using his walking stick. What about this morning?"

"He did say something about not wanting to tackle the steps up the tower. I don't remember if he had his stick. "

"Damn, neither do I."

"But he might have taken it in case of need for a walk of indefinite duration round the town, yet not for a stroll in the garden."

"True." He looked up as Ernest came out. The footman bore a silver salver on which reposed a pinkish-buff telegram envelope and a paper knife. "What now, I wonder?"

Ernest presented the telegram to Geraldine. "The evening post has come, my lady. Mr. Lowecroft said to bring you this immediately."

"Thank you, Ernest. Fresh tea and hot water, please. Please excuse me," she said to her immediate neighbours, slitting the envelope. The message took only a moment to read. She refolded the form and asked Ernest to take it to Alec.

"With her ladyship's compliments," he said, lowering his voice to add, "If there's anything doing, sir, you know as I'm game."

"I do, Ernest. I've not forgotten your assistance. Nothing at present, but I'll keep your offer in mind."

The footman bowed with a grin, then wiped it from his face and, with a suitably impassive expression, took himself off to collect teapots and hot-water jugs.

"Pearson can't make it down here till Thursday evening," Alec told Daisy, showing her the telegram.

"Bother! That means we'll have to wait till then to know what documents Sam has up his sleeve. Can you make him show you?"

"Questionable. Even if this turns out to be a case for the police, I'd probably have to get a court order. Unless there's strong evidence that they're relevant to a criminal investigation, which seems unlikely."

"But it may show us who's the real heir!"

"I must have a talk with him anyway."

215

"I'll take notes," Daisy said eagerly.

"No notes. An informal chat to put him in the picture."

"And winkle out as much information as you can."

"Of course. Perhaps he'll voluntarily tell me about the heirs. Assuming he knows. Pearson didn't actually say so, I gather."

"He's a cautious lawyer. I'm sure . . . *pretty* sure that's what he meant. I can't see why Sam wouldn't be willing to tell us—"

"Not 'us.' I don't want you getting any deeper into this imbroglio than you are already."

"But darling—"

"No. Great Scott, Daisy, most of these accidents have been minor, but now a man's dead!"

"And that's why we need to know who's the heir. In fact, everyone should be told. Then we can concentrate on protecting that one person. As it is, we can't possibly keep watch over all of them!"

"We can do a pretty good job with Ernest's help. Has it dawned on you that if Sam is the heir, he's not particularly keen to announce it and make himself a target?"

"Oh! No, it hadn't occurred to me. It would apply to all of them, too."

"Great Scott, Daisy, I hadn't thought of *that*!" Alec admitted with a wry smile.

"So, you see, you need me. . . ."

Edgar came to join them, sitting on the wall beside Daisy. "Are you comparing notes?" he whispered.

"Not exactly, sir. It's a bit too public out here." Two could keep their voices low enough not to be overheard, but three made it difficult not to look conspiratorial rather than merely casually conversing. "Also, I'm hoping for a word with Samuel before I report my observations."

"You won't give him a hard time, will you, my dear chap? Don't want to upset Martha."

"I'll do my best. Sometimes it's difficult to judge what will—"

Ernest reappeared. "Mr. Fletcher, you're wanted on the telephone, sir."

"Who . . . ? No, never mind, I'm coming."

A chilly little breeze had sprung up. Martha shivered.

Sam jumped up at once. "Come on, sweetie, let's get you indoors. We can't have you catching a chill."

"If you don't mind, Cousin Geraldine," Martha apologised. The rough edges natural to her upbringing had smoothed during her stay in Hampstead.

"Of course, dear, you mustn't catch cold. Unless anyone would like some more tea, I shall go inside now myself."

Martha gave Sam her hands and he hauled her out of her chair, undignified but effective. At six months, there wasn't really a dignified way to get out of a seat.

In the couple's wake, everyone straggled through the French window into the drawing room. Daisy glanced back and saw Vincent and Laurette coming up from the garden. Geraldine stopped to speak kindly to Laurette, suggesting she might like to lie down for a while before dinner.

"I believe I will," said Laurette. "It is a great pity the English do not use *tisanes*. *La camomille* would be soothing to me now."

"Camomile? I'll ask Mrs. Warden, but wouldn't mint do? It seems to help Martha."

"Mint, no! Mint is not for the nerves."

"I'll send a maid with a hot-water bottle."

Frank approached Daisy.

"I suppose I oughtn't to go down to the Beetle this evening," he said wistfully.

"Well, Raymond wasn't a relative of yours, except in the widest sense, but he was a fellow guest."

"Yes. Better not." He sighed. "A quiet game of snooker? No money involved? No, I mustn't drag Sam away from his wife." He brightened as he spotted Vincent, at a loose end as Laurette went out. "Vincent, snooker?"

"All right," said Vincent without enthusiasm.

Daisy had a vision of the two of them hitting each other over the head with the billiard cues. Not that Vincent could possibly have a motive for attacking Frank—unless in self-defence? Should she go with them? Or ought she to check up on the children's where-abouts?

Seeing Ernest and a maid out on the terrace clearing up the tea things, she went out. "Does either of you know where Miss Belinda and the boys are?"

The maid curtsied. "I saw them in the nurseries a few minutes ago, madam. Miss Belinda was playing with the babies. Master Derek was teaching Bla—Master Benjamin, I mean, how to play Parcheesi."

"Thanks." It sounded as if they were safely settled for the present. "Ernest, Mr. Crowley and Mr. Vincent have gone to the billiard room. Would you go and offer them drinks, and pop in now and then to see that they have all they need?"

"Consider it done, madam," said the footman, with a wink that Daisy hoped the maid hadn't noticed.

She went back in just as Alec returned from taking the phone call. He came to meet her.

"Worcester super," he answered her unspoken question. "He's offered to send a motorcycle officer with the file on Raymond's accident, including the initial medical exam. He wanted to know if it can wait till the pathologist's report is also available. He's doing the autopsy tomorrow morning."

"What did you say?"

"That I can wait for an informal postmortem report but not until an official document has been typed up. Now for Sam."

"Darling, can't I—"

"No. Sam, I'd like a word with you if you don't mind. We can use Lord Dalrymple's study."

"Sure thing." Sam rose willingly, but Martha clung to him, looking frightened.

"I want to go with him!"

"It's all right, sweetie. He's not going to arrest me. Are you, Chief Inspector?"

"I have absolutely no cause to do so."

"See?"

"Please, Alec! Let me go too."

218

Daisy could see Alec swallowing a sigh. "All right, Martha. Come along."

"And Daisy. Daisy, you'll come, won't you?"

This time Alec's sigh was overt, and Daisy, though she tried not to look too triumphant, couldn't hide her smile.

TWENTY-SIX

By the time Daisy, Alec, Sam, and Martha reached the study, Sam had reconsidered his initial willingness to cooperate.

"What's going on?" he demanded, with a hint of belligerence.

"I wish I knew."

"What the dev—deuce do you mean?"

"I mean I don't understand the situation. Could you just take it on trust that I need details of your travels? If you'll be so kind as to give me the information, then I'll explain why I'm asking."

"Go on, Sammy. Alec and Daisy have done so much for me, you can at least answer a few questions."

He smiled and her and squeezed her hand. "All right, fire away."

"I'm not going to ask about your adventures in America."

Sam grinned. "Good."

"When you made it back to Jamaica—When was that?"

"I couldn't tell you the exact date. It was what you might call an informal return. They dropped me off at night in a small cove near Runaway Bay, on the north coast. I walked most of the way to Spanish Town. Picked up a few lifts, but outside Kingston there aren't many motor vehicles, it's mostly mules and donkeys, so it was no faster. Then I took the train from Spanish Town to Kingston. End of June, that's the best I can do."

"When you reached Kingston and found Martha gone, did you write to her?"

"No." A guilty glance at his wife, who smiled forgivingly.

"Sammy's not much of a letter writer."

"I would have, but I thought I'd be here as soon as a letter. Then I looked further into the legal business and I got caught up in sorting that out."

"Sorting it out?"

"I had to go back north, to Cockpit Country in St. Elizabeth Parish, to dig up some information for the lawyer."

"Were you successful? What information did you obtain?"

"Mr. Pearson told me to keep it to myself until he gets here."

"Mr. Pearson didn't foresee that I'd have to switch over from being a guest and relative by marriage to my rôle as a copper."

"Sorry. What's the good of getting advice from a lawyer if you're going to ignore it?"

"You have a point," Alec admitted. "I'll try to contain my curiosity. On that point. When did you leave Jamaica again?"

"My ship sailed from Kingston on the tenth."

"It's a pity you didn't bring your little girls." Daisy said, ignoring Alec's frown. She had ceased to find those dark eyebrows intimidating long ago.

"If I'd had to pay for the passage, I would have. As I was first officer, it just wasn't practical. They're quite happy with their aunt and uncle, though they miss their mama."

Martha's eyes misted over.

"It shouldn't be too much longer before you see them, darling," Daisy said hurriedly, to avert a storm of tears. Whether the family would be reunited in England or in Jamaica remained to be seen.

"The tenth of July?" Alec took up his interrogation. "And what date did you arrive in England?"

"The thirtieth."

"That's a slow passage, isn't it?"

221

"For an old tub like the *Julianna* it's a pretty good time!"

"I'll take your word for it," Alec said. *Pending enquiries*, Daisy thought. "Which port did you arrive at?"

"Plymouth. Our cargo was mostly rum, so it had to be unloaded into a bonded warehouse. My contract included helping to supervise the unloading. That took all day Saturday. I spent the night in a rooming house in Plymouth—"

"Address?"

Sam shrugged. "I have no idea. One of my mates took me there. I slept late, then went to catch a train to London without looking at the house number or street name."

"I suppose you didn't keep the ticket stub."

"Good lord no. I travel light, don't stuff my pockets with odds and ends of paper. What's this all about? Why do you want to know when I got here? Look here, if you don't believe me, you can ask the harbour authorities. They're supposed to keep the crew manifest."

"I don't disbelieve you. But I may—let me stress *may*—have to check. Would the *Julietta* still be at Plymouth?"

"*Julianna*. No, she was due to sail Monday for Clydeside, to deliver the rest of the cargo. Sugar. It's not easy to sell rum to the Scots!"

"I imagine not. Is *Julianna* equipped with wireless?"

"The owner stuck in a second-hand set, but most of the time it doesn't work."

"All right, let's move on. You took the train to Paddington and went straight to see the lawyer?"

"It was Sunday. Maybe I'm a fool, but not fool enough to look for a lawyer on a Sunday! I found lodgings, then I walked up to Hampstead—Martha's letters had given me your address. Nice house you have! You weren't there and the maid couldn't be coaxed into telling me where you'd gone or when you'd be back. So I went to see the sights. When I got back to the lodging house, I found out that the next day was a bank holiday. Still no hope of seeing Mr. Pearson!"

"So you did some more sightseeing."

"I did. I can't wait to take the girls to the zoo and Madame Tussaud's. There's plenty to see in London."

" 'When a man is tired of London, he is tired of life,' " Alec said. Sam was quick to pick up his tone. "A quotation? Who said that?"

"Dr. Samuel Johnson, your namesake."

"Never heard of him. I haven't got much book learning, excepting the navigation manual."

" 'A man's a man for a' that,' " Daisy murmured.

Alec gave her a look. Sam gave her a questioning glance but turned back to Alec.

"Monday was a bank holiday, yet you went to see Mr. Pearson? At home?"

Sam grinned. "I got impatient. I found his address in a telephone directory and I thought I might as well give it a try. At least he might give me an appointment for the next day, so I wouldn't turn up at his office and find him gone."

"That's a point. I'm surprised he saw you, though. Gentlemen of the law always prefer to go about things in the proper way."

"He gave me ten minutes, maybe quarter of an hour. I showed him what I'd brought. He got about as excited as I reckon gentlemen of the law ever get, then his servant came in to say a taxi had come for him and Mrs. Pearson. He wanted me to leave the . . . papers there for him to look at later. I wasn't about to do that, with no knowing what'd become of them. I swore to the person who lent it—them—to me that I'd return them unharmed. They're irreplaceable."

"Originals. Not official records then."

"That's as may be. I was good and ready to get out of the city, begging Dr. Samuel Johnson's pardon, and I didn't want to let another day pass without seeing my gal!"

"Yet you didn't exactly hurry here from Worcester."

"I've always liked to get to know foreign places. And after being adrift in strange country in Florida, I wanted to be familiar with the territory hereabouts. You never know when it'll come in handy."

"I don't mind," Martha said earnestly. "I'm just happy that he's safe."

Safety was questionable, Daisy thought, or at least relative. If Sam was as honest and open as she would like to believe, he might be in danger. But she recognised the truth of Alec's accusation that she always, when mixed up in a case, took one of the suspects "under her wing," and found it hard to believe ill of him or her. Her faith was sometimes misplaced. For Martha's sake she wanted Sam to be innocent, so she viewed him through rose-coloured spectacles.

"What time did your train get in?" Alec asked.

"It was due at Worcester Shrub Hill at about twenty past eleven, but it arrived a few minutes late."

Sam had been in Worcester at the time of Raymond's fall. However, it would have been an astonishing coincidence for him to have happened to spot Raymond—assuming he could recognise him—at a moment when he was vulnerable.

Coincidences do happen, Daisy reminded herself. She suspected Sam had the quick wits to take advantage of an unexpected opportunity.

"You'll understand that I'm going to do some checking," Alec told him.

"I might understand if you'll tell me what this is all about!"

"Fair's fair." Alec's account of the string of odd incidents was a model of conciseness.

By the end, Sam was frowning. "Yes," he said slowly, "I see why you have to look into every possibility. I—No, I think I'd better keep my own counsel for the moment."

"And your eyes open."

"And—believe me—my eyes open! Who—" The telephone bell interrupted him.

Alec automatically reached for the receiver, hesitated with a glance at Sam, then picked it up. "Fletcher here." He listened for a moment, grimaced, said, "Yes, Ernest, put her through." Holding out the receiver and sliding the stand across the desk towards Daisy, he informed her, "Your mama."

"Blast!" She gingerly put the receiver to her ear, as Alec shepherded the others out. "Mother?"

"Daisy! What's this I hear?"

"I don't know, Mother, until you tell me."

"I gather the ne'er-do-well husband of Violet's unfortunate protégée has turned up like a bad penny."

Unfortunate in the sense of undesirable, not unlucky, Daisy felt sure. And she'd considered Martha her own protégée, not Violet's. But where the dowager was concerned, the less said the better. "Samuel Dalrymple has arrived, yes."

"The innkeeper."

"The sailor, Mother."

"Even worse. One may hope that now Violet will see the folly of becoming intimate with such impossible people."

Time to change the subject. "How is Violet?"

"If you ever came to see us, you'd know."

"I've been several times, Mother! Even though I'm rather busy helping Geraldine entertain her guests."

"What does she expect with such an ill-assorted, ill-bred party? I assume your husband hasn't yet worked out who is Edgar's heir."

"It's not his responsibility."

"What's the use of having a policeman in the family if he can't separate the pretenders from the real?"

"It's Tommy Pearson's job. The lawyer."

"If Edgar had had the sense to stay with the lawyers who served the family for centuries, all this nonsense would have been finished with years ago."

Daisy was unable to deny this assertion. "I daresay. How is Violet?"

"As well as can be expected. She was always delicate, not a hoyden like you. It's a relief not to have that noisy boy of hers about the house. I suppose I must thank Geraldine for taking him off our hands. I have been considering . . ." She paused.

"Oh?" Daisy said cautiously.

"Of all the unsuitable candidates, the jeweller is clearly the least unsuitable, the most accustomed to dealing with people of our class. This Pearson person must hurry up and confirm that he—"

"Mother, I'm sorry to have to tell you . . ." Daisy hesitated. Would Alec be furious? But the news was undoubtedly spreading by now and she couldn't let her mother continue in her misconception. "Cousin Raymond died today."

"Well, really! How inconvenient! Very inconsiderate of him to put himself in contention if he was on the point of expiring."

"Your time is about to expire, caller," said the operator, apropos. "Do you want another three minutes?"

"Yes, of course," snapped the dowager. "I am not yet in want of twopence to speak to my daughter. Where were we?"

"I'm sure Raymond didn't expect to die. He would hardly have undertaken the long sea voyage from South Africa had he known."

"People take cruises in the hope of a cure, Daisy. Surely even you are aware of that. Or possibly he wanted to consult a Harley Street medical expert in his condition. I daresay colonial doctors are all very well in their way, but they can hardly compare with the best specialists in the world. I take it Edgar will cancel his birthday party. The man was a relative, after all. Of sorts. And that reminds me, I'm told Alec's little girl fell off a donkey at the fair."

"Belinda's just a bit bruised, Mother, but thank you for enquiring."

"I wasn't enquiring. I know she wasn't badly hurt because I've seen her with that mongrel of hers and Derek and the black child, who I'm quite certain cannot possibly be a legitimate Dalrymple, playing at Red Indians in the park."

"Red Indians!"

"Or some similar game. They appeared to be sneaking after the black child's—"

"Ben. Benjamin. His guardian?"

"So I believe. He was introduced as Frank Crowley, if I remember correctly, at that appalling Sunday lunch party of Geraldine's. I could have told them where the fellow was heading. The Wedge and Beetle, playing darts in the public bar."

"Good heavens, Mother, did you see him there?"

An outraged silence was followed by the click of the dowager hanging up.

TWENTY-SEVEN

"*I shouldn't* have done it," said Daisy, "but honestly . . . I plead provocation. I'll get what-for next time I talk to her."

"She always gives you what-for, love, with or without cause, so I wouldn't worry about it."

They were in their bedroom preparing for dinner. Powdering her nose, Daisy said meditatively, "Darts. Could you kill someone with a dart, darling?"

"I doubt it. Theoretically it's possible, I imagine, but barring an unknown and instantly deadly poison of Amazonian origin, unlikely. The point is too short and narrow to do much damage."

"Trinidad is near the coast of South America."

"If someone dies of an unknown and instantly deadly Amazonian poison, I shall arrest Frank at once."

Daisy laughed. "I wouldn't be surprised if Mother considers frequenting the public bar to be an indictable offence for a guest at Fairacres. And she considers me criminally negligent for letting Bel run loose with the boys."

"Red Indians sounds quite harmless."

"Bows and arrows," she said darkly. "They learnt to use them at the fair. Gervaise used to mess about with archery. His bow and arrows are bound to be in the attics or hidden away in a cupboard somewhere. If the kids ferreted them out, the murderer could get hold of them."

"If there is a murderer. What did you think of Sam?"

"I like him. You don't need to tell me that doesn't mean anything. But I do find it difficult to see how he could be responsible for Raymond's fall when he'd only just arrived in Worcester, even if he'd actually been in England for ages."

"It would be a whopping coincidence," Alec conceded. "The diamonds are still in the running for a motive in that affair."

"If he was in England: Vincent's fall, possible; Belinda's fall, possible; Ben's, no, but Martha could have done that. It would explain why the butterfly net was placed near the bottom of the stairs. She might conceivably obey Sam's instructions up to a point. I can't see her willing to harm anyone seriously."

He shook his head. "I hoped talking to Sam would clarify matters, but I'm still completely in the dark."

"If you ask me, he's the heir. He wouldn't have gone to all that trouble to get hold of his precious 'papers' if they proved he wasn't. And it would take a lot to make Tommy excited."

"We have only his word for both. I'm just hoping tomorrow will bring a flood of information about the lot of them. Are you ready to go down?"

Daisy contemplated her shingled curls and ran the hairbrush through them one last time. "Ready."

Dinner was not a convivial occasion. Even Frank was subdued. With little conversation to distract them from eating, the meal was soon over. The sun had set, but it was still light outside. The ladies followed Geraldine to the drawing room, where the men joined them just a few minutes later. In the circumstances, Daisy wasn't surprised that they chose not to sit on at the table, passing the port in masculine cameraderie.

Vincent and Laurette at once excused themselves and went to walk in the garden.

"Dammit," Alec muttered. "I wanted to talk to Vincent."

"Why don't you follow them?" Daisy suggested.

"I don't want to talk to Laurette."

"If we both went for a stroll and happened to meet them, I could distract her."

"That would leave Geraldine's drawing room rather thin of company."

"She's far more interested in your finding out what's going on than in your fascinating conversation."

"Thanks for the compliment!"

"Geraldine, it's such a glorious evening, you won't mind if we go out, *as well*?" Daisy hoped her stress on the last two words would convey something of Alec's purpose.

Before Geraldine had time to reply, Edgar, standing at the window looking out, cried, "Good lord, a Ghost Swift!"

Martha's eyes and mouth opened wide in dismay. "A ghost?"

"A moth, my dear, I expect," Geraldine soothed her. "Too late in the day for butterflies. Edgar's rather keen on certain insects, Samuel."

Edgar plunged out in pursuit of his prey, wielding a large handkerchief in lieu of his broken net.

"Do go and enjoy the weather while it's nice, Daisy," said Geraldine. "Who knows, it may pour with rain again tomorrow."

Daisy and Alec went out. Edgar had already galloped off into the dusk and there was no sign of Vincent and Laurette.

"How did they disappear so fast?" Alec demanded crossly.

"They must have gone into the laburnum alley, I should think. Though it's an odd place to choose when it's getting dark. Do you want to follow them?"

"No, I want to be visible from the terrace in case the reports arrive from Worcester. Let's walk down to the chestnut and watch for them to reappear."

Reaching the chestnut, they stopped and turned. The sky above the house still held the colours of sunset, rose deepening to burnt orange, with a few high, fluffy, pale-pink clouds. The air was soft and still. Bats flitted after midges and moths, their swift, erratic flight reminiscent of a complicated country dance. Daisy hoped Edgar's Ghost Swift hadn't been snapped up.

"Look at the evening star, darling," she said, tucking her arm through Alec's. "I've never seen it brighter."

But his attention was elsewhere, scanning the gardens with a glance at the house now and then.

Ernest came out on the terrace, a cardboard document case under his arm. Alec waved and started towards him, and he came to meet them.

"For you, sir," he said in a conspiratorial tone, although no one was near to overhear. "A police officer on a motor bicycle brought it. Me and Mr. Lowecroft thought as it shouldn't be left unattended on his lordship's desk."

"Thank you, Ernest, quite right. Is the officer waiting?"

"Yes, sir, in case you want to send any messages. Cook's giving him a cuppa in the kitchen."

"Tell him, would you, that I'll just take a quick look and write a note for his superintendent."

"Ernest, do you know what the children are up to?"

"They went down to the river, madam, to see if the water's gone down enough for boating."

"Oh no!" Daisy swung round to chase after the errant children. "It's nearly dark. Alec, they—"

"Madam, they came in half an hour ago. I beg your pardon for alarming you. Mr. Lowecroft arranged for the garden boy to watch after 'em, me being busy serving dinner. They went up to the day nursery. Last seen playing card games under Mrs. Gilpin's eye."

"Whew! Don't give me another shock like that, Ernest!"

"I'm sure I'm very sorry, madam. But you needn't worry, we've got it covered. And I didn't tell nobody but Mr. Lowecroft what you said to me. Not but what everyone but the kitchen maid can guess there's fishy business going on."

Daisy started after Alec towards the house. "What does everyone make of it?"

"Can't make head nor tail of it, madam." The footman kept pace half a step to her rear. "It just don't seem to hang together somehow. They're a rum lot, if you don't mind me saying so. You can't choose your relatives, like Mrs. Warden says."

"That'll do, Ernest. One of them is going to become Viscount Dalrymple someday, unless another aspirant turns up unexpectedly."

"Yes, madam. I beg pardon if I spoke too free."

"I won't hold it against you. You've been very helpful and I'm much easier in my mind about the children."

"Thank you, madam."

"And please tell the staff that if anyone has any reasonable ideas to make sense of things, they should report to Mr. Fletcher."

They had reached the terrace steps, and Alec was about to enter the sitting room. Daisy saw that Geraldine was alone, knitting, while from the wireless came the strains of what Daisy guessed was a Haydn symphony. She shouldn't have assumed the others would stay to keep their hostess company. Alec could quite well have gone out by himself to fail to find Vincent and Laurette. She girded up her loins for another apology.

Before she reached the French doors, she was startled to hear Laurette's voice raised in a screech: *"Au secours! Au secours!* 'Elp! Vincent has been stabbed! *Mon dieu, qu'on nous aide!"*

Daisy peered into the near darkness. Laurette was wearing black as usual and Daisy couldn't see her. Ernest started to run, so she followed him, and she heard Alec's footsteps pounding across the paved terrace.

He easily caught up with and passed her. Though not wearing an evening dress, she was not dressed for running. She slowed down.

Vincent staggered out from the alley. Alec and Ernest went straight to him, so Daisy concentrated on Laurette.

She put her arm about the woman. "Alec and the footman are helping Vincent. Come inside and sit down. What happened?"

"Oh, I cannot talk about it! We came to the end of the *allée*—We walked slowly, you understand, talking. Near the river it is more light. Almost we walk back across the *pelouse*, the lawn, but the grass is damp, so we return to the *allée*, where is gravel. Not so bad for shoes."

Daisy glanced down guiltily at her shoes, but it was too dark by now to see any damage. "The laburnum is impenetrable. So either someone came running after you, which you would have heard on the gravel, or you reached the gap halfway, where you can turn onto the lawn or take the footpath in the opposite direction."

"Yes, yes, we come to the gap. We cross. Someone concealed himself there—*ça se voit*—this is obvious. We re-enter into the tunnel, into the darkness. The person throws himself upon my poor Vincent and thrusts a knife into his back!"

"Good heavens, how terrible! Is he badly hurt?" She looked back. Vincent was walking between Alec and Ernest, slowly but unsupported. "Not too badly, apparently. It looks as if he had a lucky escape."

"He heard a sound and started to turn himself."

"So the blow didn't strike him squarely in the back. Gosh, he really was lucky."

"Unless he bleeds slowly perhaps, unseen under the coat."

"Alec and Ernest will get him inside where we can see. It's no good fumbling in the dark."

Geraldine looked up as they went through the French doors. She jumped up, dropping her knitting, as the men appeared on the threshold. "What *now*?" she asked, in a long-suffering voice. It must be very trying to have guests so prone to dramatic upsets.

"Vincent was attacked," said Daisy. "He doesn't seem to be badly hurt."

Vincent sank limply into the nearest chair, with a slight moan. Laurette started chafing his hand, to what end Daisy wasn't sure.

"Where are Sam and Crowley?" Alec asked sharply.

"Frank quietly sloped off," Geraldine said. "I assumed to the public house."

"I told him not to go there this evening," Daisy put in. "I said it wouldn't look good after Raymond's demise. He's probably in the billiard room."

"Ernest, go and check, please. And Sam?"

"Martha felt unwell. Too much excitement, I expect. Naturally Samuel went with her to help her up the stairs."

"Naturally." Alec sighed. "Vincent, your injury must be examined. Can you make it upstairs?"

"I don't think so," Vincent said in a failing voice.

"We'll take a look at once, right here." Geraldine's no-nonsense manner reduced them all to schoolchildren. She advanced on Vincent, who couldn't repress an instinct to cower slightly. Holding out her hand to Alec, she said, "You have a clean handkerchief?"

He handed over a large white linen square. "I'll help Vincent take off his jacket."

"Unhurt side first," Geraldine directed.

They bent over their reluctant patient, Laurette hovering with little cries of distress.

Frank Crowley came in, his face lighting with interest as he observed the scene. Behind him came Ernest.

"What happened?" Frank asked Daisy.

"Vincent's hurt."

"Badly?"

"I don't know." She turned to Ernest. "You'd better bring water and a couple of towels, and brandy. Sticking plaster, bandages, lint, I don't know. . . ."

"There's a slash in your jacket," said Alec, "a clean cut. Must have been made by a pretty sharp blade."

"How lucky that you turned quickly, Vincent!" Laurette's English improved as her distress calmed.

"Very little blood on your shirt," Geraldine assured him. "We can lengthen the slit, or cut the shirt off you, or just take it off if it's not too painful."

"Take it off carefully," said Laurette, the thrifty Frenchwoman. "I shall wash and mend it."

"Nonsense. One of the maids can do it, and we'll replace both shirt and jacket as soon as possible."

Alec, now with Frank's assistance, eased Vincent out of his shirt.

"It's barely a scratch." Frank was a trifle contemptuous. "What happened?"

"Someone jumped out of the bush and attacked him," Laurette snapped. "He suffers from the shock. *I* suffer from the shock. You are not sympathetic." She stared at him suspiciously. "Where were you?"

"Playing billiards against myself."

233

Lowecroft came in with a decanter of brandy, followed by Ernest, his arms laden with first-aid supplies. Alec and Frank moved back to let Geraldine and Laurette minister to the sufferer.

Alec had appropriated Vincent's shirt and jacket. He handed them to Daisy. "Look after his clothes, will you, love? Don't let anyone start laundering or mending. I must go and hunt for the weapon." He raised his voice. "Ernest!"

"Yes, sir?" The footman joined them.

"Find me a torch, please. You'd better get one for yourself, too, and come and help me."

"At once, sir." Ernest's eyes gleamed with excitement. "Mr. Crowley was in the billiard room all right, sir, but there's no knowing how long he'd been there before I saw him." He hurried off.

"He's willing enough—"

"Eager!" said Daisy.

"But I need Tom and Ernie."

"Surely the Super will send them down now, after this."

"I hope so. Daisy, I'd like to be sure Sam is with Martha. . . ."

"Right away, Chief. I'll put Vincent's clothes in our room and then pop in to see Martha."

"You'd better take the papers as well."

Coming in supporting Vincent, Alec had dumped the document case on a small table near the French windows. Frank had noticed it and stood contemplating the Worcester police insignia and CONFIDENTIAL stamp, eyebrows raised, hands in pockets, whistling softly, tunelessly, to himself.

"Excuse me," said Daisy, "I have instructions to remove that."

"Scotland Yard taking charge, eh? I must say it was a bit of a shock finding out we have a copper among us!"

Shock, rather than mere surprise, Daisy noted. But he smiled when he said it. She smiled in return and picked up the case. It was heavier than she expected.

"Let me carry that for you. I want to go up and make sure Ben hasn't been attacked by a homicidal maniac. An incompetent one."

Not being in the running to inherit Fairacres, Daisy had no qualms about her personal safety. She caught Alec's eye and waved to him, so that Frank was aware that pinching the reports from her would immediately make him the focus of suspicion.

"I assume I'm a suspect," he said as they crossed the hall.

"I'm afraid so."

"I can't say it wouldn't be nice to have a rich stepson, or even just to have the kids off my hands without having to worry about them. But not nice enough to risk the gallows for."

"Alec will take that into account, of course."

"So he's officially investigating the poor old b—fellow's death? Raymond's, I mean?"

"He was unofficially looking into that. It may well turn out to have been an accident. But now that Vincent has been attacked . . ."

"For the second time?"

"I don't know. And I'd better not talk about all this or I'll say something Alec wants kept quiet. Ben's in the nurseries, according to Ernest. The three of them are playing cards."

Frank grinned. "That sounds safe enough, as Ben hasn't got a penny to gamble with. Not to mention Mrs. Gilpin's eagle eye."

"You've fallen afoul of Nurse Gilpin, have you?"

"She didn't like me calling Belinda Bel. 'That's Miss Belinda to you,' she said, very toffee-nosed."

"Oh dear, I'm sorry."

"Not to worry. I'm careful to call her Miss Belinda in the nursery. And Bel elsewhere. She and young Derek have been absolute bricks, as Derek would say, to Ben. Almost everyone here has been very kind and accepting—"

"Almost?"

"Except Vincent and Mrs. Vincent, who are just snooty, and the late, unlamented Raymond, who passed some nasty remarks about the horror of being related to a kaffir. I was angry, but things are different in South Africa from at home, and I wouldn't kill him for being an ignorant bigot. Do you or your husband think Ben is in danger?"

"It's possible. I was on my way up to check on them when Alec lumbered me with this stuff. I wonder how many people know he has a brother at home?"

"I see what you mean," he said thoughtfully. "I don't recall talking about Jacques to anyone. Maybe mentioning more young 'uns at home but nothing more specific. You reckon it'd be a good idea to make sure everyone hears about him?"

"It can't hurt. If we can come up with a way to encourage Ben and the others to talk about him, without alarming them . . . His name is Jack?"

"Jacques, the French name. We're a mixed bunch in Trinidad."

They reached Daisy's room. Frank handed over the documents and went on. Daisy bunged Vincent's slashed clothes into the bottom of the wardrobe, pushing them to the back, and stuffed the case of papers into one of Alec's drawers, under his socks, vests, and pants. Then she went to Martha's room. Knocking, she hoped she wasn't interrupting an intimate reunion. To her relief, Geraldine's maid came to the door.

"Oh, it's you, madam. I'm just helping Mrs. Samuel get herself to bed. She's fair exhausted what with all the excitement."

"Mr. Samuel isn't here?"

"No, madam. He stopped while she drank her tea—not that it's what I'd call tea, that nasty stuff Mrs. Warden sent up. When I came along according to her ladyship's instructions, to see if Mrs. Samuel could do with a helping hand, Mr. Samuel said he was going to look for the nurseries to meet the rest of his new relations. So I told him how to get there, seeing it's confusing what with all the passages and stairs and whatnot. I'm sure I hope I did right, madam."

Having reassured her and sent a "sweet dreams" message to Martha, Daisy followed in Sam and Frank's footsteps up to the nursery.

Had Sam gone straight there after leaving Martha, or had he sneaked out and stuck a knife into Vincent, then dashed back? It would be hard to do without someone noticing, at least hearing hurried footsteps on the stairs, even in this solidly built house. How long had the maid been with Martha? Small chance of either having noticed the time!

Frank, alone in the billiard room on the ground floor, would have found it much easier to manage the attack unseen and unheard.

The attack on Raymond also would have been much more difficult for Sam than for Frank.

If Raymond had been attacked . . .

Alec badly needed competent colleagues to help him find out who was where when.

TWENTY-EIGHT

Before she reached the nursery, Daisy could hear laughter. It made her smile, but she was going to have to spoil the fun. Though Raymond had not made himself popular, he was a relative and fellow guest. A certain sobriety was due to his memory on the day of his death, even if no one went into deep mourning.

Frank had already joined in a game of cards, sitting at the battered table with Sam and the kids. Nana snoozed at their feet. Daisy watched and listened for a minute before they noticed her presence.

Belinda saw her first. "Mummy, come and play!"

"Uncle Frank is really, really good at cheating," said Derek.

Frank rose with a rueful grimace. "I'd better point out that we're playing Cheat!"

"I recognised the game. I'm sorry to be a wet blanket, but you know, it really won't do. Uncle Raymond died just this afternoon."

"Oh Mummy, I'm sorry," Bel cried remorsefully. "He was nice to me at the fair."

"Sorry, Aunt Daisy," the boys muttered, with no signs of remorse. Frank looked equally unrepentent.

"I'm sorry," said Sam. "I never met the old chap but I ought to have known better."

"Time you kids went to bed, anyway. Put everything away neatly, please. You may read in bed till ten o'clock. I'm just going to look in on the twins."

Oliver and Miranda were sound asleep, a pair of cherubs. They didn't stir when Daisy kissed them. She realised she had hardly seen them all the long, eventful day. A light was showing under the door of the nurse's room, off the night nursery, so Mrs. Gilpin was awake.

Daisy knocked. "It's Mrs. Fletcher. If you're still up, Nurse, may I have a word?"

After a short silence came the grudging words, "You'd better come in, madam. We don't want to disturb the babies."

She had taken off her cap and apron, but still wore her uniform skirt and blouse. Daisy sometimes wondered whether she owned any personal clothes. If so, she kept them strictly for her holidays, when she went to visit a sister for a fortnight, reluctantly. She was certain Daisy and Bertha, the nurserymaid, would spoil Miranda and Oliver while she was gone.

Daisy asked how the twins' day had gone, as if Mrs. Gilpin would have acknowledged any misbehaviour. Naturally they both behaved perfectly when Mummy and Daddy and big sister didn't mess about with their routine.

"I expect you've heard about Mr. Raymond?" Daisy asked eventually.

"The maid told me, madam. Very sad, I'm sure, for them that knew the gentleman. The young people didn't ought to have been playing cards at such a time—not that I approve of card games at any time, seeing what they lead to. Gambling, and dicing, and horses!" she added darkly. "And so I told them, but them not being under my care, they wouldn't listen."

"No, I'm afraid they wouldn't."

"And then the young gentlemen, if gentlemen they may be, come along and encourage them to misbehave. . . . Well, it's not my place to say anything but that doesn't stop me thinking that there's some aren't any better than they should be!"

"Did you happen to notice what time Mr. Samuel and Mr. Crowley arrived?"

Mrs. Gilpin was affronted. "I'm not a clock-watcher, madam. I'm here and ready when the little ones need me, and I can't say fairer than that."

"No, indeed," said Daisy, and she retired defeated, as usual.

The day nursery was tidy and empty. She hadn't expected them to disappear so fast, Nana and all, and she wanted to talk to Belinda. She turned off the light and went down staircases and along corridors with mysterious jogs to right or left that were not mysterious to her because, whoever lived here, Fairacres was home. She could see how the house with its additions and sprouting of wings over the years might confuse a newcomer.

She wondered where Frank and Sam had gone, and whether they had gone together. They seemed quite friendly, not surprising really, as they were about the same age and both West Indians. In some ways they were very different, though. Frank seemed to have no regular job, yet he accepted responsibility for his stepkids—at least according to his own words. And in spite of Sam's responsible profession, he had gone off with the rumrunners, leaving his pregnant wife to manage alone—she was used to his absence on voyages, of course, and had family nearby to fall back on.

Daisy liked them both. She found it hard to believe that one of them must be either, at best, a practical joker of the nastier kind or, at worst, a murderer.

She tapped on Belinda's door. "Bel, it's Mummy."

"Come in." Bel had obviously shed a few tears.

Daisy gave her a hug. "Cheer up, darling. I didn't mean to bite your heads off."

"It's not that, Mummy. I know we shouldn't have been laughing, but Uncle Frank was so funny!"

"It was nice of him and Uncle Sam to join your game. Were they there for long?"

"No, not very. I'm really sad about Uncle Raymond. Derek said he was pushed under a tram. He overheard someone saying . . ." Bel shivered. "He told us a horrid rhyme."

"The same one my brother once told me, I bet. Try to forget it. Uncle Raymond wasn't run over. There were lots of people waiting to cross the street. He stumbled, and someone pushed him out of the way of the trams. We're not sure why he died. Daddy's trying to find out."

"Was it because . . . Derek said it was because of the 'heirs of the body' thing. Was Uncle Raymond an heir of the body?"

"Sort of. Not quite. Uncle Tommy Pearson is trying to find out about that."

"And Ben is one, too. Derek says we must never leave him alone, because of the butterfly net. They took Nana to the turret to be their watchdog."

"What a good idea."

"Ben was scared, so I said he's probably not really in danger, because the net was at the bottom of the stairs, remember? But Derek says we can't be too careful."

Belinda was probably right, Ben wasn't really in danger—because it was beginning to look more and more as if Frank was the culprit.

"I'm glad you're keeping him safe. Did you wash your face and brush your teeth? Hop into bed now. What are you reading?"

"*The Railway Children*. I've read it before, but I like it. It has a happy ending. *Black Beauty* is too sad."

"It's a good story." She kissed Bel. "Nighty-night, sleep tight, darling."

She decided not to go and disturb the boys and Nana. It sounded as if Derek had everything well in hand. They could tell Alec in the morning their impressions of how long Sam and Frank had spent with them.

Time to see whether Alec had found a knife in the bushes, a useful knife that would yield information about the wielder. Unless he or Ernest had come across it very quickly, he probably hadn't got round yet to having a crack at the reports from Worcester. Daisy went to their bedroom first, just in case he was poring over them there, but the document case was still under his underclothes. She went downstairs.

In the drawing room, she found Geraldine presiding over coffee and liqueurs. Vincent and Laurette, unsurprisingly, had gone up. Sam and Frank were there, and Edgar was showing off in a jar the

Ghost Swift he had managed to capture with his handkerchief. *Hepialus humuli* was a pretty yellow moth. Edgar's specimen was a female he informed them. The male was white and smaller.

"More ghostlike?" Frank suggested with a grin.

"Yes, particularly as the underside of the wings is brown, so it appears to flicker as it flies. Daisy, I should like to show the kids."

"They've gone to bed. Can you keep it till morning?"

Edgar reflected. "If I put it in a larger jar, it should be all right." He trotted off.

Sinking into a chair, Daisy accepted a cup of coffee and a Drambuie. "No sign of Alec?"

"As far as I know," said Geraldine, somewhat austerely, "he and Ernest are still outside. Lowecroft is a trifle perturbed at the unauthorised absence of his footman."

"Oh dear, I'd better have a word with him."

"That won't be necessary. I have explained to him the exigencies of the situation. For all practical purposes, Alec is in charge until further notice."

Frank asked, "Are we allowed to talk about what's been happening?"

"It's a free country," said Daisy, hoping she might hear something helpful. "Alec can't stop you."

"Not in my drawing room." Geraldine was firm. Frank and Sam exchanged a glance. "For an injured man to enter in search of succour is one thing. To discuss the topic casually over coffee is another matter."

"I daresay Alec will want to talk to each of you later," said Daisy.

"He won't disturb Martha," Sam said aggressively.

"Good heavens no!"

Not tonight, at least, Daisy added mentally.

Geraldine turned the subject to the West Indies and the difference between Jamaica and Trinidad. Edgar returned and joined in. The conversation was interesting, but Daisy only gave it half her attention. She was pondering that look exchanged between the two men.

Could they possibly be conspiring? How on earth could they profit jointly?

Suppose they had worked out between them that Sam and Ben were third and fourth in line. It would have to be in that order, or nothing made sense. Frank would help Sam to get rid of Raymond and Vincent, and in return, Sam would promise to take care of— perhaps even adopt—Ben and his siblings, possibly with cash for Frank thrown in to sweeten the deal.

Alec would say it was sheer speculation, and most improbable into the bargain. She ought to tell him, all the same.

Ernest came in to see whether more coffee was needed. Apart from a portentous and incomprehensible glance in Daisy's direction, his appearance would not have led anyone to imagine he'd been hunting through a shrubbery for a murderous knife. Apart from the look and a twig caught in his collar at the back, Daisy noted.

"Is Mr. Fletcher back indoors?" she asked him.

"In his lordship's study, madam." He didn't add that Alec would like to see her.

Slightly peeved, she finished her coffee, excused herself, and went to find him anyway.

Seated at the desk, he was talking on the telephone, dictating a telegram by the sound of it. He looked up when the door opened and a shade of irritation crossed his face at the sight of her, but he waved her to a chair. To her disappointment, there was no blood-stained knife on the desk, nor anything that might conceal it.

"Repeat that, please, operator." Alec listened, corrected a word, and added sternly, "Remember, this is police business. It is highly confidential." Hanging up, he leant back wearily and ran his hand through his hair. "I don't know why I bother to tell her to shut up about it. I imagine the whole household knows by now, and the village will by morning."

"I just hope we don't have the press round our ears by morning."

"Not till midday at the earliest, I should think." He took a swig from a glass of pale amber liquid—whisky, no doubt. "Truscott had better close the main gates. No doubt one or two of the most persistent will eventually find the footpaths, or conceivably arrive by water, but most will head for the pub and pick up what they can there. Which will be plenty."

"Geraldine is pretty well-respected in the village, and they think Edgar is barmy but they like him. Not to mention Mother."

"Of whom they are all scared to death."

"So they may keep their mouths closed—unless the reporters think it's a big enough story to start handing out bribes."

"We can but hope." Alec finished his whisky and looked into the delicate demitasse coffee cup that stood on a tray next to it.

"More coffee, darling?"

"I need a large mug of the stuff. I may be up most of the night. Ernest can bring me some when he comes back. I sent him to put in an appearance in the drawing room and then to fetch the papers from our room."

"I hid them in your drawer, under your clothes."

"First place a burglar would look, love, I've told you before. A footman shouldn't have any trouble."

Daisy wrinkled her nose at him. "You didn't find the knife, I take it."

"No. Unless it was immediately obvious, it was pretty hopeless searching at night, particularly as both torch batteries were failing. And as Ernest pointed out, it wouldn't have taken a minute to run down to the backwater and chuck it in, or just dump it in the woods between the end of the laburnums and the backwater. It's all blackberry brambles and stinging nettles."

"Butterflies like nettles."

"I daresay."

"Another pointer to Frank, don't you think? I mean, he's the one who knows about the wood and the inlet. He'd know it would be easy to dispose of the weapon."

"Unless Sam's been in England prospecting the lie of the land. One of the cables I've got to send tonight. Or two or three. What was his ship's name?"

"You should have let me take notes. *Juliet*?"

"*Julianna*, that's it." He reached for the phone. "I've sent another request for Tom and Piper, by the way."

"Citing the attack on Vincent."

"And the Chief Constable's request for help. I'm hoping the night superintendent will send them by the first train, not wait for Crane to put his oar in in the morning. But I must make sure Sir Nigel went ahead and called in the Yard. Is it too late to ring him?"

"Shouldn't think so."

"Sir Nigel Wookleigh, police business," Alec told the operator.

He was put through remarkably quickly. While he was talking to the Chief Constable, Ernest came in with the document case. He set it on the desk and picked up the tray. Quietly, Daisy asked him to bring Alec more coffee, in large quantities. He bowed acknowledgement, once again the very proper footman, and went out.

"Yes, very shocking," Alec was saying. "Thank you, sir. I appreciate your cooperation. Good night."

"He's already wired the Yard?" Daisy asked.

"Just a few minutes ago. The local super wasn't keen and had to be persuaded. He's agreed to send a couple of constables at first light to search for the knife." He opened the case and took out a thin manilla envelope and a fat folder with a handwritten note clipped to it. He gave Daisy a speculative look. "It would save a lot of time if you'd go through the police reports for me. Frankly, I'm not expecting to learn much from them. The Worcester police are quite capable of digging out anything of real significance and I can't do anything about it till tomorrow anyway. If you see anything even remotely promising, set it aside."

Opening the folder, Daisy groaned. "Third carbon copy. I need more light." She moved to a chair with a reading light on a table beside it.

She didn't start on them immediately. She watched Alec remove two sheets of handwritten paper from the envelope, scan them quickly, then go back and read carefully. He looked up.

"The preliminary medical report. Interesting, though not exactly helpful. Pardoe says there's no external evidence of what killed Raymond."

"He definitely wasn't stabbed like the Empress of Austria?"

"No. Given the excess weight he was carrying, Pardoe suspects he had hardening of the arteries, leading to high blood pressure. A spike in blood pressure caused by a sudden shock such as his fall between the trams could have caused a stroke if he happened to have an aortic or intracranial aneurysm."

"What's an aneurysm?"

"A weak spot in the wall of a blood vessel. A spike in pressure could make it rupture."

"Ugh!"

"*If* he had one. It's all speculative."

"And you're always telling me not to speculate. Dr. Pardoe seems to be oblivious to that rule. Let me get this straight. Strictly within the realm of speculation, the fall caused a shock, and the shock caused a fatal stroke. But what caused the fall?"

"It's possible that the stroke caused the fall in the first place. However, besides skinned knuckles and bruised knees, he had an odd bruise in the middle of his back, a small round bruise. Its appearance suggests a sudden forceful jab approximately forty minutes before his death."

"Does Dr. Pardoe suggest what might have made a bruise like that?"

"No pathologist will ever speculate on that sort of thing on paper."

"He may be the exception that proves the rule."

Alec laughed. "Perhaps. I'll talk to him tomorrow after the autopsy and suggest some possibilities, and he'll tell me yes or no. If I'm lucky."

"A walking stick," Daisy proposed. "Poked between the people waiting to cross the street. Vincent probably had his. So did Raymond himself, come to that. Frank didn't have one, but he could have bought one—"

"In which case we'll find the seller."

"Or he could have found one lying about somewhere. Men who carry one as part of their getup, not for support, are always forgetting them, especially in railway stations. I don't know whether Sam usually carries one, but he didn't have one when we met him in the park, remember?"

"He could have bunged it into a ditch or under a convenient bush anywhere between here and Worcester."

"A man dressed like a sailor, as Sam was, would have been conspicuous. Someone would remember him."

"He could have worn a suit on the train and changed somewhere after the 'accident.'"

"I suppose so," Daisy acknowledged. "By the way, I told Sam and Frank that you'd probably want to talk to them this evening."

"I do, but they'll be waiting up for me till three in the morning if we don't get on."

Thus admonished, Daisy set about puzzling over the appallingly smudged typescript. She had to concentrate too hard to catch what Alec was saying on the telephone. Ernest brought him a pot of coffee and a large cup, and he set down a smaller cup and saucer beside Daisy.

"Mr. Lowecroft thought as you might like some cocoa," he whispered.

"Perfect, thanks."

She took a sip, and then forgot to drink as she delved back into the reports. At last she came to the end. She reached for her cup, but the usual revolting skin had formed on the cocoa.

Alec finished dictating a telegram and turned to her. "Well?"

"I'm not much wiser than I was when I started. None of the bystanders the police managed to nab as witnesses could say more than that the person who prevented Raymond falling under the wheels was 'an ordinary looking man.' The same description, over and over. No one can remember whether he had a moustache, even. None of them admitted to having been that man. No one so much as mentioned Raymond's having been pushed on to the tracks in the first place. They all assumed he had stumbled on the edge of the kerb."

"What about the copper on point duty? He must have had a bird's-eye view."

"He saw Raymond falling, out of the corner of his eye, and then he focussed on stopping all the traffic as quickly as possible. I doubt you'll find anything useful in this lot."

"As expected. Thanks for reading them, love. You might as well go to—" The phone rang. "Yes, miss, DCI Fletcher speaking." He listened, made a note. "Thank you, miss." He hung up with a sigh.

"She's getting quite chatty—pleased that I've received a wire after sending so many."

"Edgar's telephone bill is going to be enormous."

"He can forward it to the county constabulary. That one was from the Yard. Tom and Ernie will be on the 8:10 express from Paddington tomorrow morning."

TWENTY-NINE

Daisy half wakened when Alec came to bed. The luminous dial of the bedside clock said it was twenty to two. To her drowsy indignation, he set the alarm for half past five.

When it duly shrilled, she was reluctantly ready to get up. Alec told her to go back to sleep.

"I have to deal with the bobbies they're sending from Worcester to search for the weapon used to attack Vincent. I don't hold out much hope of finding it, nor of it telling me much if we do, but the effort must be seen to be made."

"Good luck, darling. I hope you don't get rained on."

"It's misty out. Not foggy enough to hinder the hunt. I expect it'll be sunny later."

"It's a pity to waste this beautiful weather trying to catch a criminal. My apologies for my relatives' shenanigans!"

After the disturbed night, Daisy couldn't fall asleep again. She drowsed for a while, then got up early. She was the first down to breakfast, apart from Alec, who wasn't there.

"Mr. Fletcher's breakfasting in the study, madam," Ernest told her. "There was *five* telegrams waiting for him when he come in from the garden!"

"Did they find . . . anything out there?"

"Not as I know of, madam. The bobbies, they're to stay here, just sort of keeping an eye on things. They're having a bite in the kitchen. Mr. Fletcher's in his lordship's study. He's just called in that Smethwick, as was Mr. Raymond's driver. Champing at the bit, he is, to get back to London."

"Let me know as soon as Mr. Fletcher is alone, will you?" Daisy was itching to know what news the portentous five telegrams had brought.

Sam came down, looking worried. "Martha's not feeling at all well."

"Oh dear! She's not having an easy pregnancy, is she? I sailed through mine after a bit of morning sickness at the beginning. My sister Violet is the one who always has a hard time."

"She's told me about . . . Lady John, is it? It sounds as if she's been very kind."

"They enjoy each other's company. I'll see if Vi can come up and sit with her for a while today. Is she coming down?"

"I gather she's been breakfasting in bed. She's thinking of staying in our room this morning, if that wouldn't be rude. You'll have to excuse me not knowing the proper thing. I'm not used to such exalted company."

"Alec's a copper. Lord Dalrymple was a schoolmaster. We're not so very exalted. Though I should warn you about my mother, the dowager viscountess."

"Martha said she's very—" He grinned. "Well, that's not to be repeated." Sam rose as Geraldine and Edgar came in. Ignorance of etiquette didn't preclude good manners. "Good morning."

For the next few minutes, Lowecroft and Ernest were bustling about, in and out with fresh tea for Geraldine and freshly poached eggs for Edgar. Lowecroft, setting down a small, steaming teapot beside Geraldine, murmured something in her ear.

When he and the footman had both left the room, Geraldine said in tones of strong indignation, "Apparently Laurette told the maid who took their early tea that they're not coming out of their room until Mr. Pearson arrives!"

"One can hardly blame them, my dear," Edgar soothed her. "After all, Cousin Vincent has been attacked twice."

"Twice!" Sam exclaimed.

"On Sunday," Daisy told him. When Sam was supposedly in London. He had gone to the Hampstead house, he'd said, and spoken to Elsie. That couldn't have taken long. After that, he claimed to have toured the sights of the city. Impossible to verify! A fast car—

"I'm not convinced the first occurrence wasn't an accident," said Geraldine, with a minatory look at her sheepish husband.

Ernest popped in again with more toast. On his way out, as he passed behind Daisy's chair, he leant towards her. "The chief inspector is free," he muttered from the side of his mouth, with such discretion she wouldn't have understood if she hadn't been expecting the message.

Daisy hastily finished her coffee. "Alec," she explained apologetically to Geraldine. "I have to seize the moment."

"I must say it's comforting to have him in charge, Daisy. This . . . this whole business would be insupportable with a stranger!"

As Daisy reached the door, the kids arrived. They had all-too-clearly already been out, somewhere particularly muddy. Perfunctory efforts at cleaning themselves up had not much improved matters.

"It's all right, Mummy, we just came to say good morning to everyone. We're too mucky to sit at table."

"We had breakfast in the kitchen, Aunt Daisy," said Derek.

"Poor Cook! All right, say your good mornings from the door. Don't step on that carpet!"

Greetings were exchanged.

"Mummy, where's Daddy?"

"Busy, darling."

"Where's Uncle Frank?" Ben asked, slightly worried.

"Right here," said Frank from behind them. "You revolting creatures, what have you been up to?"

"We went down to the river, sir," Derek explained, "to see if it's gone down enough for boating."

"No boating till I've had a look," said Daisy, "and the boat'll have to be checked in case it was damaged by the flood." Or by

251

sabotage. "Off you go now. If you're staying in the house you'd better wash a bit more thoroughly."

"We're going out again, Aunt Daisy. The sun's coming out. It's going to be a capital day!"

"Off you go, now, and enjoy it," said Frank.

"I'll come and join you at the boat in half an hour," Edgar proposed. "I'll bring Truscott to give it a thorough inspection."

"Thanks, Uncle Edgar!"

As they ran off, Frank turned to Daisy and said in a low voice, "There's a couple of bobbies roaming about, did you know? I've asked one of them, a young chap, to keep an eye on the kids. On Ben in particular. He said he'd do his best."

Daisy approved. At present, Frank was the suspect with the most opportunity to carry out every attack, but some incidents were by no means proven to be attacks rather than sheer accident. The kids were the most vulnerable. They should be the first protected now that manpower was available.

Frank went into the breakfast room and Daisy headed for Edgar's den. She found Alec eating bacon, sausages, kidneys, fried bread, and fried tomatoes at the desk, surrounded by telegram forms, various papers, and a couple of volumes of an encyclopaedia.

"Nothing like exercise before breakfast to give you an appetite," she said. "Ernest said you didn't find the weapon?"

"No," he said gloomily, "nor any footprint, what with gravel on the paths and leaf litter under the bushes. It must have been the sound of a step onto the gravel that made Vincent start to turn."

"And saved his life."

"Possibly." He mashed a tomato on the fried bread, the way he did at home but not in polite company.

"And the telegrams?"

"What about the telegrams?"

"There's no need to be disagreeable, darling. You said the weapon probably wouldn't help anyway. Did you get responses from all those places?"

"Believe it or not, the farthest away have answered already: Trini-

252

dad and Jamaica—admittedly they're a few hours behind us—but Cape Town as well, and I believe they're an hour ahead."

"Ahead? I always get confused. . . ."

"When I wired them, it was already an hour or two later in the day there than here. Like Paris. In the West Indies it was still morning."

"Paris? Why Paris?"

"Your ancestor, the one responsible for this troublesome lot, was married to a Frenchwoman. His son, Vincent's grandfather, was sent to live with her family in France. And Vincent married a Frenchwoman. Doesn't he even use his wife's surname in his professional career?"

"His great-grandmother's, I think."

"The ties to France are very strong. I asked Geraldine—she was still up, writing letters—if she knew which part of France, and she told me Paris."

"Yes, that's right. But I still don't see—"

"The more I can get to know about each of them, the better chance I have of working out who's trying to do what to whom."

"Yes, I can see that. Did you find out anything about Vincent from Scarborough?"

"They're the others who haven't answered yet."

"Scotland Yard is more impressive the farther away from it you are?"

"That's the way it looks!"

"What did Trinidad and Jamaica and South Africa have to say?"

"Crowley's known to Port-of-Spain police. He's had a couple of drunk and disorderlies, and thirty days for illegal gambling. All a good few years ago, before he married Benjamin's mother. No violent offences on his record. He's a master mechanic, started in the asphalt business—"

"Road making?"

"No, extraction. They have a lake of asphalt in Trinidad, apparently. Since marrying Ben's mother, Susanna, in '22, Crowley has worked at the dockyards in Port-of-Spain. A good job, overhauling marine engines. Pays well, but intermittent, and he's pretty much lived up to his income what with four stepkids to bring up. That's not from the police—it's what he told me last night."

"The dockyards. So he could have met Sam."

"They both deny it. At that end, proving they knew each other would be difficult. At this end, we might have a chance."

"If they were in it together, it would clear up a lot of the mystery, wouldn't it? Suppose Frank agreed to help Sam become heir in return for taking the kids into his care."

"And other valuable consideration, no doubt. Yes, it's conceivable."

"It would explain the attacks on Ben—counting Bel's fall. Frank was trying to divert suspicion and didn't want to hurt him. He could have made the attempt on Vincent in the wood. And if he knew when Sam was due to arrive, he could have met him at the station and pointed out Raymond to him."

"Eleven twenty. We hadn't yet arrived in Worcester."

"Well, they could have somehow arranged to meet. You'll have to find out what Frank was up to at the Wedge and Beetle."

"I shall, believe me."

"So Frank met Sam and Sam tried to push Raymond under a tram. Then he tried to stab Vincent in the garden. . . . They're not very efficient, are they?"

"No. For two active fellows in the prime of life, they're downright incompetent."

"So perhaps it isn't them," Daisy said hopefully.

"I must find out whether Crowley's received any letters or made any telephone calls since he's been here. At the pub, perhaps, or post restante." Alec made a note. "Or he could have found out about trains when he was in London and left a message somewhere prearranged."

"Was Sam really on that ship?"

"He wasn't on the copy of the crew manifest kept in Kingston."

"Oh dear!"

"But that's explicable. The chap who's listed fell ill and Sam was taken on at the last minute. All it would take is a clerk forgetting to make the change. With everything so vague, the Admiralty won't put out a request to all ships to look out for the *Julianna*. It's a matter of waiting till she reaches Clydeside."

"What else did the Kingston coppers tell you?"

"Nothing useful. Nothing I didn't already know, except that Sam has no police record. Which could mean he's never been caught, or could mean he's never met with a big enough temptation. Other than the rumrunning caper, that is. That shows a tolerance for risk in pursuit of a sizable prize."

Daisy didn't want to pursue the idea of Frank and/or Sam as would-be murderers. Particularly Sam. She liked both, but Sam's guilt would devastate Martha. "What about South Africa?"

"Raymond was carrying rough diamonds all right. He went to Antwerp between his first call at Fairacres and this visit. He showed what he'd brought to a couple of diamond merchants, and they were to prepare bids for his consideration on his return. Or something of the sort; I'm not clear on the details."

"Anyone who knew who he was could have guessed he had them on him and followed him all the way from Cape Town, or from Antwerp, just waiting for an opportunity!"

"The middle of a busy street crossing in the heart of Worcester hardly seems the ideal opportunity."

"Perhaps not. He wasn't caught, though, was he. He could have had another try if Raymond hadn't dropped dead."

Alec looked sceptical. "I wish I thought so. As it is, we're going to have to try to check everyone's movements after they left the cathedral. I'm going to talk to the Worcester police about that." He glanced at his watch, stood up, and collected all the papers together. "I must go. Smethwick's going to drive me into Worcester in Raymond's car and go on to London. I'll meet Tom and Ernie and borrow a police car to bring them back. If you have any bright ideas, save them."

"Darling, are you actually asking me for bright ideas? Wild speculation?"

"This business is such a confounded mishmash, I have a feeling it's going to take a bit of wild speculation to solve it!"

THIRTY

Daisy decided that the weather was too good to waste, and that going for a walk was as good a way as any to inspire bright ideas. If she was going for a walk, she ought to call in at the Dower House, or she'd have her mother complaining of neglect again. If she didn't take the twins with her, Mother would complain that she never saw them.

Also, she could tell Vi that Martha was unwell and hoped for a visit.

Oliver and Miranda couldn't walk all the way, though. That meant taking the double pushchair. Getting the contraption over the hill while keeping the toddlers from straying too far was really a two-man job. Belinda would willingly help, but she had gone with the boys, Edgar, and Bill Truscott (and, no doubt, Nana and Pepper) to inspect the boat, so Nurse Gilpin would have to go with Daisy.

Mrs. Gilpin's disapproving presence would probably squelch any bright ideas at birth. However, the other reasons for the expedition still stood, and once conceived it could not easily be abandoned.

Daisy hoped her subconscious mind continued to work on the problem, because the twins had such fun on their outing that she almost forgot about Raymond's death and the inexplicable events that might or might not be connected. The dowager made it plain that she considered the whole affair beneath her notice.

In a low voice, Vi asked nervously about Derek's safety.

"Alec's letting Belinda stay." Daisy recalled the time she had broken off their engagement because he accused her of endangering Bel. "As far as we can tell, Ben himself isn't really in danger. In any case, he's safer when the others are with him. There's a bobby keeping an eye on them, not to mention Ben's stepfather, and Edgar, and Ernest, too, when they're indoors."

"Ernest?"

"The footman. He's been very helpful. And Derek's such a help with Belinda and Ben, but of course if you'd rather he came back here . . ."

Violet glanced at their mother, who had obviously had quite enough of toddler antics. "No. He'd better stay with you. I wish John were here!"

"He'll be back tomorrow, won't he? Martha was in the seventh heaven when Sam turned up at last. I presume the bush telegraph brought you the news?"

"Yes. I look forward to meeting him. Mother's dying of curiosity, too, though she won't admit it."

"You'll meet at Edgar's birthday party." If Sam hadn't been arrested by then. "If not before—Martha's feeling a bit seedy today and wondered whether you might be able to drop in later."

"I will, but it won't be till after tea. We have a luncheon invitation, and then Mother's dragging me on a round of calls."

"Rather you than me. Oliver, Miranda, it's time to go. Say bye-bye nicely to Grandmother and Aunt Violet."

"We go home now, Mama?" Miranda asked.

"To Uncle Edgar's house, darling."

"Go now," Oliver said firmly and darted towards the door.

"Master Oliver!" Mrs. Gilpin's stern voice, from the corner where she lurked, stopped him in his tracks. "Say good-bye like a gentleman."

Whatever her drawbacks, there were times when Daisy was very, very grateful for Nurse Gilpin.

When they returned to the house, Nurse whisked the babies upstairs for a nap. Daisy went to see Martha. She was lying on the chaise longue, wan and woebegone.

"It's awful being so miserable when Sammy just arrived," she said forlornly. "I told him it's no good sitting here worrying, he should go and get to know his new relations. So he went away."

Though she sympathised, Daisy couldn't find a good response to that. "Isn't the tea helping?" she asked, gesturing at the pot and cup on the table at Martha's side.

"No. Lady Dalrymple—Cousin Geraldine—came to see me and she suggested hot water bottles, but they're no help either. I'm too hot already. I just feel . . . awful. Sick, and standing up makes me dizzy."

"I'm going to call the doctor. If Dr. Hopcroft is still stuck in the floods, he'll have arranged for a locum by now."

Daisy went down to the telephone in the hall and got through to Mrs. Hopcroft.

"Yes, the water's gone down already, Mrs. Fletcher, leaving several inches of mud in the streets. The doctor is out on his morning round but I'm expecting him back any minute for his lunch. I'll tell him about . . . Mrs. *Samuel* Dalrymple, is it?"

"That's right. A sort of family gathering."

"So I've heard." Mrs. Hopcroft paused, as if hoping for further information. Daisy did not oblige. "The doctor will call at Fairacres this afternoon without fail."

Daisy thanked her. As she hung up, Ernest appeared.

"The chief inspector has returned from Worcester, madam, with two detectives from Scotland Yard. He'd like to see you in his lordship's study when convenient."

Surprised and pleased, Daisy hurried to the den. She had rather expected to be shut out of the investigation when Tom Tring and Ernie Piper arrived.

"Ernest said you asked for me, darling. Hello, Tom; hello, Ernie. How nice to see you."

DS Tring was wearing his summer suit, a vast acreage of robin's-egg blue-and-white check, topped with an expanse of forehead that continued hairless to the nape of his neck. His flourishing moustache half hid a broad smile. He loomed over Ernie Piper, a slight figure, barely regulation height, in his dark blue flannel suit. Just seeing the two of them—Tom so good with people, Ernie so good with facts—made Daisy feel better.

Greetings were exchanged, enquiries made after Tom's godson Oliver and his sisters.

"If you're *quite* ready," said Alec, a bit snarky. They all sat down. "Daisy, I want you to tell Tom and Ernie everything you can remember about the visit to Worcester, from the moment we parted in the cathedral. I'm hoping either the telling will remind you of something you saw or heard that you missed out when you reported, or one of them will spot something *I* missed."

Daisy dredged her memory for details. The three men listened in silence, Ernie writing down her words verbatim—his recent promotion to sergeant had not diminished his supply of well-sharpened pencils.

"The road was flooded," she finished, "so we turned round and came back here. Alec arrived a few minutes later."

Alec clarified: "Having been informed by Laurette—Mrs. Vincent Dalrymple—of Raymond's accident."

"Can we come back to that in a minute, Chief?" said Tom. "Mrs. Fletcher, you didn't catch even a glimpse of any of the suspects as you and Mrs. Vincent wandered about the city?"

"No. She dragged me from shop to shop, none of which satisfied her. She went on about London or Paris being the only places to buy clothes. I don't know how she survives in Scarborough."

"Did she buy anything?"

"Some aspirin, a hairnet, and a magazine, that she could have bought in any of a dozen shops."

"Was she hunting for anything in particular?"

"Not that she mentioned. She looked at clothes mostly. We went into a toy shop but she didn't seem to be particularly interested."

"Ah," said Tom profoundly.

Ernie took his turn. "Mrs. Fletcher, can you estimate how much time passed between your first awareness of something happening ahead and when you dropped Mrs. Vincent at the hotel?"

"Heavens no. I suppose it was at least fifteen minutes. Less than half an hour, though. That's the best I can do, and I wouldn't swear to it."

"You heard the deceased say he was pushed?"

"Yes. 'Someone pushed.' He was mumbling, not speaking clearly. He was in a daze. The bobby who'd helped him to the pavement assumed he was referring to the person who pushed him out of the way of the trams, so I did too. Now I come to think of it, he repeated the phrase. He might have been trying to say he didn't mean that person."

"Maybe. Mrs. Vincent offered to go and tell the rest of the party? Or did you suggest it?"

Daisy frowned. "I'm pretty sure she offered. But she wanted a lift to the hotel in Raymond's car."

"Chief," said Tom, "you haven't described their reactions when they heard."

"We'll discuss that later," said Alec, to Daisy's annoyance.

"What about Mrs. Vincent, Mrs. Fletcher? Was she very upset?"

"I was concentrating on Raymond, not Laurette. When we first realised there had been an accident, neither of us was keen to get close. Then the crowds sort of relaxed—it was really crowded, the first shopping day after the bank holiday—so I assumed nothing too serious had happened and we walked on the way we'd been going. Of course, when I saw it was Raymond, I hurried forward. I was concentrating on Raymond, not on Laurette's emotions."

"But she was tut-tutting at your side?" Tom suggested patiently. "After all, from what I gather, she was more closely related to him than you were."

"Slightly closer. Not at all close. And Raymond really didn't make any effort to get to know anyone at Fairacres, wouldn't you say, darling?"

"I agree, except for his one kindness to Belinda."

"Oh yes, at the fair. So out of character as to be memorable! He wasn't a very congenial person. No, Laurette wasn't 'tut-tutting at my side,' Tom. She stood back a little. There wasn't much room at his side, though, what with me and the coppers."

"And in the car?"

"Sorry, I really wasn't paying much attention to her. It was only a couple of minutes' drive to the Talbot. Alec, have you asked Geraldine what she observed at the hotel when Laurette told you all about Raymond?"

"No, that's a good point. I will. All right, if you can't think of anything else. . . . Do you know where the kids are?"

"No, but wherever, I'm sure they have Edgar or Frank or one of the Worcester bobbies, or all three, on guard and doubtless cramping their style. That reminds me, I promised to go and look at the river, to see whether it looks safe for boating."

"You're the expert, Mrs. Fletcher?" Tom teased, grinning.

"Experienced in the Severn's moods, at least. My brother and I used to do quite a bit of boating."

"Ah."

"Thanks, Daisy. I'll probably be asking you to go back over your impressions of the other incidents, but Raymond's being the only death—"

"So far."

"The *only* death, I trust. We're concentrating on it for the moment." Alec stood up and the others followed suit, so Daisy reluctantly accepted her dismissal and left them to their cogitations.

The all-knowing Ernest told her the kids had set up a badminton net on the lawn. Bel and Derek were teaching Ben and Frank to play. Daisy went upstairs to tell Martha that Dr. Hopcroft would call after lunch.

Sam was in their bedroom, reading poetry to Martha. She looked a bit brighter, whether because of the poems or the attention.

"John Masefield," Sam announced cheerfully. "Lady Dalrymple recommended him. Do you know *Sea Fever*? It's a cracking good poem."

"Does it begin, 'I must go down to the sea again'?"

"Seas, with an s."

"Very appropriate for you, Sam. How clever of Geraldine to think of it. I always liked that one."

"It's pretty," said Martha, clutching Sam's hand, "but I don't want you to go to sea again till the baby's born."

"I can't promise, sweetheart, but I'll do my best."

Daisy told them about the doctor, which made Sam look anxious. He went with her to the door and whispered, "Do you think she's really ill?"

"No, not for a minute. I just think it won't hurt to have him take a look. Perhaps she needs a tonic or something like that."

Satisfied, he returned to Martha's side. Daisy went down to the garden. She waved to the badminton players, but went straight on down the lawn to the river. The comparative coolness of the air near the water made her realise how hot the day was growing.

Though the river was well below the banks, swirls and eddies in the brown torrent made it too dangerous for a small rowing boat with kids at the oars. A narrow boat was barely making way upstream, the boatman standing in the bow with a boat hook to fend off floating branches, while his wife steered. She waved to Daisy. The superstructure was painted with the usual cheerful, colourful roses and castles, but Daisy thought it must be a hard life. She couldn't imagine living in such a tiny space.

She returned to the house via the backwater. The skiff looked spruce, either undamaged or repaired earlier. Clouds of midges danced about Daisy. She fanned her face with her hand to keep them away.

The winding path through the wood, along the little stream, was shady. Daisy peered into the brambles and nettle beds as she passed, not that she expected to spot a blade where Alec and his minions had failed. All the same, she walked a few yards along some of the narrow paths made by rabbits and foxes and badgers, hoping to see a glint of metal.

The soft leaf mould underfoot changed to gravel when she reached the laburnum alley. Dappled sunlight filtered through the close-woven, well-leaved vines overhead, with their dangling pods full of poisonous seeds. She must remind Nurse never to bring the little ones here in search of a shaded place to run.

Coming to the break in the alley, with the footpath leading across the park on her left and the lawn on her right, Daisy paused before stepping out into the full sun.

This was where Vincent had been stabbed. As he left the deep gloom under the laburnums for the sunset twilight, or as he moved back into the shadowy continuation of the alley? Laurette had babbled about it but Daisy couldn't remember.

It was really an odd place to choose for a stroll at dusk. Very little light would have penetrated the dense foliage above.

She looked about, trying to envisage exactly what had happened.

The attack must have occurred as Vincent and Laurette moved out of the shelter, as Daisy was about to now, because if the attacker had been lurking ahead, outside the laburnums, they might well have spotted him. Vincent had been on Laurette's left, because the cut had been on his left side. The attacker would not risk waiting on the right, the lawn side. At the time, Alec and Daisy had been walking there, where the kids and Frank were still busy with shuttlecock and battledore.

So Vincent was on Laurette's left. He had heard a sound and turned towards it. . . .

No, he had been stabbed from behind, not from the side, not in the shoulder or upper arm. It only made sense if he had mistaken the direction of the sound and swung to his right.

Unless, perhaps, the crunch of the couple's footsteps on the gravel had covered the sound of the attacker's steps, and Vincent had just happened to turn slightly towards Laurette at the moment he was struck. It wouldn't be surprising if they had been flustered enough to persuade themselves they had heard the attacker.

The attacker was certainly not a very effective murderer. Frank? Sam? Daisy had been almost convinced of Raymond's guilt until he became a victim. That demonstrated the peril Alec was always warning her about, of assuming someone one liked could not possibly be a villain, and vice versa.

Now the list of suspects had shortened to Sam and Frank.

THIRTY-ONE

The atmosphere at lunch was uneasy.

Alec, Tom, and Ernie Piper ate in Edgar's den. Vincent and Laurette persisted in their resolution not to leave their room.

"Has a tray been taken to them?" Geraldine asked Lowecroft when he delivered this news.

"Naturally, my lady."

"At least they trust my staff, it would seem! Martha's not coming down, Samuel?"

"She's feeling rotten, my l—Cousin Geraldine. Not hungry, but I made her promise to try to eat a bite or two."

"I rang Dr. Hopcroft," Daisy put in. "He's going to call this afternoon."

"Thank you, Daisy. Lowecroft, I wish to speak to the doctor after he's seen Mrs. Samuel."

"I shall inform him, my lady."

The children were present. Belinda asked anxiously, "Will Aunt Martha be all right, Mummy?"

"I'm sure she will, darling. Dr. Hopcroft will know how to make her more comfortable. Remember how he stopped your nosebleed?"

"And it didn't even swell up at all," Ben reminded her.

The children were satisfied. Raymond's death and the Vincent Dalrymples' absence from the scene hadn't made much impression on them. None of the three had asked about the stabbing so Daisy assumed everyone had had more sense than to tell them about it. She hoped Alec wouldn't want to question them.

They had reached the pudding course—a fluffy lemon mousse, sweet and tart and perfect for a hot day—when Alec came in.

"I'm sorry to interrupt, Cousin Geraldine. I wanted to catch you all together." He glanced round the table. "Where are Vincent and Laurette?"

"Barricaded in their room still. Servants-only admitted."

"They'll admit me. As you've all doubtless heard by now, my two detective sergeants have arrived from London. Geraldine, DS Tring will be talking to the servants. Would you be kind enough to instruct them to cooperate?"

"Lowecroft, you heard Mr. . . . um . . ."

"DCI."

"DCI Fletcher. Please see that everyone gives DS Tring full co-operation."

"Certainly, my lady."

Alec continued, "I'd like to ask all of you to stay within easy reach, as I may want to speak to you again this afternoon."

Edgar's face brightened. "I'll tell Wharton I can't go with him to inspect the home farm!"

"Thank you, sir." Alec preserved a straight face except for a twitch at the corner of his mouth.

"I presume coffee on the terrace is acceptable," Geraldine said.

"By all means."

Edgar brightened still further. "Then I may go to the conservatory?"

"Anywhere in the house, sir, except that I'll beg the continued use of your study. Outside, please stay close enough to be easily visible."

Even in the shade, it was as hot or hotter on the terrace, though less stuffy than in the house. No sign of thunderclouds, just the sun beating down. The air above the lawn shimmered.

Lowecroft and Ernest brought out a jug of iced coffee as well as the usual coffeepot. The children tried it but didn't like it. Edgar soon bore them off to the conservatory—or vice versa. Sam went up to see Martha, returning to say she was snoozing. A maid had told him she ate scarcely a mouthful of lunch but drank several cups of mint tea.

Geraldine went inside to write letters. Daisy was sure she ought to be writing letters, but she was too limp and lethargic to remember to whom. Frank and Sam asked whether she'd mind if they deserted her for the billiard room.

"Of course not. I'm going up to see the twins in a bit, after their nap." She moved to the wicker chaise longue.

Ernie Piper came out. "Whew, is it ever hot. You happen to know where Mr. Crowley or Mr. Samuel Dalrymple have got to?"

"They said they were going to play billiards, just a couple of minutes ago. Ernie, what's going on? What's Alec up to? Has he received any news from Scarborough or Paris? Has he any ideas about what's going on here?"

"Sorry, Mrs. Fletcher. All I'm allowed to say is the police are making progress in their investigation."

Daisy sighed. "I hope that's true. It's not at all comfortable having one's relatives attempting to do each other in."

"Happens in the best families," said Ernie. "I mean—You know what I mean."

She smiled at him. "I do."

He left. Daisy leant back against the cushions and closed her eyes against the glare.

She awoke to the sound of the grandfather clock in the drawing room striking three. Groggy, disoriented, she blinked at the sun-drenched world. She had a crick in her neck. Afternoon naps never agreed with her, and it was hotter than ever.

Pulling herself together, she struggled to her feet. Time to go up to the nursery. She was not looking forward to climbing the stairs.

"Mama!"

"Mama!"

With shrieks of glee, Miranda and Oliver scampered across the lawn towards her. Running to meet them, Daisy saw Mrs. Gilpin in the shade of the great chestnut, seated stiff as a dressmaker's dummy on a kitchen chair Ernest must have carried out for her.

Playing with the twins, Daisy managed to forget for a while that even the best families may harbour a felon.

At Nurse's decree, playtime ended at last. Daisy held Miranda's hand up the endless stairs, carrying her up the last flight. Oliver, doggedly determined, reached above his head to hold the banister rail and made it all the way on his own.

Daisy read them a story, then went down to see how Martha was doing.

Sam opened the door. He told her Dr. Hopcroft had already called. He had been very soothing. Nothing was seriously wrong, Sam assured Daisy, sounding as if he was reassuring himself. Martha should take it easy, continue to rest with her feet up and stick to small quantities of bland foods until she felt better. She must make herself eat, because though she wasn't hungry, the baby was. Nibbling a dry biscuit should quell her nausea. Plenty of liquids, he advised, particularly in this hot weather. Milk was best, most nourishing, if she could stomach it.

A plate of Marie and Bath Oliver biscuits, a dish of junket, a glass of milk, and a teapot showed that cook and housekeeper were doing their part to tempt the invalid. One biscuit showed signs of nibbling. The milk was down half an inch from the creamy ring that showed the original level.

"Maybe you can persuade her to eat?" Sam said anxiously.

"I'll try. I'll sit with her for a bit, at least, if you'd like to stretch your legs."

Daisy managed to persuade Martha to finish the nibbled biscuit and swallow most of the junket, in spite of continuing nausea. Half a cup of mint tea seemed to make her feel worse. Daisy removed the pot to the top of the chest of drawers, out of the way, so that Martha wouldn't drink more without thinking. She put a glass of water on the table.

Martha was very hot and sweaty—Daisy's nanny would have been horrified by the adjective: "Horses sweat, gentlemen perspire, ladies glow" had been one of her favourite maxims. But there it was, Martha was hot and sweaty. Daisy brought a basin of cold water and a flannel and helped her wash face, neck, and arms.

She wondered whether Alec wanted to question Martha but she didn't mention it, or talk about murder. The poor girl needed to be cheered up, not depressed.

Sam returned. "Tea on the terrace, Daisy," he said. "I'll stay with Martha till your sister . . . Oh sweetie, you've had a bite to eat. I'm so glad."

Down on the terrace, she found Geraldine alone, presiding over the tea tray. "Really, Daisy," she greeted her, "your mother!"

"What now?" Daisy accepted a cup of tea and piled a plate with cucumber and watercress sandwiches and a slice of sponge cake.

"She rang up. Now it's *my* fault Raymond died and reporters are swarming round the Dower House."

"They are?"

"Truscott and a bobby were keeping them out of Fairacres, so they're trying to wring further information from the Dower House instead. As if I could do anything about it!"

"I can't imagine what she expects of you." Daisy hoped Violet would be able to get away. She wasn't up to the walk across the park on a hot day.

Frank came out, looking disgruntled. "The same questions over and over again," he grumbled, swigging a cup of tea standing, then holding out the cup for a refill. "After a bit, you want to make up different answers, just for a change."

"Better not," Daisy advised.

"Oh, I didn't. Yet. At least I'm now allowed out of sight of the house. Lady D, would you mind if I pop down to the Wedge for a pint in a while?"

No longer a suspect, Daisy wondered, or given enough rope to hang himself? No doubt someone would be keeping an eye on him. Tom Tring, perhaps—Tom was as good in pubs as he was with servants, genial, chatty without giving anything away, picking up all sorts of information without upsetting people.

Pepper and Nana arrived, followed by Edgar and the children, all chattering happily about a Purple Emperor that had hatched today in the conservatory. They had released it in the woods, where it flitted straight to the brambles, its caterpillars' favourite food.

"It's a butterfly," Ben told Daisy when she enquired. Carefully he added, "*Apatura iris*. Is that right, Uncle Edgar?"

"To the letter, my dear boy." Edgar beamed with fond pride.

Still no sign of Vincent and Laurette. When Ernest brought out more hot water, Daisy drew him aside and asked whether Alec had been to see them in their room. He had.

Alec was being utterly infuriating. He wasn't usually quite so determined to keep her at arm's length from his investigations, once she was involved. And this one concerned her own relatives, her family! Or perhaps that was why he was keeping her in the dark, now that he had Tom and Ernie's help?

Sam arrived. "Your sister's with Martha," he told Daisy.

"I'll go up, then, and see if Violet has any ideas for making Martha more comfortable."

And while on the subject of comfort, it was past time she changed out of the skirt and blouse she had been wearing all day. She had a sleeveless linen frock, a pretty blue-and-green pattern, that would be cool and suitable for dinner, as they weren't dressing. It was sure to be creased, though. Changing course, she made for her and Alec's room, to get it out and ring for a maid to iron it.

The frock was at the back of the wardrobe. As she reached down the coat hanger, she noticed in the corner below it Vincent's slashed shirt and jacket, roughly folded, where she had deposited them.

Had Alec forgotten them, amidst the flood of information he was collecting? Abandoning the frock, she took them out and draped them over the back of a cane chair. In his haste to go and look for the weapon, he had given them only a cursory examination. Perhaps she could find something significant about them and worm her way back into the case.

She fetched a matching chair and set it side by side with the first, then dressed them, one in the shirt, one in the jacket. She looked. She frowned.

It was no good saying it couldn't have happened, because clearly it had happened. Therefore it was not impossible. But she couldn't understand how a single blow could have caused both cuts. The one in the jacket was just under the armpit, barely missing the seam. The rent in the shirt, spotted with blood that Daisy carefully avoided touching, was considerably longer, lower down, and further back, matching the graze on Vincent's back.

Daisy tried to picture the sequence of events that could have produced this result, and failed. It just wasn't possible.

She had to tell Alec at once. It was *not* just a ploy to insinuate herself into the investigation. She took the jacket off the chair—and in doing so noticed a nick in the artificial silk lining, high up inside the front of the sleeve, just where a blade entering from the back would catch it—if no arm was in the way.

With the shirt folded inside the jacket, cuts hidden, down the stairs she trudged again. After all this exercise, she ought to be slim enough to please even Lucy. In the hall she met the ubiquitous Ernest.

"Is Mr. Fletcher still in the study?" she asked. "Is anyone with him at present?"

"Yes, madam, and no, not if you mean any of them you might call suspects. There's a Dr. Pardoe, him that came to take a look at Mr. Raymond in the garage." He gave Vincent's jacket a knowing glance but didn't comment.

Daisy knocked on the study door and went in without waiting to be invited. Alec, sitting at the desk as usual, looked up in annoyance. Tom, Ernie, and the doctor stood up.

Alec rose likewise, saying, "Daisy, what—"

"Look!" She held up the clothes. "Vincent's, that he was wearing when—"

"All right, I'd forgotten them," he admitted. He took the bundle from her. "Tom and Ernie haven't seen them. We'll take a look," he said dismissively. "Thanks."

"Alec, it simply can't have happened they way they told us. In fact, it can't have happened at all. The attack on Vincent, I mean. Their story was cut out of whole cloth, in more senses than one."

He exchanged glances with Tom and Ernie. "Daisy, I said we'd take care of it. Leave it to us, will you? And don't for pity's sake talk about it."

"I wasn't going to." As an exit line, it could have been bettered, but it would do. Daisy duly made her exit. If they needed her to explain the evidence to them, they could jolly well come and find her.

She still hadn't dealt with the frock she wanted to wear. Hot and sticky, she plodded up the stairs yet again.

On her way to the bedroom, she had to pass Martha's room. She decided to pop in to say hello to Violet and see how things were going. When she knocked, to her surprise she heard rapid footsteps coming towards the door.

"Come in!" Vi sounded desperate. She flung the door open before Daisy could turn the knob. "At last—Oh, Daisy! I rang for a maid. Thank heaven you're here. Martha's bleeding and having cramps." She laid her hand on her abdomen. "Like contractions. I'm afraid. . . . Please, please, go and ring the doctor!"

"Of course, darling. Right away."

"I want Sammy!" Martha's wail followed Daisy.

This time she ran, sliding her hand down the banisters to keep her balance. Halfway down the second flight, she remembered Dr. Pardoe's presence. A doctor in the house was worth two in Upton, she thought, slightly hysterical. Dr. Pardoe was the police surgeon and pathologist, but presumably he knew a bit about difficult pregnancies as well as dead bodies.

She sped to Edgar's den and burst in without knocking. "Dr. Pardoe, I'm afraid my cousin Martha is having a miscarriage. Will you *please* come quickly!"

"I'm not really . . . But of course I'll come. Have someone fetch my bag from my car, and you'd better ring up her GP. Symptoms?" he queried, following Daisy from the room.

"Bleeding and cramps. I don't know how bad. My sister is with her."

When they reached the entrance hall, a maid was scurrying down the stairs, looking frightened. Daisy told her to show Dr. Pardoe to Mrs. Samuel's room.

By then Ernest had appeared. "Go and get the doctor's bag from his car," Daisy directed, "and take it to him."

"At once, madam."

"Half a mo, do you know where Mr. Samuel is?"

"He said just a minute ago he was going down to the river, madam, to try for a breath of cooler air."

"Thanks. Be quick now."

He dashed off.

The operator put Daisy through to Dr. Hopcroft right away. He was in the middle of his evening surgery, but he said he had only a couple of patients waiting, neither of whom he expected to occupy him for more than a few minutes. "Then I'll come straight to Fairacres," he promised, "though I have every confidence in Dr. Pardoe."

Hoping that was true, not just professional courtesy, Daisy went to look for Sam.

No one in the drawing room, no one on the terrace. Entering the alley, she could see all the way to the end: no sign of Sam. As she entered the wood the path curved and at last, through the trees, she glimpsed movement.

"Sam!" she called. There was no response, but she was breathless and the trees and undergrowth were in between. Sam—or whoever it was—might not have heard her.

Panting, she rounded the bend. Ahead, just about to disappear round the next bend, was a man's back.

Daisy drew a deep breath so that this time he'd hear her. Before she could shout, a figure darted out of the bushes. From the woods came a yell: "Uncle Sam!"

A stray ray of sun glinted on a knife blade as it rose and fell. The second man plunged back into the bushes. The first man cried out and fell, face down.

Sam—villain or victim? Daisy ran.

THIRTY-TWO

$\mathcal{N}$*o sooner* had Daisy flounced from Edgar's study, not quite slamming the door behind her, than Alec had spread Vincent's jacket and shirt on Edgar's desk. He and the sergeants bent over them, studying the pattern of cuts.

Dr. Pardoe joined them. "This is significant, Chief Inspector?" he queried. "You were rather cavalier with . . . Mrs. Fletcher, was she?"

"I just want to keep my wife out of this affair, Doctor. She has a talent for complicating matters." He pretended not to see Tom Tring's grin and shake of the head. "These clothes may or may not be material—Sorry, pun unintentional. Not material evidence of wrongdoing. But certainly indicative."

Tom put it in the vernacular: "Fishy."

"Blood on the shirt." Ernie Piper held it up to show Pardoe. "None on the jacket. And it doesn't line up."

"Are you saying someone was wearing them at the time they were damaged, Sergeant?" Pardoe examined the jacket. "At a superficial glance, anatomically impossible."

"Mrs. Fletcher is always right. Almost always."

"She's right enough this time, Chief." Tom's rumble had a questioning note.

"Mea culpa. I was in a hurry to hunt for the knife, and then I just plain forgot about them. Not that—" He looked round as the door was flung open without ceremony.

Daisy took two hasty steps across the threshold. Urgently she begged Dr. Pardoe to come and see Martha, who was showing signs of miscarrying her baby. The doctor strode out. Without another word, Daisy dashed after him.

"Sounds like an emergency," said Tom.

"Not one *we* have to deal with, thank heaven," said Alec. "Now, where were we?"

" 'Anatomically impossible,' " Piper quoted. "I'd say that just about confirms your hunch, Chief."

"Yes, I think so. It disposes of the biggest stumbling block, the supposed attacks on Vincent. Did you finish reading the reports from Scarborough and the Sûreté, Ernie?"

"The next to last page from Paris is an affidavit from the Valliers affirming that they sent copies of the letters to Vincent a couple of months ago."

"Don't tell me you read the affidavit, laddie," Tom scoffed.

The young detective sergeant grinned. "Not me. I don't parley-voo frog. The last page was a translation."

"Ah!"

"And Scarborough?"

"Not quite on their uppers: The Castle Cliff Hotel is doing well. But Vincent's father took out a whopping loan against the property towards the end of the war, when business was bad. It falls due next year. Vincent works like a dog, as both manager and maître d', and his missus is housekeeper and consy-urge."

"Then Vincent isn't exactly leading a life of leisure, as he claimed! He said the place is run by a hired manager."

"Not so, Chief. He does have a part-time undermanager, who's taking care of the place while they're here."

"What about the kids? Prep school and governess is what they talked about."

"The boy goes to a small private day school. The daughters' governess is a French relative who also helps in the hotel. Paid a pittance because she came over to learn English as much as to teach the girls. She's taken them—the boy too—to stay with her family in Paris. The French coppers missed that."

"So much for the holiday on the Continent."

"Ah." Tom ruminated for a moment. "You reckon he killed Raymond and pretended to be attacked himself to divert suspicion? But the fake attacks on the kiddies, what were they supposed to prove? I still don't get what his purpose was." He took out a blue-and-white chequered handkerchief and mopped his shining dome of a head.

"Just to sow confusion, I think," Alec said. "And he certainly succeeded. I still can't be sure that Belinda's accident wasn't just that. We don't even know that he caused Raymond's fall. We haven't got any evidence that'd hold up in court even for a manslaughter charge. Or any other charges, come to that."

Tom grinned. "Wasting police time?"

"We're wasting time, all right. What we do have is Lord Dalrymple's permission to search the house, and that includes the Vincent Dalrymples' bedroom. Time to lay down the law. Come on."

Alec knew his way about the more populated part of the house, though he didn't expect ever to master all its passages and stairways, nooks and crannies. He led the way up the stairs.

Though Tom trod lightly for his size and Ernie was slight and barely regulation height, three pairs of tramping feet made quite a racket. Alec wasn't concerned about the noise alerting Vincent to their approach. Earlier, politely requested to answer a few questions, Vincent and Laurette had refused to open the door, let alone come down to the study or even let Alec interview them in their room. He doubted they'd bolt, and if they did they wouldn't get far.

The three men had to pass Martha's bedroom to reach Vincent's. Alec was about to tell the other two to go singly, quietly, when the door opened and Dr. Pardoe came out, leaving it ajar.

"I thought I heard . . . Fletcher, Mrs. Dalrymple has been drinking pennyroyal tea. She told me it was peppermint, and it is a variety of mint, but the smell is quite distinctive. It's an abortifacient, you know."

"Great Scott, is she—has she—will she lose the baby?"

"Doubt it. The oil can be effective, an infusion rarely, especially after the first three months. And before you ask, in my opinion she is not responsible."

"Daisy said Martha had complained about the taste."

"It could be an accident," the doctor suggested. Alec, Tom, and Ernie exchanged glances. Another accident? "But I wondered if it could somehow be connected to whatever this business is you're investigating here."

"Chief," said Tom, "I told you the servants said Vincent and his wife—and Raymond, come to that—had been poking their noses all over the house the first few days they were here. What I didn't mention is that Mrs. Vincent was in and out of the pantry and the larder. The cook caught her opening jars and tins to see what was in them."

"Get down there right away, Tom, and bag anything that might have contained mint tea. With a bit of luck we might get a fingerprint. Doctor," added Alec as Tom hurried off and Pardoe turned back towards the door, "would you kindly tell Sam I'd like a quick word with him?"

"The husband? He's not here. Went out for a breath of air, I'm told. Lady John has been sitting with Mrs. Dalrymple. It was she who sent Mrs. Fletcher for a doctor. And she has been helping me very ably, I might add."

"Good," Alec said absently. "Let's go, Ernie. I should have foreseen this possibility. If Martha has a boy . . ."

He passed a couple of doors and stopped at one that had a small table beside it. On the table was a tray with a teapot, plates, and cups and saucers, all used. He knocked.

No response. He stepped back and gestured to Ernie, who put his ear to the door. After a minute's silence, Ernie shook his head, then knocked again, saying loudly, "Police! Mr. Dalrymple, please open the door."

"Who is that?" Laurette's voice sounded thin and strained.

"Detective Sergeant Piper, madam. From London. Detective Chief Inspector Fletcher would like—"

"*Ce salaud!*" she spat out. "Why does he not discover who attacked Vincent?"

"That's one thing he wants to talk to you about, madam."

"He is of the family. It is perhaps a plot to lure us out—"

"Mrs. Dalrymple," Alec said sharply, "that's nonsense. We have Lord Dalrymple's permission to search the house. If you or your husband refuses to open the door, we're coming in anyway."

Ernie took from a pocket a gadget reminiscent of a dentist's instrument of torture. As he inserted it in the lock, they heard swift footsteps inside, moving away from the door.

Always neat and quick, Ernie had the door open in a few seconds. They burst into the room. Laurette was fumbling with a key at a connecting door in the wall to their left.

Alec went to her, took the key from her shaking hand, and led her to the window overlooking the terrace. "Sit down."

Without a word, she slumped into one of the two wing chairs.

Meanwhile, Ernie glanced under the bed, in the wardrobe, and behind the curtains. "Must be in there, sir," he said, waving at the connecting door.

"Check." Alec tossed the key to him.

The door was not locked.

"Police!" Ernie flung the door open. "Bathroom. No one here, sir. But there's a door in the opposite wall. . . . It's bolted on this side." The bolt snicked. "And locked."

"Try the same key. Hotels may have a different key for each bedroom, but these country houses usually don't."

"Got it. Nothing but a corridor."

"So he's been coming and going at will! That's torn it."

"Three doors opposite. One looks like back stairs."

"Don't bother with them. Lock the door and bolt it, then come through and lock that door. Mrs. Dalrymple, I can't spare the time for you now. I'm going to leave you here, locked in."

"*Mais—*"

"For as short a period as possible. And in case you have any other keys, I'm stationing a constable at the corner where he can watch both corridors. Come on, Piper. Lock the door behind you."

Ernie obeyed. As they strode along the passage towards the main stairs, he enquired, "Which constable would that be, Chief? The one you set to follow Crowley or the one guarding Miss Belinda and her cousins?"

"One of the six others I should have asked for. No use crying over spilt milk. We have to find Vincent or Sam, or both. In a hurry."

Half aware of children's voices and a dog's bark, Daisy knelt beside Sam. A dark red patch was spreading across his shoulders. Groaning, he tried to push himself up.

"Keep still! You'll make it worse."

"Yes, ma'am! Bloody hell, it hurts."

"I can't get you out of your jacket to see how bad it is. I'm going to put pressure on, to try to stop the bleeding."

"Mummy, is Uncle Sam dead?" Belinda's quavering call came from the depths of the woods.

"No, just injured." Just? "Are the boys with you?" They had better be! "Derek, Ben, come here. I need your shirts."

"We can't, Aunt Daisy."

"Why not?" Daisy peered into the gloom of the woods. The attacker—Frank or Vincent?—in fleeing had beaten down a trail straight through the undergrowth. Fifty feet in—

"We're sitting on him."

So they were. Daisy couldn't make out much of the figure on the ground but Derek's face was a pale blob at one end, Belinda's at the other, and Ben's a dark blob between them.

"The nettles are stinging our legs."

"But *he's* got his face in them." That was Derek, deeply satisfied.

"How—?"

"Nana tripped him."

"On purpose!" Belinda claimed proudly.

"If we get up he'll get away."

"*Who?*"

"Uncle Vincent," they chorused.

278

"That bastard!" Sam sounded quite vigorous but didn't make another attempt to get up. "He tried to kill me!"

"Mrs. Fletcher!" Ernie Piper came pounding down the path.

"Thank goodness! Sam's bleeding, and the children have bagged Vincent." Afraid to lift a hand from Sam's back, she nodded towards the woods.

Already half out of his jacket, he stared, a grin spreading across his face. "Well done, young 'uns! All under control? Here, Mrs. Fletcher, use this." He handed her his shirt. "I'd better go—Ah, here comes the bobby that was supposed to be keeping an eye on 'em." Snorting, he knelt down to help Daisy staunch the flow of blood.

In the wood, a bulky figure lumbered towards the children, trailing brambles.

"He's too big to burrow through the undergrowth after them. I bet they were playing Indians. I'm not surprised he lost them."

"Unggggh," groaned Sam as Ernie's hands took over the pressure from Daisy's. "Let up a bit, mate!"

"Sorry. Better than bleeding to death. Don't think that's likely, though. The bleeding's slowing down already. You were lucky!"

"Luck, nothing! Belinda called my name so I started to turn that way and I caught a glimpse of the bastard. I started dropping to the ground before he struck. I'm a ship's officer. Something moves that shouldn't, you duck. It gets to be instinctive. Could be a broken spar or a loose hatch cover or a disgruntled seaman. Ouch, enough, dammit!"

Daisy stood up, leaving Sam to Ernie's capable hands. In the wood, the children were all talking at once. The large constable, his voice a basso continuo, bent over Vincent.

Then, through a sudden silence, came the click of handcuffs.

THIRTY-THREE

Thursday midday. Outside, a soft, steady drizzle fell.

Alec returned to Fairacres from Worcester, having taken his prisoners there the previous evening and stayed overnight. He had spent the morning tying up his investigation before seeing off Tom and Ernie at the station. Tommy Pearson came with him, having travelled from London by the ten-to-one train. Bill Truscott had fetched both of them from Worcester.

At lunch, held back half an hour as a result of Tommy's wire announcing his coming, the lawyer had excused himself for having failed to respond to Geraldine's urgent summons.

"I was called to prepare a client's deathbed will at the other end of nowhere," he said. "A country house in northern Lincolnshire—four trains, each slower than the one before, then ten miles in a pony trap. When at last I reached the place, the old gentleman had just breathed his last. By the time I returned to town and discovered your message, Lady Dalrymple, it was far too late to set out. A thoroughly unsatisfactory business. I can only present my apologies for my tardiness."

"You are clearly not to blame, Mr. Pearson," Geraldine assured him.

"Thank you. And now, perhaps, someone will explain to me just

what was going on here that required my presence several days early."
He looked—rather accusingly, Daisy thought—at Alec. "Fletcher
has given me the barest hint."

"No no, my dear fellow," said Edgar. "Bad for the digestion. After lunch, if you please, we'll have a general disclosure. I'm sure I
don't know the half of it. Would you believe I saw a Peach Blossom
this morning, before the rain started?"

There was a murmur of incredulity at this news.

"August is surely an odd time for peach blossom," Tommy observed.

"Yes, indeed. They usually fly from May to July, and sometimes
again in the autumn. They like blackberry brambles," Edgar said
pointedly.

"Ah, a butterfly!" said Tommy, enlightened.

"A moth, Mr. Pearson," Edgar gently corrected him, "and a very
attractive one. Pink spots. *Thyatira batis.*"

Conversation was desultory as everyone tried to avoid the forbidden topic. Alec alone knew the whole story.

Daisy looked round the table, as aware of those absent as of those
present: Raymond deceased; Vincent and Laurette arrested; Martha
still in bed on Dr. Hopcroft's orders, though he had pronounced
her and the unborn baby out of danger; Violet, who had nobly done
her part for Martha and returned exhausted to the Dower House
late last night; Belinda, Derek, and Ben, who had crowed over their
triumph and then moved on to more interesting pursuits.

Peach blossom was out of season, but the ripe fruit provided a
peach tart, which was consumed with appreciation. Then the adults
also moved on to a more interesting pursuit. Settled in the drawing
room, coffee served, they looked to Edgar to start the proceedings.

His lordship ceded the chair to Scotland Yard.

"Thank you, sir." Alec had no need to wait for their attention.
"Let me begin by saying that this case has been one of the most
confusing of my experience, if not *the* most confusing. Some of you
know one part, some another, so you'll forgive me if I tell you much
that you already know. I'll try to follow chronological order. The
first noteworthy incident was Vincent's report—"

Several people interrupted: "But—"

Alec held up his hand. "Vincent's tale, if you prefer, of being attacked while strolling in the woods on Sunday afternoon. He himself said it could have been an accident, a falling bough that caused him to trip in dodging it."

"I've had my bailiff and my groundsman go through the woods," Edgar said defensively, "checking for hazardous trees and dealing with them."

"I'm glad to hear it, sir. A falling bough may in fact have given him the notion of claiming he had an impression of someone swinging a branch at him. Misdirection figured largely in his plan. At any rate, there was nothing concrete enough for me to act upon, and though he limped heavily for a couple of days, with the aid of his walking stick, there was little damage done."

"I've just remembered," said Daisy, "I noticed he walked perfectly normally when carrying a tray in the refreshment tent at the fête. And he'd been limping just a minute earlier. I forgot all about it when Belinda fell off the donkey."

Alec frowned at her and resumed his narration. "Belinda's fall was the second incident."

"But Bel has nothing to do with the inheritance," Frank protested.

"True, which muddled the issue. But Daisy and I put together some odd facts. . . . Ben, with a cooperative donkey, was in the lead when he suddenly lost speed. This allowed Belinda to catch up, whereupon her donkey bucked her off."

"It doesn't sound like the kind of beast I'd let my girls ride," said Sam, a trifle censorious. His torso wrapped like an Egyptian mummy, shirtless under a borrowed blazer two sizes too large, he moved gingerly, but agreed with Drs. Pardoe and Hopcroft that his wound was nothing serious.

"The donkey man said it was very docile," Daisy assured him, "only it was afraid of flashing lights. He didn't expect any trouble in broad daylight. Then Ben said a light had flashed in his eyes and startled him, making him unintentionally rein in his mount. We guessed it must have been a reflection of the sun's rays, from a mirror, perhaps. When Ben slowed down and Bel moved ahead, it flashed in her donkey's eyes."

"Again, it could well have been an accident," Alec resumed, "though Ben's involvement made us wonder. In a sense it *was* an accident, as it was not the intended victim who got the bloody nose."

"Ben likely wouldn't have come to much harm," said Frank, "if he had been the one to fall."

"Another reason for us to dismiss it as an accident. The third incident could not be so regarded, though it had the same slapdash quality. Edgar's butterfly net was arranged near the bottom of the spiral steps to the boys' turret room, where Derek was as likely to be tripped as Ben, and again no one was likely to be badly hurt. What's more, in daylight the boys would probably have spotted it before falling over it. If not for the thunderbolt that scared them in the middle of the night, nothing at all might have come of it."

"I don't understand," Edgar said plaintively. "What did Vincent hope to gain from all this?"

"Confusion," said Alec. "And he succeeded there. Your butterfly net couldn't have placed itself in position, so at that point I had to start wondering seriously what was going on. And I couldn't make sense of it."

"I'm not surprised. What was next?"

"Raymond's death," Geraldine said flatly.

"You'll find this hard to credit, but Raymond's death was not intended. Vincent and Laurette both insist on that. Vincent claims he pushed Raymond with his stick so that he would stumble towards the tramlines, not hard enough to make him fall."

"But he fell?" Sam asked.

"He did. A quick-thinking, quick-moving citizen helped him up but didn't hang about to be thanked. Vincent had already left in a hurry, of course, for fear of being recognised. He claims Raymond had plenty of time to get out of the way of the trams, which were moving slowly. As a matter of fact, the policeman on point duty bears him out, as does one of the tram drivers."

"Then what killed him?"

"A stroke—not to get into medicalese—brought on by shock."

"Then does it count as murder?" Frank wanted to know.

"That's not for me to decide, thank goodness. Assault, yes. Manslaughter, probably. Murder, I don't know. It's up to a coroner's jury, at least initially."

"What I still don't get is what was all this in aid of?"

"Misdirection," said Geraldine. "I've known a few boys in my time who were experts at it. The spurious stabbing of Vincent was the ultimate attempt at misdirection, I assume?"

"Yes, the fifth incident. It wasn't until after tea yesterday that Daisy brought to my attention a number of inconsistencies that ruled it out as a real attack. To do myself justice, I must say that I had my suspicions much earlier, but I couldn't yet discount Sam or Frank. I still haven't heard from Sam's ship, though while you were all taking tea on the terrace yesterday, I received responses at last to my enquiries in Scarborough and Paris."

Tommy Pearson was defensive. "I myself made extensive enquiries in both places."

"But not, I think, of the police. The criminal propensities, if any, of prospective heirs were not your concern, nor their material circumstances, which were also of interest to me."

"True."

"We had just begun to study the letters from the Sûreté and the Scarborough police when Dr. Pardoe, the local police surgeon, called to discuss his findings on Raymond's death; also, truth be told, in hope of getting the whole story. DS Piper continued reading the documents while I talked to the doctor. In the meantime, the footman let us know that Mr. Crowley had declared his intention of walking over to the pub, so I sent one of the local constables to keep an eye on him."

Frank grinned. "Nice chap. He stood me a pint."

"Then Daisy came in," Alec continued, "with the evidence that the attack on Vincent was spurious. We had scarcely time to examine that before she rushed in again calling for Dr. Pardoe's assistance for Mrs. Samuel."

"Bless him!" said Sam with fervour.

"When the doctor rushed off, Piper reported to me the information from Scarborough and Paris. We—"

"What did they have to say?" Geraldine asked.

"We'll get to that in a minute, if you don't mind."

"Or if I do, no doubt," she said tartly.

Alec smiled at her. "My two sergeants and I went up to the Vincent Dalrymples' room. On the way, acting on information from Dr. Pardoe, I sent DS Tring on an errand."

"One which thoroughly upset my cook! I hope he found what he was looking for?"

"Oh yes. Fingerprints. Meanwhile DS Piper and I gained admittance to Vincent and Laurette's room and found that Vincent wasn't there. Apparently he'd been slipping in and out at will, taking care not to be seen, not difficult in a house this size. A connecting bathroom with a second door to a different hallway—"

"Which I—or my housekeeper or any of the maids—could have told you about had you asked!"

"One would hardly expect them to leave surreptitiously, Cousin Geraldine," Daisy pointed out. "Supposedly they had locked themselves in for their own safety."

"I should have demanded more men," Alec admitted, "enough to cover all exits and all eventualities. When we found that Vincent was on the loose, I locked Laurette in. Piper and I separated to hunt for him. Daisy, I'm sure you've told everyone else what happened while we were searching, but I haven't heard your story yet."

"I was looking for Sam to tell him Martha had been taken ill. I found him just as Vincent attacked. You know, I don't think he had a clue the kids were tracking him until they jumped him. Then DS Piper and the local constable turned up, in the nick of time."

"How are the children doing?" Alec asked.

"They said it was fun, once Vincent had been handcuffed and they knew Sam was going to be all right. Then they went off to start building a tree fort."

"Ben told me it was very exciting," said Frank. "He didn't seem at all upset."

285

"You needn't worry about any of them developing a complex, darling," Daisy assured Alec. "This morning, as it's raining, they were playing in the attics. Derek found a book in the library about the Himalayas, called *The Roof of the World*, and they were all being explorers up there. Or perhaps Tibetan lamas, I'm not sure."

Alec laughed. "No one will believe their story when they go back to school."

"They should get a medal," said Sam.

Geraldine disagreed. "Certainly not. They need no encouragement to attempt such dangerous exploits. They should have followed Vincent, not tackled him."

"It's easy to be wise after the event." Frank sighed. "They got caught up in the excitement of the moment." He obviously spoke from a wealth of experience. "Was Laurette arrested for conspiracy, Alec?"

"Far worse. She attempted to procure an illegal abortion. She substituted a dangerous herb, pennyroyal, for the peppermint Martha was taking for indigestion. Dr. Pardoe saw the teapot, sniffed the contents, and recognised the smell immediately."

"Martha said it tasted unpleasant," Daisy put in, "but she's not the sort to make a fuss."

"Luckily Laurette didn't realise it takes more than a simple infusion of the leaf to be reliably efficacious."

"Thank heaven!" said Sam.

"Especially as Martha is six months . . . Sorry, Geraldine, it's not a subject for mixed company."

"Nonsense, my dear man. It's no earthly use being mealy-mouthed."

"Oh!" Light dawned on Frank. "There's no point killing Sam if Martha then produces a son. That's terrible." He crossed the room to shake Sam's hand. "I'm very glad she failed, old boy. I still don't see what the other nonsense was about, though, the faked accidents and all. Alec, are you going to tell us the news from Scarborough and Paris?"

"From Scarborough, the not very surprising news that the Vincent Dalrymples are in serious financial difficulties."

"What about the children?" Geraldine asked anxiously.

"The boy's been going to a small private day school. The French relative is governess to the daughters but also helped in the hotel. She took the kids to stay with her family in Paris for a fortnight while their parents came here. As things stand, I expect they'll remain there."

Everyone was silent for a few moments.

Then Sam said ruefully, "And the moral of the story is, don't engage in criminal activities if you have a family dependent on you."

"Nothing venture, nothing win," said Frank, "though murder is taking it a bit too far! So the reason he was desperate to be the heir by fair means or foul was just money, not the glory of being a lord. I can see that the pretended attacks on himself were meant to avert suspicion. And whatever he says about Raymond, whatever Raymond actually died of, he meant to kill him if you ask me. But the butterfly net, and the pointless donkey business—if that wasn't a real accident . . ."

"It was all part of a convoluted, half-baked plan to make it appear that *all* the possible heirs were targets, which made it appear that the attacker didn't know who was the actual heir. However, he didn't want to harm anyone who didn't stand in his way."

"Good of him!" Geraldine exclaimed.

"If he had not been suspected, he'd have continued to claim ignorance of the order of birth of Julian's sons. If he found himself under serious suspicion, he'd produce evidence that he knew all along so that, as second in line, he had no reason to attack anyone but the actual heir."

"That's an explanation?" Frank protested.

"It's the best I can offer."

"Feeble!"

"He did succeed in muddying waters at first, but his efforts were ultimately unconvincing. His expertise was in hotel management, which requires careful organisation. A messy, improvised plot was very much outside his competence. He was bound to be caught in the end."

"As far as I'm concerned, the waters are still muddy. But you say he had proof of who bags the prize?"

"That's properly Mr. Pearson's side of the business," Alec said. "I'll turn it over to him."

"Thank you." Tommy bowed acknowledgment. "However, perhaps Lord Dalrymple would prefer to wait until his birthday tomorrow . . . ?"

"No," said Geraldine. "I want it settled now. Tomorrow half the county will be here for the party and we can break the news to them."

"As you wish, my dear," said Edgar with an absent smile. "I'm trying to remember what kind of caterpillar lives on pennyroyal. It grows in the herb garden, you know."

"I'll have it dug out this very afternoon," her ladyship said grimly, "whether that's where Laurette obtained it or not."

Daisy wondered silently whether Geraldine would have been equally eager to uproot the laburnum alley, had Vincent used its deadly seeds to poison someone.

Tommy cleared his throat. "Shall we proceed? Mr. Dalrymple, I trust you have kept safely the . . . item you showed me in London?"

"Of course, sir." As Sam started to struggle to his feet, Frank gave him a hand and a resigned look. Sam tried to look modest but couldn't quite hide a grin. "Lord Dalrymple let me keep it in his safe."

"Edgar!"

"Yes, dear?" His lordship emerged from his cogitation. "*Pyrausta aurata*. The mint moth, as I should have remembered. A singularly pretty creature."

"Oh *bother* your moths!" said Geraldine sacrilegiously. "Go with Samuel to open the safe. Would anyone care for more coffee?" She rang the bell.

"Champagne, don't you think, dear?" Edgar suggested from the doorway.

Lowecroft came in and was told to bring coffee and champagne. "Do go on, Mr. Pearson," said Geraldine. "We need not wait for their return."

"As you wish, Lady Dalrymple. In the car from Worcester, DCI Fletcher showed me letters he had received from France. To be precise, notarised copies of letters. They were written by Marie-Claire Dalrymple, née Vallier, wife of Julian Dalrymple, from Jamaica to her parents in Paris. Each announces the birth of one of her sons. They are dated."

"The Sûreté obtained them from the Valliers," said Alec, "who had previously sent copies to Vincent when he asked for family papers."

Tommy sighed. "They had not thought to mention them to my representative, as they naturally assumed Vincent would do so."

Edgar and Sam returned, as Lowecroft and Ernest brought in the coffee and three bottles of cellar-chilled champagne. "I ventured to bring some up after lunch, my lord," said the butler, "just in case it was called for."

"Good thinking, my dear chap. Now!" He rubbed his hands together. "Let's see what Sam has to show us."

Sam's parcel was carefully wrapped in oiled cloth and tied with a faded blue ribbon. Unwrapping it, he revealed a bible bound in black calfskin.

"This belonged to my great-grandmother, Marie-Claire," he said. "On the blank pages she kept a record of the family. She died in a cholera epidemic in 1850, along with her baby, a fifth son. After my great-grandfather, Julian, died in 1870, my grandfather moved his part of the family from the plantation to Kingston. He left this bible with his half sister, the child of Julian and a freed slave."

Frank, grinning, started to comment, then thought better of it and coughed instead.

Sam placed the bible on the table at Tommy's elbow, open at the flyleaf, and sat down beside him. "Her daughter, my great-aunt—"

"Second cousin," said Tommy.

"Aunt Lucea. This was passed on to her, and she's kept up the family records for all branches of the family still in Jamaica. I had to go over to the old plantation to beg her to lend it to me. That's why—one reason—it took me so long to get here. Don't for pity's sake get sticky fingerprints on it!"

Offended, Tommy put down his coffee, took out his handkerchief, and ostentatiously wiped his fingers. He studied the faded ink of the family tree.

Daisy was tempted to go and look over his shoulder, but she resisted the temptation. Not that she wasn't pretty sure of the answer, but she considered the lawyer to be prolonging the suspense to an unwarrantable length.

"Yes," he said at last, "this agrees with the letters from Paris. The eldest son of Julian was Alfred, born in 1832, father of James, father of Samuel. I can see no reason why the two together should not be accepted as evidence of primogeniture. Congratulations, Mr. Dalrymple. Congratulations, Lord Dalrymple, you have an heir." A buzz of congratulations arose, which he promptly interrupted. "Pending, needless to say, the decision of the College of Arms."

"Phoo to the College of Arms!" Edgar cried, shaking Sam's hand vigorously. "What about the rest of them, eh, Pearson?"

"According to the letters from Marie-Claire, her second son, Timothy was born in 1833. Her last letter dates from 1850, and seems to have been carried by Timothy to Paris, where he was sent to escape from the typhoid that killed her. He was Vincent's grandfather, who moved to England in 1870 to escape the Franco-Prussian war."

"An unsettled family," Geraldine observed. "And next?"

"The third son was Josiah, born in 1837. Perhaps Mr. Crowley can fill in some of the history of that branch of the family?"

"Not much. Ben's father, Luke—Lucas was my friend. I don't know when Josiah arrived in Trinidad, but I found a record of Luke's father's marriage, John he was, giving his father's name as Josiah Dalrymple of Jamaica. John married Luke's mama, Dolores, all right and tight. One of Ben's sisters is named after her. Luke was born in 1889—he was a bit older than me. He married Susanna, and produced four *zanfan* before—"

"*Zanfan?*" Daisy asked. "Children?"

"That's right. Creole. In 1917, Luke volunteered. He didn't come back. I'd promised to look after the *zanfan* and Susanna. We were married in 1922. She died having my baby. The baby died too." A murmur of commiseration arose. "So here I am with four stepkids and I hoped . . . Oh well, that's the way the dice roll. Lord Dalrymple, I don't suppose you'd lend me fifty quid to get me and the boy back to Port-of-Spain? Or a hundred would be even better."

"Gladly, my dear fellow, but . . . Geraldine?"

"Mr. Crowley, Edgar and I have grown quite fond of your stepson in the past few days. We would like to propose to you that he remain here at Fairacres, with his brother and sisters coming to join him. We have plenty of room, even if Sam and Martha decide to make their home here, as we hope. We'll see that they complete their schooling, and it would, I believe, solve a difficulty for you."

"Would it ever! Carlotta, here I come!" In his exuberance, Frank seized Geraldine in a hug, from which she emerged patting her hair but smiling.

By then, Lowecroft and Ernest, having lingered long enough to hear the outcome, had opened two bottles of champagne.

"Port for the servants," Daisy whispered in Edgar's ear.

He gave her a startled look. "Is it customary? Yes, by all means. Lowecroft, a bottle of port for the servants to drink to Mr. and Mrs. Samuel's health!"

The champagne bottles were empty. Sam had gone to tell Martha that the lawyer accepted his claim. Frank had gone to find out what Ben thought of Geraldine's proposal.

"Though," as he said to Daisy with a wink, "you can be sure I'll see that he's happy to agree. It's best for all of us. Sam's offered to bring the others over when he fetches his girls."

With a happy sigh, Daisy said to Alec, "All's well that ends well. Except for poor Raymond. And Laurette's children. Alec, you don't think we—"

"No! Apart from other considerations, I hardly think they'd be happy living with the police officer who arrested their parents."

"Oh dear! I suppose not. Besides, it would probably be too much for Mother's nervous system. What she'll say about Edgar and Geraldine adopting Ben and his siblings boggles the mind!"